Tangled Hearts

BY RUTH ALTAMURA-ROLL

DORRANCE
PUBLISHING CO
EST. 1920
PITTSBURGH, PENNSYLVANIA 15238

Dorrance Publishing Co
585 Alpha Drive
Pittsburgh, PA 15238
Visit our website at *www.dorrancebookstore.com*

ISBN: 978-1-6376-4007-4
eISBN: 978-1-6376-4858-2

Tangled Hearts

Tennessee, November 25, 1863

From the end of September to mid-October, General Braxton Bragg led the Army of Tennessee to lay siege at Chattanooga, cutting off the Union from its supply lines. On October 17, Major General Ulysses S. Grant received command of the Western armies from Abraham Lincoln, and he soon moved to reinforce Chattanooga with a new supply line. Major General William Tecumseh Sherman arrived with his four divisions in November and the Federal offensive began. Late in November, Union forces struck out capturing Orchard Knob and Lookout Mountain. November 25th, Union soldiers assaulted the Confederate Army's impenetrable lines on Missionary Ridge. Outnumbered four to one, English-born Confederate General Patrick Cleburne fought with particular stubbornness. In his retreat, he planned to destroy the only bridge over Chickamauga Creek.

CHAPTER 1

Musket balls whizzed across the battlefield. The cannonade pounded as Sherman's Division closed-in on General Cleburne's bedraggled troops. Putrid sulfur hung pungent in the air. Thick smoke swirled with the heavy fog which settled low over the damp ground on that cool November evening. Fighting valiantly, they could no longer hold their line. Ordered to retreat, Captain Miles Pembroke, his sword held high, led his men through the heavy mist towards Chickamauga Creek. He knew the sooner they found cover the sooner they could regroup to bring down the bridge as ordered. Forty-nine men of his unit remained. It had been a hard and bloody day, and it wasn't over yet. Minie' balls and scattershot threatened to end more lives if they did not move quickly.

"Corporal Malin!" he ordered back, "Keep the men close," his voice mingled with the din of battle.

"Close up!" Corporal Charles Malin echoed down the line.

The war-weary men ran double quick in semi-broken rows through the smoke over their own dead and wounded towards an unknown destination. Fear gripped their hearts as grapeshot and exploding shells screamed around them. The excruciating cries of newly fallen men joined with the chaotic roar of battle. Captain Pembroke needed to get his men to safety.

Stopped suddenly, Pembroke arched back. His arms lifted skyward as he slowly fell to his knees. Dark blood gushed from a hole in his chest. As if in slow motion, he crumpled, his face struck the hard ground. His troops scattered, confused as frightened sheep. Their leader was down.

"Follow me!" Corporal Malin cried, trying to get order back into the shattered ranks.

The weary men scrambled after him down the slimy creek embankment, the whiz of musket balls buzzing overhead as they slid, breathlessly, into the muck. " We'll wait here `till nightfall!" Malin shouted breathlessly to his exhausted troops.

"Has anyone seen Captain Pembroke?" Malin asked the muddied Rebs squatting next to him.

"Yes, Suh," a sweat-stained soldier panted, "I thank that last round 'a scattashot got him raht in the back, Suh. Saw'm go down. He might be dead, Suh."

"No!" Charles moaned in shock, "Not Miles!"

"I'm truly sorry Suh, I know'd you was kin."

Charles fell back against the soft bank. The war faded into the background, memories of their childhood home in England flooded his head. They were friends and cousins; played war games together, swam in crystal streams and rode in deep green fields together. They came to the Confederate United States for the cause and for glory. England did not agree with the rebellion but hated the United States more. Plus, Charles wanted to get into the fight. The loss of the colonies and the defeat in 1812 left a bitter taste in the mouths of many a British man. Charles felt a twinge of guilt. He was the older of the two. Miles idolized him and was easy to convince. Trade with the South was so well developed that the Confederate States were almost British Colonies. It was the right thing for England. But Charles never considered death for either of them even a remote possibility. They were invincible.

The battle calmed as night fell. The scent of hickory cook fires permeated the air, bringing him back to the present. He decided to send out several pickets to scout for a safe place to set up camp.

"Suh, there is a small clear'n on the otha side of the bridge. It looks lahk a good, drah place," reported the returning scout, eager to get out of the cold murky creek.

"Good, move out of this mire and set up camp." Charles was now in charge. "We've work to do in the morning, so let's get something to eat and a good night's sleep, shall we?"

The exhausted men climbed up the embankment and crossed the soon-to-be demolished Chickamauga Creek Bridge. The sound of heel plates and clanking tin cups blended with the sounds of the low voices of the camps.

Pulling one of the men aside, Charles whispered, "I've got to find Captain Pembroke. Set up a picket, I'll join you shortly."

A white autumn moon broke through the overcast sky illuminating the gray battle-charred landscape. Dark plumes of smoke and smoldering embers floated above the once raging fires of trees and war wagons. Charles didn't notice the silver-lined clouds that glistened in the night sky as he searched the battered field scattered with ruined bodies of men and motionless horses. The occasional moan did not give him pause. He had to find Miles.

Recognizing the stand of trees where Miles had fallen, he made his way through the thick grasses, and came upon the tall oaks. He focused in the dim moonlight. The fallen body of his cousin lay still and crumpled. He nudged the corpse with the toe of his boot. He felt numb. It surprised him. He knelt down and turned the body over. Shock and pain were frozen on the once handsome face of his cousin. Charles grimaced at the taste of bile in his mouth.

"Well, Miles," he said to the corpse, "We did have some fun. Sorry to see you go like this, ol' chap." Emotionless, he rifled through Miles' blood-soaked sack coat and haversack pulling out family letters, foodstuffs, and tobacco. Finally, he found the Victoria Cross with its silver bars, the unofficial honor from the Queen given for bravery to all nobles who volunteered for the Confederate cause.

Stuffing the items into his own bag, Charles looked into the dead face of his boyhood friend. "This is going to be hard on the family," he thought.

He reached over to close the blue lifeless eyes. Pulling the blanket from the dead man's knapsack, he covered the body. Remembering Miles' ring, he pulled hard, but it did not budge. He could hear the bones in his cousin's hand break under the pressure. He winced. Still it would not come off. Taking out his knife he prepared to cut the finger from its owner. He raised the knife, but quickly stopped. A rustling in the nearby trees startled him. The ring had to stay where it was. He quickly returned to his men to prepare their orders for the following day.

Charles entered the tent of General Cleburne at headquarters. It was well-appointed with a bed, lanterns, dressing stand, chairs, and a field desk set upon a ground carpet of a red India rug. It was a vast contrast to the meager living conditions he and his men endured, but Charles hoped that would not last much longer. Corporal Malin stood at attention waiting to be addressed. Finally, the General lifted his head from his desk.

"At ease, Corporal."

"Sir," he said, shifting his position, his hands at his side.

"Corporal Charles Malin, is that right?"

"Yes, sir, General Cleburne."

"First I wish to commend you for a job well done in dismantling the bridge at Chickamauga Creek. You saved quite a few men."

"Thank you, sir!" he answered, standing taller with pride.

"I've been informed that you wish to be dismissed from your post, extenuating family circumstances?

"Yes, sir."

"Which are?" he asked, only slightly curious.

"I came with my cousin Miles Pembroke, the son of Sir William Pembroke, Baron of Milford. Miles was the only direct heir, sir. He was killed, now which leaves me, sir."

"I see," Cleburne said thoughtfully. "Convenient for you, I dare say."

"No sir, it's not like that. My cousin and I were close, very close. It's a great loss for me, sir," Charles explained with heartfelt emotion.

"Yes, I see that." Cleburne squinted at Charles to size him up.

"Sir, I'm concerned for my family and the preservation of our inheritance. Miles has only sisters." Cleburne was getting annoying.

"So, Corporal, you wish to claim your inheritance then?"

"Yes sir," he said, feeling relieved.

"Has your family been notified of the death?"

"Yes, sir, I believe they're expecting my return."

Cleburne thought.

"We're very shorthanded here."

"Yes, sir," Charles answered, keeping his emotions in check though his jaw was beginning to tighten with unspoken anger.

The General was pensive for a few moments. At last he replied, "Well, I understand these situations, Malin. Permission granted. Corporal, you are re-lieved of your duties at dawn. But leave your musket and rounds, we are in short supply."

"Yes sir. Thank you, sir!" Charles said, relieved by more than Cleburne's salute.

Though he was uncomfortable at the prospect of leaving Miles behind, buried in foreign soil, Charles had seen enough war and was glad to be return-ing home.

The long trip to England gave him time to think of home and family. He might even make it home for Christmas. He wondered if he'd receive a soldier's wel-come. In truth, the mood most likely would be somber at best. Though glad for his return, Aunt Margaret and Uncle William would be devastated with the loss of their son. Then there was the matter of his cousin Eliza, her hus-band Henry, and their growing brood.

Of all those left behind in England however, Charles was most eager to see Ana. He had always thought of her as more than just his youngest cousin. As long as he could remember, Ana made him run hot with passion. He had been living with his cousin's family since age twelve following his parents' death, but since the day they met when she was a mere child of five, he wanted her and waited for her. He remembered attempting to steal kisses from her, but she always managed to keep out of reach, teasing him, taunting him with her turquoise eyes and auburn curls. He enjoyed watching her grow from a plump girl into a sensuous beauty. Even Uncle William knew she was too spe-cial for just anyone. Maybe now that he was the heir apparent, she would agree to marriage. The very idea of taking her stirred him. Soon he would be home and he would make Ana his.

The black bunting was harsh against the white stone row home in Berkeley Square. Paying the carriage driver, Charles walked up the steps and braced for his homecoming reception. Breathing in the thick incomparable London air, he rang the bell; the familiar footsteps of the family butler drew near.

Sedgewick recognized Charles immediately, his expressionless face unchangeable but for the twinkle in his eyes. "Lord Malin, welcome home sir, welcome home! Sir William and Lady Margaret have been expecting you. They'll be so pleased that you've arrived, and with Christmas just a few days away."

Taking his coat and hat he said, "Wait in the drawing room, Sir, I'll announce you at once."

"Thank you, Sedgewick," Charles answered as he entered the familiar room. *Lord* Malin. He had always been Master, but now that he was heir, he would be Lord. *Lord Charles Malin, Baron of Milford.* He practiced the sound of it in his head. It fit him like a comfortable glove. He smiled to himself.

A welcoming fire radiated in the grate. Charles realized there was no Christmas tree, the new tradition from Victoria and Albert. Understandable, he thought, as he poured a measure of claret into a crystal goblet and admired its ruby color. He meandered around the room appreciating the wall paintings and slightly shabby furnishings that would someday be his. Uncle William had not been the best steward to his title, lands and fortune. But Charles would see to the restorations. For now, however, this was much preferable to war tents.

"Charles? Charles!" Ana exclaimed as she and her parents quickly entered the room. To his pleasant surprise, Ana threw her arms around his neck and their lips met briefly. Aunt Margaret gave a warm hug and a cheek. She held him at arm's length to look at him. He was safe at home.

After clearing his throat, Uncle William gave a hardy handshake. "Welcome home my boy, welcome home!" he said, his eyes moist with emotion. "Thank you, sir. It's so good to see you all. Aunt Margaret you are as ever."

"Ana," he continued, as he took in her fine delicate features, large turquoise eyes and dark ginger curls for the first time in many long months, "You look ravishing, cousin, a balm for these war-weary eyes."

Ana's long black lashes fluttered to her cheeks as a barely perceptible smile flitted across her full sensual mouth. She blushed.

An awkward silence filled the room. Aunt Margaret began to dab at her eyes. "I should be welcoming my son home too," she said, desperately trying to hold back her tears, not wanting to spoil Charles' homecoming.

"It's not that we aren't happy to see you Charles, of course we are my boy," explained Sir William. "We're pleased to see you healthy and unhurt by that terrible ordeal. It is just that Miles is ... was ..." his voice cracked.

"What Father is trying to say is that we are just so glad that you're home, Charles, safe and sound," Ana said. She was subdued as she took his hand. The news of her brother's death was almost more than any of them could bear, though they were glad to see Charles unharmed.

"Charles, I wish to thank you for returning Miles' Victoria Cross," Sir William said, giving Charles a firm pat on his shoulder. "It's meant so much to Mother and I."

"Yes," Charles said, "I knew you must have it. This has been difficult for me also. Miles was like a brother to me."

Still teary, Lady Margaret added, "Charles you are now our son, you know, our true son."

Charles hung his head, feeling a sense of awe at the prospect. "Thank you, Aunt."

"Charles, you must be starved from your journey," Ana said. "Let me ring the kitchen and we'll get you some food. I know Mother could use some tea."

"You look different Charles. Thinner. Older," Aunt Margaret said with some concern. "Was the war hard on you?"

"Yes, yes it was. Mostly tedious marching and drilling. We never really had enough supplies. Poor food, wet powder. Many men were barefoot. The battles were so bloody. I have memories I'll never forget." He shuddered. "And now with Miles gone…" he drifted off.

"My poor boy, I'm sure war does something to a man," Aunt Margaret said and again began to tear. Ana placed her arm around her mother's thin shoulders. "What Miles must have been through …" Aunt Margaret drifted off.

"It's been hard on Mother," Ana said. "I'm glad Father's taking her to visit her sister in Spain," patting her mother's thin frail hand.

"Yes," added Sir William giving his rather large gray mustache a tug, "A change of scenery; the Mediterranean climate will help us both."

"When do you plan on leaving?" Charles asked, hoping it was not too soon.

"The day after Christmas," Sir William answered. "Few festivities this year, I'm afraid."

"Yes, naturally." Charles felt disappointed, hoping to receive a better reception. Maybe Miles was gone but at least he had returned.

Sedgewick brought out refreshments. Ana poured tea as Charles loaded his plate with the bounty.

Clearing his throat, Sir William said, "Charles, Mother and I have thought long and hard about this. We want you to have Miles' Victoria Cross. You fought together and now that you will be … Well, it is yours."

"Thank you, sir. You don't know how much this means to me," he said looking at the silver and gold medal in his hand. Remembering Miles bloodless face in the moonlight, he pushed the image away.

His uncle added, "We thought you might like your apartments ready, so we took the liberty to open your rooms."

"Uncle, you and Aunt Margaret are so generous. It has been a long day, and with rooms waiting, I think I'll retire. Good night Aunt, Uncle." Putting his empty plate on the tray, he kissed his aunt on the cheek. "Ana, will you walk me out?" he asked with a pleading look in his eyes.

Ana followed Charles to the door. When he stopped, he stood uncomfortably close. She felt herself lean away.

"I hope now that I'm home we'll see much more of each other. I am, as always, looking forward to being with you." His voice was deep with emotion as he bent down to give her a kiss. But Ana turned, giving him her cheek rather than her lips.

"In time, Ana," he said coolly, putting his hat on his head, "In time."

She shook her head. "*He'll have to wait forever*," she thought, but instead she answered simply, "Good night Charles. We're glad you're home."

"Thank you," he said flatly as he turned and walked into the dark, foggy streets.

CHAPTER 2

*I*t was as somber and gray in as it was out. One month had passed since Miles was killed at Chickamauga and Christmas Day was gloomy indeed. The usual family holiday conversations were subdued. All but Henry and Charles passed on the Christmas pudding. Even the children, Sarah and Ana Jane, mirrored the muted mood of the adults around the table.

As they were preparing to leave for the salon, Sedgewick brought a letter and a small package which had just arrived special delivery.

"Thank you, Sedgewick," Lord William said as he inspected the correspondence. Flipping it over, his brow creased. He placed the package in front of him.

"Father, what is it?" asked Ana, her curiosity piqued by her father's expression.

Exasperated, he said, "I don't know yet, girl. Let me open it." Pulling his glass from his vest pocket, he placed it over his left eye. He opened the letter and read it silently, tugging on his mustache as he did so. Clearing his throat, he nodded.

All the family sat in quiet anticipation as he folded the letter and removed his glass.

"Business, my dears, just business," he said nonchalantly, tapping the lens on the parchment then placing it into the breast pocket of his jacket along with the small parcel.

"And on Christmas Day, too," Lady Margaret sighed and shook her head, oblivious to her husband's mood. "Shall we go through then? We can forget about business in the drawing room. We'll be leaving tomorrow, and business will just have to wait." They began to rise from their places.

"Oh, Charles," Sir William said, "I wonder if you would kindly join me in my study. We'll have our cigars and brandy there. The ladies can occupy themselves tonight with Henry. Henry, if you wouldn't mind keeping our women entertained?" He smiled through cool blue eyes.

"Of course not, Sir William, it's always a pleasure to entertain the ladies," Henry said with a wink and broad smile on his handsome face. He took his mother-in-law's elbow and led her from the room, followed by his wife Eliza, then Ana, and finally his young daughters.

In less than a half hour Charles and Sir William rejoined the family. Ana was seated at the pianoforte providing holiday entertainment.

As the evening progressed, Henry kept Charles deep in conversation about the war in the States. Henry told him about several shipping deals in which he was involved to help the Confederate cause. He greatly hoped that he could entice Charles to participate in the project. Sir William tried his best to do his grandfatherly duty by playing simple magic tricks with the girls, while Eliza discussed the upcoming trip with her mother.

Tiring of playing, Ana went to sit next her sister and mother on the settee. Charles followed her with his eyes, admiring her as she walked.

"Henry, dear," Eliza said, "as today is Christmas let's not talk any more about war. It brings too many sad memories. Besides, Mother, Father, we have something of a present to share with you both before you leave tomorrow."

"Oh, I have nothing to give," Ana said. "Now I feel badly. I knew I should've purchased something." She frowned, knowing they had all agreed to keep things simple this Christmas.

"We didn't buy this one. We hope it brings good tidings and joy for the New Year and speeds your return home."

"Oh Eliza, good news is so needed!" Ana was excited at the prospect.

"We're expecting." Eliza's pretty face blushed at divulging such personal news as she looked at their eager faces.

"Oh, Eliza, another baby, how marvelous!" Lady Margaret's weary eyes sparkled for the first time in weeks as she hugged Eliza tightly. "You're right, this is just the gift our family needed."

Henry and Eliza were pelted with questions and congratulations.

"Here, here for Henry and Eliza! To health, to life and prosperity!" Charles said as he raised his glass, the flat smile pasted on his face unnoticed by others.

"I hope it's a boy," Sir William said. "To the new Baron."

"Thank you everyone, thank you," Henry stood up. "Let's all raise a glass to wish a bon voyage. To Lady Margaret and Sir William, may their trip be safe. May they return with light hearts and hopeful futures."

"Here, here!" all chimed, sipping from their glasses.

"Well done, Henry, thank you," Sir William, added wiping the moisture from his eyes.

Charles finally found a few moments alone with Ana. "You're as beautiful as ever and quite the woman in that blue silk dress," he said as his eyes wandered over her exposed white shoulders and lingered on the full mounds of her breasts that pushed up from the turquoise fabric. Ana felt repugnant by his wandering gaze.

"I'm surprised to find you still unattached." He added coyly, "Admit it, you're waiting for me."

Ana took a step back. As always, Charles was too close for comfort, his scrutiny too personal. Charles was not the attractive man he thought himself to be. He was thin and wiry, with hair cropped close to his head. His small black darting eyes made him appear cold and hard.

"Yes, Charles, still unattached, and no it's not about you," she answered coolly, now feeling edgy with his question of marriage. At twenty-four, if she did not find a husband soon, she would most definitely be an old maiden aunt, and that prospect was anything but pleasant.

"You know how I feel about you Ana. Now that I've returned, I had hoped you would've missed me as I missed you. I thought of you every day on those battlefields. I believe you kept me alive. And though this sounds a bit clumsy, someday I'll be Baron. Ana, your future would be secure with me."

Ana couldn't believe her ears. "Charles, I find your offer uncivilized. My brother is barely cold. Sometimes I don't understand you. Besides, you're more a brother to me and we've always been good friends. I couldn't think of you that way. Anyway, Eliza and Henry might have a son." The thought of kissing his thin lips brought a shiver of disgust.

He took a step closer. "Well, remember the offer is open for now," his icy finger tracing its way along the rounded flesh above the fabric of her dress. She slapped at his hand.

"Consider it." He bent down to brush her lips with his, but as always, she turned her head just in time, so he kissed her cheek instead. Ana's stomach churned at the liberties he was taking and would have stepped back further if she was not already against the wall.

"Hey you two." Eliza had come to the rescue. "Come and say good-bye, we're returning home."

Thank God for Eliza, Ana thought as she looped her arm in her sister's and gallantly walked away from Charles who followed a few steps behind, glaring cold daggers into Eliza's straight back.

"I too must return to my apartments. Ana, I shall come to visit tomorrow. We can catch up on all the latest town gossip. I've missed so much." Ana did not relish being alone with Charles and did not reply to his invitation but held her head high with her nose just a bit into the air.

Soon all stood in the door with much hugging and kissing and even some tears, hoping for God's speed on all journeys home and abroad.

The house felt lonely and quiet in the few hours since Lord and Lady Pembroke left for their journey. The rain turned to ice and snow during the night making the roads slick and treacherous. Ana was not pleased at the idea of her parents leaving for Spain under such harsh conditions. She was convinced that even the sturdy ship in which they were to travel was going to struggle in the rough winter seas.

Ana sat alone finishing her morning tea and making plans. With Eliza expecting and Charles now at home, Ana knew her days would be full of family life and appointments. Unsettled by Charles' behavior the previous evening, Ana admitted to herself that she was, in reality, looking forward to bringing him up to date on the latest news of their crowd. Lost in her thoughts, Ana, suddenly became aware of a commotion in the hall and went to investigate.

"Eliza? Henry? Eliza, you're as pale as ghost?!" Ana noticed Eliza's swollen eyes. "What's happened? Is it the girls? The baby?"

Throwing her arms around Ana's neck, Eliza began to cry. Instinctively hugging in return, Ana looked at Henry's drawn face.

"No, it's not the girls and Eliza is fine … for now," he stated categorically. "Let's move into the drawing room, shall we." He gathered the sisters in his arms gently pushing them towards the settee. Eliza's sobs subsided some, but her tears continued to flow as the women sat down; Ana caressed her sister's hand as she held it in her lap.

"Henry, please. Tell me! What's happened?" Seeing the depth of her sister's grief, tears began to run down Ana's flushed cheeks and she became petrified at the possible news.

Henry pulled up a chair so that he could be closer the women. "Brace yourself Ana."

"Is it Charles? Something has happened to Charles!" Ana cried, knowing him a scoundrel.

"No, Ana," he said. Ana's eyes were wide with fear. "It's the worst. There was an accident on the Dover Road. Lord and Lady Pembroke …"

"No!" Ana's face turned white as a sheet, "Not Mother and Father. No, Henry you're mistaken." She shook her head as if to dislodge the news she had just heard, her trembling hand covering her mouth.

"Eliza? Is this true?" Ana's eyes widened as Eliza's welled up again as she nodded.

"Eliza it's not true! They are only hurt."

"Oh Ana, we have been orphaned!" Eliza cried.

Ana could not breathe. "How could this be?" she gasped. "They just left. They will be returning in three months."

"No Ana, their coach overturned," Henry continued slowly letting the information sink in.

"What do you mean overturned?" she wept, horror on her face.

"Ana, something must have spooked the horses. The coach was run off the road and overturned. The roads were so icy. It slid down a sharp ravine. All were killed, the coachman as well. They were all killed." Henry looked down at his hands, struggling himself with the news for he loved both of his in-laws dearly.

"No! No, it's not true!" Ana could not believe her ears, "First Miles and now this?"

Ana felt lightheaded as if the room was crashing in. She clutched Eliza. The two sisters held each other tightly as they sobbed into each other's arms. Henry felt helpless to ease their pain. Their family had been through so much in such a short span of time. He reached out and patted each one on the back.

"I'll get you both a glass of claret," Henry said. "I know I can use one."

"What's happening here?" Charles had come for his visit with Ana, but instead came upon a scene of weeping women. He was troubled and concerned. Henry stood up and told him of the untimely and tragic deaths of his Aunt and Uncle. He went over to his two cousins reaching out and joining them in their sorrow. Lord and Lady Pembroke had been like parents to him.

"How could this be?" he asked. His face paled at the news.

"Apparently," Henry explained again, "while on the Dover Road, something spooked their horses. The carriage went out of control, careened off the road and rolled down into a ravine. No one survived." Charles shook his head in disbelief as he dropped down in Henry's now vacated chair, his own eyes filling with tears.

"Oh, my dearest cousins! First Miles, and now this. It's too much to bear." His head hung into his hands.

For a time, they sat in silence at the shock and what it meant. Charles looked ashen. There were dark circles under his eyes.

Eliza was the first to speak, "Charles … this makes you … Baron of Milford," realizing the full weight of her parents' death.

"What?" Suddenly all eyes were on Charles.

"Charles … Baron? How strange. It had always been Father," Ana's eyes filled again, unsure of the consequences of this new realization. "And we would have all expected that Miles would … Henry?" She looked to Henry for answers.

"It means this is now your home Charles, and Picton Hall also. The title, the lands, all yours," Henry said. "You are now Lord Charles Malin, Baron of Milford." Henry frowned, uneasy now at this turn of events. But Charles was family; his mother and Sir William were siblings. Following his parents' death, Charles came to live at Picton Hall and Lord and Lady Pembroke raised him as their own. Henry scrutinized the new Baron for a few more moments. In time, he decided Charles appeared sincere in his sorrow.

"Ana, until things settle, it would be best for you to return home … with us," Eliza said. "I need you with me. We need each other." Eliza knew fully well that if Charles were to move into the residence, Ana, a single woman, could not stay alone with an eligible bachelor.

Ana looked confused by this turn of events. "What do you mean? This is my home. Why should I leave? I need to be here. I was planning on coming to visit, but this is my home," she said, her wide eyes again filling with tears.

Henry took Ana's hand. "Ana, now that Charles is Baron, this is his home. You must come with us."

"No. Wait. I don't want Ana to leave on my account. She's lost enough. Don't deny her her home too," Charles pleaded.

A calm settled over Eliza, her thoughts clear at once, despite the trauma of the day. "Ana, I need you with me," she said firmly. Eliza had never approved of Charles' pursuit of Ana.

"Yes, Ana. Eliza will need you," Henry parroted.

"But I don't want to go," she protested, as a tear rolled down her soft cheek.

"Just for a bit, until things settle. Acceptable?" Henry encouraged.

There was to be no arguing about this decision. Within the next few tearful hours, Ana was packed and off to live with Eliza and Henry, leaving Charles to his new title, home and duties as Baron.

CHAPTER 3

*A*na missed home, yet she knew she needed to be with Eliza. She spent her time helping their governess, Tess. But Ana was depressed and it did not go unnoticed by Eliza.

"Ana, you're so quiet these days," said Eliza, her pretty face clouded with concern.

"I guess I'm homesick. I refuse to marry Charles and I have no other prospects." Wistfully she added, "I wonder what's to become of me?"

"Oh Ana, I understand, but I'm really glad you are here. You've been such a comfort to me these past months."

"Eliza, I love you dearly, but I feel I'm in the way," she said sighing deeply and looking down at her hands. "You're planning the nursery. You have your daughters to look after, not to mention Henry. I know I've been a help but I'm observing your life, not living my own."

Eliza put an arm around Ana. "Don't you want to be part of this?" she asked, rubbing her now expanding belly.

"Oh, yes Liza, I do. But it's so hard to watch the way you are together."

"Ana, you make it sound like you don't belong. You're family."

"I understand and appreciate it. But ..." she sighed, "I don't know."

"You can't go back to Picton Hall. You never know when he'll return to Berkeley Square. You are a single woman and Charles is ... well, Charles."

"You know he's asked for my hand so many times now. I could always marry him and return home." Her lilting voice and twinkling turquoise eyes told Eliza she was not serious.

"Ana, you wouldn't. You couldn't," Both sisters crinkled their noses. "Poor Charles," Eliza added. "He means well, I think."

Ana sighed, "I know I can't go back. But I can't stay here, becoming the old maiden aunt, longing for what you have, watching your family grow. I would become bitter like so many old spinsters," her eyes began to fill. "I've lost so much! Miles, Mother and Father, my home … my dreams."

"Ana, please," Eliza hugged her sister, feeling her pain. "Let Henry find a suitable match. He has connections. Your dreams are not lost."

"No Liza. I must find another way. I don't want a "match." I'm almost twenty-five. No man has shown interest and why should they? I have little annual income now. I'd be a burden to most. Maybe I have a good education and come from a good noble family, but nothing else. Besides, I want … I want love."

"Ana, I'm afraid you'll do something foolish."

"Eliza, I'll come up with a plan, I know it. I'll find my way. In the meantime, I'll stay here and help you and Henry. I do love you all. I know I'll be fine," said Ana, trying to convince herself even more then her sister.

Eliza shook her head, giving her sister another hug. "I pray you someday find the happiness that Henry and I have. You deserve it."

"I don't know what God has in store for my life, but I trust His plan is going to be in my best interest. I just have to find His direction." She smiled at her sister lovingly, "I just hope it's not Charles."

Ana consoled herself with her young nieces and helped Tess with their schooling, finding enjoyment in their eager young minds. Yet she could not envision herself a spinster aunt and financial burden to her family. She was grateful that her father provided a modest income, however it was insufficient to sustain a single woman with no other means of support.

Both daughters had been well loved by their parents, but Ana had a special bond with her father. They spent hours discussing books and fables of gallant knights, chivalry and medieval conquests. "Ana there are so many possibilities from which to find a suitable situation," Father would say with a twinkle in his eye. "For you we must find the best and brightest knight." But that knight had not been found. Ana spent a long time deciding upon the direction of her life. It was now time to share it with Eliza.

Standing behind Eliza and brushing her long luxurious black hair, Ana admired her sister's reflection in the mirror. With bright blue eyes and a perfect straight nose, Eliza looked so much like Father. She was tall and willowy like Father too. Ana viewed her own reflection in comparison. She had mother's light olive complexion, was shorter and what she considered plump next to Eliza's statuesque frame. She much preferred Eliza's crystal blue eyes over her own large turquoise ones. Plus no one in the family had her unruly auburn curls that refused to remain in place.

"Eliza, I do appreciate your offer. But you have a fine governess in Tess, and I feel in the way."

"Ana, just give Henry a chance. I'm sure he'll find a suitable match," Eliza said frustrated with the repeated conversation.

Ana shook her head. "No, not this again. If Father wasn't able to, neither will Henry."

Ana saw Eliza's worried face reflected in the mirror, "I know you mean well but you married at eighteen. I'm an old maid and a burden," she sighed, quickly shaking her head, "No, I've thought this through. I've watched Tess. I've helped her. We're well educated, Father saw to that. Looking for a position as a governess will fulfill my life. I will be useful and make my own way." Ana set her jaw firmly, "I may even have adventure. Besides, I've decided, marriage is not for me."

"Now you're being nonsensical. As girls we always dreamed about weddings and children … about falling in love. I can't believe you no longer desire that."

"For whatever reason, Liza, that dream is not to be mine. It's your destiny. I see that now."

"I still think you're wrong. You're young and beautiful; frankly, anyone would be lucky to have you." Eliza always thought of Ana as a beauty and couldn't understand why her hand had not been taken. "Anyway, how can we get along without you? You're part of our family," Eliza argued, "and I have this baby on the way."

"Oh, sweet Liza!" Ana softened. "Please, don't make this harder than it is. Just speak to Henry about a letter of recommendation. I'll take care of the rest," she said with purpose. "There are always positions in the *Times* or maybe I can try an agency…" she added, thinking out loud, resolved to get her way.

Eliza knew by the determined look in Ana's eyes and the set of her chin that arguing was futile. Eliza's own blue eyes welled with tears as she stretched out her arms to embrace her stubborn sister.

"I'll speak to Henry," she said, folding Ana into her arms. Eliza knew Ana; though the youngest, she was the strongest of the two of them. Now that Ana's mind was set, she was impossible to dissuade. And in some ways Ana was right. With Mother and Father gone and Charles the new Baron, her chances of marriage were more limited than ever.

"I just wish you would wait until the birth of the baby," Eliza said, trying one last time to dissuade her.

"No, Liza, the sooner the better. I need to do this before I lose my nerve," she confessed. Her bright eyes twinkled. Ana was at once excited by Eliza's support and frightened by the future she was determined to make for herself. She was about to embark on an adventure which would determine the rest of her life.

Ana came down to breakfast hopeful and with not the least doubt that Eliza had kept her word.

"Good morning Liza, Henry," she said brightly as she made her way to the sideboard in the sun-filled dining room.

"Oh, the eggs look wonderful. I'm starved!" Ana sounded a bit too cheerful and she knew it.

Henry cleared his voice from his own uneasy tensions, "Ana, what's this nonsense I'm hearing?" His tone stern.

Ana looked at him through the reflection in the mirror and could see his red face and drawn brow. So much for clearing this with Henry, she thought. Henry was a handsome man but this morning he looked very out of sorts. She would have to win him over if she was going to move forward. Sighing, she slowly placed a kipper on her plate and deliberately turned towards her place at the table. Her eyes never left Henry's gaze. She could feel Eliza silently following her every move.

"Now Henry, brother, dearest...." she started demurely, placing her plate on the table.

"Don't 'brother dearest' me!" His fist came down heavy upon the table. The tenor of his deep voice made both Ana and Eliza jump.

"Your sister has informed me of your foolishness. No sister of mine … in-law or not … will be employed as common governess. You're under my care and I won't have it!" His face twisted dark in anger.

"Henry, stop! I know what I'm doing. I'll do this with or without your help and I certainly don't need your permission or blessing if that's what you think. I'm not a child!" She stood abruptly, leaving her breakfast untouched. Her appetite had vanished. With head held high, Ana walked from the table, stopped and turned at the door to re-address her brother-in-law, her skirts flaring around her ankles.

"I just thought you might support me … you might have some information to help me secure a position. I … I don't want pity from family and friends, and I will not live by your leave!" Her voice quivered with high emotion. "Poor Ana," they'll say. "She never found a suitable match. Isn't it so generous of Eliza and Henry to care for her?" she cried, stomping her foot. "Henry, don't confine me to that. I'll … I'll go crazy!" Her eyes welled with tears that she did not want him to see. She turned and dashed into the hall.

"Henry, how could you?! You've not even heard her out," Eliza said. Pushing back her chair she quickly followed Ana into the hall.

"Damnation!" Henry muttered under his breath as his wife called, "Ana wait! Henry will hear you out. I insist upon it."

Stopping at the base of the stairs, Ana turned towards her sister.

Smiling through unshed tears Ana said, "Oh Liza, I knew you'd understand."

"Ana, I don't understand. But I accept it. Now, let's get back to breakfast. You must eat something," she coaxed, extending her hand.

Rolling his eyes, "God's teeth!" he muttered, certain now he was going to lose this fight as he watched them reenter hand in hand.

"Henry, please," Eliza gently chided. "Just listen. Maybe you'll understand. I don't like this any more than you do. But, Ana's right. She's not a child." Eliza motioned Ana back to the table as she sat next to Henry. Taking his hand, she continued. "If you're willing to help, she'll be able to find a much more secure position with people we know who have good reputations."

Ana sat quietly fiddling with the corner of her napkin as she listened to her sister. Henry's face began to soften. She bit the inside of her lip with anticipation.

"I know Ana, and when she gets an idea that she believes in ... well there is no stopping her. You know that. If you don't help her Henry, I am afraid she'll move forward and end up in some distant forsaken place. I will lose her forever. Henry, I can't lose more family." Eliza's voice began to break. "I just can't."

Henry opened his mouth to speak but Ana beat him to it.

"Henry, I can't be a burden to you and Eliza. Our family has been through enough. I need to make my own way. I have no marriage prospects and with Mother and Father gone, I just can't see anyone of our society finding me a suitable match. I'd be a burden to anyone. I'll not take pity."

Henry was outnumbered. "I don't pity you Ana," he softened. "But I can't fight you both either," he sighed shaking his head, "I don't believe I'm going to say this but ... I'll ask around at the club this afternoon. Someone must surely know of a family in need of a governess," he yielded.

"Oh Henry! Thank you, thank you!" her turquoise eyes twinkled as her face brightened into a beautiful wide grin. She leaned over and gave Henry a big kiss on the cheek. He blushed.

"Oh, I AM hungry," Ana smiled taking a forkful of cold eggs.

The dark mahogany chambers of Henry's club in Whitehall were thick with the smell of tobacco and brandy. Men were sitting around small tables or lounging in large soft leather chairs deep in conversation, playing cards, or just reading the day's *Times*. Waiters in formal attire and starched collars scampered around meeting the needs of their wealthy patrons.

"Ah, Jacob Sumner, just the man I was hoping to find," Henry said as he sat down at the table. Jacob Sumner was Henry's solicitor as well as his friend.

"Well, good afternoon, ole' chum. How is your growing family?"

"Never better," he said with a hint of sarcasm. He ordered a port.

"I've been reading up on that war in the Colonies. Bloody mess, I'd say. I think that Lincoln chap needs to concede and stop the bloodbath."

"Listen Jacob, I would love to talk about war, but Eliza has me on a mission."

"A mission, you say," Jacob laughed. Not being married himself, he thought the whole idea of running and jumping to the beck and call of a woman utterly ridiculous.

"That wife of yours has you wrapped around her little finger," he teased as his eyes laughed, twirling his pinkie at Henry.

"Jake, you don't know the half of it," Henry sighed shaking his head, "now that Ana has been living with us."

"That's right. Two of them! You poor fellow," Jacob quipped with a crooked smile, his left brow raised.

"Well, Eliza insists I ask around about this preposterous scheme Ana's hatched." Henry felt as if he had been shaking his head all day trying to get the idea to sink into his brain.

Jacob sat back in his chair giving his beleaguered friend a gap-toothed grin and sipped on his brandy. "Oh, this is going to be bloody good."

"Ana's decided she wants to be a governess."

"A governess!" Keeping the grin in place, his eyes mocked at his friend's dilemma. He took a long drag on his enormous cigar, enjoying the aroma, watching the smoke swirl in the air as he slowly blew it out.

"Jacob, she's serious. Stop laughing!" Now perturbed, Henry took a gulp of his port.

"Sorry, ole' chum." Serious now, he sat upright. "Alright, tell me more."

"Well, Ana thinks she's an old maid and a burden. So, she came up with this … this scheme to … oh yes, 'make her way' in the world. With both women badgering me this morning I agreed to ask around. So I'm asking."

Jacob struggled to stay serious.

"She thinks it's a position she's qualified for. She does help us a great deal with our own girls and has a splendid education. However, she has no other experience. And for heaven's sake, she is a daughter of a Baron. This has a potential for scandal."

"I realize this might be gauche; how old is she?"

"Twenty-four."

"Hmmm." Jacob scratched his chin. "I remember when your in-laws had that tragic accident last December. It still saddens me."

"Yes," Henry said, shaking his head at the thought of all the pain and sadness the family had endured in the course of a few short months.

"Left a good income then?"

"Meager."

With gentle truth Jacob replied, "I hate to say this, my friend, but she's probably right about the old maid thing. Personally, if I were the marrying type, I'd prefer a more experienced woman rather than the children most men marry these days. But that's me."

"Any way to get you to be the marrying type?" Henry looked up, fleetingly hopeful.

"Ah, nope, I decided to be a bachelor long ago and I'm not going to change my mind now. I've seen too many men become weak-kneed ninnies over a woman; example at hand."

"Jacob, when you meet the right one, you'll fall hard, my friend," Henry laughed. "Mark my words."

Ignoring him Jacob now answered thoughtfully, "You know, I actually have a client who recently inquired about a governess. Who was that?" he said as he tapped his lower lip. "Oh, yes, a Lady Catherine Luttrell of Dunster, near Minehead, I believe. Her son is Duke of Exmoor or something."

"A Duke you say?" Henry was impressed.

"Well, wait, before you jump in here. You might remember this chap, a Sir Alexander Luttrell?"

"Luttrell, Luttrell. Now that you mention it the name's a bit familiar. Wasn't there some scandal? A divorce? Wife took a lover and ran off or some such thing before his return from India?"

"The very one."

"He hasn't remarried?"

"I think he's 'confirmed' like myself, if memory serves."

"Frequents brothels, does he?" Henry was suspicious, knowing his friend's own predilection towards the same.

"Wouldn't be surprised, but it's not part of the rumor mill," Jacob added with a wink. "But I have heard he's brought back some black girl from India. I am sure she is useful to him, if you get my meaning."

Henry tapped his fingers on the table. "Well, Ana's certainly not returning to her childhood home."

"Henry, it's Lady Catherine doing the retaining, not the Duke, although it's his sons. There are two young boys, you know. It is quite a bit for one old gal to handle by herself, especially when the Duke's in town on the Queen's business."

Henry sat quietly and thought, a slow smile crossing his face. "You know this just might be the ticket. Give her a bit of a scare … two rambunctious boys, a disgraced divorcé who has an apparent problem with women, girls from India, old Lady Catherine … I like it! She'll be home again in no time. Governess … bah!" Henry downed the last of his cup. "Let's do it!" he resolved, bringing his empty glass down loudly upon the table.

The two men left for Jacob's offices to close the deal and send a letter off to Lady Catherine. Ana was going to get her wish, and if all goes to plan, she'll return in a fortnight.

CHAPTER 4

Though quite sure he had made the right decision, Henry knew Eliza was not going to be pleased. He couldn't imagine Ana accepting the post. But if she did take the position, she was sure to see the folly of her ways and quickly return home. Most likely she'd be furious with him for making arrangements without consulting her first. He wasn't looking forward to spending the evening with two angry women, yet he felt secure his scheme was worth it.

Ana was waiting for him in the hall like an eager pup, filled with anticipation.

"Henry, would you like a brandy? I'll take your hat. Can I get your paper? I'll fluff the pillows on your chair. Would you like a cigar?"

"God's teeth, Ana, let me be!" Henry barked. "Where's Eliza?"

"She's upstairs with the girls, seeing them to bed," Ana said anxiously. "So, do you have any news?"

"Pour a brandy. I'm going to see my family," he said sternly, ignoring her questions. "And pour one for yourself," eyeing her up and down. "You look like you need it. When I return, I want you seated and quiet! Do you understand?"

"Henry, I just ..."

"Enough!" he bellowed turning on his heels toward the stairs. "Sit!"

"Oh dear!" Ana exclaimed as she plunked herself down on the settee, "He's found nothing." Her heart dropped to the pit of her stomach. Her fingers tapped on the arm of the chair. "Sit! What, am I a dog?" she thought out loud. "This is not fair."

Spying his paper on the footrest Ana resolved to peruse the ads herself. Surely someone had to be looking for a governess. Deciding to pour the brandy Henry had suggested, just to steady her nerves, she took a sip. The alcohol burned her throat. "Oh! How can they drink this stuff?" she said scrunching her face in disgust. Putting the glass down, she picked up the paper.

But hearing Eliza and Henry coming down the stairs, she quickly returned to her seat. Eliza entered first, joining Ana on the couch.

"Ana," she said cheerfully. "Henry has some good news."

Ana's turquoise eyes opened wide with excitement and her face flushed, bringing out the natural pink in her light olive completion.

"Henry, you devil! Leading me on as if there was nothing! Do tell all!" she exclaimed breathlessly while taking Eliza's hand in hers.

"Let me get the brandy that I thought YOU were pouring for me." He took his time, enjoying the anticipation on their faces while at the same time dreading the ire he was sure to receive. Finishing the drink, he placed the empty glass on the table and considered pouring another.

He slowly pulled the footrest in front them. With his elbows on his knees, he looked squarely into their eager faces as if he were going to tell the sweetest gossip of the season.

Clearing his voice, he began, "Do you remember that scandal several years ago about a Lord Alexander Luttrell, Duke of Exmoor?"

Ana shook her head as Eliza nodded. "Ana you were too young to be interested. What does he have to do with it? Henry?" Suspicious of her husband, she squinted her blue eyes.

"Well, I saw Jacob Sumner at the club this afternoon. He informed me that the Duke's mother, Lady Catherine Luttrell, sent an inquiry to hire a governess for her two young grandsons." Henry sat back with a satisfied smile. He had said it.

"Henry! How could you?" Eliza said, looking shocked. "He's divorced!"

"So?"

"Tell me. What are you talking about?" Ana pleaded her interest sparked. They ignored her.

"I will not have my sister living and working in a home with a divorced, unattached man, especially a man with a scandal connected to his name. What were you thinking?"

"Henry?" Ana tried to break in.

"It's his mother, the Lady Catherine who is employing though it is for the Duke's two young sons." Henry explained.

"What scandal?" Ana asked looking from Eliza to Henry.

"Besides," Henry continued, "he has an estate near Minehead in Somerset, a Dunster Castle or something. It's barely a two-day ride, one if you don't stop. I believe he also has a house here in town." He smiled thinking it was already working towards his advantage.

"Henry, how could you!" Eliza exclaimed with anger and astonishment. "I will not have my sister employed by that scoundrel. I've heard it said that he is so hard and cold it forced his poor wife to leave!"

"Scoundrel? Please, won't someone tell me what is going on?" Ana demanded.

"Why else would a woman leave her children? And then there's that Indian girl he brought back with him," Eliza added.

"What?" Ana asserted, "What do you mean, Indian girl?"

"His wife left him, Eliza, of her own accord. In light of the situation, he had little or no choice but to divorce her," Henry argued. "Anyway, I have it by good authority that he has sworn off women." This was just what he wanted. Eliza was not pleased. It would not bode well for Ana.

"Why did his wife leave?" Ana felt like she was talking to herself. "That's an interesting twist," she thought.

"No, absolutely, not!" Eliza stood up and began to pace, ignoring Ana's question. "A man swearing off women … I have never heard of anything so ridiculous. He's not a monk. I suppose it's why he has that … that … black Indian girl."

Henry looked over at Ana hoping to see the same dismay but instead saw a slight smile and her eyes bright with the intrigue.

"Eliza, don't be silly, I think it sounds fine. Besides, maybe she is just a servant girl," Ana exclaimed, finally getting the attention of her sister.

Stunned, Eliza suddenly looked over at Ana. Her mouth dropped open at what she heard.

"It's just what I want," Ana continued. "Anyway, I'll be working for Lady Luttrell, not her scandalous son, just like Henry said. So, I'll take the position." Her face was flushed with excitement.

"Ana, no!" Eliza said sternly looking directly at her sister, her hands on her hips. "No sister of mine is going to work for …. a … libertine! I forbid it!"

"Well, Eliza, it's a bit too late." Henry added though he felt his plan was going a bit awry with Ana's excitement.

"What do you mean?" Eliza's blue eyes flashed fire in his direction.

Knowing he was going to take a big hit for this one, Henry cleared his throat and said tentatively, "Well, after Jake told me of their circumstances, I thought it was exactly what Ana wanted. So, we went to his office and sent a letter of agreement."

"What? You did what? And without my consent?" Eliza's voice rose several decibels.

"I don't need your consent," Ana stated quietly. She was being completely ignored.

"Now, now dear, don't get too upset. The baby you know," Henry cooed.

"Don't you patronize me, Henry Colwell. This is scandalous for us! What were you thinking?"

Eliza began wringing her hands as she paced, her mind filled with the consequences of Henry's dealings. She felt responsible for her younger sister. It felt as if they were throwing her to the wolves, or at least one wolf, one big unattached male wolf. With a prospect of scandal this great, it would be better to send her to live with Charles! Though she was level-headed, Eliza knew Ana was sometimes impetuous and definitely ignorant of the world. This was not one of her sister's shining moments, and Eliza glared at her.

"Who's going to protect her? What about her reputation, not to mention the reputation of our own two daughters?" Eliza demanded. "And … and who is going to protect her?"

"Eliza, don't I have a say in this? We are speaking of my life after all," Ana said quietly.

Eliza stared at her sister, aghast at her foolishness.

"Ana, I was willing to support you in this, but this is just too much," she said pursing her lips and shaking her head in disbelief.

"Eliza, it will be all right. There'll not be a scandal. Besides, Lady Catherine also wants Ana as a paid companion, not just as governess for the boys," Henry continued. "Anyway, that old scandal has well passed interest and other, more juicy tidbits are now afoot."

Eliza let out a sigh of frustration.

It was too late to make Ana see the foolishness of her ways but Henry was convinced that she would return posthaste to her home with them. In fact, he would bet on it.

Henry stood up and took his wife by the shoulders. "Eliza, my dearest, all will be well. You know my stand on this issue so I would never place Ana in harm's way," he said as he took her into his arms. "Besides if Ana finds herself unhappy, she can always return home ... to us."

Eliza began to relax at that thought, "Yes, Ana can always return home."

Ana always felt uncomfortable with their closeness. It had been something she dreamt of for herself, but the sudden death of her parents made her keenly aware that her life had changed forever. If adventure was all she would have, then so be it. Love and security would never be hers now and she would have to fulfill her natural maternal instincts with someone else's children.

"Henry?" Ana asked quietly watching the tenderness between them. "When do I start?'

"Two weeks."

"Two weeks?!" she exclaimed. "Why that's barely enough time to get ready. Oh, Eliza, who ever thought my life would take such an exciting turn, and in only two weeks!" Now determined, Ana stood up. "I must go and begin to prepare."

She stopped at the door and turned towards Eliza and Henry, her eyes glistening, her voice filled with gratitude. "Thank you! Thank you both!"

The next weeks were filled with a flurry of activity and anticipation as Ana prepared for her new life as governess at Dunster Castle. "Travel light," Henry suggested. So, she packed only a few of her best dresses and donated the rest to charity.

"What you are taking?" Eliza asked helping her sister pack.

"These two dresses for dinner; the turquoise that Mother gave me last Christmas, and this brown silk from you and Henry. I think this gray one and this brown plaid, a governess must be modest you know," the sisters laughed, "Several collars and cuffs. How many bonnets should I take?"

"Maybe two. Don't forget a good pair of walking shoes," Eliza added. Though she did not agree, Eliza had accepted that this was her sister's decision and did not want her to leave with a rift between them. Anyway, she could not stay mad at Ana for long. "Gloves and cloak too."

"Yes, and my silver brush set from Mother and Father."

Ana placed her folded garments in the large wooden trunk Henry had provided for her and looked lovingly at her sister. "Eliza, I must confess, I'm a bit frightened by this whole proposition. What if they don't like me?"

"You can always come home. You know how Henry and I really feel about this." Eliza hoped she might be changing her mind.

"Staying here is out of the question. This is something I must do for myself. But it doesn't mean that I don't have feelings about leaving you all. And I'm a bit nervous." Ana was clearly worried but quickly added, "However, I'm determined to succeed."

"I can't imagine you won't be liked. But I'm wary about this Duke. I don't like the fact that he is divorced and remains unattached. I think it's too dangerous."

"Oh Liza, don't be silly. He's most likely never remarried because he is old and fat. You know how those Dukes can get." They laughed.

"Yes, and with the gout."

"And I'm sure he wears those horrible outdated wigs …"

"No, his mother wears wigs and paints her face white with a dark mole on her chin."

"You think he's a fop? He does have a French name."

"Oh yes, of the worst kind. Sniffing snuff and drinking claret all day."

"And don't forget those French pastries which made him so fat."

"You mean the ones that gave him the gout?"

"The very ones!" They giggled like young girls as they painted a picture of the old and feeble Duke of Exmoor.

"Do you think he chases his servants around the house looking for favors?" Eliza's eyes widened in horror at the thought.

"Oh no, he is much too fat to catch any of them." Ana blew out her cheeks, held her arms out around her middle and lumbered around the room mimicking the fat old duke in pursuit of a poor housemaid.

They laughed so hard it brought tears to their eyes.

"Oh," Eliza stopped and placed her hand on her belly. "We made the baby kick."

"Let me feel," Ana said as she placed her hand on Eliza's expanding belly. "I feel it," she smiled at her sister.

Eliza's face became somber. "Ana I'm going to miss this. I'm going to miss you. I can't believe you're leaving so early tomorrow morning." Her eyes welled up with tears, ending their laughter. The two sisters embraced.

"I'm not moving too far away. I'll write and visit. You know I will," Ana assured her sister. "We shall write pages and pages. I can be home in a day and a half."

"I do look forward to hearing about this fat old Duke. You must give me as clear a picture as you can. But Ana, what if he is handsome?" Her blue eyes widened.

"No, he's fat, most definitely old and fat." Ana convinced herself as she smiled at Eliza.

It was difficult to sleep. The excitement of the next days' journey and new life rushed through Ana's head. She wondered if Lady Catherine was old and cranky or sweet and friendly. Then there were the two young boys. Other than Miles and Charles, Ana had to admit she had no experience with young boys. She decided she must be firm with them; establish firm rules from the beginning. Of course, spiders and frogs would be part of their lives. Plus, boys play at war, the very thing that killed Miles in the end; the foolish idea that war is glory. If it was not for that, she would have her family around her now. She might have even found a husband and had her own family. But because of war, she was going to start a new life, a different life.

Ana smiled thinking of her conversation with Eliza. Any Duke named Alexander had to be old and fat. He was most likely indulged and spoiled as a child. "Oh, Alexander?" she could hear his mother calling, "Pastries, dear." She chuckled.

But what if he was young and handsome as Eliza said? Would he be dark and brooding like Mr. Rochester? Cold and prejudiced like Mr. Darcy? Maybe stormy and savage like Heathcliff. He most definitely had a torrid history and sullied reputation. Whatever he was, she was going to teach his sons and be his mother's companion and not to have silly fanciful dreams about an old Duke.

CHAPTER 5

*T*he early April fields were tipped white with glistening frost as the golden rays, struggling to break through morning clouds, danced across the twinkling landscape. But Ana did not notice the cold or the view from her coach window. She was dreaming of Dunster Castle in Exmoor with its exotic and romantic fantasies: riding on the moors, walking on the moors, being rescued on the moors. Despite Eliza's concerns about silly scandals and Tess's warning about the boring life of a governess, Ana believed that this was the beginning of a new life filled with excitement and adventure. Maybe not love, but adventure.

It was hard leaving Eliza and her family behind yesterday morning. Even Charles came to bid her farewell. He was not pleased by her decision either but had no choice but to accept it. Ana hoped Charles would soon find a more suitable match. Even he had the right to happiness.

Barely noticing the passing countryside and small hamlets, Ana continued to wonder. Would the boys be a challenge? Would she and Lady Catherine become friends? Then there was Sir Alexander Luttrell, the man of scandal, with a jaded and cynical reputation where women were concerned. It made him very intriguing and a bit dangerous. As tantalizing as it was, she determined it would be best to just follow the sound advice given to her by Tess: *Remember you're a servant now and take the direction given by your master.*

A servant, Ana thought. She was not used to taking orders from others and hoped she could manage to keep her tongue and her temper.

After an overnight is Salisbury, Ana's journey was over before she knew it. Ahead Ana could see a shimmering outline of the castle keep floating above the fresh spring green plain. Turning off Loxhole Bridge, the orange sun hung low in the sky as the coach turned onto Dunster Steep towards the castle. A single hilltop tower was visible through the trees to the right; the ancient dark turrets of the castle gleamed golden high in the distance to the left. As the carriage turned, they entered the small town of Dunster nestled at the base of the castle mount. Ana searched out both sides of her coach glancing at quaint thatched-roof cottages, the stuff of fairytales. There was an interesting hexagon building situated in the middle of the road and wood framed Tudor-style shops with white stucco facades lining the streets. At the steep incline, the carriage came to a halt.

"Dunster Castle, Miss," the coachman announced through the hatch door. Helping her down, he placed her luggage on the ground and with a tip of his hat and flick of his whip was off.

Ana stood at the entrance of an ancient stone gatehouse, her heart beating feverously with anticipation. Ivy-lined walls led to an iron gateway welcoming all who entered. There was an ancient seal set into the stonework above the sally port. If the castle itself had any likeness to its gatehouse it would be magnificent.

As she made her way through the arched gateway and wound her way up the stairs to her right, the castle came into view. The mauves and yellows from the sunset glistened on the many windows, turrets and chimneys. There were numerous floors and the building's pink sandstone walls gleamed in the late afternoon sun. The same curious crest of two chained swans surrounding a shield emblazoned on the helmet of an impressive stone knight posted guard above the entrance door of the castle.

"So, this is to be home," she sighed. "I think I can do this," she said out loud, giving herself reassurance and encouragement, "No," she said even more determinedly, "I know that I can do this."

"Hmmm, no knocker," she said under her breath. She noticed a small chain and gave it a pull. Somewhere, deep within the recesses of the castle she heard the faint tinkle of bells. She adjusted her bonnet and gloves and smoothed out her skirts. The anticipated moment had arrived. The knob turned. The large wooden door opened on what was to be her new life.

"May I help you, Miss?" an elderly and very formal butler said.

"Yes, sir, I am Miss Ana Pembroke … the new governess?" She made a small curtsey.

"Do come in," he said, opening the door for her entrance. "We have been expecting you."

"Thank you, sir," she said following him into the great hall. The fading light created dust beams that streamed through the large glazed panes giving the cavernous hall an ethereal glow. The walls were a soft cream color with wooden panel overlays. A red Turkish carpet set off the exquisite white plasterwork of the ceilings. There were large marble fireplaces to one side and two wooden carved arches, with the head of a large trophy deer mounted in between. She could envision the knights as they sat around the long tables in the center of the room. It felt very grand and very ancient.

"I'm Chesterton," he said nodding his head. "You must be tired from your journey. Follow me to the kitchens."

Walking to the next hall past the magnificently carved sweeping oak staircase, Ana glanced at the ornately framed portraits of Luttrell family ancestors. They walked through the grand dining room and Ana couldn't help but notice two life-size statues of Indian servants on either side of the large fireplace. "My, this is a grand estate," she said.

"Yes Miss," was all he said. Entering an inconspicuous door at the end of the dining room, Ana followed Chesterton down a few winding steps through the pantry. Large cupboards with locked glass doors housed ornate china suitable for enormous dinner parties, along with crystal goblets, and gold and silver bowls. She suddenly felt like a rustic rather than a daughter of a Baron.

At the end of a long hall, they entered the scullery and large kitchen. Great gray slates made up the floor. There were three lancet windows at the head of the room, large sinks against one wall, cabinets for storage, baskets for laundry and such, and herbs and flowers hung to dry. There was also a rather large fireplace with a very modern stepped black iron cook stove, heavy iron kettles and copper pans and an imposing but well-worn wooden table in the center of the room. There several frightening rows of bells for summoning the many servants.

Wordlessly Chesterton pulled out a chair. Ana sat obediently.

"Mrs. C. will be in momentarily," he said stiffly. "I suspect you have luggage?"

"Oh, yes sir, my trunk is by the gate. Thank you," she said politely.

"I'll have it brought to your room," he said formally. His face suddenly softened as an older woman entered the kitchen. "Ah, Mrs. C., Miss Pembroke has finally arrived. I believe she is tired and may be hungry."

"Yes dearest," Mrs. C. replied with a soft smile. Ana decided they must be married and made quite a nice couple.

Mrs. C. was a tall matronly woman with graying red hair stuffed into a clean white cap. Her face was lined from satisfaction rather than worry. The keys attached to the chain on her waist demonstrated her efficiency. Her cheeks were rosy pink and she had the clearest blue smiling eyes. "Don't mind Mr. C.," she began, "He takes his position very seriously as should we all, but sometimes I think he likes to act quite stuffy to intimidate. It's really all show you know."

Ana smiled. *I'm going to like them*, she thought.

"Are you hungry, my dear?"

"Yes, thank you, I am," Ana replied realizing she had nothing substantial to eat since the early breakfast at the inn.

"I have some cold meat pies, cheese and fruit. I put the kettle on as soon as I heard the bell," she said as she placed the food and a china cup on the table. "Have your fill, my dear and when you are done, I'll take you to your room as the sun will soon set. Tomorrow you shall meet Lady Catherine, Geoffrey and Hugh. I'll give you a bit of a tour. It's a large home as you can see, so I wouldn't want you to get lost. Now eat up."

"It's delicious," Ana said, "I didn't realize I was so hungry."

"I'll tell Cook. Do you like history my dear?"

"Why yes, I do."

"Well then you'll love this place. We have such a grand history here. The Luttrells have been here for over four hundred and fifty years." Mrs. C. continued to chat proudly on about Dunster Castle, the Village of Dunster and Exmoor Park while Ana had her meal. "And you'll enjoy exploring our local ruins, the mill and bridges." When she saw that Ana had finished, she led her up the back steps to the upper floors of the castle and her room.

"Lady Catherine and Lord Alexander have their apartments down that hall. Your room is by the nursery in this direction," Mrs. C. said. Ana followed silently, in awe of the art and architecture in her new home.

"Yes, here you are, dear," she said as she opened the door. "I'll wake you on the morrow at six. Have a good rest. I'm sure we will get along just fine." Mrs. C. gave her a warm smile.

"Thank you, Mrs. C. I like it here already. Good night and thank you again for the refreshment," Ana said returning the smile.

The candle by the bed gave a soft golden glow to the room. It was not large but cheery and comfortable enough. It had an adequate bed with long red curtains and blue canopy, a dressing stand, wardrobe and drawers and a writing table with a small chair. A warm fire burned to ward off the cold and damp of the spring night. The window had beautiful blue draperies that complimented the coverlet. Her trunk was neatly placed at the foot of her bed. The plush red and blue Turkish rugs felt warm and soft under her tired feet. Yes, she thought, this will do just fine. "Welcome home, Ana," she said to herself as she placed her gloves and bonnet on the desk.

"Good morning, my dear," Mrs. C. said with a cheery smile. Soft pink morning light streamed into the room making it look larger than she remembered.

"Good morning Mrs. C."

"How did you sleep?"

"Very well thank you. I must've been exhausted," Ana stretched and yawned.

"There is breakfast waiting for you in our kitchen. Do you remember your way down?"

Ana nodded.

"Good. Lady Catherine would like to meet you promptly at eight. Following breakfast, I'll show you the castle then take you to Lady Catherine."

"Yes, thank you," Ana said as her eyes adjusted to the morning light.

"I'll see you downstairs," Mrs. C. smiled closing the door behind her.

Ana quickly saw to her toilet and dressed in her plain gray dress, her collar and cuffs, white and clean. She plaited her long unruly hair and fastened it to the back of her head. With a final look in the mirror she decided she was ready to face her first day. She took in a deep breath and slowly let it out. She found her way to the kitchen where she had been the night before.

"Good morning," Ana said shyly. Mrs. C. swiftly and kindly made introductions to the other castle staff.

"This is Cook. Bess works upstairs and helps with the boys. Rollins drives the coaches and oversees the stables." She also introduced a few of the footmen and other household workers.

"Welcome," Bess said. "I'm glad you got here safely. We can sure use help with them boys. I know Lady Catherine'll be glad of it." She had a nice smile and warm brown eyes.

"How was your carriage ride?" Rollins asked.

"It was well enough, thank you," Ana responded. She was pleased to meet all the new faces and feeling very welcome indeed.

Following breakfast, Mrs. C. took Ana through the castle. The dining room had dark paneled walls and long beautiful windows. They passed the magnificent carved oak staircase off the inner hall and impressive outer hall. There was a conservatory, drawing room, and library where Lord Luttrell saw tenants of the estate.

"Is Lord Luttrell here?" Ana asked, her curiosity piqued.

"No, he's in London. As a Knight of Bath, he has military duties to perform for Her Majesty, you know."

"Oh," Ana said, much humbled by his posts. "I didn't know he was also a knight."

"Yes, the Luttrell family has quite a history. I believe they came with William the Conqueror and fought in the Battle of Hastings. They were originally granted lands and castle in Nottingham," she added.

"Oh my!" Ana exclaimed.

"And here is the orangery." Mrs. C. led her into a beautifully sun lit room with orange and lemon trees in enormous pots. Outside the windows were rows of palm trees.

"Real palm trees? And what is that distant tower way over there?" she asked.

"That is Conygar tower, Miss. That was put up as a folly by Henry Luttrell over a century ago. It has a beautiful view of the Bristol Bay."

"It's impressive I must say," Ana said. "When was this castle built?"

"There's been castle here since William the Conqueror's invasion. It was built by William de Mohun in 1068."

"No wonder it looks so ancient," Ana said as she followed Mrs. C. from room to room.

Each room was grander than the next, like in a fine museum. As they walked through the home, Mrs. C. instructed servants busy polishing and cleaning. She pointed out portraits of Luttrell family ancestors.

"Is there a portrait of the current Lord Luttrell?" She could not help but be curious.

"No, he has not had one commissioned. I hope he does. It would be a shame not to have his likeness. He's very impressive."

"Yes." Ana could not bring herself to ask if it was his titles or the man himself. The question had to wait. Somewhere within the castle a clock chimed eight.

CHAPTER 6

*M*rs. C. looked at the timepiece pinned to her apron. "Eight o'clock on the dot and Lady Catherine's sitting room is right here."

"Thank you for the tour. What an impressive family, Mrs. C. It's such a grand historic house. Overwhelming actually," Ana said, her turquoise eyes wide.

"You'll get used to it. I did," she smiled as she knocked on the door. "You will find Lady Catherine and the boys make it quite a home."

A muffled "Enter" was heard through the door and Mrs. C. opened it. "You'll do fine," she whispered giving Ana the assurance she needed.

The room was filled with colors of soft pastel greens and peach. There were white bookshelves, an ornate white German stove, plush floral chairs and a beautiful French writing desk in the middle of the room. Sitting behind the desk was Lady Catherine Luttrell. Ana could feel her heart beat wildly as she walked and stood before the grand lady, who was deeply engaged in writing, purposefully giving Ana a moment for study. She was a small elderly woman, a little overly plump, bedecked in a grand china blue organdy dress. Her gray hair was piled high on her head in a very old-fashioned coiffure topped with a lace cap. She had fine Austrian lace around her neck and wrists. Her fingers were encircled with some of the most beautiful glistening jeweled rings that Ana had ever seen. But what was most impressive was the long strand of gleaming gray pearls that hung down around her neck and fell into her lap. To Ana, Lady Catherine was as opulent as the castle in which she lived.

Dusting her letter, with a gentle blow Lady Catherine finally looked up. Ana could see by her dancing bright blue eyes that she would like her at once. They immediately smiled at each other.

"Have a seat my dear, you don't need to stand in front of me." She motioned one of her bejeweled hands towards a finely upholstered chair.

Ana gave her a small curtsy and took the seat. "Thank you, Milady."

"So you are Miss Ana Pembroke, daughter of the late Sir William Pembroke, Baron of Milford. I'm sorry to hear about the untimely death of your parents; how sad for you."

"Thank you, Lady Luttrell." Ana felt a touch of sorrow and appreciated the compassion.

"And now you wish to be our governess."

"Yes, Lady Luttrell." Ana sat straight as an arrow; her hands folded neatly in the creases of her gray skirt.

"Oh, no dear, please call me Catherine." She gave her a warm smile.

"Yes, ma'am, Lady Catherine," Ana felt a sense of regard at the request.

Walking around her desk, Lady Catherine took the chair next to Ana as if they were long lost friends.

"I'm so pleased to make your acquaintance. I have been so looking forward to having help with my rambunctious grandsons. As an old woman I don't have the energy a young girl would have." Ana smiled as Lady Catherine continued, "I hope your journey here was uneventful?"

"Yes, Lady Catherine. It went very well. Thank you."

"And your first night my dear?"

"Very comfortable, thank you."

"Good. This is to be your home now and I want you to be comfortable. So, what do you think of our humble abode, Ana?"

"It's magnificent. I would hardly call it humble."

Ana quickly pursed her lips, realizing she may have overstepped her bounds in correcting the great lady. "Oh, I am sorry!"

Instead of taking offense, Lady Catherine chuckled. "Yes, dear, you are right. A bit overwhelming, but that's what comes being married to a Duke." She gave Ana's hand a pat.

Ana could not help but smile back at her. Yes, they were going to get along very well.

Changing the conversation, Lady Catherine said, "I read your letter of introduction. Mr. Sumner explained your losses and the reason you desire work. I think it's very commendable." She looked tenderly at Ana. "First your brother to that infernal war in the States, then both of your parents in that horrid coach accident. I do hope that you are up for this, my dear."

"Thank you, Lady Catherine. I assure you I have healed sufficiently and am ready to take on life's new challenges."

"I'm curious though, why a governess? You are so young and pretty, I would think you would want marriage; a family of your own."

"I had wanted that once, however, with all that's happened I felt I needed to make my own way in the world. I didn't wish to be a burden on my sister and her family." Ana felt the old twinge in her heart about her decision, but determined to become self-sufficient.

The smile returned to Lady Catherine's face. "Yes. Good for you, girl! That is just what I liked about the letter. It said you were looking for challenges. Well they're here. I do have several expectations of you. I want my grandsons to be challenged, literature, the classics, you know, Shakespeare, Homer, Virgil; and history, very important. Geoffrey's the oldest. He needs special attention—one day he'll be Duke." Looking askance at Ana she added, "Some of which I think should be his father's job, don't you?"

Ana nodded in agreement, hoping Lady Catherine would talk about her son.

"Good. You will dine with us. Teach those boys etiquette. I have tried, but Lord knows, I'm only their grandmother. I'm sure I have spoiled them terribly. And their father ... Well, we'll talk about him some other time." Lady Catherine shook her head and made several short 'clicks' of her tongue.

Ana's hopes fell with Lady Catherine's comments, realizing now she would have to wait. The Duke of Exmoor would remain an enigma for the immediate future.

"Finally, I do hope that you will provide an old woman with some companionship," Lady Catherine continued, smiling at Ana. "I do get lonely for some female company from time to time."

"Oh, yes, Lady Catherine. It would give me great pleasure. I'm enjoying your company already," she said, returning the smile.

"You're a good girl." Lady Catherine leaned over, again patting Ana on the hand.

"You have free reign of the library. It's filled with books and journals of all sorts. My dear Albert loved to read and thought books were a gateway into the minds and souls of men. And there are lovely novels too. Do you enjoy reading, Ana?"

"Yes, Lady Catherine, my father too was an avid reader and he instilled his love for fine literature in all his children. He also dabbled with botany I dare say for all those dried flowers and insects in his library." Ana smiled at the memory of her father's intent study over a butterfly or flower.

"You know, with all the fine books we have, I still find myself drawn to our newest romances by the Bronte sisters, and Mr. Dickens. I find that I can read *Great Expectations* again and again and never tire of it. And of course, there is always Byron."

"I admit they are some of my favorites also."

"Splendid. Splendid. We can talk about them too." Lady Catherine clapped her hands like a young girl making Ana grin from ear to ear.

"Why, child, you have a lovely smile. We'll see to it that you smile quite a bit."

"Thank you, ma'am," Ana blushed, a bit uncomfortable with the compliment.

"Well, enough with our chat for today. I think it's time to meet the rest of the family, my dear. Shall we?" Lady Catherine stood up and went to the bell pull on the wall by the stove. Ana could hear a faint bell jingle in the deep recess of the castle. Soon, an exotic, girl of about sixteen came to the door. She was dressed in English garb except for large hoop earrings, a long black braid at her back and no shoes upon her feet.

"Yes, Missus Sahib?" the figure said, her accent thick.

"Riya, bring the boys around." Whispering to Ana, "Alexander brought her back from India you know. Took pity on her, poor thing."

"Yes, Missus Sahib," Riya curtsied as she looked over at Ana.

"Riya, this is Miss Pembroke. She's the new governess. I expect you to help her and follow her instructions."

As Riya curtsied again, Ana could not help but feel uncomfortable seeing this Indian girl. Knowing why Lord Luttrell had brought her, Ana found herself wondering what would make a man be interested in someone of such a different race. Not only that, but this young girl was a mere child. Ana thought it was most definitely indecent. Giving Riya a slight nod, she returned her attention back to Lady Catherine with a slight yet undiscernible lift of her nose.

"Let me tell you about Geoffrey and Hugh. Geoffrey is fourteen sometimes going on seven and sometimes going on forty. He is headstrong like his father. So, I suspect he'll be somewhat of a handful. Hugh, who is nine, on the other hand really is in need of attention. He was so young when his mother left, I'm truly concerned for him. He is such a sweet boy and Geoffrey sometimes just runs circle around him teasing him to distraction."

Both women looked up towards the door at hearing the ruckus from the hall. Suddenly, the door flew open with a crash and two rather disheveled and unruly boys unceremoniously fell into the room. The smaller of the two ran to his grandmother and threw his arms around her waist looking for protection. The other older boy gave the younger a quick slap on the head.

"What?" Hugh said to Geoffrey from his Lady Catherine's skirts.

"Geoffrey!" Lady Catherine reprimanded.

"Don't be such a sot, Hugh. We're here to meet our new governess." Geoffrey pointed at Ana who was now standing awaiting introductions and rather surprised by their unruly antics. Geoffrey had dark steely blue eyes and auburn hair which was most unkempt. It was obvious that he was going to be tall and handsome someday and was already eye level to Ana. Hugh had big brown eyes and sandy brown curls, and when he smiled his face lit up with the excitement and innocence of his youth. Geoffrey, however, appeared sadly jaded for a lad of his age.

Lady Catherine looked at Ana with apologetic eyes. "You can see what I mean. Stand up straight boys and behave yourselves, you should both know better. I'm ashamed at your behavior," she said firmly. The boys were instantly quiet.

"This is Miss Pembroke."

Geoffrey eyed Ana with a cool squint filled with suspicion while Hugh opened into a big dimpled grin revealing a missing tooth.

"Hello, Geoffrey, Hugh. I am so pleased to meet you both at last." Sticking her hand out for a shake, Ana knew it was going to be her job to make them comfortable with her, rather than the other way around.

"Welcome to Dunster Castle, Miss Pembroke," Geoffrey said flatly but very properly trying to be the gentleman. He pointedly did not take the hand she offered him.

"Why thank you Geoffrey. You have a lovely home and a most impressive ancestry." She casually let her hand drop to her side stung though she was by the rejection.

"Yes, it has been in our family for centuries. I come from a long line of Exmoor Dukes, you know. I will be the fourteenth Duke."

"I'm very impressed," Ana answered. *He's going to be a tough challenge* she thought.

"And how are you Hugh?"

"I'm hungry," he said, turning to Lady Catherine. "Grandmama, when is tea?" Geoffrey again gave his brother another swift slap to the head.

"What?" Hugh whined and twisted his face as he glared at his older brother.

Lady Catherine shook her head. "Geoffrey and Hugh, I want you both to take Miss Pembroke up to your nursery and show her where you study. I also want you both to show Miss Pembroke respect. She is here to teach you so it is important that you follow her instructions. Is that clear?"

"Yes, ma'am. Follow me," Hugh said, happy to lead the way, though oblivious to his grandmother's words of admonishment or direction.

"Thank you, Lady Catherine. I'm looking forward to getting started with them and looking forward to spending some time with you." And with a quick curtsey, Ana turned to follow the boys out of the room since they barely gave her time to show her respect.

"Good luck, Ana," Lady Catherine called after her.

"Thank you, Lady Catherine," Ana smiled at her new friend and was soon out the door.

She trailed the unruly boys up the grand staircase, past her room and down the long corridor to the nursery where they had their sleeping chamber, a play room, and a study. The study room had a long walnut table with four chairs, several bookcases, and a large dusty slate board with chalk bits on its sill. There was a bank of windows overlooking the gardens and walks. Papers were thrown about the table and books were askew everywhere and in dire jeopardy of getting their bindings permanently ruined. Ana could see she had her work cut out for her from the start as she bent over to pick up one of the mistreated volumes.

"This is a lovely room for lessons," Ana said looking about. "However, the first thing we're going to do today is tidy up."

"I don't tidy up. Riya can tidy up. We have servants for that, and you are one of them. So you can 'tidy up,'" Geoffrey said arrogantly, his chin up in the air. "Besides, I don't need a governess. I am fourteen and almost a man. A governess is for little boys like Hugh."

"That is true Geoffrey. You are almost a man. But you know, this is the room where we can learn all kinds of wonderful things, things that will help you to be the fourteenth Duke of Exmoor. We'll explore numbers and practice letters. I really want to see what you already know. Plus, we will learn about knights and castles and history. We will read exciting adventure stories. And we will learn responsibility. All of these things, Geoffrey, will help you become a proud and wonderful Duke, just like your father is today. Besides, you can help me with Hugh."

Geoffrey stopped to think about her offer. Adventure stories sounded quite interesting as did knights and castles. He especially liked the idea of helping with Hugh. But above he idolized his father and to be like him was his dream.

"I'm not going to be a Duke so Geoffrey you get to tidy up," Hugh said. Geoffrey glared at his brother through hard gray eyes, his lips pursed tightly together. Hugh stepped back as his brother's hand flew out to give him another whack on the head, but this time he missed.

"Ha!" Hugh pointed and exclaimed at the miss.

"No Hugh, you might be a doctor or a barrister, or a great scholar exploring the world for buried treasures for England," Ana explained.

"Ha! Ha! And Geoffrey, you get to be just a stupid Duke," Hugh jibed sticking out his tongue.

"Oh, you're going to get it now," Geoffrey threatened as he leaned in for another blow.

"Before anyone 'gets it' again, I think we need to settle down and set some rules. And the best rules are ones we make for ourselves," Ana suggested hoping to stave off any further attacks of violence on poor Hugh's head. "OK rule number one, cooperation. We all work together. Like a team," she said.

"Rule number two," Geoffrey chimed "we end classes by dinner," knowing dinner was at noon.

"OK, but we must then start very early in the morning. Shall we say five in the morning?" Ana asked knowing that wouldn't go over well.

Geoffrey thought about starting that early and didn't like the sound of it. "I would like to change that rule."

"Why of course. Would you prefer that we start at eight and end, let's say, around three in the afternoon, before tea?"

"Yes, that sounds better," Geoffrey made a face at Hugh.

"We can play after three, can't we?" asked Hugh.

"Yes of course you can play after three," Ana agreed. "And rule number three is we all work at keeping this room clean and tidy."

"I want to make a rule," Hugh whined. "My rule is we play after three o'clock."

Geoffrey was obviously frustrated with Hugh. "You are such a sot. You already said play after three."

"But we didn't make it a rule," Hugh whined.

"All right, rule number four—playing after three o'clock. And one last rule is, listen to your teacher. So there are five rules. Agreed?

Both boys nodded their heads. "Agreed."

"Let's begin by getting this room into shape and then you can both show me your work. Do we have an accord?" And they set about to accomplish their task.

Soon the room was neat and tidy with each boy demonstrating his skills. Time passed quickly and as the clock struck three, the boys went off to play, leaving Ana satisfied with her first day's work and contemplating her new life.

CHAPTER 7

The weeks flew by. Ana acclimated herself to her new surroundings and routine. Each morning she ate breakfast with the other servants which gave her the opportunity to make additional acquaintances with the many house staff. The Chestertons were a warm and loving couple who performed miracles with the grand house and with those in its service.

Bess was one of the servants who attended to general family needs. In addition, she served as ladies' maid to the Duchess. She had gentle brown eyes, unruly curls which she managed to keep neatly under her cap, and a distinct Irish brogue. She had been with the family for a number of years.

"Miss Pembroke, the boys'll be havin' their bath today. Linens will be changed in the nursery. So they will be a wee bit late for their studies," she informed Ana.

"Thank you, Bess," Ana said. She liked the woman and was pleased to find acceptance. She never had the inclination to engage with the servants in her own home and found the genuine spirits of the Luttrell staff refreshing. "I so appreciate all you do Bess. No one should ever take you for granted."

"Ach, go on Miss, I'm just doin' me' job's all. It's an honor to be of service to such a great family." Her face blushed pink at the compliment.

"All the same, I wanted to thank you," Ana said, reminding herself to do the same when she returned home for a visit.

Though she was a tremendous help, Ana remained uncomfortable around Ryia. She wondered about her odd connection with the Duke and therefore did not know how to have a relationship with the girl. So Ana remained suspicious and distant. But Riya was willing to do whatever was asked of her and appeared grateful for it.

"Riya, if you would dust the chalk board?" It was one of Riya's usual tasks.

"Yes Miss," was the most Riya said to Ana. She tidied up, kept the boys occupied when needed, and played with them in the afternoons. Otherwise Riya kept to herself.

Ana spent her days instructing the boys. She enjoyed discovering their skills and abilities and was finding it challenging to stay ahead of their lessons. Geoffrey excelled in his numbers and letters; he was so logical it was easy to see he would make a wonderful Member of Parliament someday. Hugh was sensitive; he loved the romance of history and might fill the British museums with wonderful artifacts. Ana was pleased to see Geoffrey becoming less critical of Hugh. For his part, Hugh was lapping-up the attention he so craved.

"Miss Pembroke, may I sit next to you today?" Hugh often asked, sometimes several times per day. Geoffrey responded by shaking his head, his eyes looking skyward.

"Geoffrey would you like to sit on this side?" Ana would offer.

"No thank you," was his reply, now always polite though always wary. He held fast to his opinion of not needing a governess.

Every afternoon after lessons, Ana enjoyed tea with Lady Catherine. They chatted about novels, fashions and the boys' progress with their studies. Lady Catherine also loved to share stories about Albert, her late and beloved husband. She enjoyed telling tales of their love and romance. Ana found herself drawn into the dream world of Dunster Castle, filled with balls, dinner parties and the warmth they shared as a family.

"Albert was such a wonderful man. I miss him so much," Lady Catherine said. "I wish you had the opportunity to meet him. He would've liked you very much I'm sure."

"Lady Catherine, that is so kind of you. I too wish I could have met him," Ana said. "Your life together sounds wonderful. I can tell you loved each other dearly."

"It wasn't like that in the beginning though."

"What do you mean?" It had sounded as if they always were in love.

"We were not a love match, Ana. We were arranged by our families. It was very uncomfortable at first. I didn't know what to expect. I don't think Albert wanted to marry me. We had to get to know each other. But with time we could see we were meant for each other," she explained. "Not all arranged marriages work though," she said wistfully.

"I know what you mean," Ana responded. "My brother-in-law wished to arrange one for me but I dared not risk it. He and my sister have such a wonderful, loving relationship. If I were to ever marry, I would want to do it for love. You were so lucky Lady Catherine that it worked for you."

"Yes, that I was, that I was. And I think you were wise. Sometimes arranged marriages leave people bitter and hurt. I was very lucky. I just wish my Alexander had the same luck. But that's a story for another time my dear," she concluded, leaving Ana to once again wonder about the mysterious Alexander Luttrell.

As was now her habit, Ana entered the large oak-paneled library to read and prepare for the next day's lessons. The warmth of the mid-spring day had lifted and a cool soft breeze came in from the distant bay. The boys were safely tucked into their rooms thanks to Bess's assistance, and the house was quiet from the daily bustle. Lady Catherine had been right, Lord Albert's extensive library was an impressive asset for any man of means. Ana found several books that she could use for Geoffrey's growing interest in Rome including the complete translated works of Virgil.

That task completed she began to explore the vast array of bookshelves. It was a practice that often had Ana lost in reading something quite different than what she had originally intended. She found a lovely book of poems by Byron and had been enthralled with Mary Shelley's *Frankenstein*. But tonight, Ana was excited to find a beautiful gold leaf copy of one of her favorites. She curled up on one of the cushioned seats of the large deep window. She lit a sconce on the nearby wall to provide reading light. With the house so quiet, Ana decided to make herself comfortable. She loosened the pins from her hair allowing her thick chestnut curls to fall about her back and shoulders. She then removed her shoes so she could tuck her feet under her skirts. She was now quite comfortable and ready to settle down and delve into her newfound treasure, *Jane Eyre*.

Sir Alexander Luttrell, Duke of Exmoor, Knight of the Order of Bath, Lord of Dunster Castle had returned late in the evening from his long journey to London. The Queen had requested his presence to provide advice on several issues regarding the dire situation in the Confederate States of America. He didn't agree with the current policies which the Crown had adopted. He felt, to maintain trade, the British Navy should break the blockades established by the Union and escort trade ships through to New Orleans.

Affairs of State always left him feeling wretched and exhausted. His head ached. He was glad to return home and knew he had been away longer than he had anticipated. Chesterton, as always, saw to it that he was fed and had a hot bath made ready to remove the dust of the road. Alexander informed him to have his sons prepared for an outing the next day. Perhaps some riding and fishing in this good clean country air with his boys would help remove the kinks in his neck and the pain in his back along with the fog in his brain from the foul city stench.

"What about their lessons, sir?" Chesterton queried, knowing full well that Lord Alexander had no idea of lessons.

Alexander looked puzzled. "Lessons, what lessons? What are you talking about?"

Chesterton cleared his throat, "Sir, Lady Catherine has hired a governess in your absence."

"Did she now? Well, governess be damned! Tell Bess to have the boys ready by eight." His headache was returning. "Just see to my request."

Chesterton met all his master's requests with the customary, "Yes, sir," "As you wish, sir," and "Very good, sir." And though he knew he could pump Chesterton for more information about this governess, Alexander decided he was too tired and would rather get the estate news in the morning.

Following his meal and hot bath, Alexander decided that a good book and a brandy would be just the thing to get him off to sleep and alleviate the return of his throbbing head, despite his ablutions.

It was nearing midnight and all were asleep. The brilliant moon was full and white, flooding the rooms with so much light that he did not need a candle to find his way into the dark library; his footsteps silenced by his brocade slippers. The library was one of his favorite rooms, a place of refuge and quiet away from the servants, his sons, and his meddlesome mother. It was where he could go to think, read, and manage his affairs, completely undisturbed.

As he pushed open the library door, he was dismayed to find a sputtering candle lit by the draped window. His brows knitted together in concern. He was going to have to speak with Mrs. C. about this. It was too dangerous to have an unattended candle in this room. The staff surely must know better than this. These books, some over five-hundred years old, were too precious to be lost in a careless fire. As he moved towards the light, his eyes were drawn to the sleeping figure of a young woman on the window cushion below. He most definitely needed to speak with Mrs. C. He began to feel the anger tightening his jaw, his tentative grasp on relaxation slipping away. It must be some new servant girl hired while he was in London. No respect these days, he thought. She will have to go. He then remembered Chesterton remarking on some governess his mother had hired. He decided to roust her and get her out of his way. As he reached over to shake her he stumbled over something on the floor.

"Damnation," he whispered through clenched teeth. He looked around to see what he tripped over. He saw a book: a copy of *Jane Eyre*. He frowned and picked it up checking for bent pages and broken bindings from its apparent fall. He was glad to see there was no damage. A governess who does not respect books; he shook his head. He closed the book and placed it on a nearby table.

Reaching down to roust her, the woman on the window seat shifted, her face partially exposed by the dwindling candlelight. She was young. Not what he would expect in a governess. They were usually angular old battle axes. Suddenly he was oddly intrigued to see this "governess" his mother had brought into his house without his approval. He felt strangely concerned about waking her. She looked so peaceful sleeping there. Yet something about her made him curious. He wanted a closer look. The candle gently illuminated her features, but the thick spill of auburn curls blocked her face from his view. His gaze traveled. He watched the rise and fall of her more than ample bosom as she breathed. His eyes shifted down to her slim waist and over the womanly curve of her hip. He noticed the white flounce of her petticoat which had lifted exposing part of a shapely calf, ankle and foot. His left brow lifted as an odd smile appeared on his face. This did not look like any governess he'd ever known. He felt oddly attracted to her, a complete stranger sleeping in the window of his library. He wanted to see more of her face. Slowly, his hand reached out to remove the curls blocking his view. He could see that she had fine features: a smooth forehead, a fine brow, long black lashes laid against her cheek. She had a slightly upturned nose with just a few freckles. Just as he was about to lift the curls from her mouth to see her lips, her eyes fluttered open. They were the most exotic turquoise eyes he had ever seen. They widened with surprise and shock at the sight of him. His heart skipped a beat. He'd been caught by an enemy.

"Geoffrey? What are you doing?" She said and closed her eyes tight, placing her hand over her face to block the light. Stealthily, Alexander quickly jumped back and moved into the shadows of the room. He watched as the young woman sat up and looked around the room. She didn't see him against the shadowed wall. He held his breath.

"Geoffrey?" she called again. He watched her shake her head, curls bouncing around her face. She rubbed the sleep from her eyes. "I must be dreaming," she said to herself. She stood up, stretching her arms forward. He wanted her to be still so he could see her clearly.

Ana began searching around herself. "Where is it?" She bent down to see if she could find the book but noticed one of her shoes on the floor and picked it up. Alexander watched with curiosity as she continued searching the floor for the other shoe.

"Where in the world?" She dropped to her hands and knees and began to look. Alexander was definitely enjoying the angle of her search as he watched her backside sway back and forth.

When she finally stood, Alexander could see both shoes in her hand.

"How did that get over here?" she said as she noticed the book on the table. She quickly glanced around the room. "Geoffrey?" she again asked the darkness, her voice a bit stern. She shook her head and picked up the book, finally turning so that he could see her face clearly in the soft candlelight. He was stunned. Her lips were full, crimson and sensuous. Her dark curls and almond shaped eyes made him think of an exotic harem beauty. She then leaned over and blew out the candle. The room suddenly darkened. Yet slits of moonlight beaming through the draperies provided some illumination. Alexander hoped she would not see him in the dark corner as she passed by and pressed even closer to the wall. With a slow sigh of relief, he watched her leave the library, book and shoes in hand, never knowing he was there.

Alone in the darkness, he frowned at his foolishness, a grown man hiding in his own library as if from some war enemy. Not only was he hiding, but hiding from a subordinate, a governess. What was his mother thinking? A governess was not like a new upstairs maid. She was an integral part of the family. She was going to influence his sons and they were going to become attached to her. Plus, this young woman did not look like the typical governess. He could see that. Not since Elizabeth left had there been a woman so closely involved with his family. And that was just the way he liked it. No women. His temples throbbed.

"Brandy be damned, where's that bloody whiskey?" He reached for the crystal decanter with the amber liquid and grabbed a glass, "Mother, you are up to something," he snarled. He took the bottle and his pounding head and made his way up to his rooms.

Ana knew it was late into the night and was angry with herself for falling asleep in the library. She had run up the stairs in her stocking feet and threw her shoes into the corner of her room. Quickly changing into her nightclothes, she plaited her hair and climbed under the soft down covers of her bed. Deep in the house she heard the clock strike twelve-thirty. She knew she was going to have an early start teaching Geoffrey and Hugh and hoped that she was not going to be too tired in the morning for her foolishness.

As she closed her weary eyes, her mind wandered back to the library. How odd. Why would she dream of Geoffrey staring so intently at her? Keeping her eyes closed, she began to picture the intense dark grayish blue eyes rimmed with thick black lashes that met hers. But it was not really Geoffrey's face at all. The eyes were the same but somehow older. It was much more a man's face, not that of boy at all. No, this face had a dark black mustache. Geoffrey was only fourteen with barely signs of a mustache. She began to remember the well-defined jaw and strong chin. He had a straight nose and strong brow. She remembered the dark hair that framed his face.

Suddenly, Ana opened her eyes and sat straight up in her bed wide awake with the realization. That was no boy. It was a man who had been staring so intently at her. But who, she wondered? It felt too real to just be a dream. A shiver ran down her spine as she thought of who might be inspecting her so closely. So closely that she could almost smell the nearness of him. His face was so close to hers, then he was gone. Ana sighed with confusion; it had to be a dream. She shook her head. There was no other explanation.

"I am reading too many novels," she said to herself as she lay back into her pillows with a plop.

"Too many silly talks with Lady Catherine of romance and love." I'm getting muddleheaded, she thought.

Within a few moments her eyes grew heavy, and she drifted off into a fitful sleep filled with dreams of mysterious men. Tall, dark haired, blue eyed men.

CHAPTER 8

*M*rs. C. entered Ana's room to throw open the thick drapes, allowing the brilliant morning sunshine to spill across the floor.

"Good morning, dear. You have a day off," Mrs. C. said brightly." I thought breakfast in your room might be a treat. You were sleeping so soundly I just couldn't wake you."

"A day off?" Ana said surprised, rubbing the sleep from her eyes and feeling exhausted from the late hour she retired to her bed. "What time is it?" she said, realizing it was much later than six.

"Dear it's almost seven-thirty. Lord Luttrell returned late last evening and will be taking the boys for the day. So, you are free to explore or relax to your heart's content."

"Thank you, Mrs. C. You're so kind to think of it," she said sincerely though she was somewhat confused.

"Your breakfast is on your dresser."

Ana sat up on the edge of her bed and stretched. Suddenly, she remembered her dream in the library. No, it couldn't have been Geoffrey. Feeling a bit uneasy, she frowned and bit her bottom lip. It must have been some kind of strange coincidence. Though she had never met Lord Luttrell nor seen a likeness of him, a man of his breeding would never spy on a sleeping woman. But then there was his sullied reputation to consider. She raised a brow in concern. It had to be a fanciful dream. There was no other explanation. So Ana decided to put the situation out of her head and enjoy her first, real day off in weeks.

Breakfast in her room was a luxurious treat. Pulling out several sheets of paper she decided to write to Eliza. Once satisfied with her report of the latest news, Ana began to dress. She put on her brown plaid dress and starched white collar and cuffs; cotton stockings and sturdy shoes for walking. Ana pulled on her gloves and stored her letter in her reticule. Giving herself a quick look in the mirror, she felt satisfied for the day's outing. She made sure that she shared her plan to walk into the town of Dunster with Mrs. C.

Leaving through the large front doors, Ana stood at the edge of the portico under the family crest taking in the beauty of the day. A light breeze off the distant bay fluttered the few exposed curls from under her straw bonnet. Her eyes delighted in the well-manicured gardens and fountains of the estate and she breathed deeply filling her lungs with the clean fresh air. Enjoying the crunch of the red gravel under her feet as she walked, she squinted up into the bright sunlit sky filled with billowy white clouds. It was going to be a perfect day. Suddenly, she realized that she had not felt this "normal" since before her brother's death and quickly felt guilty for it.

It was an especially warm morning for early June but the sun on her back felt invigorating. She came to the ancient gate where she entered all those weeks ago and rather than turning down High Street towards the main part of town, Ana decided to walk left around the castle mount towards the mill.

As she walked along swinging her arms to her gait, she began to whistle a lively tune. She knew she was being completely unladylike but she was fine with it. She noticed the thick forests of trees that opened wide onto fields filled with heath begging to bloom.

"So this is Exmoor," she said to herself. The meadows smelled heavenly to her, hinting at the scent of heather, wildflowers, and grasses. Her thoughts began to stray to the many romance stories she loved to read. Maybe it was a road just like this where Jane Eyre first encountered the dark and brooding Mr. Rochester. Perhaps it was a spot like this where his horse went down. She imagined Jane Eyre sitting on a 'style' just over there. She giggled at her fantasy.

She walked past several stone farm cottages with their neat whitewashed fences and colorful flower gardens. Pastures were filled with fluffy white horn

sheep and great shaggy Vernon red cattle. There was the occasional horse graz-
ing calmly on green clover. A small gaggle of geese ran loudly by in the direction of the babbling Avill River.

Finally, she came to the mill. She stood and watched the two wheels as it
pulled green-brown water from the river. The brilliant sun glistened gold and
white on the mesmerizing spray. The scent of the warm earth was intoxicating.
She noticed the geese swimming off the shore along with a longnecked swan.
She was filled with a sense of peace and calm.

Moving on, she saw the ancient stone bridge, Gallox Bridge, as Mrs. C.
called it, in the distance. The bridge curved gracefully over the river almost as
if it had been placed there by God. At further inspection of the bridge, she
could see the stones through the shallow water used for horse and cart while
the bridge itself was filled with the traffic of ancient and medieval pedestrians
coming to town to do their business. A beautiful thatched cottage sat in the
meadow on the other side of the bridge. Ana could not help but admire the
wholesomeness of the countryside. It was all so bright and beautiful. She waved
to a young boy with a dog tending his flock; he waved in reply. There was a
large outcropping of rock in the distance making some of landscape appear
jagged and raw. She could feel herself falling in love with Exmoor. All the while
Dunster Castle loomed high above her, standing guardian and protector to
the moors, the fields and hill and even to the Bristol Bay itself.

As she rounded the bend from Mill Lane to West Street, she stopped to
take in the view of the small village of Dunster with its pristine tower of St.
George's Church and its medieval buildings. She could see the gray haze of
the Bristol Channel off in the distance, bright billowy clouds hanging lazily in
the crystal blue sky.

Ana walked into the main town. The architecture of some of the structures
were very old indeed. Looking down High Street she could see Conygar tower
in the distance at the top of the hill to the left. She passed many whitewashed
cottages adorned with ivy and lovely English rose gardens. Some gardens were
encircled with high stone walls and fanciful antiquated wooden door entrances.
The streets were paved with ancient brown cobblestones.

Ana found her way to the center of town. The square was festooned with
colorful market tents of various shapes and sizes surrounding the eight-sided
building called the Yarn Market. She began to make her way through the tables

and displays looking at the colorful fruits and vegetables and beautiful fresh flowers in large buckets of water. She laughed as several young children ran past her chasing a cat and stopped to watch an old woman weave a basket, admiring her skill. She then noticed another group of women making lace. She walked over and watched in awe as the white threads and bobbins weaved in and out of the pins creating the most delicate patterns.

"May I help you Miss?" one of the women asked.

"Oh, no, thank you ma'am. I'm just admiring your handiwork," Ana smiled.

"We can make a collar for you that would enhance your beauty," another woman said.

"No, not today, but thank you kindly." Not having known that it was market day, Ana had come unprepared to shop. "Maybe I'll return."

"Friday's always market day. Been market day forever," the first woman said.

"Well, thank you. I'll keep that in mind for the future," Ana replied, "By the way, do you know where I may post a letter?"

"Why yes Miss," the first woman said. "Go to the Dunster Mercantile further down on High Street past Priory Green. Tis down that way Miss," the woman pointed a long bony finger down towards the street.

"Thank you," she smiled gave them a small curtsey. "Have a good day."

As she came upon Priory Green, she could see the shops lined with the regular array of town merchants. She passed the butcher shop with its chickens, sausages and hams hanging in the window. Then there was the bakery, with aromas of fresh breads and baked sweets wafting into the road enticing strollers to enter. There was a cheese shop and a haberdashery. Finally, she came upon Dunster Mercantile, a dry goods store with cloth, ribbons, shoes, a small apothecary, soaps, candles, and all sorts of necessary items for living. She entered the store and slowly meandered around the tables looking at the items of interest.

"Good afternoon Miss," the shopkeeper said. "Ow can I elp you this fine daie?"

"Good day sir. I'd like to post a letter.

"Well you've come to the right plice Miss," he said. "Just step right over 'ere and I will take care of it for ye."

The man walked behind the iron grilled counter and stood inside a booth that was filled with pigeon hole boxes. Ana pulled out her letter and slid it through the slot. "Here you are, sir."

"Let's see, to Londontown then. That will be a half p. Miss." Looking at the letter he continued, "Miss Pembroke is it then, from Dunster Castle?"

"Why, yes, sir."

"Ye are the new governess then?" he inquired. "I know every soul 'bout town, I do."

"Yes," Ana felt a bit wary by his friendly manner, something she was not used to from London merchants.

"Well I am pleased to make your acquaintance, Miss. I'm Bob Goodall, proprietor, and postman," he said with a nod of his head and a click of his cheek.

Ana could not help but smile at his friendly countenance.

"Anything you need Miss, all ye 'ave to do is just ask and good ol' Bob will do 'is best for ye."

"Thank you, sir, but just for today, posting my letter is all that is required," she said as she handed him the coin he requested.

Suddenly he looked a bit pensive. "Wait a minute … Pembroke, Pembroke. You know Miss, something about that name is a bit familiar to me," he said placing a finger on the side of his nose and continuing under his breath. "Pembroke."

"I know," he finally said. "There was a bloke in 'ere a few weeks past asking after a Miss Pembroke. Said she was the new governess at Dunster Castle. That be ye, Miss!"

"Why, yes. Yes, it is." Ana was startled and taken aback. "I wonder who was asking after me. Did this man give you a name?"

"No Miss, 'e was just asking, is all."

"What did he look like?" she said, her brows knitted together.

"A regular sort of bloke, medium 'ite, brown 'air, nothin' special I'd say. Well dressed, though. Spoke the King's English 'e did."

Ana shook her head and shrugged her shoulders. "I wonder who it could have been."

"Well if'n 'e turns up again I know who ye be now, Miss." he said with a crooked smile showing his yellow teeth.

"Yes, well, thank you Mr. Goodall. Have a good day." She left quickly with an uneasy smile on her face.

The bright midday sun was almost blinding as Ana left the dark shop. As her eyes adjusted to the sunlight, she thought that she saw a man from across the street watching her, as she blinked to focus, he was gone. With the information that was shared by Mr. Goodall, Ana began to feel anxiety clouding her day, and now thinking she was seeing a man across the street, a shudder ran down her back. "Silly fantasies," she said to herself, resolving to remain calm.

Ana decided it best to return home. She realized she was now being watchful of the same friendly faces that had greeted her just minutes before and decided that she was being foolish. "Why would anyone be watching me?" she thought. She was no one of interest.

"Well it is too beautiful a day to be concerned about such nonsense," she said to herself, determined to put it out of her mind. Ana picked up her pace for home.

It was warm and still hours before dusk. Having put her anxieties to rest, she determined to enjoy her walk home. Ana decided to venture from the road and look for some of the castle ruins that Mrs. C. had mentioned. Taking a deep breath, she made her way down a small side path she found. In a short time, the road and any semblance of civilization faded away.

"I could grow to love this country," she said aloud as she twirled, arms outstretched in the sunlight feeling young, free and easy. Her bonnet slid from her unruly hair onto her back. She stopped and inhaled deeply the sweet aromas of the earth. A gentle breeze fluttered her dark curls against her cheeks. Meadow birds sang sweetly as bees and butterflies buzzed through the air.

She stood listening and thought she could hear water. She moved towards the sound.

"Oh," she said, "what a beautiful spot." There amongst trees and shrubs growing close to the water's edge, she found a clump of soft green moss and sat down by the crystal-clear river water. Gathering her skirts, she sat down, encircling her knees within her arms. She watched as the water ran swiftly over the flat gray and brown stones. Several colorful dragonflies skimmed the water's cool surface along the shallow banks of the stream. It was relaxing just to watch the rush of water. It appeared so refreshing. After sitting for a while, with the water looking so inviting, she decided to remove her shoes and stockings and dip her feet into the water, something she had not done since she was a child.

She hoisted up her skirts, hoops and petticoats and waded into the gurgling stream. The cool water felt invigorating on her hot and tired feet. She stood and watched the water flow around her ankles and wiggled her toes to get the full effects of the rushing water; a swirl of the soft brown silt whirled up in the water's flow.

As she stood in the water, her eyes were drawn to movement further upstream. The shimmering light on the water made it difficult to see. Thinking it a deer, she craned her neck to get a better view. It was two boys and a man. She tried to make out their faces but they were too far away. The boys were on the opposite bank sitting on some flat rocks tossing pebbles into the dark swirling water, while the man was floating peacefully obviously enjoying himself as he occasionally tried to catch the lightly hurled missiles tossed his direction. She did not hear any words over the sound of the gurgling water, only the laughter from the boys and the deep and rich tones of the man. Ana could not help but smile to watch them at play.

Suddenly, one of the boys spotted her standing in the stream and pointed. "Look," she heard him say as he stood up and pointed in her direction. Ana's jaw dropped slightly and her eyes opened wide as she realized she had been spotted spying on their fun.

The man stood up and turned towards her direction. The water came to his hips. His tan body glistened in the sunlight as streams of water ran into the river, his dark hair dripped over his face. Ana froze not knowing what to do. She'd been caught. But what amazed her, what kept her from running, was the beautiful muscular definition of his exposed arms, chest and shoulders which she couldn't help but admire.

She couldn't see his face clearly even though he pushed back his wet hair with his hand. The sun was just too bright. It was obvious that he couldn't see her either since the light gleamed directly onto his face. Ana could feel her heart beat. Her breath quickened and she swallowed hard as she allowed her gaze to run down from his face to his muscular neck and broad shoulders. She found her eyes slowly and instinctively moving downward towards his narrow hips. A small shiver ran through her body but it was not related to the cool water flowing over her feet. Her mouth felt dry. She moistened her lips with her tongue.

"Ho there," he called out to her.

Even at this distance, her eyes connected with his. Impulsively, she turned to look behind her before realizing he was calling to her. Breaking from her trance, she quickly lifted her skirts higher and scampered to the bank. Gathering up her shoes and stockings Ana took off, running barefoot towards the road, bruising her feet on the pebbles and twigs.

Breathless, she stopped, believing she was now safely out of sight of the swimmers. Ana found a large flat rock and sat down to collect herself. Though she was embarrassed about being seen, she couldn't help but feel intrigued by the vision of a naked man. She sat there for a few minutes as the pounding in her chest began to quiet. But as the beating of her heart settled, Ana felt a sudden sadness take its place. "This may be the only time I'll ever see a man unclothed," she realized. Marriage was simply out of the question.

"Well, it's been too beautiful a day to feel sorry for myself," she said, resigned. She shook off the somber mood and began to dust the debris from the bottom of her damp feet. Leaning down to replace her stockings, she discovered one was missing.

"Damn! I must have lost it."

Feeling a bit sheepish and knowing she could not retrace her steps, she slipped her bare foot into her shoe and stood up. Unfortunately, she faced a long walk back on sore and bruised feet.

"Well, I don't remember this from any of the books I've read," she said to herself with a chuckle shaking the leaves off her rumpled and muddied dress. She had enough adventure for one day, and took off down the road towards home.

CHAPTER 9

*I*t had been a long confounding day. Ana's sockless foot was chafed and blistered from rubbing in her shoe and she developed a slight limp as she plodded home.

"Miss Pembroke?" Chesterton held the door. His brows lifted over the rims of his spectacles as he noticed her flushed face and disheveled attire. Her hat was askew and wild curls were peeping from under the brim. The hem of her dress was caked in mud and leaves, her limp pronounced. "Did you have a good day?" There was a hint of both humor and concern in his expression.

Ana looked him in the eye. "Do I look as if I had a good day?" she asked.

"Well, it is hard to say," he said as he watched her remove her bonnet. "Have you been hurt?"

"Mr. C., it was most definitely a day of adventure, but I am fine and glad to be home." She smiled wearily, realizing she looked a fright.

"I'll have Mrs. C. prepare a bath for you."

"Oh, Mr. C., thank you!" She said throwing her arms around his neck making him blush.

Ana laughed, "I think I have just embarrassed you."

"No my dear, I just rarely get such a greeting," he lied. He was embarrassed to the quick.

Ana limped off to her room. Soon Mrs. C. came in with a tray of tea and biscuits. Several servants followed with a tub and buckets of steaming water in tow.

"Mr. C. said you might need this," she smiled noticing Ana's disarray. "And I must say I agree."

"You're both so kind," Ana grinned. "I'm a fright. This bath is just what I need. Thank you."

"Yes my dear. By the way, this evening you will be dining with the Duke, so you'll want to look your best." Mrs. C. informed her. "I would suggest something more formal."

Ana's eyes became large at the thought. She wanted nothing more than just to stay in her room. "What do you mean?"

"You remember dear, I told you this morning Lord Luttrell has returned. The first dinner home with Lord Luttrell is always most impressive."

"Lord Luttrell! Oh, Mrs. C. I've had enough adventure today. And now this," Ana sighed, bringing her hands to her flushed cheeks.

"Don't worry dear," Mrs. C. said kindly. "He doesn't bite."

"Maybe so, but what is he really like?"

"Well, he's always been a good master. He saved Riya from a terrible fate in India. He's very kind and generous to his tenants. And he's always been a loving son to Lady Catherine and a doting father to his sons. He protects them fiercely." Mrs. C. smiled. "I think you will like him right off."

"Yes, but what does he look like?" Curiosity was getting the better of her as she pictured him as Eliza had described, old and fat.

Mrs. C. smiled, "Oh, you will find him attractive enough, I would suspect. Most ladies do." Then, with an unsettled look she continued, "However, since his divorce ..." and she drifted off. "Well, never you mind."

Ana suspected that Mrs. C. was inferring to the terrible effects of drink and food on his physique. Or maybe she was uncomfortable with his relationship with such a young girl from India. Ana knew *she* found it unsettling.

"Ana, my dear," her smile returning, "You will find him pleasant and a gentleman at all times. I am sure you will get along fine as you both have Geoffrey and Hugh's best interests at heart." She gave Ana a reassuring pat on her arm. "I'll leave you to your bath."

Quickly undressing from her ruined clothes Ana slipped into the welcoming tub of warm water. The fresh lavender floating on top filled the room with its fragrance. She could feel the heat and tension leave her body as she closed her eyes; the water eased her sore tired feet.

She lay in the tub thinking of her dream in the library and the man at the stream. Suddenly, she giggled to herself thinking "wouldn't it be funny if it was Lord Luttrell both in the dream and the man in the river?" Suddenly her mood changed with the impact of that possibility. What if that was the Duke of Exmoor? Her turquoise eyes widened at the thought. Mrs. C. said he returned last night. Why wouldn't he come into the library? It is his library. Her heart began to pound. Then there was the man with two boys who were about the ages of Geoffrey and Hugh. Ana held her breath and slid under the water as if to wash away the fear of what was materializing in her brain.

"It WAS Lord Luttrell!"

She pushed back up sputtering for air, a sense of panic set in. "It was dark last night. Maybe he won't recognize me. And today I was such a far distance up the stream. He can't know it was me. And now in a few short hours I will be dining with him."

"What if they identified me?" Ana was mortified.

She took the bar of soap and quickly lathered her face and hair, scrubbing hard as if to remove her features so he would not recognize her. But it only made her face glow a healthy pink.

Stepping out of the tub she wrapped herself in a large soft towel and began the laborious task of brushing the tangles from her long thick hair, all the while feeling a great lump in her throat at the dread of being recognized. Her hands would not stop shaking. She wished she had Eliza to calm her down. What would Eliza do? She was always so poised. Yes, poise, dignity, composure, self-assurance was what was needed. "As long as I look composed then I'll be fine."

"Oh, thank you Eliza," Ana said out loud feeling some relief from her anxiety.

Ana chose the deep brown silk taffeta that she and Eliza had picked out for just such an occasion. It was as if her sister was holding her hand. At her bosom she pinned the turquoise brooch and attached the matching ear bobs her father had given to her for her sixteenth birthday. She so missed her parents. She smoothed and plaited her hair creating loops over her ears to pull into the tight knot at the nape of her neck. Taking one last look in the mirror, she readjusted her skirts over her hoops and petticoats. Feeling a bit exposed from the events of the day, she pulled up at the sleeves of her dress trying to hide her soft smooth shoulders. Satisfied with the reflection, she took in and held a deep breath. Noting the rise in her breasts she decided not to do that again.

Ana went to the nursery to collect the boys. "Miss Pembroke, you look very pretty tonight," Hugh said. Geoffrey nodded in agreement, which was odd since he was not generally short on words.

"Why thank you Hugh. You both look very handsome." Ana said taking their arms, "Shall we go down then?"

Meeting them in the inner hall, Chesterton led them into the dining room.

"You look very lovely this evening, Miss Ana." Mr. C. said as he nodded approval.

Ana blushed prettily "Thank you."

They walked through the wooden paneled doors. The table was much more formally set than usual with golden bowls and golden tableware. The freshly polished silver sconces that hung from the walls were ablaze with candles, their light reflecting on the white marble of the sculpted fireplace and the gleaming molded plaster ceiling. The Indian statues looked alive in their yellow garb, waiting to provide aide to the well liveried footmen who stood at the ready. The wooden floor shined from the many coats of wax that must have been applied earlier that day.

"How different from home," Ana thought. The Pembrokes were much less formal.

There were several large golden candelabras on the table making the china and crystal glisten with the shimmer of light. Mr. C. showed her to the chair which was next to the head of the table. Realizing she was to sit next to the Duke, the lump returned to her throat.

Geoffrey, Hugh and Ana stood behind their chairs waiting for the others to arrive. Ana heard voices coming from the inner hall. As they moved closer, she recognized that of Lady Catherine and heard a man's deep rich tones. Her heart was beating faster as they approached. She prayed that her conclusions were wrong. Holding onto the back of the chair for support, her knuckles turned white under the pressure. As they entered the room Ana's eyes widened. It was the face of the man in her library dream and the same from the swimming hole. She felt her face flush hot with embarrassment. She had to fight the urge to slip under the table. "Poise, dignity, composure," she repeated silently.

"Ana," Lady Catherine said proudly, "This is my son, Lord Alexander Luttrell, the thirteenth Duke of Exmoor. Alexander, this is Miss Ana Pembroke, the young governess I've been telling you about. She's been doing a wonderful job with your boys and is a welcome addition to the household." Ana gave a small curtsey but kept her eyes on the floor for fear he might see her embarrassment.

Lord Luttrell gave a cool bow from the waist and nodded his head. He was dressed very formally in a black cutaway coat and trousers, starched white shirt, and white cravat. "Good evening Miss Pembroke." His voice was terse, his blue gray eyes hard and cold.

"Good evening My Lord," she said, finally looking up. He was nothing like she and Eliza had imagined. In fact, he was quite the opposite.

"It was my mother's idea to hire a governess." He seemed cross. Maybe he did recognize her. Ana's knees felt weak. Thankfully one of the footmen had pulled out her chair. They all sat.

Geoffrey and Hugh did not seem to remember seeing her at the river. If they recognized her then all was lost. Hugh took his seat next to Ana and Geoffrey sat opposite her with Lord Luttrell at the head and Lady Catherine at the foot.

The footmen silently began to ladle soup in to the bowls. "I trust you boys had a good day with your father?" Lady Catherine began.

"Oh, no here it comes," Ana thought as she watched the warm liquid swirl in her bowl.

"Oh, yes," said Hugh. "First we took a walk down to the mill to explore. Then we went fishing. I caught the biggest."

"You did not." Geoffrey interrupted. "Father caught the biggest fish."

"No, I caught it, he just helped."

"Boys, silence!" Lord Luttrell said sternly. "It appears your governess has not yet taught you table manners."

Ana nearly choked on her soup; "Poise, composure," she thought. Her first instinct was to defend herself as well as the boys but thought twice about confronting an apparently disgruntled Duke. Lady Catherine thankfully changed the subject.

"Alexander, dear, do tell us of your trip to London. How is our lovely Queen?" She smiled sweetly in his direction.

This gave Ana the opportunity to glance in the Duke's direction. She remembered Mrs. C.'s description of him as kind and generous, but instead he seemed cold and angry. But Mrs. C. was correct on one account. He was attractive, very attractive and definitely the complete opposite of what Eliza had imagined. Eliza wasn't going to like this.

As she ate, she listened to their discussion. She could not help but glance over at him. So intent was he in conversation with his mother that he didn't seem to take any notice of her. She studied him further. Thick black lashes rimed his expressive blue eyes that would grow dark gray with his emotions and gleam with his deep laughter. When he laughed, his face brightened with a most engaging smile and handsome creases on each cheek. The less interest he took in her presence, the more relaxed Ana felt and the more she examined him. She watched his mouth move as he spoke and thought of what it might be like to kiss his full lips. The thought shocked her.

"Miss Pembroke."

Ana jumped. He was addressing her. She felt her face grow hot as she looked into his darkening eyes.

"How do you find your position here?" He was looking directly at her.

"Very well, your Lordship. "Her hand was shaking as she reached for her goblet.

"And my sons…are they learning?"

"I find them to be eager, sir. I enjoy working with them." Ana took a swallow of her wine hoping to steady her nerves.

"Do you think that they needed a governess?"

What an odd question, Ana thought replacing the shaking glass on the table.

"I'm pleased to teach them sir, and all children need a good education to prepare them for adulthood." She began to smooth the napkin in her lap.

"I believe they were getting along fine without a governess." His eyes turned cold and hard as he glared towards his mother.

It was obvious that she was unwelcome in his household.

"Yes, sir, my Lord, I did respond to Lady Catherine's inquiry." Poise, Ana, she told herself. Her mounting anger at his inquiries would require tact.

"Well, I would've never inquired after a governess as I don't believe in them," he said curtly.

Ana could feel the color rush to her cheeks. Generous and kind?! The man was a boor, especially towards his mother!

"Sir, it has been my pleasure to help Lady Catherine. She obviously needed my help or she wouldn't have placed such an advertisement."

He ignored her.

"Now Alexander," Lady Catherine gently chided but decided not to take it any further when she saw his steel cold gaze across the table.

"I'm sorry Mother, but I do wish you had waited for my return to hire this, this governess." Ana was dumbfounded by his lack of respect in front of his sons.

"But Father, I like her." Hugh's eyes began to fill with tears fearing his father would make Ana leave.

Alexander's eyes looked heavenward as he shook his head. He looked at his youngest son; just what he wanted to avoid, his sons becoming attached to a woman who would ultimately leave them as their mother had done.

"I don't need a governess, Father." Geoffrey said his chin jutting out, wanting his father's approval. "I don't need anyone."

Looking from his mother to Hugh, Lord Alexander said sternly, "We will end this discussion for tonight. As for now, we have a governess. I'd suggest you both learn your lessons. Your grandmother's good money is going towards this teacher. So take advantage of her while she is here." His voice was filled with sarcasm as he looked at Ana with dark gray eyes.

Geoffrey scowled and hit the table with his fist while Hugh looked relieved as he looked at Ana who smiled back at him.

Lord Alexander's voice softened, "I want you both to know I had a good time with you today. We must do that more often. Now off with you both, dinner is finished and it's time for bed."

The boys looked pleased by their father's acceptance. Hugh came around the table to give his father a hug, but Lord Luttrell declined. Geoffrey knew he was too old for that sort of nonsense. But Ana could see the affection in the exchange of glances between them. As they began to rush out of the dining room their father's deep voice boomed, "Walk!" Immediately the boys slowed down.

Ana sat still waiting to be dismissed. Lord Luttrell stood up and said, "I've had a long day. We'll discuss my sons' education tomorrow morning, eight, sharp," leaving Ana to feel very dismissed.

"Mother?" he said as he steered Lady Catherine towards the drawing room.

Ana, feeling exhausted by the emotional events of the day, followed Lady Catherine and Lord Alexander into the inner hall. Lady Catherine took her hand saying quietly, "Don't worry about Alexander. He's in a mood tonight. But he'll come around. Have a good night, dear."

"Good night Lady Catherine, Lord Luttrell." Ana curtsied and started up the grand stairs to the sanctuary of her room.

"One moment Miss Pembroke." Ana swallowed hard at the sound of Lord Luttrell's voice

"Sir?" She stopped on the first step and turned towards him. Though they were nearly eye to eye he still seemed to loom over her, standing most uncomfortably close, he leaned closer still.

"I believe I have something of yours." His face was cold as marble, his eyes smoldering, and his voice a seductive whisper. She could almost feel the warmth of his breath near her cheek as he spoke. The masculine smell of him filled her nostrils.

"Something of mine, sir?" Ana swallowed hard, her heart beating wildly.

"Hold out your hand."

Tentatively, Ana lifted her hand. He cradled it in his palm. The warmth of his touch reverberated up her arm at his liberties. Her eyes fluttered slightly as she found herself holding her breath at the nearness of him. Suddenly, a cold shudder ran down her back. It was her lost stocking. He studied her as her turquoise eyes widened.

"Good evening," he said and turned to follow his mother into the drawing room, apparently completely unaffected by what had just transpired. Ana felt lightheaded. He knew. All through dinner he knew. And tomorrow he wanted to meet with her. How could she possibly face him?

Clutching the ill-fated stocking, Ana quickly returned to her room. The door barely closed as she pulled her trunk from the corner. She could not stay. Eliza was right. She was leaving at first light. She'll take what she could carry and send for the rest. How could she face this man after seeing him naked? She decided to leave a note explaining that she was suddenly called away. Lady Catherine would understand. Lord Luttrell would most certainly be glad of it. Hugh would be crushed and Geoffrey…

Ana stopped. What was it Geoffrey said? He did not need anyone? Ana closed the lid to her trunk and sat on top of it. She needed to think. She had only been at Dunster Castle for a short time and already both boys had grown attached to her in some way and admittedly she to them. If she were to leave now Hugh would be devastated. How would he learn to trust? Geoffrey was already closing his heart. He must have been so hurt by his mother. He would become cold and hard like his father. That would be no life for either of the boys. Ana could not be part of their heartache. She stood up to unpack with a renewed sense of determination. She had to find another way. Besides, she did not run that easily.

CHAPTER 10

*F*ollowing his mother into the drawing room after his encounter with Ana on the stairs, Alexander found her agitated with him about his behavior during dinner. It was his first night home with his family in many weeks and instead of finding peace he found his household turned upside down by his mother's decision, made without consulting him first. And now she was irritated for what he felt was her irresponsibility; meddling with the parenting of his sons.

"Mother, I know you meant well, but they're my sons. I'll decide about their education. They are my responsibility," Alexander closed the doors loudly to the drawing room. He looked cross and uneasy. He hated confrontations with his mother. But this time she had gone too far. Somehow, the women in his life didn't understand that he was the Lord of this Castle.

Lady Catherine took a seat by an open window hoping to get some night air as she felt flushed by the discord between the two of them. She began to cool herself with a rose scented fan she had taken from her pocket.

"Son, I'm an old woman. You have two young, strong and energetic sons. When you're away they're too much for me." She looked tired and weary.

"There are plenty of servants in this household to help you, Mother. Riya is here for you, as well as Bess." His voice was stern.

"I'm not looking for help from servants such as Bess. Riya is a nice girl, but she's just that, a girl. Plus, I have a difficult time understanding her thick accent.

She may give you some needed companionship, some fond memories of India, even make you feel altruistic. I don't know. But I do know that she's not what I need. Alexander, Miss Pembroke comes from a good family, her father was Baron of Milford. She is well educated, and besides I enjoy her company."

"Mother, I want to understand. You have many friends in this district." He shook his head. "Good family or not, I needed you to consult with me first. A governess? My sons have been hurt enough." His blue eyes were growing dark gray with anger at the thought of Elizabeth's abandonment of her own sons, "How can I trust my sons to another woman? They'll become attached. She'll hurt them."

"Alexander, you forget. I too am a woman." Lady Catherine looked hurt.

"Mother, I'm sorry. You're different to them. You're their grandmother. It's just … different."

Lady Catherine shook her head, and looked sadly at her son through eyes much like his own. It had been four years since Elizabeth had run off. It was painful to see Alexander return home from the wars in India, wounded and changed, finding his wife had abandoned her family for a lover. The scandal still haunted him.

"When Mr. Sumner responded to my request informing me about Miss Pembroke, it just felt right. Shall we call it woman's intuition?"

"Please mother…woman's intuition? I'll not accept hocus pocus as logic." Alexander was losing his patience with his mother's fanciful ideas.

"Well, I thought I might fill two positions nicely with one person. Miss Pembroke seemed to fit the bill. I'll say she fills it perfectly."

"Two positions? What in the name of all that is holy are you talking about now?" It was not the first time Lady Catherine had romantic schemes to find him a match and his mother's response hinted of a new plan. He knew her too well to let it drop.

"I told you, a governess for the boys and a companion for me," she responded sounding exasperated.

"A companion for you," he said sarcastically. Alexander was amazed, needing to repeat her statement just to know he heard her correctly, yet somehow, he found her hard to believe.

"Son, I'm a lonely old woman. I don't have the energy to entertain company nor to go visiting. You're a busy man. There are times you spend months in London. I'm as proud of you as I was of your father. I miss your father deeply. I have no one else. I need adult companionship and I most certainly need help with those boys." The look on her face told Alexander that the discussion was over. Lady Catherine stood up and walked over to her son who was leaning with his elbow against the cold white marble fireplace.

"Give her a chance. You may grow as fond of her as I have."

Alexander looked at his mother, suspicion glowing from the squint in his eyes, his voice booming "Ha!" Pointing a strong finger, he added "Mother, you see women cannot be trusted."

She looked up at her tall handsome son, "Nonsense. I've learned all too well not to play that game with you. Anyway. it's late and this old woman needs her sleep. Bend down and give me a kiss like a good boy. All will be well, you'll see."

Obediently, Alexander kissed his mother's forehead. "Have a pleasant rest Mother." He added with sarcasm, "And I still don't trust you."

"Thank you, son. I love you too. Welcome home," Lady Catherine said, getting the last word in as she closed the door leaving Alexander to his thoughts.

"Welcome home," he stormed. "Companion, bloody hell!"

Alexander walked to the table and picked up a decanter of ruddy liquid, opened it and sniffed. Sherry. He put it down and picked up another. Whiskey. He filled a large tumbler. Opening the humidor and selected a thick Cuban cigar. Cutting off the tip, he struck a match and took several long drags, watching the end glow red. Slowly he exhaled the smoke, studying its circles in the air. He picked up his glass and downed half the tumbler. Refilling the glass, he walked over to the sofa and stretched out, crossing his feet at the end. He needed to think.

There was a knock at the door.

"Come in," he called out, exasperated about not having a moment alone.

It was Chesterson. "Is there anything else for this evening, mi' Lord.

"No, Chesterton."

"May I suggest sending for Riya?"

"Actually, yes. Thank you. Somehow, you always know what I need."

"Very good then, sir."

"Good evening, Chesterton."

The house was quieting down. Alexander lay on the sofa enjoying his 'whiskey and cigar when Riya quietly came into the room. He watched her as she moved a large brocade cushioned stool over to the fire. She threw some incense onto the dying embers. The aromatic smoke filled the air with another worldly scent. She motioned for him to sit. He stood up and removed his waistcoat, cravat and shirt sitting crossed leg taking the seat offered him. Slowly, Riya began to work the kinks from his neck and shoulders with her dark, strong fingers. It was what she learned from her grandmother, ancient ways of healing. She knew to keep her silence as she worked out his stress.

Alexander pondered the situation at hand. He had other female servants in his household, maids and charwomen. Riya most definitely interacted regularly with his sons, a mere child herself. Then there were Mrs. C. and Bess. And of course, Mother. But a governess? A governess plays quite a different role. She'd be too involved. What did he know of this Miss Pembroke anyway?

Riya stopped her work. Her hands dropped to her sides.

"Why did you stop?"

"Sir, your mind, it works too hard. Your neck is too tight," Riya said in her native tongue.

"Riya, you are right. I have too much on my mind," He returned in Hindi. "Some other time perhaps."

"Yes, Sahib."

"Life seemed much easier in India."

"Yes, Sahib, for you."

"Everything was regimented, orders were never questioned. But here … I guess you wouldn't understand; you've always taken orders." He took a gulp from his glass, remembering the conditions in which he found her. "Life here is much safer for you, isn't it? Are you happy here, Riya?"

"Oh yes, Sahib, very happy," she replied as her black eyes studied the carpeted floor.

He studied her young face. She still wore her long black braid and looked uncomfortable in her western clothes. She wore no shoes, as was her preference.

"Are they treating you well, the others I mean? Of course, they are. Anything must be better than that squalor you came from." He pondered their particular and even peculiar relationship.

"Yes Sahib."

"Go to bed Riya, it is getting late," he said, downing the rest of his drink. Riya bowed and left as quietly as she came in.

Alexander's thoughts quickly returned to its preoccupation before the door fully closed. "Well, this governess is easily flustered by me. That's perfectly clear by the way she acted on the stairs when I returned her stocking. She was obviously mortified by what had happened at the river. She probably finds me intriguing," he thought and smiled slightly, remembering her study of him during dinner. He raised one well defined brow. "That could be to my advantage." His glass now empty, he decided to pour another.

Pacing the floor, he continued to ponder this new and unsolicited situation.

"Companion!" he shook his head again. "Mother's up to something!"

Still, Miss Pembroke was his mother's servant, not his. She paid her salary. Mother would have to let her go and he would have to convince her to do so. "Mother seems to like her too much. She's committed to keeping her." So that was out of the question.

Suddenly, Alexander stopped pacing. A slow smile crossed his face.

"Intimidation!" he whispered.

He swallowed the last of his whiskey. His mind raced, "That's it. She'll be so uncomfortable she'll quit. I'll not be the cause of their pain by asking her to leave. She'll leave on her own accord. I'll deal with Hugh's broken heart, and Mother'll get over it. Geoffrey will be glad to get rid of her. That's obvious from his sentiment at dinner." He sighed in relief and his shoulders relaxed.

Alexander felt satisfied with himself for what he considered a brilliant solution. He'll find fault with her, be flippant with her, and even trifle with her a bit if necessary. It was extreme and against his nature. But this was war. He had to protect his sons from the fickle heart of a woman. If he demanded she leave outright he would be the cause of their pain and that he would never do.

He poured another glass to celebrate. He felt the burn of the alcohol slide down his throat and noticed its effects mellowing his mood. He stretched out on the couch to relax. He should have had Riya stay. He gave his neck a twist, hearing the bones crack.

His thoughts returned to finding Ana sleeping in his library, her exotic turquoise eyes opening wide in surprise and the sway of her hips as she searched for her shoes on the floor. Then tonight at dinner … He paused as he remembered her exposed shoulders and the soft ample mounds that pushed up from her bodice, the fullness of her crimson lips.

Shaking his head to banish the memory, he attributed his awakening passion to the whiskey weakening his resolve. Taking a last drag on his cigar, he reminded himself that he too needed to be wary of the wiles of women. He would have to stay on his guard for himself as well as his sons.

Up earlier than usual, Ana was tired from a fitful night's sleep. Trying not to think of the previous day's events, she still felt mortified by what had transpired between her and the Duke and was more than apprehensive about their meeting. She could not decide. Would it be best to explain that her coming upon them in the river had been an accident or just to remain silent on the subject unless he brought it up? But the main thing to remember was that the meeting was to discuss the education of Geoffrey and Hugh. If nothing else, she was glad she had not runaway last night.

Wearing her plain gray dress, Ana pulled her hair back to hide her thick heavy curls. "Plain," she thought. "Plain, plain, plain, is the mode for the day."

"If I am to be a governess, I must look like a governess and act like a governess," she said, giving herself courage to face the day as she left to meet her destiny.

"My but you're up early," Mrs. C. greeted her as she entered the large kitchen and sat at the table.

"I didn't sleep well last night." There were dark circles under her eyes.

"I'm surprised, with all the fresh air and exercise you took yesterday," Mrs. C. looked concerned. "Are you feeling well, my dear?"

"Actually, yesterday was a very trying day." Ana took the cup of hot tea and buttered bread offered to her.

Mrs. C. poured herself some tea and sat next to Ana hoping she might share some of her distress. "Sometimes I find that when I talk about something it is not as I thought."

"Well, I suppose I can share some of what happened." Breakfast and Mrs. C. might help to lessen Ana's anxiety about the upcoming meeting with Lord Luttrell.

"My day began with such hope and excitement. I was so glad of it, to be in the clean air and explore. I wrote a letter to my sister and took it to post. And you know a very strange thing occurred. I didn't think of it until this very minute," Ana looked deeply perplexed.

"What happened?"

"Well, I met Mr. Goodall."

"How's that so strange?"

"It was not meeting him that was strange but what he told me."

"Go on, dear," Mrs. C. said.

"It appears as if there have been several inquiries about me. Some man has been asking of my whereabouts." Ana held her cup to her lips.

"My, that is disconcerting. Did he say who?"

"That's just it. The man didn't leave a name."

"What do you think that means?"

Ana shook her head. "I don't know."

"Well this is most unusual. I insist you inform Lord Luttrell." Mrs. C. felt very distressed, "He'll get to the bottom of this and see to it that you are not in danger."

"Oh, Mrs. C., I don't think I'm in any danger." Ana laughed pushing away feelings of trepidation. Besides she didn't believe Lord Luttrell would to be very sympathetic to this situation and would think her a silly child rather than a responsible governess.

"When a strange man is lurking about asking questions concerning an un-attached, pretty, young woman, I do think there is danger," Mrs. C. stated sternly.

Trying to assuage Mrs. C.'s fears, Ana said, "I'm perfectly capable of taking care of myself. But I'll mention it to Lord Luttrell if it will make you feel better," she conceded.

Ana intentionally neglected to mention the encounter by the river. What would she say? How would she explain it?

She was brought back to the present when Mrs. C. asked, "What of your meeting with Lord Luttrell at dinner?"

"Actually, I don't think we got off to a good start. I don't think he wants me here," Ana said, her anxiety returning.

"Ana, I think you must be mistaken. Both Lord Luttrell and Lady Catherine have been personally involved in Geoffrey and Hugh's education. In fact,

Lord Luttrell handled much of it himself. He's very devoted, especially since their mother left."

"Maybe he's concerned that they'll become too attached to me?" She remembered his response to Hugh's tears.

"Nonsense! They're his sons. He would want the best for them."

"Yes, I suppose so. Anyway, I'm meeting with him this morning. Hopefully we can get off to a better start." As long as the river incident is put behind them, she thought.

"Ana, I think he was just tired from his journey home. But you'll see. He'll be the kind and generous Master that we all know and love," Mrs. C. said, smiling warmly.

"Thank you, Mrs. C. You're right. It's been very helpful to have someone listen. I'll most definitely give it another go," Ana smiled back at her friend.

With a bit of time before eight, Ana decided to take a garden stroll to quiet her nerves before the upcoming meeting. As she walked along the dewy paths, she reminded herself to stop and take a deep breath to smell the peonies even though the butterflies in her stomach continued to do somersaults at the thought of her upcoming meeting. So much had transpired between them even before they met formally. Now they had an unsavory past and Ana was concerned that it was bound to set the tone for the future. Finally, the clock struck eight. Her meeting with Lord Alexander Luttrell had come. Taking in one more deep breath, Ana walked into the house to face the Duke of Exmoor.

C H A P T E R   1 1

*A*lexander stood at the long windows of the dining room with his second cup of coffee in his hand. His head throbbed from too many libations the previous night. He hated whiskey, especially when he drank too much of it. But this infernal governess in his household brought up too many memories which he thought were long buried. He vowed not to let another woman get close to his family and a governess was too close for comfort. The decision he made was unsavory. However, Hugh was already attached to her. His mother was up to no good. They were doing just fine alone. "Damn Mother," he muttered, "and damn this Miss Ana Pembroke." In a few weeks she had wormed her way into the fabric of his family.

Though deep in thought, he noticed Ana walking in the garden. He watched her as she slowly made her way around the fountain. He watched her smell some of the flowers. He noticed that the bright morning sunlight shining on her head created brilliant stands of red and gold intertwined through her hair. Though she was dressed plainly, he found her female shape most appealing. She looked natural in his garden. Still, he was angry that he was not informed of this change in his household that now walked his gardens. He took another sip of coffee as his head pounded at his temples. Alexander scarcely admitted to himself that she was pleasing to the eye when his cynicism reared up inside him.

They were up to something. Of course, his mother would pick a young and beautiful daughter of some Baron to pose as a governess. His eyes squinted as he watched her meander down the walkways. It would not be the first time his mother had tried to form an alliance. He fell for it at eighteen when he married Elizabeth at his parent's urgings. But he would not fall again. He was young and gullible then. "No, women cannot be trusted, not even Mother." He continued brooding, "I tried marriage. It is not for me. I have heirs. I don't need anyone now, especially a woman."

"Good morning, Alexander." He hadn't noticed his mother entering the dining room, her voice overly cheerful for his taste. She walked over to the window to see what he was looking at so intently. She saw Ana and smiled. Then she looked up at her son, who obviously was watching Ana too. But one look at his dark scowl told her that it was not a good morning for him.

"Alexander! You look awful this morning," Lady Catherine said with feigned concern.

"Thanks to you, Mother. Your concern is most touching," he answered coolly.

"And testy too," she said as she walked towards the sideboard. "The eggs look good this morning."

"I don't know I haven't eaten." His was voice flat and unemotional.

"Son, are you ill?" she turned to look at him over her shoulder.

"No Mother. I'm not ill," Alexander responded, his mood darkening further at his mother's interrogation.

"Alexander, then stop being such a boor," she replied, now exasperated with him.

"Am I Mother? Am I being a boor?" Pointing his cup towards the garden he gestured, "You're the one that hired her."

"Alexander, not again. I thought we had settled this last night." She took her filled plate to the table and took her seat.

"You thought wrong then. I have my sons to look after. But you were just looking after yourself as you usually do." He was angry with her constant meddling in his life.

"That is not fair." Lady Catherine felt hurt and angry at her son's lack of understanding for her own situation. "You're the one that's selfish." She stood up to leave. "And now I have completely lost my appetite, thank you very much. I think it's long overdue for you to let go of the past and move on. It's time to forget Elizabeth. I certainly have."

"You knew she was no innocent," he growled. "How her family kept that secret so well is beyond me. Yet you and father both knew why she was gone all those months. Who knows what happened to the child she bore? My God, when I found out the truth, I looked for Lizbeth to no avail, that poor child. It tugs at my very soul to think that … that woman could put her own infant into some workhouse." He shook his head in disbelief and disgust. "Mother, your fantastical romantic ideas and father's desire to expand his fortune were poor reasons to subject me to that sham of a marriage. I was so naïve … you and Father were cruel and heartless!" He glared at his mother.

"I agree with you about Lizbeth. That situation was and is disgraceful and tragic. I am not heartless. But I was hopeful. Your father and I fell in love after a match. I can be hopeful, can't I? Besides, Alexander, you never loved her; she only hurt your pride and nothing else." With that, Lady Catherine swept from the room leaving her breakfast unfinished and cold on her plate.

Alexander did feel like a boor, and somewhere, he knew she was right. But he was not ready to admit to it. He remembered the mortification he felt on their wedding night when she laughed at his inexperience. She was cruel and coldblooded. And it was her unholy lusts that made her leave her sons. Now he needed to protect them. It had been hard for them when their mother left.

"Maybe she hurt my pride but she crushed my sons. Mother should know this. This governess is a threat," he said quietly.

As the clock struck eight, Alexander made his way towards the library to set in motion his plan of intimidation. He did not look forward the task. It was not his style. But he knew it must be done if he was going to get her to quit. His mother had hired her and as a result he could not fire her. But he could lay the groundwork to get her to leave her position voluntarily.

Ana was waiting in the hall. Her heart fluttered upon seeing him; she had been anticipating their meeting. She noticed his informal dress of black trousers and riding boots, a white shirt open at the collar and buff vest. He looked calm and self-assured which was in sharp contrast to her jitters. His cool blue eyes pierced her very being.

"Good morning sir," she said. Way too cheery, she thought.

He stopped at the door and motioned with his hand for her to enter. She gave a small curtsey to honor his post. He did not respond as it was not a good morning for him. Glaring at her as she walked past, he noted that she barely came up to his shoulders. Pointing towards a dark red leather chair, he made his way around the big mahogany desk and took a seat. For interrogation, there was no better position than from behind a massive desk.

"So, Miss Pembroke, is it? I understand you are a daughter of some Baron. How then, did you come to gain experience as a governess? Did you bring references? Or did my mother pull you out of a hat?" his voice was cold and flat, his gray eyes dark and menacing.

Ana's face paled, stunned by his caustic attitude. "My father was the Baron of Milford, yes. As for official experience as a governess I … I have none, however," she stuttered, looking confused.

He did not let her finish. "Oh, so why then are you here?"

Ana's large turquoise eyes widened. Her heart began to beat faster. "I responded to your mother's inquiry through Mr. Sumner. I believe our families share the same solicitor," she answered as she felt anger begin to kindle. "Situations in my life changed. I decided employment as a governess would suit me." She tried to sound matter of fact.

"So now that we have established that you've never done this before, what makes you think you are qualified?" He continued to glare at her.

Ana's vexation began to calm her nerves, helping her feel stronger. "I've helped my sister with her two children. I enjoy children and I'm well educated."

"Well educated." His voice was sarcastic.

"Yes, I attended Bedford College for Women. My father believed in education."

"I see, college, very unusual and radical … for a woman," he sounded skeptical.

"Bedford College and I enjoy children," his tone mocked. "Why is it then you never married if you love children so much?" he said as he leaned over his desk, searching her face.

"Sir, that is my affair!" she answered immediately, her voice strong. Amazed at his scrutiny of her, Ana could not see how this question applied to her position of governess. Her turquoise eyes flashed with emotion. His question stabbed her in the heart. She looked down at her hands that were neatly folded in her lap to hide her reaction and regain a sense of composure.

He could see from Ana's expression that the topic of marriage was a sensitive subject. Marriage was what all women wanted and if that was her goal she would have to search elsewhere.

"I see it as an important question Miss Pembroke. It is curious, if you love children, I would think that you would seek out marriage rather than be governess to another woman's children." He studied her reaction but was taken aback at the green fire in her eyes as she looked directly into his.

"I made a choice to work." Her voice was steady and unintimidated.

"I have been father, mother and teacher to my sons. What could you bring to them that I can't?" he challenged her.

"A different perspective." Her eyes calmly met his icy stare, and this time she knew it was will against will.

"You mean a woman's point of view?" he glared at her.

"If you like," she said, holding her head higher.

"They have their grandmother for that."

"True, however, I bring life experiences that are particular to me, my Lord."

"I see, you are a world traveler then," he retorted, knowing this to be most likely false.

"No, sir, I've not traveled." Ana felt cornered but not defeated.

"What life experiences could you possibly have that would benefit my sons? You have been sheltered by your upbringing. You've never even been married. Children of your own to support?" He knew this was an insult.

"How dare you infer …" Ana was highly offended by his inference and felt more than irritated with his continuous references to her spinsterhood. "My choice to marry or not is completely my concern, sir. And if I had married, the only Christian way to have children, I certainly would not leave them to be raised by another." She could throw a barb just as well as he and she knew this was most likely a sore spot.

Her turquoise eyes glistened with anger.

Alexander scowled as he leaned back in his chair and studied Ana through the gray slit of his own eyes. This marriage thing was a sensitive topic, he could see. It angered her, but he could also see it pained her. However, her barb did not go unnoticed and it hit its mark with him. He wanted to strike back. He continued.

"So here you are a nobleman's daughter, never wed and working as a commoner?" He shook his head convinced she was conjuring a plan. He eyed her up and down. She looked normal enough and had a most agreeable countenance. But she had to be up to something. Women always were. And she was a spitfire who could hold her own with him.

"My mother put you up to this, didn't she?" he charged her, now leaning forward over his desk, this time with his hand in a fist.

"Sir? I don't understand your meaning," she answered, perplexed by his statement. "Other than hiring me as governess and a companion, there is no other motive. I'm here to discuss the education of your sons, not the choices I've made for my personal life or the motives of your mother. Whether I married or chose work is my affair."

"Oh, but the choices that you have made directly impact the lives and well-being of my sons. Don't you agree? Had you married you would never have come here."

Ana could not believe his coldness nor his cruel line of questioning. She was stunned into silence. She looked directly into his steel eyes for a moment and held his stare. They were his mother's eyes. But Lady Catherine's eyes were warm and friendly. She wondered how he would look if he was not so hard and cold. Ana remembered coming upon him and the boys in the stream. She felt her face begin to flush and hoped he would not notice. But he did.

Seeing her face turn pink, he leaning closer, "I hope I'm not making you … uncomfortable. However, I have a right to know what sort of person is going to be teaching my sons. Don't you agree? You will have a great deal of influence over them, wouldn't you say? I have the right to be particular, which is why I'm not pleased by this arrangement my mother has made with you, nor of your behavior thus far." His eyes cast dark shadows of disdain in her direction.

Ana felt she had found the opportunity to return the focus to her purpose in the household, though her heart beat wildly. "Lord Luttrell, I do agree. I will have influence with your sons however, you mean more to them than I ever will." A little flattery might help, she thought. "Having been with them for the past weeks, it is obvious you have given them a lot of time and care. I only wish to continue in their progress, teaching them about literature and history, not to mention basics in mathematics and reading. I'm so looking forward to opening their young minds."

"Opening their young minds … so how does your behavior of yesterday benefit their young minds?" He watched her closely.

Her face flushed a deep crimson, her lips parted, her clear turquoise eyes grew large and dark. "Sir?" she answered, her breath quickening.

"I would call it spying, wouldn't you?" His face was dark with suspicion. He watched her as she bit her lower lip but her gaze remained steady on him.

Ana wanted to melt into the chair. She had hoped this subject would remain buried. Deciding to be as honest as possible, Ana bolstered her courage and looked directly into those cold eyes.

"Yes, that. Lord Luttrell, I was just exploring. It was such a warm day and I came across the river. It looked so inviting that I decided to dip my feet in the cool water. It was not until I was in the water that I noticed swimmers. And no, I would not call it spying. It was happenstance, mere happenstance."

"So how do you propose to explain this to a fourteen-year-old boy?' He was enjoying watching her squirm, hoping this was the charm. "His governess found him swimming, naked. As a matter of fact, his governess found his father naked." He watched her crimson mouth as she ran her tongue over her dry lips.

"Sir, had I known, I would never ..." Ana felt cornered. He had the upper hand. Her face paled.

"So how are you going to explain it to him?" he pressed on. "Well, I can see how your—what did you call it—yes, 'life experiences'—are going to help in this situation."

Ana was speechless. She found herself looking at her hands, forcing back tears of embarrassment and rage. She willed herself to look directly into his cold face and return his gaze measure for measure. She hoped he could not hear the rapid beating of her heart.

"As for myself," he added, "I might consider your explanation as true. I have little concern for being seen naked by a woman, as it has been my pleasure to do so many times," he raised his left brow and presented her with a small crooked grin letting the statement sink into her head. "But how are you going to explain this to a young boy who has never been exposed to the, shall we say, gentler sex in such a way."

Never had a man spoke so dishonorably to her. Sitting straight up, Ana decided not to let him intimidate her. She held her head proud though her nerves were raw. "I shall ask him about his adventures with you and Hugh. If he brings up the subject, I shall be honest with him, as I have been with you.

If he appears shy or embarrassed, I shall let him have his feelings. And I will accept any consequence of his feelings to the situation … if he brings it up."

Knowing that neither Geoffrey nor Hugh had recognized Ana at the stream, Alexander knew this was one topic she would not have to contend with. However, it may be just enough to send this little chit packing.

"Good luck with that. You will surely have a great deal to explain to them. It is getting late into the morning and my mother is paying you a good salary. Your charges await their teacher. I do hope they enjoy their lessons of your 'life experiences.' By the way, my boys notice everything," he said. With that the meeting was over. Ana was coolly dismissed.

Horrified, she stood up and walked purposefully towards the door. Never had she been so unceremoniously dismissed. Suddenly, Ana stopped and returned to his desk, the anger flashing in her large turquoise eyes surprised him.

"Spying? Spying?" She couldn't believe that she was confronting him but her ire was up "What about you, spying on me?"

"What in God's teeth are you talking about?" His fury was apparent, his fists tight on his desk at her impudence.

"Right there, in this very room, the other night," she said, pointing towards the window cushion where she had fallen asleep. Alexander scowled. She remembered after all.

"That was you! And here I thought it was Geoffrey. You accuse me, sir, but I suggest you look to yourself!" With that Ana turned and stormed victorious from the room. Alexander's blood was boiling, yet he was impressed by her temper. The war was on.

CHAPTER 12

Several weeks had passed since the first confrontation in the library. Ana and Lord Luttrell continued to be at odds. He criticized every lesson she wished to teach. And this morning was no different.

"No, I don't think you do understand the consequences to the Crown," he argued.

"Oh, I do understand. I don't think you understand why the colonies desired freedom from tyranny. And why would you? You are a nobleman, not a commoner. On the other hand, as a woman I most definitely understand the constraints of men," she spit back.

"Oh, please," he rolled his eyes in exasperation. "Next thing, women are going to ask for the vote," he snapped.

"And what is wrong with that?"

"Everything! Now go. I will see to it that my sons are fully aware of what the colonies have done." With that Ana was dismissed, infuriated by another morning of discord over lessons.

Ana surmised the cause of the problem. It was clear that Lord Alexander Luttrell did not like her and wanted her gone. He didn't trust her with his children. She had never encountered the person that Mrs. C. had described— warm, generous and caring for those that worked under him. To Ana he was cold, callous and often insulting. She was most sure she did not like him. But never a quitter, Ana was determined to stay.

"Miss Ana, are you alright?" Chesterton had come into the great hall where she was pacing after their last round. He could see she was distressed.

"No, I'm not alright," she confessed clasping her hands together and bringing them up to her chin in exasperation. She had just left the library. "But I will be fine shortly," she replied, taking in a deep breath.

"This might cheer your day Miss." He handed Ana two letters. One was from Charles and the other in an unfamiliar hand.

"Thank you, Chesterton, yes, these will cheer me up." Though she preferred a letter from Eliza, a letter from Charles would do. She tucked them into her sleeve to read later. She returned to the nursery, deeply concerned over the continuing tensions she was experiencing with Lord Luttrell.

Riya was minding the boys. "Thank you, Riya, you can go now," she dismissed her coolly. Always unsettled in her presence, she watched Riya as she silently left the nursery, amazed she never wore shoes. Yes, she was helpful with the boys, seeing to many of their needs as well as keeping watch over them while they played. Yet she couldn't put her finger on what made it so uncomfortable. She never considered herself a snob, but this quiet girl from India was out of place. Plus, she didn't know exactly what the relationship was between Riya and Lord Luttrell; Ana was convinced that it was not holy. She had never seen the two of them actually together, but she could not help but notice the gentle way that Lord Luttrell would look at Riya if she passed by. Ana admitted that she might even be a bit jealous of this mere slip of a girl who had no real standing yet had somehow gained the affections of the Duke of Exmoor. Ana, in contrast, had only known his wrath.

"Miss Pembroke, are you alright?" Hugh asked. He had noticed and was concerned by Ana's furrowed brow.

"Yes, Hugh, I'm fine." She gave him a bright smile to shake off her mood. "I didn't sleep well last night so I'm a bit tired," she added to mask her feelings.

"I didn't sleep well either. I was too hot," Hugh said in sympathy.

"You slept last night. You snored so loudly you could've awoken the dead," Geoffrey said, shoving his brother with disgust.

"Hey! How would you know if I slept or not, you were sleeping too," Hugh whined.

Geoffrey cast his gray eyes skyward in frustration. He looked so much like his father.

"Geoffrey, you must stop pushing your brother, we've already had this discussion," Ana chided, struggling to control her own irritation.

"It sounds as if we're all tired and out of sorts. So we'll keep our lessons simple today. We'll continue reading our book. Let's see, we left off ending at chapter three. Geoffrey if you would please?"

Opening the book, Geoffrey settled down to read, his strong voice echoing through the nursery.

"Chapter 4. D'artagnan, in a state of rage, crossed the antechamber in three bounds ..."

Hugh moved his chair next to Ana while his brother read. Ana was pleased. Hugh was gaining a sense of trust in her. She still hoped that Geoffrey would come around, though her tone with him today was of no help.

She wanted to lose herself in the story. But her mind continued to wander.

"Geoffrey resembles his father in temperament; stubborn and belligerent," she mused. "He's leery of me, uncertain of whether if I'm trustworthy. He has so obviously been hurt. And Hugh just wants to be loved and accepted. Lord Luttrell is a puzzle. Could he still be holding a grudge from the swimming incident weeks ago? Is he nursing a broken heart from his previous marriage? Or jealous of my time spent with his sons? If so, he's proving to be childish."

Ana sighed and forced herself to refocus on the task at hand. She smiled down at Hugh who was studying her intently. "Focus," she silently mouthed to him as well as to herself.

"But at the street gate Porthos was talking with the soldiers on guard. Between the two talkers there was room for just one man to pass ..." Geoffrey read.

The day had become warm. Chesterton left the week's post on Lord Luttrell's desk as was his custom. It was the first time Alexander could relax, read his mail, and catch-up on the latest news. His morning meeting with Ana was cantankerous at best. He thought of her turquoise eyes and how they flashed at him when she became angry. She challenged him at every turn. It was oddly stimulating. The more she fought, the more he wanted to win. He had to come up with some other tactics. She had awakened his warrior instincts. He poured himself a glass of claret. Picking up the *London Time*s he settled into a plush armchair near a window to catch the bright afternoon light.

"Bloody war," he said shaking his head as he read the latest on the War in the States.

> *Bloody Battle of the Wilderness, Casualties in Thousands, 18,000 Union and 7,500 Confederates.* This was the first in a series of battles that took place in the woods near Chancellorsville, Virginia. The first Union attack was made in an area about 50 miles from Richmond. Both Confederate and Union soldiers were trapped in the blazing woods. The Union gained little ground but lost much in casualties.

Wanting to clearly locate Virginia on a map he looked towards the corner of the room for his globe. But, it was gone. He quickly scanned the library to search for the object.

"Where the devil …?" he said aloud, his brows drawn. Suddenly his jaw hardened as anger replaced curiosity.

He knew where the globe was.

"Miss Pembroke!" he snarled under his breath, smacking the now folded paper on the arm of his chair and knocking over his glass of claret.

"Damn her!" he said, pulling off his neckerchief to sop up the red liquid. "That little thief," he said with contempt as he noticed his ruined shirt. "Look at this mess!"

Exasperated, he stood up. Pulling the servant's bell to have the spill properly cleaned, he unceremoniously marched out of the room, through the halls, up the stairs, and burst uninvited into the nursery.

Ana and her charges looked up, surprised by his abrupt entrance. "My Lord, as you can see, we are in session. May I help you with something?" she asked as politely as possible to hide her own irritation and annoyance at his rude entrance. However, upon seeing the ruby stains on his shirtsleeves, his missing cravat and the all too familiar dark look on his face, Ana realized it was not to be a friendly call. She braced herself for round two of the day.

"Miss Pembroke," he growled, "since when have you come into the habit of stealing my things?"

Ana's turquoise eyes opened wide in disbelief of his fabricated accusation. "My Lord, I have no knowledge of what you are missing," she replied, wondering at what nonsensical thing he could be referring.

His steel blue eyes flashed in anger as he noticed his library globe neatly tucked into the corner of the room. Alexander took several long strides over to the globe.

"Why, Miss Pembroke, what a lovely globe you have," he said, his voice thick with sarcasm. "Do you know I had one just like this in my library?" He paused to study the object in question. "No, wait," he continued sardonically pointing a finger in the air, "I do believe this IS my globe from my library," he said giving it a twirl with a strong well-formed hand. "Well, I want it returned!" his voice boomed as he placed his hand on the spinning orb, stopping it abruptly.

Geoffrey and Hugh sheepishly glanced at each other. Feeling anxious, they began to snicker but stopped suddenly as they caught their father's glare in their direction. Quickly they returned to busying themselves in their books as if they could not hear the ensuing conversation.

"Well, sir, it is such a lovely globe. That is true," she answered sweetly with just a hint of her own sarcasm. Then her tone changed, "I did ask Mr. Chesterson to have it brought up as I'm teaching your sons geography. I thought it would be a valuable addition and a useful tool to our classroom, knowing how you would want your children to learn about geography. So, as you can see I have not stolen it. It is still under your roof and you found it, placed here." Adding through her teeth, "I just had it moved." Then returning to her sugary tone, "I can also see that you are a student of geography yourself or you would not own such a fine globe," she continued with polite disdain. "Your sons and I wish to thank you for allowing us to use your precious globe and learn from it, my Lord." She finished with a short curtsey.

Feeling at once ready to throttle her, yet caught in front of his sons, he knew she had won this argument. He cleared his throat. "Yes," he hissed, definitely uncomfortable with keeping his emotions in check.

"Geography, very necessary," he again cleared his throat. He knew both boys, though looking innocently occupied, were fully aware of the tension between the two of them.

In a few long strides he made his way back to the door. "Do carry on but in the future do NOT move anything of MINE without my permission!" he commanded, slamming the door loudly behind him as he left. He stood in the long hallway for a moment shaking with anger and at the same time feeling rather foolish. And still he felt infuriated that he had not been asked for his globe. After all was he not the Lord of this Castle? He took long hard strides towards his chambers to change his ruined clothes.

As soon as the door slammed shut, the boys began to snicker again over what they had observed between their father and Ana; their own tensions over the event were obvious. But the fire in Ana's eyes and her stern brow brought them back to their books. "Keep reading," she said firmly. "I'll be back momentarily."

"Yes' m." their eyes were as big as saucers, for it was unusual to have Ana speak to them in such a stern manner.

"How dare he reprimand me in front of my charges like a common servant," she thought angrily. "And the impertinence of him; breaking into one of my teaching sessions, angry, unannounced and filled with such false accusations. No one calls me a thief." After this morning's battle, this was more than she was going to tolerate. She had to confront him. Closing the door more softly, she followed him out into the corridor and called down to him.

"Lord Luttrell, might I have one moment, sir?"

He stopped and turned, watching her as she strode towards him. He couldn't help but notice how well she filled out her dress. She could see the anger still drawn across his strong brow. And though his height and broad shoulders were somewhat intimidating, she knew she must face him if she was to retain any semblance of self-respect.

"My Lord, if, in the future you wish to chide me as if I were an errant child," she said looking up at him, "I would appreciate that you not do so in front of your sons. It undermines my authority. I have their young minds to look after, you know."

As a cool anger clouded into his dark eyes he sneered, "I shall say what I please, when I please, in my own house," He said as he hit his chest with his finger. It was the third time today that she crossed him and his fuse was getting short.

"Yes, my Lord, except when you are in my classroom. That is my domain," Ana stated with authority and then turned abruptly to leave. She chose purposely not to engage him any further in conversation and was fully prepared to leave him in the dust.

But Alexander grabbed her by the arm, pulling her close. His face was so close he could look directly into her eyes.

"Do not anger me further Miss Pembroke," he reprimanded. She could feel the warmth of his breath on her forehead and noticed that he smelled of spice and claret. She watched his mouth as he formed the words. Ana bit her bottom lip as something unknown was stirred inside her by his closeness but returned his hard gaze unflinching.

"I have no need of a governess here and despite my mother, I have a good mind to let you go," knowing full well that it was not in his power to do so, their eyes locked in battle.

Ana slowly drew her eyes away from his and looked down at his tanned hand firmly wrapped around her upper arm, "Then do so, sir," she answered, her voice quiet and steady.

He suddenly realized that his grip was pushing hard into the soft flesh of her arm. He released his hold. Ana glared once more into his steel cold eyes, her own eyes reflecting back his anger. He stepped back, suppressing an urge to take her in his arms and kiss her, hard. He was shocked by his own reaction towards this small hellion standing in front of him.

"As for your need of a governess, sir, yes, you might need one yourself just to teach you some decorum." And with that Ana turned and walked deliberately back to the schoolroom. She could feel his gaze burning into her back, her heart beating frantically, her arm hot from his touch. Her mind reeled from disbelief at her own words.

Though thoroughly angry, Alexander found her fire tantalizing. His strong desire to kiss her surprised him. Holding her so close was uncomfortably arousing. He could feel his blood coursing through his veins. These confrontations were not working. If he was going to intimidate her, he needed to find another way. Thoroughly enjoying the sway of her hips as she walked away, he thought, "maybe I do need a governess, especially one that needs to be taught a lesson herself," he thought to himself, his left brow rising with a slight churlish upturn of a grin.

CHAPTER 13

*F*inally alone, Ana reflected on her encounters with Lord Luttrell. She felt unusually uncomfortable in a way she had never experienced. His eyes seemed penetrating as if he could see into her very soul. She touched her arm where he had held it so tightly. Standing close to him was unnerving. She felt glad she had not run, yet decided it would be best to keep her distance.

Leaning out her bedroom window for a breath of fresh air Ana felt something in her sleeve, her forgotten letters. She moved the chair to the window and opened the letter from Charles hoping news from home would distract her from her worries.

My Dearest Ana,

It feels an eternity since we were together.

I had the pleasure of visiting with your sister several weeks ago. As you can imagine, I was keenly aware of your absence. I miss you terribly and hope the feelings I have for you will someday be returned.

I have spent some time doing much needed work at home. Your father had let so much go to ruin. You would hardly recognize the gardens. I can see you gracing them by your presence. Ana, my darling, I think of you often.

I hope you come to your senses and reconsider my proposal of marriage. Life is not the same without you. I know you have rebuffed me in the past. However, I find it harder to be without you, my love.

I cannot conceive of you employed as a common governess especially in a household with such a sullied reputation. You are degrading our family, my darling. I am amazed that Eliza approved of such nonsense. Please come to your senses, my dearest and return home to me.

Your faithful and loving,
Charles

"Ooo ... that insolent ..." Ana crumpled the letter and tossed it into the fire. "How dare he think he can dictate my life? And he calls that love?" she mumbled. Then, to insult her father on top of it was too much. Maybe he did let things go a bit, but her father had raised him and loved him like a son.

"First Lord Luttrell," she sighed angrily, "and now Charles? One tells me I am degrading the family and the other is ... is just ... well, just degrading. Well, neither will win." Ana was determined, her anger brimming against the whole lot of them.

Hearing the distant clock chimes, Ana realized it was past four. She had spent too much of her precious time brooding. Not having time to read the other note, she placed it on the table by her bed. She quickly left her room to seek out Lady Catherine for tea. Maybe Lady Catherine would be able provide some useful suggestions and insights to the many dilemmas of her day.

Ana took tea with Lady Catherine in her small study. Over the many weeks, they had had the opportunity to share and to grow close. In some ways Lady Catherine had become a surrogate mother and Ana found herself growing fonder of her by the day.

"There you are my dear! You are late today." Ana greeted Lady Catherine with a small curtsey.

"Yes, Lady Catherine I do apologize. I was reading a letter from home."

"Oh, how wonderful. Good news from your sister, I hope?" she said as she poured steaming tea into a delicate blue fine bone china cup rimmed with pink rosebuds and tinges of gold leaf.

Taking the cup, Ana said, "Well it wasn't newsworthy at all. It's from my cousin, Charles, the new Baron." Ana sighed, "Lady Catherine, I must admit he infuriates me," she said, as she looked into the steaming cup as the swirling cream turned it into a light brown.

"What happened, dear?" Lady Catherine was all ears for juicy gossip, something she so rarely had the opportunity in which to indulge.

"Charles continues to propose marriage, which I always turn down. He doesn't seem to understand that I do NOT wish to marry him."

"You don't love him?"

"I do love him but not in that way. We grew up together. He's more like a brother to me. And the thought of ... well I just can't see it."

"You know, my marriage to my dear Alfred was arranged. But we grew to love each other. Alfred was so easy to love. Would you grow to love Charles if you married him?"

"Lady Catherine, I've known Charles all my life. If I could ever love him the way a woman loves her husband, I believe I would've realized it by now." Ana sipped her tea feeling a blush cross her cheeks.

"Hmm, yes, I suppose that's true. I know you chose employment, however if the right man came along, you'd reconsider?" Lady Catherine studied Ana's face but could not see into her lowered eyes.

"That had been my dream to have marriage and family, but since the death of my parents ..." Ana went silent. "I had to put it behind me." She sounded discouraged yet resolved. Lady Catherine watched her for a few moments over her own cup.

"Ana, you know I'm a hopeless romantic." Putting her cup down with determination, her blue eyes were twinkling when she confessed, "It would please me to no end if you were to become my daughter-in-law."

Ana nearly choked on her cucumber sandwich as her turquoise eyes grew large. She couldn't believe what she just heard. "Oh, Lady Catherine, I wouldn't even entertain such a thing. Whatever would make you have such an idea? We'd never be a good match. No. Besides, his Lordship doesn't like me. We're always at loggerheads."

"Nonsense! He just doesn't know that he likes you." Lady Catherine looked at Ana like the cat that just ate the canary.

"No, he's made it perfectly clear. He wishes I were gone. It's only because you are my employer that I'm still here." Ana shook her head. "Lady Catherine, my conversations with your son have been anything but pleasant. He interrogates me and I … I feel so uncomfortable in his presence."

Lady Catherine smiled and nodded, "That's good. I've seen him watching you. I know my son. He may be pushing you away but give him time. He'll warm up to you. He was so hurt by his first wife, that awful woman. I never liked her. Alfred thought he was doing the right thing, you know. Linking our families together through marriage was so right at the time. However, Elizabeth was all wrong. Hugh and Geoffrey had such a hard time of it. And now …" She drifted off, adding, "He is protecting them and protecting himself from being hurt. That's all."

That's all? She couldn't believe what she was hearing. *It doesn't excuse his behavior.* Ana had shared little of her exchanges with Lord Luttrell. "Lady Catherine, I know so little of what happened." Lady Catherine loved to tell stories and Ana hoped this would both put the topic of marriage behind them and put his behavior in context.

Smoothing her napkin on her lap, Lady Catherine settled in to tell the story, "Hugh was two when Alexander was given his commission in India. I believe it was in fifty-seven. A Mr. Abernathy had been hired by Alexander to oversee the estate and family. Rufus Abernathy, that scoundrel. Well, Alexander was gone for three years. He was in a nasty battle. A blood bath really. Never speaks of it, but I know it affected him. He was wounded you know, almost died." Lady Catherine faded off looking distracted. "That's where he met Riya."

"I didn't know he was wounded," Ana said, truly feeling the cost of war. "What happened when he returned?"

"Abernathy and Elizabeth ran off leaving young Hugh and Geoffrey in my care, those poor children. Hugh cried endlessly for his mother, long into the nights. And Geoffrey took to fits of rage, hurting himself, breaking things. Alexander was a stranger to his own sons. Oh it was a terrible homecoming. Alexander had no other recourse but to divorce her. It took him almost a year to get the boys settled down. They are still so wounded … so needy."

"Oh my!" Ana felt deep empathy for the boys. Knowing loss herself, she knew the pain they must have suffered. Even her negative opinion towards Lord Luttrell shifted upon learning that he had been wounded in India and of the many hurdles he had to overcome when he returned.

"One of the most painful aspects of this whole story, my dear, is that Alexander can't let the past go. He blames it on the annual income he must pay her. As long as she remains unmarried, he is obliged to pay her five thousand pounds a year. To make matters worse, that Abernathy is still with her. So every time he draws up a draft the whole incident becomes an open sore. I believe that's why he refuses to open his heart. It's his pride you know."

"Lady Catherine, it is so sad. Your family has been through so much."

"Ana my dear, it is so easy to like you. You have made such a difference in the lives of those boys already as well as in the life of this old woman." Lady Catherine gave Ana a pat on the hand. "Give my Alexander a chance. I know you'll be good for him."

That was something Ana knew she would not do. She needed to change the subject quickly. "Lady Catherine, tell me about being a bride in this house." Lady Catherine loved to reminisce and it was an easy way to change the subject.

"Well, I will never forget the night of our first wedding anniversary. We planned to have a grand party to celebrate. All of our families were invited as well as many guests in the district. My Alfred wanted us to dance and have a grand banquet. There was a superb orchestra. I'll never forget the music. It was like magic. We danced until dawn." She smiled lost in her memory, sipping her tea." Several days following the event I realized that the orchestra had left the beautiful pianoforte. So, I ran to inform Alfred," she chuckled. "He followed me into the grand salon—it was blue then you know. He asked me to sit and play for him. Well, I sat at the box and opened the case to expose those beautiful ivory keys. Then I saw a beautiful blue satin ribbon, the very color of the room, and attached was the most beautiful note professing his love for me. He had purchased the pianoforte for our anniversary. It still sits in the grand salon where he had it placed. He spent many hours listening to me play. I never decline when asked to play, for when I do, I'm playing for my Alfred." She looked at Ana whose eyes were filled with tears.

"My child, I've made you sad," she said, seeing the emotion on Ana's face.

Ana wiped away her tears. "No, Milady, your story is so beautiful that it touched my heart."

"Ana, you too deserve such happiness. And I believe you'll get it."

The moonlight streamed through the window as the curtains fluttered in gentle night breeze. Ana was finding it hard to sleep. Her interactions with Lord Luttrell and Lady Catherine weighed heavy upon her mind. The thought of marrying Lord Luttrell was preposterous. How could Lady Catherine propose such nonsense? If marriage was all she was after, she would have married Charles. But she wanted more. She wanted what Eliza and Henry had, a deep abiding love. She winced. The very thought of touching Charles made her skin crawl. She wondered what it would be like to be touched by Lord Alexander Luttrell. His eyes were so intriguing and expressive. If only he would look at her the way he looked at Riya. Ana instinctively moved her hand to the place on her arm where his hand had been earlier that day. He had stood so close. She remembered the scent of him. She thought about his mouth as he spoke. She wondered what it would have been like to have kissed him and she slowly ran her fingers over her lips. She turned onto her side and closed her eyes tight. What foolish thoughts, making love to the Duke.

She needed to distract her mind. It was late. Everyone had to be in bed. A trip to the library to find a book might be helpful.

Slowly she turned the knob of her door and gently pushed it open. She stuck her head into the hallway looking for signs of life. Only the light from the moon streamed from windows. Silently, Ana made her way past the darkened rooms of other sleeping household members and down the grand stairs. The bright moonlight illuminated the portraits, drawing her attention to their eerie blue faces as she went past. She was oblivious to the dim light coming from beneath the library door.

Pushing the door open, Ana stopped short by what met her eyes. There in the glow by the library fireplace sat Lord Luttrell cross legged on a floor cushion, shirtless. And behind him was Riya, kneeling with her hands on his naked back. She was leaning into him as if whispering in his ear.

"Oh!" Ana exclaimed, bringing her hand to her mouth, her face a deep crimson, her turquoise eyes large with surprise.

Both turned and appeared frozen at seeing Ana. They were as startled to see her as she them.

"Excuse me!" Ana blurted out and quickly turned to run from the room, shocked and disgusted by the open display of affection between the two of them. Her thoughts raced as fast has her feet could carry her away from what she had just witnessed.

How could Lady Catherine condone such behavior and then suggest the possibility of a marriage to him? Did she even know? The very idea of a union to such a perverted and disgusting man was more than she could comprehend. How dare he act so condescending towards her, shaming her for innocently stumbling upon them in the river? Riya was barely seventeen and of a different race. Lord Luttrell was obviously a twisted man. To think she felt some sense of sympathy towards his situation disgusted her.

Finding the safety of her room, Ana began to pace the floor, her mind whirling. How could she stay in this house filled with deceit and perversion? Eliza was right. This was no place for her. She was out of her league. She remembered Eliza had mentioned something of Luttrell's despicable nature, but she could not believe that people really were this perverse. It was no wonder Lord Luttrell did not want her here. He wanted her gone so that he could perform his unholy deeds with Riya. Poor Riya, she most likely did not even understand that he was corrupting her.

The pity of it was the prospect of those innocent boys growing up as debauched as their father. But Ana knew she could not take part in their demise. What could she possibly do to help them not take the same dark road their father had taken? What kind of life would they have, destroyed by their mother's abandonment and their father's depravity?

She needed to leave. She needed to think. She continued to pace, wringing her hands in the anxiety.

Where was she to go, into the arms of Charles? How could that be better than this? She didn't love him. She would be just as perverted to give herself in marriage to a man who made her skin crawl, and for what? Money? Security? She couldn't return to Eliza and Henry with her tail between her legs. It would only prove to them that they were right and that she was unable to take care of herself. The reality was that without a position she was homeless. She had to stick this out until she found herself a new situation.

Suddenly, Ana stopped. She heard Riya and Lord Luttrell in the hall. It was clear that they were not speaking English. A chill went down Ana's spine at the thought of that man with such a girl. Yet she could not resist putting her ear to the door to gain any information.

"Good night Riya, don't worry. I'll take care of it," Lord Luttrell finally said in English, his voice was soft and gentle.

"Yes Sahib. Thank you," Riya responded quietly.

Ana heard the door to Riya's room close. She heard Lord Luttrell coming closer to her own door. He stopped directly in front of her room as if deciding to knock. If he did, Ana was determined not to let him in. Who knew what he was capable of? All was silent for a moment. Then she heard him move on towards his own apartments. To Ana's relief his door finally closed in the distance.

Take care of it? What could that mean? Riya must have felt such shame at being discovered in such a compromising position. It's Lord Luttrell who should be ashamed. How was he going to take care of it? It must be that he planned on saying something to her about it. He might even wonder what Ana thought about it, not that it mattered.

As Ana lay back in her bed, she wondered what he must be thinking, knowing she had witnessed their torrid relationship. Now he would truly believe her to be a spy, sneaking around late at night. Who wouldn't come to that conclusion? He would never trust her. And why did it concern her what he thought? He meant nothing to her, and she knew beyond a shadow of a doubt that she meant nothing to him. What was Lady Catherine thinking?

CHAPTER 14

*A*na awoke exhausted from disturbing dreams. She was already worn out from the previous day's events when she and Lord Luttrell had gone through two rounds of arguments. Lady Catherine had suggested the most preposterous notion of marriage. There was an obnoxious letter from Charles. And, to top it all off, her belief in the unholy relationship between Riya and the Duke was confirmed.

Meeting with him first thing in the morning was not going to calm her throbbing temples.

Upon awakening her, Mrs. C. had announced that Ana was expected in the library at Lord Luttrell's request and as soon as possible. Ana was sure it was about "taking care" of whatever "it" was.

She made herself as presentable as possible in her brown plaid dress. After a last glance around her room to check that all was in place, she spotted the note left unread on the table by her bed. Being a few minutes late was not going to change the Duke's disgruntled attitude. Opening the neatly folded letter Ana began to read the unfamiliar hand.

Miss Pembroke,

This is to inform you that you are in grave danger. It is imperative that you leave Dunster Castle immediately. Return at once to London for your safety and protection before you are sorry.

A concerned friend.

Irritated, Ana turned the parchment over to review the seal. There was nothing significant about it and provided no indication of who this "concerned friend" might be.

"Danger? How could I possibly be in danger? I have no enemies," she said to herself.

It must be some childish note from Geoffrey trying to scare her away. "Boys," she thought as she placed the note into a box on her table. She would have to address this later. Her stomach churned with emotion about the upcoming meeting.

Ana realized she could no longer stall the inevitable. Swallowing the sense of trepidation that was percolating, Ana made one final check in the mirror and went to keep her appointment.

At this early point in the day, Ana couldn't imagine how her day could get any worse. Between childish notes, a headache, and now the Duke to contend with, Ana dreaded what was going to happen in the next few minutes. She was sure he was going to admonish her for sneaking around the house yet again. But how could she have known about the clandestine relationship between Riya and Lord Luttrell?

Knocking on the open door of the library, Ana anxiously waited to be invited in.

Alexander sorted through his own thoughts and shuffled papers on his desk knowing Ana was waiting at the door. He'd been surprised by his physical response to her when he grabbed her by the arm and pulled her close the day before. Having found her attractive from the first day he saw her, he had kept her more than arm's length way. But yesterday, he had held her so close that he caught the scent of her.

He realized his next request from her was either going to make or break the situation, especially after last night. He hoped it would make her leave. He repressed the feelings of attraction that were beginning to stir.

"Come in and close the door," the Lord said. His deep voice resonated from behind his desk.

Ana swallowed hard and entered. "I would feel better with the door open," she thought, but she took her seat on the red leather chair. Folding her hands demurely in her lap, she waited for him to speak. She noticed that he too looked tired and drawn. He should, she thought.

"Miss Pembroke," he said, finally breaking the silence. "I want you to teach Riya to read and write plus some simple mathematics. I want you to teach her to be an English lady."

"What?!" she cried. Ana could not believe what she was hearing, her face paling at the request.

"You heard me," he replied flatly.

"Sir, after what I witnessed last night, I could not possibly fulfill your request," Ana stated in disbelief. She was astounded at her own words. What was the purpose? What was he preparing her for? She could only imagine and the thought horrified her.

"First, you don't know what you saw last night," he added with little emotion though knowing she thought him a cad, "Second, you will do as I say or you will leave my house. This will place you under my employ, not my mothers."

"But…"

"If you do not take this addition to your post, I'll consider it insubordination, and I'll tell my sons you decided to resign." His gray eyes were hard and cold.

"But …"

"Do as I say or leave; it's that simple," his voice growing colder.

Ana stood up in disbelief and watched him return his focus to the papers on his desk. She felt frozen to the floor, recognizing the ultimatum as a challenge to a duel. Glancing down at the papers on his desk, she realized that the parchments were similar to the ridiculous note that she had just read in her room. Her mouth dropped open in astonishment at the game he was playing.

"He's doing his best to make me leave. Well, I don't give in easily," she thought, now determined to stay more than ever.

"Is there something else?" he asked, never once looking up from his work.

"You amaze me," she said, her turquoise eyes blinking in disbelief.

"What?" He looked up at her face and saw the bewilderment there.

"You are willing to go to any lengths to make me leave, won't you?"

"What are you talking about?" he responded though he knew full well she was correct.

"Oh, you know very well. You can't deny it!" Ana was incredulous.

"Miss Pembroke, have you gone mad?" A storm of gathering anger crossed his brow.

"Not I, but I've some strong concerns about *you*," she said pointing.

"Again, what are you talking about? I have no time for your foolishness."

"Foolishness? I'm not the one sending threatening notes to myself."

"Miss Pembroke. I believe you are deranged. I've sent you no note." He stood up from his chair, his face moving closer to hers as he leaned over his desk.

"I, sir, may be many things, but deranged is not one of them, whereas you are most certainly sophomoric." Her anger was such that she had completely forgotten her station.

Lord Alexander stood in disbelief at the barb that was just thrown his way. Never, in his lifetime had anyone, especially some snit of a girl and a subordinate at that, dared to speak to him with such a tone. He was rendered momentarily speechless. As he stared into her large turquoise eyes, he realized that the fire from her anger made them glimmer like finely cut gems. No one made his blood boil like this, not even his mother in her finest moments. His jaw rippled through clenched teeth.

"You, Miss Pembroke are dismissed," he said, his tone ice cold.

"Well, it's going to take a lot more than teaching Riya how to be a proper English lady or sending threatening adolescent notes to get me to leave." Ana stormed out of the room. This was more then she could tolerate. Leave? Well, the truth was that she should leave, but where would she go? The same old dilemma presented itself. Even if she wanted to find another position, she sincerely doubted she would get a glowing letter of recommendation from this family. She was trapped. Even Charles had never made her so angry. How dare he call her deranged? By all that was holy, it was Lord Luttrell who suffered from some malady of thinking.

Standing outside the nursery, Ana took a minute to calm her jangled nerves. Riya would be inside keeping the boys occupied and quiet until her arrival. Today she was not to dismiss her as usual. She was going to request that she stay so she could teach her to read and write and become an English lady. And what would be the purpose of that? Was Lord Luttrell planning on marrying Riya? Ana raised her clenched fists to her throbbing temples. She took a deep breath and opened the door.

"Good morning Hugh, Geoffrey. Today Riya is going to stay with us. I'm going to teach you to read and write as requested by Lord Luttrell," she said calmly though it felt as if her head was going to explode. Rather than taking up this infernal challenge she really should be packing and leaving for home where it was, as the note said, "safe."

"Oh, Miss Ana, thank you, thank you," Riya's eyes welled up with tears of joy.

The last thing she wanted to do was teach Riya anything and now she was acting grateful. Ana had expected Riya to at least show some shame or embarrassment for being found out last night. But this gratitude was too hard to comprehend.

"There's no need to thank me, Riya. Just take a seat next to Geoffrey and we will get started." Somehow, Ana felt small.

"Does this mean Riya would be able to read to me at night?" Hugh asked hopefully. How in the world she was to teach this Indian girl how to be an English lady was beyond her, but now she had taken up the challenge and needed to start.

"Yes, it does, Hugh. Now, let's open our books, shall we?"

Alexander was furious. Once again, Ana did not take the bait and resign her position. Further, he could hardly believe the pointed accusations which spewed from the mouth of a mere governess. The false fabrication startled him. How could she even consider a man of his station stooping so low as to write such tripe? There was only one explanation. Geoffrey was trying to scare her off. Who else would write something so childish and foolhardy?

That Geoffrey, he most definitely was learning to protect himself against the wiles of women. Alexander almost felt proud of his son's scheme. He had learned the hard way not to trust women. Sadly, Elizabeth provided the first lesson with the deepest cut of all.

Women in general were most definitely deranged. He could come up with no better word for this Miss Pembroke and her insane accusations, for his mother and her scheming. And now he had to leave for London to make another payment to his whore of an ex-wife and her weasel lover.

Women were a necessary evil in what he considered two areas of life, bearing children and giving men pleasure. Women should be banished to an island for breeding or left in the brothels for whoring. That is just where this Miss Pembroke should be. She was built for giving men pleasure. That was easy to see. She was not supposed to be teaching his sons. That was his responsibility and he had been doing a fine job of it, despite his mother's meddling. And no matter what he'd done thus far, she would not quit her position.

At three o'clock, Ana's head was still throbbing from the emotion of the day, and she sent word to Lady Catherine that she would not be down for tea. She needed time to think.

Even in one day, Riya proved herself to be an eager and quick student. Ana could see she was still so innocent in so many ways. In fact, Ana decided Riya most likely did not even understand what Lord Luttrell was doing. She did know that in India girls were treated as property and were forced into marriage. But Lord Luttrell should know better than to take advantage of her culture, inexperience, and youth.

She needed to educate Riya that English ladies had the opportunity for choice, limited choice, but choice all the same. She could help her understand that she had a say in what happens in her life and whom she chose to marry, if she wished to marry. She did not have to give in to the demands of a libertine. Maybe teaching Riya was a gift. She most likely didn't know that being in the arms of the Duke was an option. There were other opportunities. Maybe she had never given Riya a chance. But now she could do something for Riya.

A much-concerned Mrs. C. brought her meal to her room. As Ana took a sip of her tea, her thoughts returned to the previous night. She became acutely aware that it was the second time she had seen the Duke naked; more than she had seen of any other man. She had to admit that he had a very muscular and becoming physique. She wondered what it would be like to touch him the way she had seen Riya touch him, to feel the smoothness of his skin, to feel the warmth of his embrace. She closed her eyes as her thoughts began to stimulate her senses.

The gentle and persistent knock at her door broke her deep concentration. Lady Catherine's muffled voice asked "Ana? Ana are you all right?"

Placing her cup on the table Ana sighed as she stood up to answer the door. "Yes, Lady Catherine, I'm well."

"My dear, you are not well," she replied as a look of genuine concern covered her face. "You look pale and drawn. When I received your message about tea, I spoke to Mrs. C. We all agreed that you must be ill."

"I didn't wish to alarm you. I have had a rather trying day, Lady Catherine, that is all. Other than a slight headache, I'm fine. Really, I am," Ana answered. She was plainly exhausted.

Nonsense! You look terrible," she said pushing her way into Ana's room. "Before he left, Alexander told me that he charged you to teach Riya. Is that what's troubling you? I think he was hoping you would not take up the challenge. But you did take it up—you aren't leaving! Oh, he can be such a boor," Lady Catherine said.

"I am staying," Ana said flatly. "Lord Luttrell is gone?" she added on an upturned note.

"Why yes. He was called to town."

"Oh." What a relief, she thought to herself.

"Yes, Ana, just for a fortnight." She looked at Ana closely, studying her eyes. "Have you been thinking about my suggestion?" she ventured, cocking her head to one side.

"Oh, Lady Catherine this is preposterous. If you only knew ..." Ana's voice drifted off.

"If I only knew what?" Her curiosity piqued, Lady Catherine took the only seat in the room, excited to hear more lovely gossip.

"Lady Catherine, your son ... well ... I will not nor could I ever marry anyone out of convenience. I think that's what would happen. Anyway, your son has no feelings for me," she added, turning to look out her window so that Lady Catherine would not see her face and read her distain.

"He threatened that if I did not teach Riya he'd force me to leave, and said that I was now under his employ and not yours. He has stolen me from you and now has the power to send me packing at his whim."

"He threatened you?" Lady Catherine looked shocked yet was secretly pleased at the same time. "But he did not send you packing did he? No wonder you are not well. He is being such a cad. I'm so sorry for that, my dear."

"Lady Catherine, you know I cannot return home. The reality is … I have no home to return to. So there it is and here I am," she said in a flat matter-of-fact tone of voice.

With a hand on her chin, Lady Catherine took a moment and studied Ana closer. "Ana, I think there's an attachment forming."

Ana shook her head vigorously against the ghastly idea.

"There is. Yes, I see it. You are protesting too much! Oh, I am so glad." Pausing for a minute she added, "And I suspect he has feelings for you. Otherwise he would not have challenged you with this infernal position." Lady Catherine stood up and clapped her hands. "Don't you see? He wants you to stay. By pushing you away he's as much as told you that you have become too close for comfort. This is wonderful!" She again clapped her hands like a silly school girl.

"No. No, I think he really wants me gone. I don't think that has changed. I … I think his interests lie elsewhere," she added quietly, wishing she could tell Lady Catherine the ungodly truth about her son's lechery with Riya.

"If I know anything, I know my son," Lady Catherine said as she took Ana's hand. "His heart's not elsewhere. It's just been locked up. Oh, I know the two of you have been arguing like cats and dogs, but that's just the challenge he's needed, someone to get his blood up. And I believe it's you. Why, his boorish behavior is the way he's been keeping you at bay. Oh, Ana, I'm so pleased!" And with that, Lady Catherine swept out of her room.

It was apparent that Lady Catherine had no knowledge of what was happening under her own roof. She had no clue of the relationship her son had with Riya, and Ana was not going to burst her bubble. No matter what her personal feelings were for the Duke, he was not the type of man that Ana wanted to marry. But Lady Catherine was entitled to her fantasy. Ana shook her head in disbelief, now convinced that the whole family was deranged.

CHAPTER 15

With Lord Luttrell away for weeks in London, Ana finally relaxed and actually began enjoying teaching Riya. But this summer day was a humid one. An afternoon storm was brewing over the bay. Geoffrey and Hugh were having trouble focusing on their sums and Ana was feeling challenged by Riya's spelling.

"Boys, stop fidgeting and concentrate," Ana repeated sternly. Within a few minutes they were at it again, poking and prodding; Ana glared at them.

"What?" Geoffrey replied, assuming a pained look of innocence for Riya's benefit.

"He started it," Hugh whined, pushing Geoffrey's shoulder.

Ana loudly slapped the book in her lap closed.

Smiling at Riya, she said, "We've done enough spelling for today. You did well and can go."

"Thank you, Miss Pembroke." Riya stood up and organized the papers on the table before giving a small curtsy and leaving the room.

Turning her attention to the boys, Ana was as peeved with them as she was with the weather. "This isn't working," she thought. Putting her book down on the desk with a thud, she said, "Let's find something else to release today's pent up energy." Both boys looked at each other, their eyes wide with excitement. "Hooray!" they cheered, racing towards the door.

Ana wondered what had happened to the well-groomed boys that began the day, their hair neatly slicked back and their shirts firmly tucked into their brown knickers. The damp weather wreaked havoc on Geoffrey's dark curls. And Hugh … he could never keep his blonde cowlick from sticking up. Cravats askew, shirt collars undone, and shirttails hanging crumpled from the back, they both looked a fright. Ana could not help smiling to herself thinking how different boys were from the tidy nieces she had left behind.

"Hold on now," Ana chided. "I did give you leave of your lessons. However, we'll find something else to do. This is not playtime." Their hopes of play crushed, they slowly meandered back to their seats. Hugh flopped into his chair while Geoffrey sat with his ankle over his knee, his foot anxiously bouncing up and down. Sitting quietly in deep thought, Ana could see their young minds at work.

"I know!" Always the leader, Geoffrey sat up abruptly and said, "Let's play war. Hugh, you be Napoleon. I'll be Lord Nelson. We'll get Riya to play Josephine."

Hugh whined, "Why do you always get to be Lord Nelson? I want to be Lord Nelson!"

"Boys you *are not* playing war," Ana said firmly believing it was the very same childhood folly that eventually took the life of Miles and ultimately her parents. "There's no glory in war." She thought for a moment, biting her bottom lip. "I know," she said having a small epiphany of her own. "Today we learn how to waltz."

"Waltz?" they chorused with faces screwed up in utter disgust.

"Yes, waltz. All well-bred gentlemen must learn the fine art of dance. How else will you woo your lady love?" she asked, smiling, knowing the thought of "wooing" was not yet an interest and she fully expected the reaction that she received.

"Lady love? Never!" Geoffrey grabbed his stomach and winced. Hugh laughed as he watched his brother's animations. Ana shook her head.

"Besides it's much cooler downstairs. Meet me in the drawing room in fifteen minutes. Make yourselves presentable. I don't know how you two ended up looking so frightful. Oh, and bring Riya." By then Hugh joined the gyrations and the boys continued their agony death scene at the thought of a "lady love." Ana knew they would follow her instructions. Ignoring their antics, she left to find Lady Catherine who would surely agree to play the pianoforte.

Lady Catherine was pleased to participate and looked forward to watching her grandsons learn to dance. She played a few chords to limber up her bejeweled hands. She was dressed in a fine, sky blue silk taffeta trimmed with a cream lace collar and cuffs. A beautiful brocade bodice completed her outfit. Her gray hair was piled high on her head and crowned with a cream lace and blue-ribbon cap. She looked magnificent and surprisingly cool as she settled herself before the finely carved instrument, her delicate blue satin slipper resting on a pedal.

She smiled as her two young grandsons entered the drawing room. They looked uncomfortable at this prospect of learning to waltz. Riya, several inches taller than Geoffrey, stood quietly behind them, obviously wanting to hide in the shadows.

"Geoffrey, Hugh, stand up straight," Lady Catherine instructed. "I think this is a grand idea. Miss Pembroke is proving to be a very positive influence." She smiled, nodding at Ana who had shared with her the boys' silly behavior at the idea of dance. "And Riya, I'm so glad you're joining in. You look lovely my dear," commenting on her proper attire and noticing she was wearing shoes. "What a grand family we are." It was clear that Lady Catherine was completely unaware of the situation between the Duke and Riya and had oddly embraced Riya as a member of the family.

Lady Catherine was delighted with Ana's results. There was much improvement in the boys' demeanor and social graces. And now dance lessons too. Yes, Lady Catherine was very pleased. If only her son would stop his nonsense and begin to see the benefit of Ana's presence instead of being suspicious and impossible. Soon Geoffrey would be old enough to join in pleasant society and her prior concern that he would lack the graces to do so was quickly diminishing.

"Your grandmother has graciously agreed to play for us this afternoon, Thank you Lady Catherine. Thank your grandmother boys," Ana instructed.

"Thanks Grams," Geoffrey said, shifting his feet and looking every bit like a belligerent teen. Ana shook her head.

"Now you can do better than that, Geoffrey. Lady Catherine is being very kind to play for us on this hot day," she scolded.

Hugh piped-in, "Thank you Grandmother for playing the waltz for us. I enjoy when you play." Showing his big brother up, he sent a toothless grin in Geoffrey's direction as if he won the grand prize.

"Hugh, that was beautifully done! I would gladly play for you at any time. All you need do is ask."

Enjoying the praise, he added, "And you look lovely today, Grandmother." Geoffrey's gray eyes glared at Hugh with the same cool look Ana had so often received from his father. The similarity startled her.

Laughing at his young charm, Lady Catherine added, "Oh, thank you kind sir! Come, both of you and give me a big hug."

They ran to the piano. Ana was warmed to see their caring and open relationship. Riya, for her part, remained behind, feeling uncomfortable and oddly out of place.

Hugh is right, Ana thought, Lady Catherine did look lovely today. She looked down at her own plain gray cotton dress which was in mean contrast to that of Lady Catherine's fine gown. Ana began to feel a bit wistful and unbecoming for the lessons to be given. She looked at her black leather walking shoes and sighed. It had been a long time since she was at a ball, she thought, missing the enjoyment of her youth and the beautiful clothes she left behind.

She remembered her life as a Baron's daughter with balls, parties and theater. She and Eliza would spend hours planning their gowns and ribbons, curling their hair and laughing in preparation. But that was a lifetime ago. She was no longer the Baron's daughter. She was employed as a governess and she was beginning to feel as dreary as the day. Snapping out of her malaise, she prepared for the waltz lesson. Her dress may be drab, but least it was cotton and cool. *Enough self-pity, best get on with it.*

The settee needed to be moved so as not to damage the furniture. The room was beautifully decorated with deep Turkish carpets covering a magnificent Italianate tiled floor, light green walls, and furnishings upholstered in deep reds, golds and forest greens. Matching heavy green taffeta draperies laced with golden fringe decorated the windows and enormous French doors that opened to the gardens and conservatory. Portraits and country scenes adorned the towering walls. Plasterwork encircled the high ceiling from which hung several glistening crystal chandeliers. Large flowing ferns brightened the corners of the room. The pianoforte was magnificently placed near one of the two finely carved gleaming marble fireplaces.

"Boys, help me clear a space for a dance floor." They jumped in gallantly taking a side, happy to show off their growing strength in front of the ladies.

Once a space was cleared, Ana began instruction, "Now, Geoffrey you stand here like this," picking up his arms and placing them into position. "Keep your arms steady and elbows up and out. Riya come here. Stand in front of Geoffrey. Take his hand."

Geoffrey looked horrified. "You mean I have to dance with HER? Oh, I'm not dancing with a girl," he scowled and his arms dropped in defiance.

"Would you rather dance with Hugh?"

Hugh protested vigorously, shaking his head and folding his arms tightly against his chest, his eyes wide in horror. "I'm not dancing with HIM!"

Ana sighed and seeing the situation as hopeless stated, "Well we're off to a fine start." Conceding she said, "Geoffrey, I'll be your dance partner. Raise your arms as I showed you. Come on, I'm not going to bite." She took his cold and clammy hands in hers. "Lady Catherine, a waltz if you please." Lady Catherine began to play an old favorite. The light and airy tones of the pianoforte filled the room with cheery melodious sounds which echoed out into the hallways of the castle.

"Now, with your left foot … listen to the rhythm of the music. One Two Three, One Two Three … move your feet, with the beat …" they began to move with the music.

"Ouch!" Ana exclaimed as Geoffrey stomped on her foot. Rubbing her sore foot. she said, "Don't watch your feet. Look at me. And just follow the music."

"But …"

Exasperated, she said, "look at me; follow the music. Again! Lady Catherine, music please. One Two Three, One Two Three." They began to move.

"Geoffrey!" Ana yelped. He mistakenly pushed her into a group of chairs where she fell ungracefully into one of them, her feet in the air and her petticoats above her knees.

"Be careful!" she said as she stood up, dusting off her skirts.

"But, Miss Pembroke …!"

All were startled as deep melodic tones of laughter rang into the room. Alexander had returned. He had been drawn to the music and was leaning against the doorway, his traveling coat thrown over his left shoulder, watching Ana's feeble attempts with Geoffrey. She noted he was simply dressed: dark trousers, white shirt, and buff waistcoat. His shirt collar was open exposing his muscular neck and dark curls. His high brown leather riding boots accentuated his muscular calves. His hair, damp from his ride home, hung unruly on his forehead and down his collar making him look the rogue. Ana felt exposed realizing he had been standing there watching her dance. Her face flushed.

Alexander was just as surprised to find Ana still in residence. Secure in the belief that his request of her to teach Riya would be more then she could tolerate, he expected to find her gone when he returned from London. But as he watched the fumbling lesson, he admired the way she filled out her dress. His eyes looked almost black as he allowed them to slowly roam over her, noticing the fullness and roundness of her breasts, her small waist, and the sway of her hips as she moved with the rhythm of the waltz. He wished her skirts flew higher at her spill onto the chair to show off more of her shapely legs.

Quelling his passions, he decided this was a good time to give her a lesson she so obviously deserved. Though it had been several weeks since the encounter in the library, his trip to London only deepened his resolve to make her leave. As luck would have it, she was presenting him with a perfect opportunity and in front of his family.

"Alexander, you're home!" Lady Catherine exclaimed, happy to see the safe return of her son. The boys smiled in agreement.

"Geoffrey. Step aside," he ordered, tossing his coat on a nearby chair. To the surprise of all he strode into the room, dismissing the greetings from his family, determined to fulfill his mission.

"May I?" He took Ana's hand, leading her to the center of the floor. Realizing his intentions, the heat of the day became oppressive. Embarrassed now by her stumbling around with the boys, she allowed the Duke to lead.

"Mother, if you please..."

Lady Catherine began to play, her eyes gleaming hopefully with these new circumstances as the lilting waltz filled the room.

"First, sons, you must ask the lady if she desires to dance thusly: Miss Pembroke, may I have this dance?" He bowed deeply from the waist, a look of mockery in his steely eyes.

"Yes, My Lord," Ana answered giving a small modest curtsy though suspicious of his intentions.

"Now that the dance is agreed upon you place your hand so. Allow your lady's hand to rest gently on yours. See?" He looked over at his sons as they watched intently.

Ana timidly placed her hand under his. It was warm and strong. Even with the heat, shivers ran up her arm as their skin touched. She was quite aware of their lack of gloves. He noticed how delicate her fingers were. Unwittingly, he ran his thumb gently over her velvet soft skin secretly enjoying the feel of her hand against his.

"Then you take your right arm and slip it around your lady's waist, placing your hand firmly on her back." His smoldering eyes now burned into Ana's turquoise ones as his hand slid, caressingly yet firmly against the smallness of her waist. Her heart skipped at the nearness of him. Aware of the heat from her exotic eyes, his arm pulled her close to him. He instinctively wanted to press her to him but kept his distance for the dance. Ana's face began to feel flush with excitement, and her breath quickened with the pounding of her heart. He hoped it was not the temperature but the effect of his hands on her person. He held her so close that she could feel his breath against the hair on the top of her head as he spoke; she struggled to keep clear eye contact for fear of having her emotions read.

The drapes began to billow with the growing wind as the summer storm approached. The room exploded with light as electricity streaked across the sky and the pianoforte began to pound out the waltz.

"You see, it is your job in the dance to control the fair lady in your arms." He continued searching her face for the effects of his touch. She was blushing, and he felt pleased with himself for her discomfort. Suddenly the crash of thunder pealed from across the bay. He felt Ana flinch in his arms. All the better, her nerves were raw.

"You control her; protect her from the other dancers." He looked at Riya and his sons, all looking on, uncomfortably intrigued. His return gaze was more intent. His cool gray eyes flashed with blue fire. Ana felt as if he could read her every thought. Her mouth felt dry. She licked her lips. They glistened with desire. He imagined covering her mouth with his. Just what she wants, he thought with contempt. The music played on. Another flash of lightning and deep rumble brought the storm closer.

"And if she is a good dancer, she will let you lead and do as you direct," he pretended to smile but it never reached his eyes. There was something in them that was a mixture of ridicule and taunting. Ana felt hot.

Ignoring the darkening of the room from the impending storm, Alexander twirled Ana about the floor to the music, his hand on her slim waist guiding her across the room. "You see? You're the master on the dance floor," he instructed the boys, his eyes never leaving Ana's face. Her knees felt weak. The mood was changing, becoming more intense, more passionate. Something deep inside her began to burn. This was much more than a dance lesson.

"Never let your eyes wander from hers," he continued. His gaze was intense, burning into hers.

The music continued to rise through the air. "You move her in and out with the pressure you place on her body through your hands. You both move to the rhythm of the music. In and out, One, Two, Three, to the rhythm, of the music," his voice grew deeper, more intense, keeping time with the music, caressing, playing with the words. A lightening crack flashed brilliance into the room. Rain began to pelt the open windows and doors. The curtains rippled like watery sails. The music soared. His closeness was making her head spin. She wanted him to stop. She wanted him to continue.

Is he making love to me? Ana thought, bewildered as he spun her around and around, his eyes searching hers, his arms holding her decadently closer, feeling the heat of his body against hers. She felt unnerved, excited, and out of control. She was acutely aware of being watched by the others. She felt embarrassed. The storm's passion mounted as if to prepare her for the rest of the dance.

He picked up his pace as the music intensified towards its climax. Pulling her even closer, he circled her around the room, their bodies converging, igniting a fire between them. "Keep her close but be on your guard," he warned, his voice full of emotion. "Dancing can be dangerous," he said, his breath hot in her ear.

She felt breathless and lost in his arms. The scent of him mixed with the pungent spice of his cologne made her head spin with unfamiliar feelings.

As Lady Catherine played the final notes, Alexander gave Ana one more spin around the room. They had moved deeper into the darkening shadows created by the tempest. As the music ended, he allowed himself to hold her close against his body for a moment, searching her exotic eyes, taking pleasure in the feel of the rise and fall of her chest against his. He felt the hot pulse of her blood coursing through her wrist. He felt her breasts pressed against him, his own heart beating fast, his passion beginning to rise. He struggled hard against the urge to kiss her open mouth and felt he was losing his battle with his own desire.

Suddenly, a potted fern crashed to the floor with the gusts of the storm. He stepped back, regaining his senses, and took her hand in his. She was speechless, yearning for cool air. She watched as he brought her naked fingers to his warm lips, brushing them ever so lightly with a soft kiss. She inhaled at his touch. Her whole body shivered with excitement, the storm now as intense and dark as the passions raging within her.

Finally, after what felt like an eternity to Ana, Alexander withdrew his icy blue gaze, dropped her hand and turned to the others who were standing at the other end of the room, spellbound by the intense and intimate nature of what they had witnessed.

"Now that is how you waltz." He turned to Ana and bowed coolly as if nothing had happened. Flushed and confused, she gave a small curtsey, her long dark lashes fluttered to her cheeks as her gaze fixed on the floor, afraid of what he might find in her eyes.

From the other side of the salon, Lady Catherine clapped her hands, "Ana dear that was beautiful. Alexander, magnificent."

"Can I go next?" asked Geoffrey, the boy transfixed by the unknown passion he had witnessed.

Alexander looked at Ana's rosy cheeks, the delicate glistening of her moist skin, and her downcast eyes. He knew that she was feeling more than just the effects of the exercise, a feeling he himself needed to repress. Alexander smiled at himself, satisfied with his efforts at her discomfort.

"No, I think we've had enough lessons for today. Lord Luttrell, Lady Catherine." Humiliated, Ana curtsied and turned on her heels, quickly removing herself from the room. She knew her departure was inappropriate but she couldn't stay and remain in control of her feelings, hot tears teetering at the brink.

"What just happened here?" Lady Catherine asked sternly, concerned for Ana's speedy and seemingly painful departure. "Alexander, what did you say to her?"

"Nothing Mother, we just danced," he said with all innocence.

Lady Catherine stood up closing the pianoforte with a bang. "Boys, return to the nursery. I need to speak with your father." Feeling relieved that the lessons were over, the boys quickly turned and left the room resuming their banter about being Lord Nelson or Napoleon and calling to Riya who slowly followed behind. "Do you want to be Josephine?"

"Alexander, you did not just dance with that young woman for if you had she would not have left so abruptly. I know you did something or said something," she chided.

"Mother, I want her gone, from this house and from our lives. She needs to leave." he said scornfully.

"I don't understand, Alexander, she's been doing such a fine job. I thought you put that silly nonsense from your head."

"From the time she arrived she has been nothing but trouble for me," he said, his strong jaw set and one eyebrow raised. "Mother, I am through, I tell you. Through. I have had a belly full of her arguments and challenges to my authority. Let her go!" his voice boomed, "or I'll make her go."

"No, son. I like her too much," she stated softly. "I wish to keep her as my companion.

"She infuriates me! It is like having an argument on the Parliament floor. I don't get such contentions from the men at my club.

"So, she is passionate and invigorating?" Lady Catherine said, hoping to put a new spin on it.

"No, she is a cancerous social climber and a nag," he spouted.

"Alexander, have you lost your mind? What would give you such a ridiculous idea?" she said in disbelief.

"I spoke to Sumner while in town. I don't believe she's down on her luck. She's had numerous opportunities to marry her cousin. But she refuses. I don't trust her and I don't trust you. I'm sure you've been concocting something," he answered with disgust.

"Son, you cut me to the quick." Lady Catherine placed her hand on his arm and looked directly into his face. His eyes were dark with an unspoken rage.

"Alexander, this woman comes from a good family, and she has suffered great tragedy. Besides she doesn't love her cousin."

"You prove my point. She's a social climber." His own feelings were as hard and cold as his face. "You act naive. But no! You want it all. You take it all," he breathed with disgust.

"Oh son, you must give this up. This is about Elizabeth isn't it?" She was well aware of her son's resentments over his first wife. "You never loved her. She only hurt your pride."

"Give it up, you say?" His mood was now as dark as the raging summer storm. "I have to give up five thousand a year from that damn divorce. She gets my money and keeps that puny stinking … in her bed at my expense." Rage and pain twisted his face. "Give it up? I returned from the battlefields of India to find she's left her babies, my sons, in your care so she can dally with that snake in the grass and he is lavished upon with MY MONEY. She ruined their lives and she ruined my life. I will NOT be taken in by an argumentative social climber. I'll not forget and will never GIVE IT UP!

Alexander headed towards the door and abruptly faced his mother, "Besides, she is a pain in my … Arrrgh … I want her gone!" With that Alexander turned on his heels and stormed from the room leaving his mother dually concerned about his frame of mind as well as the emotional well-being of his apparent target of revenge, Ana. Her hopes for a union between them had been dashed.

CHAPTER 16

Ana had barely reached the top of the grand staircase when Geoffrey and Hugh raced past her. Normally she would have chided them for being unruly. But she hardly noticed them scamper down the hall.

"Is he toying with me?" she thought as hot tears over-spilled her eyes. She knew he was mocking her. She felt used, played with. And yet she wanted more than anything to feel his arms around her once more. The scent of him lingered about her. His steely blue eyes penetrated her as if he could see into her very soul. He frightened her and excited her at the same time. Never before had the nearness of a man caused such turmoil of emotions and passions. Realizing that she wanted a man who was so vulgar, Ana felt a deep self-loathing.

Entering the safety of her room, Ana sat on the edge of her bed and began to weep, her hands covering her face. This was not what she expected. She missed the companionship of Eliza and her family. She missed Miles. She missed her mother's understanding and her father's strength. She missed her old life with her family. She even missed Charles. Maybe she should have stayed with Eliza and helped with the girls.

"What did you expect, Ana?" she asked out loud, blowing into her handkerchief. "Love?"

She stood up and viewed herself in the looking glass wondering why she could not find love and be loved. *Maybe I should marry Charles.* The very thought of that brought fresh tears streaming down her already wet face. She threw herself on the bed to have a good cry. She felt as if she had lost everything and more.

After a time, she rolled on her back and stared at the ceiling of her room. "I have to make the best of this," she said to herself. "I can't just wallow. What's done is done." Her thoughts continued, "I've made my choice. Anyway, those boys need me. Lady Catherine needs me. What would Father say? Probably, *don't give a fig about the Duke and stay out of his way*. Well, I'll do just that. I'll do my best to stay out of his way, the boor. I'll just focus on my work and stay as far away from him as possible. He may not want me around but those boys need me. And, I must admit, I need them too."

The storm had finally passed. A deep orange glow hung on the horizon under the vanishing gray clouds as the sun began to set, making way for a new day.

There was a knock on her door. "Yes?" Ana said, her dark lashes still showing signs of tears.

"Miss Pembroke?" She recognized Riya's gentle voice at the door.

"Yes?" Ana blew her nose again.

The door slowly opened as Riya pushed her head into the room. She looked over at Ana who was sitting on her bed in the remaining gloom of the afternoon storm. She noticed her swollen eyes. "May I come in? Lady Catherine asked me to bring to you some tea."

"Yes, thank you, Riya. Place it there. That was very kind of her."

"Is everything fine?" she asked, genuine concern crossing her brown brow.

"Yes, fine, just having a bout of self-pity, I think. I'll get over it soon."

"Self-pity?" Riya asked as if unclear of the concept.

"I'm feeling sorry for myself because I have lost much of my family and I don't have a family of my own. Now that I say it, it sounds rather silly doesn't it?" She gave Riya a small unconvincing smile.

"Miss Pembroke, come, sit in chair … this chair. I help with self-pity."

Why not, Ana thought as she moved to the small chair by the cold fire grate. Riya stepped behind her and began to gently knead the kinks from her neck. To Ana's surprise it was warm and relaxing. Riya's fingers were gentle but strong and sure, almost knowing where her shoulders were tight and aching. As she felt the tension easy from Ana's neck, Riya began to speak.

"I too lost my family, in the wars from my country. My brothers and uncles were taken to the armies to fighting the English. My mother was already dead and my aunts took their children and returned to their families. I was left with my Nanni, you say, grandmother. She was very, very old and very wise. She taught me ancient healing."

"Like what you're doing now?" Ana asked her voice regaining calm, her head leaning forward.

"Yes, like this," she continued. "One day there was a very bad battle close to my house. Many soldiers killed and hurt. One English came into my house. He had a big cut in his back from a knife. I was very much afraid. I hid with my Nanni in the closet. It was so hot and she was so very old. I kept praying to Vishnu that he would leave. There was little air. But he did not go. I could see the blood from his back through the cracks in the door. He looked in our cupboards. He tried to mend to his wound but could not. He was there much, very long time. I think it was the heat of the closet that killed my Nanni. I was too much afraid to come out to save her." Her voice was quiet and somber.

"Oh, Riya. No, no it wasn't your fault," Ana cried, hoping the young girl would understand.

"Sit still. Don't move," she directed continuing her work. "I could not stay in the closet. So, I came out. The soldier was not strong from the bleeding. I could see he could not hurt me. I began to use the arts my grandmother taught me. I stopped the bleeding and cleaned his wounds. I made buti, um, herbs for his back to prevent sickness. His will must have been very strong to live. I gave him food and tended to him until he was stronger. Even in his weak feeling, he helped me bury my Nanni."

"Riya, what happened to him?"

"Miss Pembroke, it was Lord Luttrell."

"What?" Ana turned in her chair to look directly into Riya's dark beautiful face.

"Yes, Miss. He was so grateful for … to me that he rescued me to … from India."

"I don't understand?"

"He saved me from a life of shame," Riya stated quietly, her large honey brown eyes downcast.

"But Riya has he not brought you here to a life of shame?" Ana asked, genuinely concerned for the well-being of this young woman whom she began to esteem.

"Oh, no Miss. At home, I have no more family. A man would have made me a slave."

"A slave? Oh no Riya, you must be mistaken. The only place left in the world where there is slavery is in America and they are fighting a great war to stop it. You must be mistaken." Ana could not believe what she had heard.

"I would have been a slave for the pleasure of men." Riya continued to knead Ana's back. Ana became quiet as she thought of this awful prospect.

"That's terrible. But what if you were with child? Surely you would be taken care of,"

"I would have been forced to take herbs to make baby die," Riya answered, voice soft and sad.

"What? I have never heard of such a thing. Oh Riya, that is terrible."

"If I was old or sick, they would throw me out in the street to beg and die, to be Pariah outcast. But most do not get old, just sick."

"But wouldn't you have some say, some choice in what happened to you?"

"No Miss Pembroke, it's not like you teach. I would have no choice in my whole life. That's why I say Luttrell Lord he saved me. He has been very kind to me. He wants me to be ... to learn English ways so I marry someday. He is Luttrell Uncle to me." There was some silence between them as Riya began to rub Ana's temples. "Sometimes the old wounds on his back give him pain. It is what you saw that night. I was putting medicine to help ease the pain."

Suddenly, Ana stood up and gathered Riya into her arms. "Oh, Riya, Riya. I have been such a fool, such a fool. I'm so sorry. Please. Please can you forgive me?" The tears streaming down her face mixed with shame and in some odd sense, joy.

"Miss Pembroke, there is nothing to forgive. You have been good teacher to me." Riya assured her.

"No, Riya I thought ... I misunderstood. He was right. I did not know what I saw. Oh, he must think I'm such a fool." Ana began to pace as her mind raged with humiliation.

"I don't think so Miss Ana. I think he respects you very much. That is why he wanted you to teach me."

"I wish that were so, Riya. I'm resolved to do all I can to teach you. I too want the best for you, just as I want the best for Geoffrey and Hugh. You have helped me with my self-pity. You do have healing arts." She added with determination, "I will gain his respect."

"I am glad you feel better, Miss. I will leave you now." The two young women embraced one final time with the knowledge that a deep friendship had just formed that would hopefully last for many years to come.

Ana was both ashamed and embarrassed by what she had learned from Riya. She realized that Lord Luttrell was the better person for not having the petty prejudices which had prevented her from befriending Riya. She was ashamed by her small-mindedness and was determined to get to know Riya better. Plus, it would be fascinating to learn about the healing arts she had demonstrated earlier. Ana was amazed how Riya's hands had melted away her tensions. If taught, she might even be able to practice on Eliza when it came time for her to give birth.

The great hall clock struck seven telling her it was soon time for supper. Filled with new anxiety, how was she to act in front of Lord Luttrell after what had transpired between them that afternoon? Butterflies filled her stomach in dreaded anticipation of the upcoming meal. And then there was the rest of the family to address. She wanted to disappear.

As Ana prepared for supper, she continued to fabricate possible excuses to evade an evening of embarrassment and ultimate indigestion. However, she could not get around the fact that hiding was the coward's way out. Ana was determined not to be labeled a coward, not by the family and especially not by Lord Luttrell.

Finally, after changing her clothes several times, she settled on her brown taffeta. It was elegant enough for dinner yet plain enough to remain, hopefully, unnoticed, as hiding in the corner or under the table had not yet been ruled out.

However, it was Lord Luttrell who chose to not join the family that evening. As Lady Catherine relayed, he was most likely sulking in the library over his affairs with the lawyers.

To Ana's relief the dance lesson was never mentioned. It was as if the afternoon storm and the humiliating waltz had never happened.

Claiming to have a slight headache from fatigue, Ana retired to her room earlier than usual to be alone with her thoughts. She realized she had terribly misjudged Riya and her relationship with the Duke. He had been right. She did not know what she thought she saw that night in the library all those weeks ago. Her conclusions had been costly. She didn't like what she saw in herself, noting it was an area for growth. However, it left her with many unanswered questions and feelings. She needed to sort out both.

Ana began to slowly walk about her room. As best as she could figure, maybe he was a good man. He obviously did not hold the kind of small-minded beliefs that troubled her. Mrs. C. told her weeks ago that he was kind to his servants and generous with his tenants. He appeared to be well-liked and respected by his household. He served the Queen and country in both war and council. He was even with the Queen when she first came to Dunster Castle. And he was painfully wounded in her service on a battlefield. Even through his pain, he helped Riya and saved Riya from what would certainly have been a life of shame and degradation. What sort of man had such concern for his fellow beings?

Ana shook her head. Miles and Charles went to war for the insignificant glory of battle. Not because of a cause they believed in. But not only did Lord Luttrell rescue Riya, he wanted to educate her so she could better her future. Again, she felt a hot twinge of shame at her own poor behavior towards Riya, all because her skin color and culture were different from hers. Ana opened the window to catch the cool evening breeze that remained after the storm. As she pondered tense thoughts, she changed into her nightclothes, slipping on a soft white cotton shift.

Then there were his sons. She and the Duke would often argue over the direction of their education. He frustrated her at every turn. It was so obvious he didn't trust her with their care and education. He most defiantly did his best to keep her at arm's length. He didn't want to get to know her at all and she felt frustrated by it. Instinctively, Ana stomped her foot feeling annoyed with his hardheadedness. It made it harder for the boys to come to trust her as she had hoped, because they implicitly felt their father's animosity towards her presence in their lives.

Geoffrey so much respected his father. It was obvious in watching the two of them together that Lord Luttrell was his hero. It was Geoffrey's mission to please his father and therefore he often took his side. And Hugh, dear, sweet, Hugh, just craved to be near him and be loved by him. Lord Luttrell so obviously loved his sons he wanted to protect them the best way he knew. She could see it in his expressive steel blue eyes, the way he looked at them with such warmth and kindness. Even when he chastised them, he was loving and gentle. He knew that they had been sorely wounded by their mother's abandonment and Ana could see he didn't want them to hurt again. Ana understood that and agreed with him.

But he too must have been very hurt. He must have loved his wife very much. They had two children together. How devastating to return from serving your Queen, wounded almost to the point of death, only to find your wife had left for another. What type of woman would leave her children and the man who loved her for some other? What could possibly have been better? That woman had everything Ana ever wanted. She couldn't fathom a lower deed. Ana knew that she would do anything to have what that woman threw away; a loving husband, two wonderful children and beautiful home. Instead, here she was looking after three wounded souls the other woman had left in her wake; two boys who feared abandonment and a man who could not trust. Feeling some returning self-pity, Ana sat down and sighed. She took the pins from her hair and began to brush out her long auburn curls.

She had misjudged him more than she realized. Ana stood up and resumed her pacing, absently hitting the brush in the palm of her hand. She moved to the open window, and placing her elbows on the sill, she leaned her head on her hands. The cool night air felt refreshing through her light shift. The smell of the damp clean earth filled her nostrils. Remembering the storm, she couldn't help but recall what had happened that afternoon in the drawing room. The intensity of his expression-filled eyes brought a shiver down her back. She thought of his beautiful blue gray eyes, she thought of how he smelled and the warmth of his breath in her hair as he spoke to her, the melodic tone of his deep voice with the music. Oh, to be in his arms! The closeness of their bodies while they danced had excited and thrilled her.

"And then he ever so gently brushed his lips on my fingers," Ana said wistfully. "Stop! You foolish girl," she told herself trying to shake the fanciful thoughts from her head.

"Oh!" she exclaimed as she watched her silver hairbrush fall from her hands down to the wet lawn below. She sighed in exasperation. It was too late and too wet outside to retrieve it now. Beside she was in her night shift. Ana would ask Mrs. C. to have it brought up in the morning. Anyway, she was exhausted by the day's events. She climbed into bed and blew out her candle hoping to fall asleep.

Though the moon was waning, its brilliant light was enough to see clearly. Ana lifted her hand in front of her face and studied the place where his lips had brushed her fingers. She brought it towards her, placing her lips where his had been only a few hours before. Her heart began to race. She realized she had misjudged him. She felt hopeless. *He is still at war*, she thought. *Protecting his sons and protecting himself from the enemy. And somehow, I'm his enemy.* Her heart skipped a beat. *And I love him.*

CHAPTER 17

It was late and the household had long retired for the night. Following the afternoon's raging storm, the gentle rain finally stopped, leaving the night damp and cool. A soft breeze blew in from the open windows bringing with it the scent of the wet earth, the delicate fragrance of roses and the salt air of the bay. The waning moon had broken through the remaining clouds, spreading its light over the gardens.

Alexander had remained in the library since his confrontation with his mother that afternoon, trying to clear his mind of his troubles and the resentments of his past. He knew he was disappointing his sons by not joining them, and he hated himself for it. But he had to think. He hoped the several large tumblers of whiskey he had consumed would help settle his raging emotions.

Having spent the last several weeks with his solicitor, Jake Sumner, to settle up this year's accounts from the divorce, he returned home to find that other woman still in residence. Feeling used by the women in his life set his blood to boil—first his mother, then Elizabeth, and now this governess. Alexander was at his wits end trying to concoct ways to make her leave. He knew he could just dismiss her; however, his sons were already attached. The idea that he would be the cause of breaking their hearts again was more than he could bear. Plus, his mother was up to her old romantic tricks. He was positive she had formulated a love scheme for his future and it included this governess.

While in London, he was able to discover that Ana had a previous offer of marriage which was still open but she chose not to take it. There was only one reason a woman would decline such an offer and it was to gain something better, something more lucrative. By marrying this other man, a cousin he understood, her income would not meet what he could provide. He paid much more to his former wife alone and was worth five times that himself. He knew his income was no secret around society. And it galled him to think this common knowledge was the brunt of his current troubles.

He never did love Elizabeth. Maybe it was his pride as mother said. He was young and his father thought it a suitable match to a good family with additional income. However, his parents were wrong. Arranged marriages don't always end in love. Some people never find love. He felt cold and cynical as he stared into empty glass.

And now his family was disgraced by a divorce, by a woman who had used him for his money, and by a stigma that would follow his sons into their adult lives. They'd never trust their hearts to a woman. He'd see to that. Alexander knew he never could. He'd be damned if he would. He hurt for his sons because of the frivolous behavior of their worthless whore of a mother, a circumstance that mitigated any chance they might have for happiness. He had to teach them to be wary and not trust women, especially beautiful ones. There were so many reasons not to trust.

He swirled the whiskey around and around watching as the light from the candle reflected sparkling beams in the glass. The money he paid his ex-wife annually tore at him each time he revisited the arrangements. He hated her for using him for his money. He hated that puny excuse of a man she took up with; that sniveling bastard he himself engaged to watch over his family while he was almost killed in battle. Instead, he smashed the family into bits. Alexander felt stabbed in the back. Thank God they did not steal his sons. He remained dumfounded that any woman could leave her children the way she had, to cast her illegitimate daughter Lizbeth into a workhouse and her sons … A cold-hearted bitch was what she was.

And now he had another problem. This Miss Pembroke knew what she was doing. She obviously came with intentions, another one scheming for money and title. "Mother should have asked!" he said aloud, bringing his fist down forcefully against the arm of the chair. He threw back the remnants of whiskey left in his glass and decided it was time for another in hopes of deadening the pain that was both mental and physical.

"They're most likely in cahoots," he snarled. How can people be trusted at all? Even the troops in India betrayed him, leaving him for dead. The sound of battle rang in his ears. He could smell the stench of the battlefield and see the dead strung across the landscape. It felt so real. Again, he felt the blade cut into his flesh. The memories wouldn't stop.

How could he ever trust? He rubbed his temples hoping to refocus.

As he stood up, he could feel the alcohol at work. He poured another and quickly gulped it down. His vision blurred. He rubbed his eyes. The room was closing in as the battle raged on. The searing heat of the blade slicing into his back felt so real. He stumbled outside into the night hoping the air might clear his head. The cool breeze hit his damp skin and felt refreshing. The landscape glistened from the rain as the moonlight sparkled on the droplets left on each blade of grass. He breathed in deeply. The whiskey and evening air were taking effect as he felt his shoulders drop. He was at Dunster. As he turned, he noticed the open window on the floor above. It was Ana's window.

"Why did I have to dance with her?" he questioned silently. He remembered the feel of her in his arms, the blush of her cheek, her firm breasts as they pushed against his chest, the moistness of her lips demanding to be kissed, the smell of lavender in her hair. The memory of kissing her soft fingers burned his lips. Clearly, she was shaken by what he had done. He shook his head. It had to be the whiskey weakening his resolve. She too was his enemy.

As he turned toward the house, his foot hit something hard in the grass. He bent to pick it up. Dizzy now, he staggered forward a bit. It was a silver hair brush with a *P* engraved on the handle. Looking at the brown curls it held in its bristles, he wondered how it got there. He looked up. Ana must have dropped it from her window. *I'll just take it up to her*, he thought, feeling the effects of the drink. Cautiously he made his way up the grand stairs and down the corridor. Swaying, he stopped in front of her door wondering if he should knock or just go in. *This is my house. I can do as I please.* Alexander opened the door and stepped inside.

He closed the door. Her room was dark. It took a few seconds for his eyes to adjust to the light provided by the fading moonlight that came through the crack of the drapes. He stood there, brush in hand, noticing the curve of her hip under her covers. Taking a step forward he stumbled over her chair.

"Damn!" he cursed.

Ana awoke startled and sat up in bed.

"Who's there?" she asked tentatively. She saw the outlined shadow of a man. Her heart raced with fear.

"I have a brass candle stick!" she threatened, hoping to scare the intruder away.

"Oh, a candle stick. Now I'm really scared," he mocked her, his words slurring together.

She recognized his voice instantly. The intrusion of the Duke into her room shocked her. She quickly climbed from her bed, pulling the blanket up with her for protection, and putting the bed between them.

"Sir, what are you doing in my room?" she demanded, her eyes wide. "Is there something wrong? Do the boys need me?"

Alexander stood for a moment. He felt himself wobble a little, and as he studied the situation, the room spun. He noticed her thick auburn tresses tumbling over her shoulders and down her arms. He moved around the bed, closing the distance between them as if being pulled by some unknown force.

"Stay where you are!" Ana warned. But he paid no heed to her command. She stepped back as he approached but soon, he was standing directly in front of her; her back against the wall.

The dim moonlight revealed the sleeve of her shift had fallen aside exposing the creamy white skin of her shoulder. He instinctively moved closer to bring the fallen garment up into place. His hand brushed the warm softness of her naked arm bringing with it a shiver down her sides. His cool fingers lingered on her silky round shoulder. His eyes looked heavy and dark as he gazed down at her, his passion kindling.

"I believe this is yours, madame?" he said as he held up her brush. She could smell the whiskey on his breath. He seemed to be swaying gently.

"I think you've been drinking," she said with concern.

"Oh, one or two," he responded, slurring a bit.

"I think you should leave. Kindly place the brush on the table on your way out," she said with a commanding tone. She swallowed hard as the nearness of him was making her legs weak. But he wasn't listening. Throwing the brush onto her bed, his hand moved towards her hair. Slowly he began to twist his fingers around her silken curls.

"So soft," he whispered, bringing several curls to his nose. "Lavender."

"Lord Luttrell, please. Please leave," she again pleaded in a loud whisper.

He studied her face, searching out her eyes. "Why are you here?" His hand, entangled in her hair, cupped her chin. His voice was deep with emotion, "Why won't you go?" His thumb softly caressed her lips. She caught her breath. His touch brought a blaze of passion to her belly, her own desire catching fire. He dampened his lips with his tongue. She needed to stop him.

"Lord Alexander! Stop this!" Her voice was quiet and controlled. His other hand slipped to the small of her back. Her body ached with his nearness as he drew her close, his steel blue eyes dark with passion. His face was so close, so warm, so hot. He felt the soft mounds of her breasts pushed up against the muscles of his chest. She struggled to keep her head about her—he had, apparently, lost his.

"Ana," he whispered, his mouth so close to hers she could almost feel his lips move against hers as he whispered her name. She could feel his passion throbbing against her belly as he pushed his hips into her. Her heart raced. His hand moved behind her head, guiding her towards him. His lips lightly brushed hers with a tease of a kiss. He searched her face to see her reaction, her own eyes darkened by desire, drawing him in. Again, his lips met hers, but this time with more passion. His mouth began searching, opening, longing. She felt out of control. She responded to him as her arms slowly entwined behind his neck. She felt lost and helpless to surrender. She was melting into the feelings he was stirring up in her. Her mouth opened in eager response to his. His tongue slowly, seductively slid into her mouth, tasting her, mingling with her. He tasted of whiskey. She had never been kissed in such a fashion and it stimulated her beyond her wildest dreams. The musky scent of him filled her nostrils. She ached for him to continue, but somewhere she knew he had to stop. His hand at the small of her back began to slip down from its place. He cupped her firm rounded cheek and pressed her into him. A deep moan intermingled with his kiss at the feeling of her warm body pushed against him, his passion raging to be released. He wanted her. She could feel his hardening manhood through her thin shift. And she was unsure if she wanted him to stop. She ached for him to continue.

Suddenly, Alexander began to slump in her arms.

"My Lord?"

The alcohol had taken its toll as last. The weight too much to bear, she pushed him off of her and he fell gently onto her bed. "My Lord?" she asked again, concerned that he had passed out. He looked up at her in a drunken stupor.

"Why are you in my room?" He was obviously confused, his passion waning quickly from the drink.

Ana gave a sigh of relief and thanked God that the whiskey had intervened when she knew she could not, her own body still quivering from his kiss. She leaned against the wall, gaining hold of her own raging emotions. He could not stay here. That was obvious. She needed to get him to his rooms down the hall.

"Why are you in my room?" his demanding voice getting louder.

"No sir, you are in my room. Keep your voice low. Others are sleeping." Having regained some of her own senses, Ana grabbed her robe from the end of the bed and quickly pulled it on.

"I think you are intoxicated," she added feeling very concerned for the circumstances of this most uncomfortable situation.

"Nah, I never get tight. Hate it. Gives me a headache," his voice was just a little too loud for comfort, his words slurred. "'s room's spinning." He rubbed his eyes with the back of his hand.

"My Lord, let me help you to your rooms." She struggled to get him to sit up.

"Get away from me you she-devil," he said as he pushed her away.

"Come sir, we must get you to your rooms. You can't stay here." Ana was flustered. He was tall and muscular and his heaviness might be more then she could bear, especially if he gave her a struggle.

"Why do you have to get me to my room?" His glazed eyes darted about her chamber.

"Sir, you are in my room," she answered fully exasperated with the situation.

"Well, I sure am. How'd I get here?" he slurred as he realized where he was.

"It's a long story. Here, let me help you up," she said as she stretched out her arm to give him support and balance.

"All right," he said lightly. The weight of him leaning on her made her knees give a little. She took hold of his arm, draping it over her shoulder as they began to move to the door, his frame towering over her.

"Lord Alexander, please open the door."

"Why?"

"Just open the door."

He fumbled with the knob and finally the door opened. Using her foot, she swung the door wide hoping no one heard it bang against the wall as she maneuvered him into the hall. Never before had the corridor appeared so long. They slowly made their way down the hall, stumbling and weaving towards his chambers; he because of his state of inebriation and she because of the sheer weight of him over her shoulders.

"Oops," he said as they bumped against a hall table.

"Keep quiet," she ordered in a whisper.

His finger slowly and lazily came up to his lips, "Shhhhh," he whispered loudly and with a slur of words. "You don't want to waken the household."

"Ahh, I shall not do the awakening, sir," she responded. Finally at his rooms, she pushed open the door, and led him to his bed. He fell back onto the large soft mattress.

"Yes, this is better. My bed's bigger." Again, feeling a bit frisky, he reached for her, grabbing hold of her robe to pull her close.

"Oh, no you don't!" She pulled his hand from the soft fabric. Standing back out of arm's reach, she thought that he looked like a little boy, vulnerable and befuddled. But she knew by what had transpired in her room that he was no little boy and that she needed to keep him at a safe distance.

"Take off my boots," he drawled. Leaning back on his elbows he lifted his left leg so she could remove the boot.

"Maybe we should call for Chesterton," she answered, feeling wary of his command.

"Take off my boots!" he demanded, his voice getting louder.

"Well … behave then!" The first boot came off easily. She threw it into the corner. As much as she tugged, the second would not budge.

"Wait," she said as she struggled to find a different grip. She turned around and hoisted her gown. With her back to him, she straddled his leg.

"I think you should always take my boots off," he chuckled admiring her backside.

"Relax your foot," she commanded, not finding the situation amusing at all. As she straddled his right leg, she felt his warm foot press against her bottom giving her aid as she tugged. She slipped the boot off and threw it into the corner with the other.

"Can't sleep with shirt," he said, raising his arms in the air.

"Put your arms down so I can get the buttons."

"I like this," he drawled, responding to her direction.

"I just hope you don't remember this," Ana added under her breath as she began to undo the many buttons of his white linen shirt and exposing his muscular chest.

"Let me have your hands." She undid the buttons at his wrists and removed his shirt. She couldn't help but admire his strong naked frame and well-shaped muscular arms.

"Now, lie down," she commanded. "Go on, lie down." He followed her direction and rolled onto his stomach, his cheek on the pillow.

"Come to bed," he said, looking at her through hazy eyes.

"No sir. I'm returning to my own bed. Go to sleep." He closed his eyes, but then opened them suddenly. "Ana? 's room keeps spinning."

"Yes, I know, sir. Now go to sleep," again he closed his eyes.

She stayed and waited for his breathing to become heavy as he drifted off into a deep sleep brought on by the whiskey. Ana stood looking down at him, admiring his handsome features. As she pulled the coverlet over his back, she noticed the red jagged scar. She gently traced its path. A shiver ran down her back. It was a miracle he survived. He shifted. Her heart went out to him. He was not going to awaken until morning. She bent down, pushing away some of his dark curls and ever so softly kissed his forehead.

"I am afraid I have fallen in love with you," she whispered in his ear. "And I don't know what to do about it."

Quietly closing his door, she returned to her room and her now cold bed. Her thoughts were in turmoil, the hope of any sleep this night fading into the distance.

Ana knew that she could never return to her home. The idea of marrying Charles was completely out of the question. She could never feel for Charles what she felt for Lord Luttrell. She had never felt such passion for any man as she had felt this night. She realized that she had been willing to give all she had to him. And if he had not stopped, she too would not have stopped. The thought frightened her and excited her. Maybe she did have a future here. Maybe he did have feelings for her or why else would he have kissed her so passionately. Maybe, Lady Catherine was right and her dreams of marriage could be realized. Ana's spirits began to soar. Maybe there was love for her after all. She tasted the whiskey still on her lips as she fell into a deep sleep.

CHAPTER 18

"Oh, God," Alexander awoke, holding his pounding head. "I hate whiskey." His mouth felt stuffed with a bale of cotton. His stomach churned. Rolling on his back he squinted at the sunshine beaming into his room. *Whoever opened those damn drapes will be sacked.* Rubbing his hand across his bleary eyes and face, he felt the stubble of his beard. Breakfast was out of the question. But coffee, a shave, and a bath were most definitely in order. Groaning, he slowly sat up and set his stocking feet onto the floor. *Where's Chesterton?* He groaned once more as he slowly stood and reached for the bell. Seeing himself in the mirror he realized was still in his trousers. He scratched his naked chest as he rang the bell. The light was too much, he continued to squint and sat back on the bed.

"There you are. I need a bath and shave … and coffee, strong coffee. I feel God-awful this morning."

"Yes, sir," Chesterton said.

"And close those damn drapes!" he ordered, his head pounding at the sound of his own voice.

"Shall I bring up some breakfast sir?" Chesterton asked as he closed the drapes.

"No, just coffee … and quietly. My head is exploding."

"Yes sir." Chesterton left to attend to his duties as quietly as he had entered.

Alexander laid back on his bed covering his eyes with his arm. As he lay there waiting for his morning ablutions to be prepared, he began to piece together the events of the previous night. He clearly remembered the storm and the waltz. An impish smile crossed his lips at the thought of how he had intimidated that governess. Her response was exactly what he wanted. However, he also remembered how alluring she felt in his arms and his smile morphed into a frown. He was angry at his own carnal response to her. "Women," he said with disdain.

"Sir?" Chesterton had returned.

"Nothing Chesterton," he responded flatly.

"Your bath is prepared sir, and there is hot coffee next to your tub."

"Chesterton, you know just how to take care of me," he said as he slowly stood up.

"Do you need anything else sir?" Chesterton asked.

"That will be all."

Chesterton left Alexander to himself. He slowly removed the remainder of his clothes and with a groan gently eased himself into the steamy tub. After a sip of black coffee, he closed his eyes and placed a warm wet cloth over his face hoping to ease the throbbing in his temples. He lay there quietly letting the water ease the tension in his body. He took a deep breath, remembering retiring to the library to think and find retreat. "Damn whiskey," he said as he reached for the brush and soap. Looking at the brush in his hand, he sat up abruptly, water spilling onto the floor.

"My God, what have I done?" He scolded himself as memories of his nighttime encounter with Ana flooded back into his consciousness. He remembered finding her silver hair brush on the lawn, taking it to her room, entering unannounced. She was afraid. Yet, he remembered seeing her in her thin night shift, a passionate kiss, the taste of her, the feel of her firm breasts pushing up against his chest, hungry, yearning, eager, he had wanted her ... And she? But he didn't remember anything more. His memory was a blank. How did he return to his room? It concerned him. What had he done? Had he forced himself on her? He shook his head in an effort to sweep out the cobwebs of last night's drink. He felt sick. His memory did not return.

"My God man, this is not what you want ..." He was angry at his own body for such betrayal. He was disgusted with himself. Never had he forced a woman, and he was appalled by any man who did. He took a sip of his coffee, now starting to cool, to settle the bile rising in his mouth. His head throbbed relentlessly. How to handle this was the question. He couldn't dismiss her now. That would risk the prospect that she'd spread tales in polite society. He would be known as a drunken libertine or worse.

"Oh my God," he thought. He slipped back into the water with a groan and stared up at the ceiling. Had he ruined her? Had he ruined his family? He needed another plan. It had become complicated now. How would this be taken at Court? Victoria would be horrified to say the least.

"Reputation be damned," he said through clenched teeth. "I'm the Duke of Exmoor. But … It's not my reputation I'm worried about." He then added solemnly to himself, "It's my sons'." His heart sank with the knowledge that he may have hurt them and hurt them permanently. How could he shield them from the damage this may do to them? They were already so burdened by the actions of their whore of a mother and now they have a libertine as a father. He swallowed hard as the pain for his sons gripped his heart. He was angry with his behavior and lack of willpower. He had taken a personal vow to protect his sons. What kind of knight was he? He felt himself a disgrace. He knew he had to come up with a new tactic.

Maybe nothing happened. Maybe, it was a dream brought on by too many libations. He remembered clearly: dark memories of war had flooded his thoughts. He had taken the whiskey to clear them. Yet, he knew deep in his gut that was only partial truth. He needed to think and he needed a new plan.

In the meantime, he determined to not speak of it. A new plan would come to light. He would observe her for any damages he had done, if any were done. "Damn that whiskey. Damn that woman. Damn all women. Damn. Damn. Damn!" And he braced himself for the day ahead, resolved that he would come up with an answer.

Ana spent the next morning filled with a mixture of joy and trepidation, realizing how she felt toward Lord Luttrell. She had learned so much about him from Riya. She knew she had been mistaken in her opinions of him, though he did little to show that side of himself with her. She wanted to share her love of him with the world yet knew she must hold back. Her feelings most likely would not be reciprocated. He was just toying with her. Lady

Catherine would take Ana's change of heart and run wild with romantic fancies if she knew. She couldn't share it with Riya either. Eliza would be outraged and humiliated! Henry would demand she return home. And Charles? She shuddered at the thought.

She needed to keep all of it in her heart. What if Lord Luttrell didn't remember? She hoped he didn't, for he might think her a loose and wanton woman. That would only reinforce his disgruntled feeling toward her. Last night he had called her a "she-devil." But what if he did remember? How could she face him? She'd have to leave if he didn't return her feelings and was only interested in the physical passion. What would she tell people? Her reputation would be sullied. She would be ruined. Any chances she had of a normal future would be dashed. Even being a governess in another household would not likely happen. Doors would be closed to her. She and her family would be shrouded in shame.

Ana picked up her hair brush to smooth down her unruly curls. "Damn brush," she cursed. "It's all your fault," she told it as if it had a life of its own. She shook her head. The thought of leaving broke her heart now that she recognized her feelings towards the Duke. She couldn't imagine a life without him in it, even if she was only the silent governess loving him from afar. She did not know what the future held. Her only hope was that his inebriated state would prevent him from having any memory at all.

He didn't appear for breakfast. She was grateful for a few more moments without being in his presence, and she barely touched her food for the butterflies in her stomach. However, she was soon summoned to the library for what she hoped to be the usual morning trials on lessons. As she stood at the door, she studied Lord Luttrell as he preoccupied himself with papers on his desk. He was well dressed, freshly shaven, and appeared cool, rested and nonplussed by the past evening's goings on. Realizing her palms were damp from nerves she smoothed out her the skirts of her gray frock.

"Come in." His voice was strong and clear. She walked towards the desk, her heart beating rapidly. Finally, he looked up from his work. His jaw looked set for battle. Ana's heart skipped a beat as their eyes met. Maybe he didn't remember. He motioned for her to sit. She obeyed quietly. He seemed to study her for a moment as if deciding as to whether to ruin her by dismissal or not.

He noted that she was not hysterical, accusatory, or fainting away as women so often do. For that he was grateful. As a matter of fact, she appeared subdued, a change from the usual firebrand that would confront him every morning.

"You're exceptionally demure today," he said sardonically.

"Sir?" Ana responded with a sense of panic. *Oh God, he remembers!*

"You are generally ready for bear. Never mind. My head is pounding and I don't have patience for you this morning. Remember I hold your employ and I can end it at any moment. So, don't argue with me today," he said, knowing fully well that sacking her would only lead to painful consequences for his family.

He doesn't remember! She thought, feeling relieved.

Still, Ana was uncertain. The pounding head was an indication of the drink from the previous night. But did he remember? She unconsciously bit her bottom lip. She didn't think so. She knew him well enough that he would have said something, done something. He would have either taken her into his arms or dismissed her to a life of humiliation. And so far, he did neither. Ana felt her shoulders drop with both relief and disappointment. She sat quietly listening to his directions, she didn't argue with him at his suggestions, and said "Yes sir" at the appropriate times and "Thank you" when dismissed.

"Ana," he said as she got to the door. *Oh, here it comes just like my stocking, at the last moment*, she thought as she turned towards him, bracing for the worst.

"Thank you for not arguing," he said quietly then returned to his papers.

"You're welcome, sir," Ana replied softly and with a quick curtsey left the room. She stopped halfway up the grand stair confused at what had transpired between them, her hand on her beating heart. He called her Ana. He had never been that familiar with her. It was the first civilized conversation they had had since they began morning meetings or at any interaction for that matter. Maybe he remembers. But he would have said something. Something. He did say his head was pounding, undoubtedly from the residual effects of inebriation.

Unless he says something or does something differently, Ana decided she would act as if nothing had happened between the two of them.

"Act as if nothing happened," she repeated softly. "Take you heart and tuck it away. Nothing happened." *I'll follow his lead. And until then what happened between us last night will remain my secret.* Gathering her skirts, she slowly climbed the stairs to teach her charges.

CHAPTER 19

*A*s if nothing happened, they both returned to their familiar morning pattern. Lord Luttrell remained inflexible and distant while Ana continued to argue for what she believed to be the right education for the boys, often being reminded that as a servant under his employ he held her future in his hands.

Oddly, however, he continued to call her Ana. Not out of familiarity, Ana decided, but from lack of respect. Since neither had mentioned the dance lesson nor the tremendous "headache" Lord Luttrell possessed the following day, Ana concluded he had no recollection of the kiss that had transpired between them.

Riya and Ana were becoming fast friends. Teaching her about being an English lady turned out to be a great deal of fun. In return, Ana was being taught the ancient Indian arts of healing by her student. She was fascinated by herbs and poultices and was intrigued by breathing exercises and massage and found that some of the things she was learning was helping her manage her stress.

Learning what she had about Lord Luttrell from Riya, Ana continued to realize how quickly she misjudged others. Maybe Mrs. C. had been correct about his character with the others of his employ. And though he remained dismissive of her, she couldn't forget being in his arms as they danced or the passion of his kiss. She looked for times to be alone to think about his smoldering eyes or the way his hair curled at the base of his neck and around his ears. Her love for him was a bittersweet realization which she couldn't share with Eliza, who always reminded her she could return home to those who truly loved her.

"Miss Pembroke?"

Geoffrey's inquiry immediately brought Ana back to task.

"As today is my birthday, I asked Father if we could target practice with my new bow. Would it be alright if we stopped early?" Even Geoffrey's attitude towards Ana was changing and he was showing her greater regard.

"Yes, Geoffrey. Let's first finish our lessons. You help Riya with her sums. I'll help Hugh." Ana had also noticed that Geoffrey was developing a greater adolescent infatuation towards Riya. Though she believed nothing would come of it, she thought it sweet watching his boyhood fascination with the fairer sex.

Shortly, there was a knock at the door.

"It's Father! Miss Pembroke, may I let him in?" Hugh immediately became giddy with expectation of bow practice.

"Yes, Hugh. Remember, walk," Ana admonished gently.

Lord Luttrell entered, smiling at his sons and placing his arm around Hugh's shoulder. Ana was taken with the softness of his face, his bright smile and gleaming gentle eyes as he looked at Hugh, an expression she loved but rarely saw and never towards her.

"Well, has your governess given you leave of your studies for the afternoon?" he said, noting Geoffrey and Riya in close study of their books.

"Oh, yes, Father," Hugh beamed at the thought of spending the afternoon with his father.

"May Riya and Miss Pembroke join us?"

"Yes, of course. Riya and Miss Pembroke may join us. We'll be in the front garden." he added flashing a dazzling smile towards Riya. Ana was again taken with his boyish good looks.

"Well, Riya," as Ana collected herself, "let's get our bonnets and gloves, shall we? A little target practice should be a good diversion."

Ana relished the prospect of spending time with the Duke. Walking towards the front garden, they could see Lady Catherine, beautifully dressed in pink, seated at a well-appointed table with sandwiches, cakes, punch and beautiful flowers.

"Riya, I thought this was to be the birthday celebration for Geoffrey. I'm glad I brought his gift," Ana whispered.

"I have a gift too," Riya smiled back at Ana, their growing friendship apparent.

As Hugh spotted the two young women walking towards them, he broke away from the group and ran to greet them. "Miss Pembroke, Miss Pembroke! We are to have a party here on the lawn, a birthday party for Geoffrey." His excitement was contagious.

"Yes, Hugh, I see!" Ana took Hugh's offered hand as they walked.

"Miss Pembroke, what a splendid surprise. Don't you think?" Geoffrey asked her. "Wasn't it grand of Father to plan this?"

"Yes Geoffrey, it was," she answered feeling Lord Luttrell's cool eyes upon her at their interchange.

"Look at these lovely cakes, Miss Pembroke," Hugh said as he dragging her to the table.

"They are lovely. Do you know which one you'll eat?" she asked smiling down at him with interest.

"Yes, the one with the blue rose, mmmm." he licked his lips and rubbed his tummy in anticipation of the treat.

"I think that would've been the very one I'd pick for you too," she added rumpling his hair and smiling down at her young charge.

Taking hold of her hand again, he pulled her around the table. "And look at this bowl of punch. I love punch. Do you like punch?"

Ana chuckled at Hugh's boyish enthusiasm, "Oh Hugh, you're very excited, aren't you?"

"Oh, yes. I just love birthdays. Mine is in January. I can't wait. But we never have a picnic for mine because it's in the winter," he prattled on.

"Hugh," Lord Luttrell broke in. "Let Miss Pembroke be. You're making us deaf with your chatter."

Severely disappointed, he looked down at his shoes, "Yes, Father." Then perking up, and with hope filling his eyes he said, "Miss Pembroke sit over here next to me."

"Hugh, did you hear Father?" Geoffrey chimed in. "Besides that's where I'm sitting. I've asked Riya to sit beside me," glancing back in her direction. "Is that OK Miss Pembroke?"

"All right, enough!" Lady Catherine raised her hands in feigned exasperation. "Hugh, sit here next to me. Ana, dear, you can then sit next to Hugh. Riya you can sit in front of me. Then Geoffrey and Alexander you sit across from Ana. There, it's all settled. Now sit down. Let's enjoy Geoffrey's birthday picnic."

Quickly all took their seats as commanded. But today, Lord Luttrell walked around the table and pulled the chair out for Ana, not one of the footmen in attendance.

With a look of surprise, Ana said, "Thank you, sir." Their eyes met briefly.

"You're welcome, Ana." There was something different in his eyes she thought. They were a warmer blue. Even his voice seemed softer. Maybe it was Geoffrey's birthday and he was on his best behavior for Geoffrey's sake.

"Father," Geoffrey began, "Miss Pembroke has been teaching me about Henry VIII. He was a most interesting King. Don't you think? He had six wives you know? And he ruined so many monasteries too."

"And Miss Pembroke has been teaching me about King Arthur and Lancelot," Hugh piped in. "Geoffrey, maybe we can play at knights after we eat?"

"Hugh, we are getting too old to play such silly games." Geoffrey glanced at Riya. It was obvious he was trying to appear mature for her sake.

Not to be left out Riya added, "Miss Ana and I have been studying Byron and English."

"It sounds like you are all enjoying your studies with Miss Pembroke," Alexander said, looking coolly at Ana as he passed her a plate of small sandwiches. Ana felt self-conscious from all the attention and realized it had not gone unnoticed by the Duke.

"Oh, yes Father," Hugh added, his mouth full of food. "I love Miss Pembroke."

Looking down at her plate, Ana could feel her face beginning to turn hot with embarrassment. Alexander's eyes winced at Hugh's statement. She could sense Lord Luttrell's jaw clench as she removed a sandwich from the platter.

Not one to miss an opportunity to further her cause, Lady Catherine added, "Alexander isn't it grand the way your sons have taken to Ana? I knew she would do them good. I can't remember when I've seen them happier," she said, smiling at both her grandsons.

Glancing at his mother, Alexander conceded, "Yes, Mother. Thank you for pointing that out," before continuing with a slight cock of his head and a raised left brow to clarify that she should not interfere. But he had heard too many mentions of "Miss Pembroke this" and "Miss Pembroke that" that he had to admit that his sons were flourishing under her tutelage.

Embarrassed at being cast into the spotlight, Ana moved to change the subject. The attention from Lord Luttrell was making her unsteady. Turning towards Lady Catherine she said, "Lady Catherine, this is such a wonderful treat. What a beautiful place for a picnic."

"Yes, my dear. We have such lovely gardens. We used to picnic here quite often, didn't we, Alexander? However, since my Alfred passed, I've found it hard to enjoy the roses quite as much. You see them over there? Alfred planted them just for me."

"Oh, how lovely," Ana said, relieved now that attention was finally shifting from her and onto one of Lady Catherine's love stories.

"My Alfred knew I loved pink roses. So, he had all the red roses removed. We were Lancastrians you know. Then, he planted these wonderful gardens filled with pink roses. You're such a dear to remind me."

She couldn't help glance at her son, who had crossed his arms and closed his eyes feigning sleep and feeling completely defeated by his family's embrace of this "Miss Pembroke." He well realized he needed some other tactic to get her to leave, or failing that, stay permanently. He knew he could not destroy his sons' hearts again. Though the strategic challenges piqued his military prowess, this type of warfare was far beyond his ken and wearing on his soul. He needed to make a tactical decision and soon.

"Alexander don't you go to sleep," his mother chided. "You're being a boor and on Geoffrey's birthday too."

Keeping his eyes closed, Alexander dutifully answered, "Yes Mum," her admonishments bringing him back to the present.

"Really Alexander, you can be such a rake and in front of your sons too," she added shaking her head.

"Father, may I open my gifts?" Geoffrey asked hoping to lighten the conversation.

Alexander opened one eye in his son's direction. "Yes, yes open them." He opened the other eye and stretched. He sat forward with his elbows on his knees and focused on his son.

Geoffrey received a beautiful pocket watch from Lady Catherine, who told him it was one of his grandfather's favorites. Blushing he opened a lovely pencil box from Riya. He was very pleased with Shakespeare's Complete Works from Ana. But the gift that thrilled him the most was the Enfield rifle from his father.

"Well, Geoffrey you wanted to target practice today. It's time you learn how to shoot firearms. Put those bows away for today."

As father and sons spent time reviewing the firing mechanisms on the stock of Geoffrey's gift, the servants cleared the tables and set up several targets in the distance. Chesterton brought out several of Lord Luttrell's pistols and revolvers and gently laid them out on the white cloth as he had been directed.

"Alexander, do be careful." Lady Catherine chided, turning to Ana she added, "I do hate it when men play with those awful things. Come dear let's take a stroll amongst my roses."

Arm-in-arm they quietly began to meander through the garden paths. The swan fountain bubbled merrily as the water glistened in the afternoon sunlight. They wound their way down the side of the motte and far above the distant green deer park below. The palms swayed in the gentle breeze as it came off the bay.

"I think things are going well. Don't you?" Lady Catherine asked, breaking the long silence.

"Oh, yes, the boys have come around at last. They're doing so well. And it's been grand teaching Riya; we're becoming fast friends," Ana shared smiling over at the group around the table as they came back into view.

"No, no dear. What you say is true, but I mean Alexander. I think he's finally getting used to the idea of you. He can't deny the rest of us love you. He has to yield. He has no other recourse. I'm so pleased. You know I'm holding onto my wish of happiness for you both."

"Ahh, Lady Catherine, I don't know what to say," Ana answered as she glanced in Lord Luttrell's direction from under her bonnet.

"Nonsense, I see the way you look at my son. I know how you feel. I believe you've fallen in love." She patted Ana's hand, "Remember, I too have been in love, I know."

"Lady Catherine, even if it were true, and I'm not saying it is, he still sees me as some type of enemy." She glanced in his direction and caught him watching the two of them.

"Listen to you—even if it were true! I say it *is* true. He's coming around. He finds you intellectually challenging which I will say is attractive to him. I catch him watching you with an admiring glint in his eyes. He can't deny the boys love you. As a matter of fact, he is watching us now is he not? Don't look. Oh, I know he doesn't trust me. But I have his best interest at heart. You'll win him over. You already have won the rest of us, my dear."

"Lady Catherine, I don't want to marry someone who wants me because I won over his family and he finds me 'challenging.' Besides, I would've married my cousin if all I wanted was security. I just …"

"Never you mind, I know what I'm doing. Let's take another go around. It'll show off your figure to its best advantage. Shall we?" Picking a pink rose, she placed it in the belt of her dress and began to walk once more through the garden, leaving Ana disturbed as she walked quietly by her side.

Ana was troubled that her feelings for Lord Luttrell had become obvious to Lady Catherine. Who else knew? Wide-eyed, she glanced across the lawn at the Duke as they walked.

Finally, they sat to watch as Geoffrey and Lord Alexander took aim at the distant targets. Hugh was anxious to participate, but was being strongly admonished to stay back with Ana for safety.

"Father, may I please have a chance?" he would break in.

Finally, Lord Alexander called Hugh over. He carefully explained the dangers of firearms and gently walked him through his first firing. To everyone's surprise, Hugh hit the target on his first attempt, perturbing Geoffrey to no end. To distract himself he decided to give Riya a more detailed look at his Enfield.

"Hugh, rejoin your grandmother. Ana," Lord Luttrell called to her. "Have you ever fired?"

"No sir," she answered, surprised by his query.

"Come over, I'll teach you. You should learn." Feeling a bit nervous, Ana looked over at Lady Catherine.

"Go on dear, he is calling to you," she whispered in her ear.

Ana gave Lady Catherine an uneasy glance as she walked to where Lord Luttrell was standing. He picked up a small ivory-handled revolver from the table. "This should fit your hand nicely."

"Let's move over here." He took her elbow to lead her to face the target, he handed her the gun, and moved to stand behind her. His physical closeness made her heady.

"Here. Place the gun in your hands like this." His arms encircled her as he took hold of her hands. "Point it towards the target. Now look at the sights."

She looked at him in confusion, not knowing what he meant.

"See that small knob on the end?"

She nodded.

"That's the sight. It gives you your target." As he moved in closer, she could feel herself leaning into him. His head was almost resting on her shoulder as he leaned down so close to hers. "No, put your finger here on the trigger. Like this. That's right." His voice was calm and gentle in her ear making it difficult to concentrate.

"It seems my sons have taken to you."

Shocked, Ana looked at him directly. "Sir?"

"Keep your eyes on the target and hold steady," he commanded. She returned her gaze to the target.

"You're doing a fine job with them." Ana did not notice his frown.

"Thank you, sir." Ana swallowed hard forcing herself to frown at the distant target.

"Take aim," Ana closed one eye and looked at the target using the small knob at the end of the pistol as he had directed.

"With your thumb, slowly pull back on the hammer. Good. Now slowly pull the trigger."

Though her hands were shaking, Alexander held them steady in his. She held her breath, closed her eyes and let off a shot. The power of the shot pushed her further back into his arms. The target was hit but on the far side of the bullseye.

"Oh! I hit it," she couldn't help but jump a little with excitement.

"Whoa. Be careful, there's still a charge in that." Alexander stepped back, smiling at her success. He looked so much like Geoffrey in that moment, young and fresh.

"Oh, I'm sorry. Can we do that again?" The flush of excitement was over her face, her emerald eyes sparkling with delight.

"Take aim," he said placing his arms around her to steady her aim. She stretched out her arms.

"No, wait," he commanded again, stepping back.

"Am I doing something wrong?"

"No, it's your bonnet. It's in my way."

Not accepting the pistol she tried to hand him, he began to undo the bow around her chin, his fingers lightly brushing her cheek and neck. While he was intent on the knot she had created, she studied his face. He noticed her full crimson lips as they opened slightly in surprise at his touch. Finally, he tossed her hat on the lawn and returned her to her task. He leaned in closely catching the scent of lavender from her uncovered hair. He encircled her in his arms and took her hands into his. The pistol was hot to the touch from the previous fire. He was acutely aware of her leaning into him for balance. Its effect was tantalizing, making him think that conceding to his desires would not be so bad.

"Stop shaking, you'll miss the target," he whispered softly into her ear. Ana's heart skipped. "And this time, keep both eyes open."

This afternoon's events were turning out to be much more than a birthday party, Ana thought as she took aim. She was keenly aware of his arms around her and his chest up against her back. She felt warm, safe and steadied by his strength. Taking a deep breath, she took aim and pulled the trigger. Bull's eye!

The sheer excitement of the hit took Ana by surprise and she quickly turned in his arms. Just as quickly, she was flooded with embarrassment for her exuberance and pushed away from his chest. Alexander, equally surprised by her response, took a step back and dropped his hands by his sides. His mouth went wide before quickly turning up a knowing smile at Ana's unsettled demeanor.

Placing the gun on the table and feeling the fool, Ana gathered up her skirts in one hand and swiftly scooped up her bonnet from the lawn. As she walked back to the castle, Ana looked over her shoulder only once at the man who stood watching her depart—the man who had captured her heart.

Lady Catherine sat with Hugh by her side watching the events unfold in front of them.

"Grandmother, did Father just hug Miss Pembroke?" Hugh asked.

"She hit the bullseye Hugh," she answered, smiling quietly to herself.

"Oh," he responded quietly, a frown crossed his young brow.

"Chesterton?" He was standing beside her chair looking on.

"Yes' mum?"

"They make a lovely couple don't you think?"

"Yes' mum, that they do," and glancing at Riya and Geoffrey sitting closely together at the table added "Young Geoffrey also appears to be thusly engaged, Mum."

"Isn't love grand Chesterton?"

"Yes' mum."

"Come Hugh, let's go back to the house," Lady Catherine said as she took the hand of her youngest grandson. She gave her son a sweet knowing smile as she passed him by. It was unspoken, but she knew her scheme was working.

CHAPTER 20

"Mrs. C., I have letters to mail. Do you need anything from town?" Ana asked tying on her infamous bonnet from the day before, and looking forward to an afternoon of quiet and exploration.

"No Ana, thank you." Looking up from her work she added, "By the way, how's your sister? Her time should be close."

"Yes, a few more weeks I would guess. Our family's been through so much. We need a new baby."

"You know I never asked, did you ever tell Lord Luttrell about that man spying on you a while back?

"Mrs. C., I completely forgot. It must've been nothing as nothing has come of it," she answered. Surely it was just a mistake.

"Mr. Goodall hasn't reported anything since?"

"Not a word. I'm sure if someone had continued to inquire after me, he would've most definitely told me."

"'Tis true, be careful just the same," Mrs. C. chided. "I still think you should've said something to His Lordship."

"Oh, Mrs. C.," Ana laughed. "I'll be fine," she assured the anxious woman.

"Well, at the least I'm going to inform Lord Luttrell you went to town. He needs to know." *Even if I'm being overprotective*, she added to herself.

"Very well, but I assure you I'll be home before tea," Ana said, hugging her before leaving.

Mrs. C. shook her head as she watched from the window as Ana walked briskly down the stone drive, admiring her for her self-sufficiency. She had become such a part of the household.

Ana decided today she would visit Conygar Tower once she completed her errands in town. With so much on her mind, she thought it might be a good distraction. It was a warm summer's day with clouds and humidity that suggested a threat of an afternoon squall. Her thoughts returned to Lord Luttrell as she walked along the road hardly noticing the dark clouds on the horizon.

The Duke hadn't called her into the library for their usual morning discussion. His behavior was decidedly odd and unusual during Geoffrey's birthday party. Showing her how to shoot a pistol and being so close with his arms about her had left Ana unsettled and stimulated at the same time. She couldn't decide if he was being genuinely kind or again toying with her. He had even complimented her work with his sons. The idea that he had finally settled on asking her to leave filled Ana with unknown anxieties.

The smell of fresh bread from the bakery made Ana realize how hungry she was following her walk into town. Sitting by the window, Ana enjoyed a cup of tea and a fresh scone smothered in strawberry jam, though it way before teatime. She enjoyed watching the pedestrian housewives doing their shopping, the children playing street games, and vendors selling their wares. Ana smiled seeing the everyday lives of her fellow Englishmen.

Suddenly, the image of a man peeking from behind a curtain in the shop window on the other side of the street caught her attention. Startled, she choked on a sip of tea. But in a flash, he disappeared. His hat had covered his face, but she knew he was looking directly at her. She felt incredibly uncomfortable. Yet, coughing, she shook her head and decided Mrs. C.'s anxieties were playing tricks on her imagination. All the same, to be safe she would ask Mr. Goodall if there had been any other inquires.

"No Miss. I 'aven't 'ad any inquiries since that first daiy," Mr. Goodall informed her as she posted her letters. "But I think you're wise t' be cautious. If

I remember, that bloke didn't sit too comfortable wif me, askin' after a fine young lady as yerself."

"Thank you, Mr. Goodall. It was very good to see you today. And please give my wishes to Missus Goodall and the children."

"That I will, Miss, that I will. And 'ave a good daiy to ye," giving a tip of his head.

Feeling relieved of her foolishness, Ana set off to explore the countryside. She had some time before tea and would be sure to keep her promise to Mrs. C.

"Good afternoon, Ana," a familiar deep voice behind caught her unawares and she flinched. She felt silly at her unwarranted jitters.

"Oh, sir, you startled me!" Lord Luttrell was standing behind her. "What brings you to town?" she inquired, quickly gaining back some of her composure.

"Business. It was not my intention to startle you." There was an uncomfortable silence between them. He cleared his throat. "May I walk with you?" he said uneasily.

"Why yes," she said, giving a small curtsey which he returned with a stiff nod. Her face flushed a slight pink.

They began to stroll down the streets of Dunster. The lack of conversation was awkward for them both as they ambled towards the outskirts of town watching the cobblestones disappear from under their feet.

"Mrs. C. told you I would be in town?" Ana finally broke the silence.

"No," was his short uncommunicative answer.

Uneasy with the return of silence and also a bit inquisitive, she prodded "You weren't in the shop across the way from the bakery per chance, were you, sir?"

"No. Why do you ask?" Alexander answered, thinking it an odd question.

"I thought I saw someone I might've recognized. I guess I have a good imagination," Ana again shrugged off the curiously uncomfortable feeling.

"Perhaps." He added, "You are taking the long way back to the castle?"

"Actually sir, I plan on doing some exploring today."

"Exploring?" he glanced sideways in her direction from under the brim of his hat which sat slightly askance on his head. His eyes studied the profile of her face.

"Yes, I'm eager to see Conygar Tower. I haven't yet had the opportunity. I understand from Mrs. C. that it gives an excellent perspective of Bristol Bay," she said glancing at him, and seeing that she piqued his interest.

"There are none better in these parts, I must agree, especially if you have a liking for that type of architecture and landscape. You can climb up into the tower ramparts and look out over the bay."

"I love the history of this place. Dunster and Dunster Castle and the romance of history!"

"The romance of history?" He looked over at her quizzically as he walked, his hands comfortably folded behind his back.

"Yes, wondering whose hand touched all those walls and what their lives were like; their joys and pains. It's so intriguing. Each person and place, it's made us who we are."

"It's an interesting philosophy. Where did you learn that?"

"I don't think I learned it anywhere. It's the way I feel about these ancient places. Don't you find ancient places stirring?" She was amazed that they were having such a pleasant conversation and glanced again in his direction.

They came to a stop at the turn in the road, one fork leading to Dunster Castle, the other to a grassy path to the tower. The silence between them returned but was no longer strained.

"Ana, may I be your guide this afternoon?" Alexander offered. He looked down the lane as if he wished to return to Dunster Castle.

"That would be kind of you, sir. Only I don't wish to be a bother. I'm sure you are very busy," Ana answered, thoroughly surprised by his offer. Though she admitted to herself that she was enjoying their pleasant conversation.

"No bother. I have nothing waiting for me at home and it is a pleasant day." He glanced down at her as he motioned for her to pass. "Besides I haven't been to the tower in ages." He too had been thinking that the discussion with her was amiable and found he wanted to continue their discourse.

"This's very generous of you, sir," she said with a small curtsey.

They began to walk down the winding path. The first tensions eased to a congenial stroll. The scent of wildflowers mingled with that of sea air. Meadow birds were singing happily as they searched for seeds and bugs in the fields. As the trail became steep and rocky, Lord Luttrell offered a strong arm for assistance. The field gave way to wooded incline and forest.

"Thank you. This is such a lovely area of England." Ana said to break the silence. She was enjoying the terrain and didn't know quite what to say.

"Yes, it is. Watch your step through the gate." Alexander too was feeling less self-conscious as he guided her through the ancient stone archway.

"Gate?" she said as they walked under the crumbling stonework covered in wild vine.

"Yes, this is all that's left of the gatehouse. This leads us up to the tower." He said as he pointed further up the forest path.

"The history of Dunster Castle and your family is so fascinating to me," she said, as they wound their way through the lush trees and brush. Ana was glad of his company as the climb was more strenuous then she had realized.

"It is," he said, adding, "Dunster Castle was built during the Saxon times, on an old motte and bailey in the eleventh century, the time of William the Conqueror. The Luttrells originated in France, you know. We played a part of the Battle of Hastings. Then in 1403 John Luttrell took up arms on Henry IV's behalf and was knighted into the Order of Bath. My family have been here at Dunster for almost five centuries." He was clearly proud of his illustrious heritage.

As they rounded the top of the hill, Ana thought back to her father and his proclamation that "only the best and bravest knight will be worthy of your hand."

"So, are you a Knight of Bath?" she said, her heart fluttering at the memory of her father's words.

"Why, of course," he chuckled.

The view of the tower rose up in a clearing from the crest. Blue streaks of sky broke through the gathering thick gray clouds. Shafts of golden light reflected in the aqua swells of the water on the distant bay. The stone structure stood in front of them in all its majesty, its brown and mauve stone walls outlined against its magnificent backdrop. The steady bay breeze blew softly into their faces.

"Oh my, what a beautiful spot!" Ana said as she stopped to catch her breath from the climb. She looked over the towards the bay and up at the peak of the tower they were yet to climb.

Seeing the vista through her eyes, Alexander answered "Yes, it is beautiful. Here," he said as he offered his hand. "I don't want you to fall."

Her heart began to ache just a little as their hands touched. But she was too apprehensive to hope for anything more.

"Watch your step," he said as he pointed to several loose stones and reached out again to steady her as they reached the entrance.

"What else do you know of this place?" Ana inquired, longing to hear more.

"My great, great, grandfather built this tower, just for the view I understand. I like it. It adds to the landscape. I remember coming here to play as a boy. I haven't been here for years though." He sounded pensive.

"Five hundred years for your family to live here. What must their lives have been like?" Ana wondered. "To think they lived and died here, loved and probably hated too."

"I'm sure. As a matter of fact, King Stephen laid siege to Empress Matilda right here." He smiled down at her curiosity, intrigued by it. "I believe during our Civil War, Dunster Castle became a Royalist stronghold under a Colonel Wyndham. In 1646 the castle surrendered to Parliamentary forces and almost all of its defenses were destroyed. Actually, most of the original castle where Matilda lived was destroyed."

"Really, how sad … I would never have known and would've loved to have seen the ancient structure." Ana stood and looked back at Dunster Castle's outline against the graying sky as it sat atop the distant hill with the town nestled at its base. "You see? If it were not for this place, you wouldn't be here."

He stood silently looking out to the bay. Ana stood by his side keenly aware of his presence. Except for elements of the breeze, the dark threatening clouds, and the cry of circling gulls, Ana felt as if they were the only two people on earth.

"Ana," he said, his voice a bit pensive.

"Sir?" she turned towards him. Seeing his brow heavy with emotion as he stared out over the darkening bay, Ana felt a slight shiver run down the length of her back. She was sure he was going to ask her to leave Dunster Castle.

"I have a request to make of you," his voice suddenly was business-like, devoid of all emotion.

"Yes, sir?" Ana held her breath.

"Having been married before and having it end in such disgrace … I've been against the idea of recommitting to such a union," he said as he continued to stare out over the water.

"Sir, I…"

"No let me speak. I've never believed in the foolhardy notion of fanciful love that my mother so loves to prattle about. I don't expect I ever will believe in it.

It's just not in me. However, I have come to the realization that my sons love you. My mother, the great manipulator, loves you." He continued to stare out over the bay, the tone of his voice distant, "I determined long ago that my sons shall never re-experience the pain and shame of being abandoned by a woman."

"I wouldn't wish that on them either, sir," she agreed, though she was completely confused by the direction of the conversation.

"I don't deny that I find you ... shall I say, alluring, if you don't mind the use of word. So that should make this easier."

"Easier? I don't understand." Ana was surprised and bewildered by his words.

He continued as if she had said nothing. "Therefore, after long consideration, I offer my hand in marriage. You will gain a fine income ... the financial security I know you're looking for, title of course above a baroness. Consequently, I feel assured by accepting this offer you would not leave my sons for another, for I also don't believe you to be wanton as Elizabeth. You'll be bound to them through me. If you need a few days to consider, I will understand." He turned to study her face. His own was completely cold and emotionless.

Ana stood motionless for a few moments, shocked by what she heard. Her face paled and her mouth opened in shock. A sudden gust of wind blew her bonnet from her head, loosening several curls and bringing her back to her senses. Her head began to swim with anger at his cruel insult. She felt as dark as the looming clouds above them.

"Sir, a few days to consider!?" Green daggers of rage and hurt sprang into her turquoise eyes. "I have no need to consider such a farce of a request. I do believe in the foolish notion of love. And I abhor the very idea of marriage for money, or title for that matter, as I would be no more than a common ..."

Stunned by her anger he took a step back, his eyes wide with surprise.

"A loveless marriage has been offered to me before, sir, and as a result I chose to be self-sustaining and independent. You have no need to fear my leaving your sons for any other match as there is no love in my life. It has become apparent to me that love is not my destiny. So, spinster governess is my lot. Oh, how you insult me." Ana stomped her foot as rage and anger took hold.

"Ana, this was not meant as an insult. I am offering you a comfortable life," He was visibly confused and agitated by her response. Wasn't marriage what all women wanted? Alexander had struggled for days to make this decision, but after yesterday's display of "Miss Pembrokes" by his family he was certain this was the best recourse for his son's safety.

"And after your sons have grown and found families of their own," she continued, her voice rising, "What then, sir? Shall I be chained to a cold love-less marriage? Chained like the swans on your crest? Is that what Lutrells do? Will you find solace in the arms of other women? Shall I find my life with the disgrace of a divorce of my own? Is that why Elizabeth left you, for warmth and love of another because you are cold, heartless, and hateful, and could not give her love?" Ana knew her words were cutting yet couldn't stop herself.

"Ana, you go too far!" he warned, his eyes turning a steely dark gray with his own growing rage. His heart was racing with unspoken pain. His military instincts told him to counterattack and he stepped closer.

"What you say is true. It is your lot in life to be an unloved spinster! Who would want such a … shrew?" he hissed. Suddenly, her hand flew out towards him taking aim at his cheek, for he had hit his target full on. But he caught her by the wrist.

"Don't you strike at me, you witch!" he sneered. But instead of pushing her away, he pulled her to him, his other hand wrapping around her back, bringing her closer, pulling her against his body. His icy gray eyes searched out her cold turquoise ones. He bent his head down and found her mouth, kissing her hard, parting her lips, tasting the sweetness of her with his tongue. His mouth moved with fierce hunger over hers, drinking her in, feeling the heat of her body against his, hot passion igniting both their senses. Ana was ashamed by her immediate response to his touch. Yet she met his passion with her own.

Suddenly he thrust her away. He glared at her as he wiped his mouth with the back of his hand as if she were some foul-tasting thing. Ana stood back stunned by his look of disgust.

"That is what you'll be missing," he jeered tauntingly before he turned on his heels and left her standing alone in the darkening wind at the base of the tower.

Ana watched him depart, struggling to catch her breath, angry, hurt, and confused by their exchange, appalled at her body's reaction to his kiss, and shaken by his violence and revulsion of her.

Hot tears of shame and pain began to cascade down her crimson cheeks, her heart throbbing. She ran into the tower. Her vision blurred as she began to ascend the darkening stair to gain as much distance from him as possible. His cruel mocking words ripped into her very soul. *Unloved, spinster, shrew.* Grief tightened her chest. It was hard to breathe. She grasped at the damp and clammy walls for emotional support, finding it hard to climb as sobs wracked her body. Her world was imploding. Reaching an open window, she wanted to scream but instead, she could only wail as she struggled to catch her breath.

Suddenly, something thrust against her back, shoving her forward. The stones of the tower widow began to give way. She was being pushed. Ana grabbed for the threatening dark figure to no avail. She couldn't stop herself from the treacherous fall from the crumbling window. She screamed as she hit the ground, tumbling downward towards the ravine below, fear gripping at her. Branches grabbed at her skirts as she fell forward, pulling and ripping, slowing the plunge. She grasped at brush and roots to stop her descent as she rolled down the steep incline, but could not stop. The impact on the wet, cold ground was quick and hard. Her world went dark.

CHAPTER 21

*A*lexander returned to Dunster Castle, dark and brooding as the skies. He immediately stormed into his library and poured a large whiskey. He hated whiskey and hated that he was drinking it. He hated everything. Gulping a second glass, he hurled it towards the fireplace in rage and disgust, shattering the glass into a thousand tiny pieces.

How dare she refuse his offer of marriage? He would never open himself up to a woman again. He had been willing to take a risk and this was his consequence. Women could not be trusted and she proved it. She had to leave. He would have her things packed even before she returned. Damn her to hell! He picked up the decanter of whiskey wishing he had not broken the glass, then looked at it and hurled the whole bottle into the fireplace to join the glass. Exhausted by the rage of emotions that wracked his brain, he rubbed his aching eyes. The taste of her lingered in his mind.

"Chesterton," he yelled out into the hall. "Chesterton! Where the devil?! Has everyone gone mad!" he roared? "Chesterton!" Who did she think she was, turning down a proposal from the Duke of Exmoor? What did she want, a king? His head pounded from anger. He could feel the tension grabbing at his back.

"Yes, sir," Chesterton said, a bit out of breath as he rushed in.

"Get Riya. Now!" he ordered. His head had been throbbing since he left Ana at the tower, the ungrateful witch. And now his neck and shoulders were stiffening sending shooting pains down his back. He began to remove his coat and cravat.

"Riya!" he growled under his breath, "What the hell is taking her so long," he muttered to himself.

"Here I am Sahib," she said entering breathless from her quick climb down the stairs.

"Riya, I need you to give me a rub. My head and back are killing me." He began to unbutton his shirt. Riya had the art to ease the tension and he needed it desperately.

"I'm sorry Sahib. I cannot give you rub today," she said quietly yet firmly, her face set in determination.

"I beg your pardon?" he was astounded by what he was hearing, and his eyes opened wide in astonishment at the tenor of her insubordination. Never since the time he knew this child had she defied him as she did now.

"Miss Ana, she told me I had choice, English ladies have choice. So today I choose. No rub," giving a respectful curtsey. She was, however, unprepared for his response.

"Out!" he bellowed pointing to the door, the rough sound of his voice making Riya jump.

"But sir, I have choice," she tried to explain, her eyes brimming with tears of fear at his outburst.

"Get out!" And in three long strides he loudly slammed the door directly behind her as she scurried fearfully from the library into the hall. He then picked up an oriental vase and launched it into the fireplace to join the shattered glass and decanter. In two strides he was by his desk, the humidor banging open. He pulled out a cigar. Cutting off the end, he placed the thick roll of tobacco in his mouth and lit it. He inhaled deeply of the fragrant smoke. Blowing out the match, he walked to the window more calmly and pulled back the sash. The sky was dark and ominous reflecting his mood. The wind had picked up as the gathering storm built in intensity. He took another drag on his cigar and began to feel the whiskey relax his throbbing temples, regretting now having thrown the decanter into the fire grate. Heavy drops of rain began to pelt the window panes.

"She will be gone by the morrow," he resolved.

"Something is very wrong with Lord Alexander. I have never seen him so angry. And now, poor Riya, she's in tears," Mrs. C. said breathlessly as she knocked on the door to Lady Catherine's room. She didn't wait to be invited in, pushing through the door, her face red from emotion.

"Whatever do you mean?" Lady Catherine said with concern.

"He's locked himself in his library and it sounds as if he is destroying the room."

"Destroying the room?" Lady Catherine quickly followed the overanxious Mrs. C. into the hall. Putting her ear to the library door, Lady Catherine could hear her son pacing and muttering to himself.

"Ma'am, I've never seen him so angry. He has frightened poor Riya half to death. She is crying in the kitchen right now, poor dear. We can hardly console her."

"Shhh," Lady Catherine waved towards Mrs. C. "I can't hear." She again placed her ear by the door for a few moments. "Mrs. C.," she whispered, "it is almost time for tea. Please get things ready. I'll go in and talk to him," she soothed.

"Yes, ma'am," Mrs. C. said as she wiped a tear from the corner of her eye with her white apron, gave a small curtsey, and went off to attend to her assignment.

"Alexander? Alexander, let me in." Lady Catherine knocked gently at the door and awaited a response. "Alexander, let me in."

"Mother, go away."

"I'll not, now let me in." She tried the door and found it had never been locked.

Slowly she opened the door. She could see that her son's face was dark and damp with perspiration. The room was lit only with light coming from the storm's blackened sky.

"Son, what has happened?" She gently closed the door behind her giving them privacy from the prying servants and walked to the desk to light a lamp.

"Mother, this is *your* fault. *You* did this ..." His voice was cold and cruel as he pointed at her, his hand shaking.

"What are you talking about?" she answered, shocked by his accusation.

"I've watched my sons grow in affection for that ... that woman you brought into my household. I have watched you oil your way around hoping that I would "fall in love" with her. Love! Ha! So, I thought how bad would it be if I did ask this ... this woman to marry me? I found her attractive enough, the idea of bringing her to my bed not abhorrent. Marrying her would protect my sons from the pain of her leaving for another position. I knew she would stay for the money. So, I asked her." His gray eyes narrowed into slits of rage as he glowered down at his mother.

"Oh Alexander, I'm so pleased!" Lady Catherine said as she began to grin from ear to ear.

Alexander shook his head at his mother's absurd reaction.

"Do you know what she said?" he answered.

"Why, yes, of course." Lady Catherine was not only buoyed with hope, but completely oblivious to her son's dark mood.

"No, Mother, she said NO!" Alexander exclaimed, barely keeping his rage in control.

"No? Alexander, how did you ask her? What do you mean?" she was shocked at what she heard.

Raising his eyes skyward, "No mother, I was honest."

"Honest?" She was incredulous.

"Yes, honest. Honest, Mother. I told her that I found her attractive, that my sons loved her, and that I would not want her to leave them."

"What else did you say?"

"I told her I would give her a good life."

"Yes, yes, that's good. And she turned you down anyway? Unbelievable." Lady Catherine couldn't grasp the reason for Ana's rejection of her son.

"Yes, she turned me down. So now you can see why I hate women. They are all treacherous snakes," he snarled.

"Did you tell her that too? You told her you hate women?"

His mother's naivete astounded him. "No Mother. But I did tell her I did not love her. I don't believe in love." His voice was laced with sarcasm. "If this is love Mother, I want none of it."

"Alexander, no wonder she turned you down!" Lady Catherine threw her hands up. She was speechless at what she heard.

"Well, it's tea time. I'm hungry and I'm going to enjoy my tea." She looked at her son and shook her head in disbelief. "Will you join me?"

Alexander realized his mother was clueless.

"No Mother. I think I'm going to pass on tea today. I strongly suggest you say your goodbyes to her when she returns. I cannot and will not abide having her under my roof one hour more than needed. You will obey me in this." His voice was controlled and resolute. "And I will deal with my sons."

"Alexander, you're a boor. I just don't understand you. How did you become so hard and uncaring?" she said sadly. "You were so tender as a child." Lady Catherine shook her head. "Well, I plan on having my tea."

With that Lady Catherine swept from the room only to stop at the door and turn towards her disgruntled son. "By the way, your sons are behaving shamefully." Glancing towards the pile of glass shards in the fire grate, she added, "Which I would say is something they inherited from their father." She then turned left her son alone to brood.

"Mrs. C., has Ana not yet returned?" Lady Catherine asked as she was picking up the tray with remnants of her repast.

"No ma'am. She promised she would be home before tea. She always keeps her word. And now with this awful weather and it's nearly six, I'm concerned."

Lady Catherine walked over to the window and pushed aside one of the heavy drapes to assess the raging storm. "Yes, it does look mean. Are you sure you haven't heard her return?" she asked, echoing her housekeeper's concern for Ana's well-being.

"No ma'am, 'tis not like her to be so late."

"And you checked her room?" Lady Catherine frowned.

"Yes, ma'am, she's not there."

With growing concern, Lady Catherine was not, however, surprised at all that Ana had not yet returned. She most likely needed some time to be alone with her thoughts and feelings and possibly had found safe shelter to wait out the storm.

"Well, don't worry. I'm sure she'll be home shortly. She would not stay out with a storm like this. Did Lord Luttrell order her things packed?"

"Why no Milady," she answered, extremely worried now at this line of questioning.

"You can go now. Let me know the moment she returns. I want to speak with her," Lady Catherine insisted, determined to give her warning of Alexander's decision to terminate her position.

"Yes ma'am," Mrs. C. said, her anxiety heightening as the storm continued to grow more menacing with each passing moment. Lightning flashed across the blackening clouds. The palm trees swayed restlessly in the wind. Mrs. C. turned to leave but paused a moment and gnawed at her lower lip. Knowing Ana had not mentioned anything to Lord Luttrell about the stranger asking for her in town and herself not having had the opportunity, her apprehension only worsened at the thought that she might be in danger.

"Is there something more?" Lady Catherine asked, seeing her hesitation.

Feeling compelled, Mrs. C. said timidly, "Lady Catherine, I must speak." Worry creased her brow.

"Yes, what is it now?" Lady Catherine responded, feeling a bit perturbed at Mrs. C.'s hesitation.

She placed the tea set back on the table and approached Lady Catherine wringing her hands from her anxieties.

"Well, out with it, madam!" Lady Catherine was near the end of her own rope.

"I told her and told her. I thought she needed to speak to someone. But she thought it was all stuff and nonsense."

"You told her what?" Lady Catherine said in dismay.

"I know I should've said something sooner, Milady," Mrs. C. shook her head. "When Miss Pembroke first arrived, there was someone in town asking after her. A stranger had talked with Mr. Goodall—a strange man—he said. Mr. Goodall didn't know him. I was uneasy about it and told Miss Ana she needed to tell you or Lord Luttrell. I reminded her just today before she left. I would've told him but he too had already left." Tears filled her eyes, "Oh your ladyship, I'm sure something terrible has happened!"

"Yes, you should have said something right away," Lady Catherine scolded. "But thank you for telling me now. I'll go and speak to Lord Luttrell at once, if he will see me." She agreed that something may very well be amiss. She was apprehensive about approaching her son given his current mood. But it had to be done. Ana was under their protection and therefore she was their responsibility.

Lady Catherine returned to the library only to find that Alexander was not there.

"Chesterton," she called. "Where is Lord Luttrell?"

"Up in the nursery ma'am."

"Thank you, Chesterton."

Knowing he must be attending his sons, she let herself into the room. Hugh was teary-eyed, stifling his sobs while Geoffrey stood cross-armed and angry. What Alexander had said to them was not the reason for her entrance, but she surmised by the looks on the boys faces that he was trying to prepare them for Ana's departure.

Not wanting to fan the flames towards hysterics in her grandsons she said quietly, "Son, I need to speak to you, in private."

Hugh's lower lip began to quiver at the thought of his father leaving him alone with his angry brother.

"Hugh it's time to stop crying...now! Life's not always easy nor is it fair and it's time to learn this lesson," Alexander said coldly as he followed his mother into the long gallery.

"Alexander, we have a new situation we must deal with. I believe Ana is in real danger," grave concern lined her face.

"Oh, now I've heard it all," he spit back, exasperated and fatigued by the day's events. "You really are too much, Mother. You are willing to do anything. You just don't stop, do you?" His eyes flashed at her.

"Son, she's not returned," she answered quietly, though she was unnerved at his accusation.

"She's playing a game. All women play games." He squinted at his mother.

"Alexander, I'm serious. Mrs. C. told me of a stranger who had been asking after Ana around town. That does not seem odd to you?"

"No. People often ask about newcomers to this area."

"Alexander, this person was a stranger. Don't you understand? Look at the weather. This is a bad storm. It doesn't matter what transpired between you both. She should've returned by now. She's not a fool." Lady Catherine couldn't believe she needed to beg.

Closing his eyes Alexander rubbed his throbbing temples. "Will this day never end?'

"Alexander, please. She's your responsibility." His mother rarely pleaded. He stood for a moment dreading the thought of going out into the storm. Women and their histrionics, he thought to himself. But it was getting darker and more violent by the minute. His shoulders slumped. He had to concede. As long as Ana was under his roof, he was responsible for her, no matter how he felt and no matter how angry she made him. His whole household had been unhinged by the day's events and now he needed to go out into this raging storm to track down a deranged and emotional female.

"Deranged," he said quietly.

"Deranged? Alexander what are you talking about?" Lady Catherine was beginning to lose her temper.

"Yes, deranged, mother, I called her deranged a while back when she accused me of writing some sophomoric letter, saying I was trying to scare her into leaving. She called me juvenile or something." He shook his head to clear himself of this line of thought. "Let's not go to pieces. She's most likely weathering the storm in one of the tenants' farms." He was satisfied with his answer.

Completely exasperated by her son, "Alexander, sometimes you are juvenile," she answered as she clicked her tongue in exasperation. She was at a loss as to how to reach her stubborn and thickheaded son.

Suddenly, his demeanor changed. Alexander was on the move.

"Chesterton!" he yelled "Get Cesar saddled. Mother, you may be right. Send for Doctor Pendleton."

"Where are you going? Do you know where to look?" Lady Catherine was surprised and excited at his abrupt change of mood. She followed him as he rushed into him into the library.

"I'm going back to where I left her, Conygar Tower." Alexander threw on his discarded coat and hat which had been strewn about the library.

"Damn, she said something about someone spying on her just today," he said under his breath as he opened his gun case and pulled out a revolver. Loading it, quickly, he tucked into his belt.

"Guns? Alexander! What are you about?" She was frantic. Something was amiss or Alexander would not have changed so dramatically and he would not have taken guns.

But he ran past her saying, "Mother, attend to the boys. I'll return shortly. And get the doctor." He repeated his order again but his words were barely audible above the wind as he ran out the door. He leapt onto his black stallion and raced off down the stone drive towards the Conygar Woods, the tower, and Ana.

CHAPTER 22

Wild gusts of wind and cold hard rain pelted Alexander's face as he raced down the muddy road towards the once tranquil path they had trod only a few short hours ago. Clumps of mud flew as Cesar's hoofs quickly ate into the distance to Conygar Tower. He remembered that Ana had asked if he had been watching her from a shop window just that afternoon. It made the urgency of his ride all the more real. He knew she was in danger. Leaning into the flying black mane of his stallion, Alexander felt his heart racing in his chest as fast as his steed bounded toward its destination. Turning off the road, Cesar vaulted over the hedgerow onto the soft earth of the soggy pasture, his speed now hampered by the high meadow grasses, his rider cursing under his breath at the impediments. Seeing the outline of the towering structure in the shadowy distance, Alexander kicked his heels hard into Cesar's side to spur him on. The steed, seeming to understand the urgency, accelerated forward up the rocky terrain. Reaching the tower, Alexander jumped to the ground running.

"Ana," the wind ripped the words from his mouth, the salty rain blurring his vision. "Ana!" he called again. He should have never left her alone in this desolate place. He was angry at his behavior and his own mindless stupidity. He remembered that she had headed towards the tower as he left and now, he began to climb the slippery steps; the darkness made the way all the more treacherous. He wished he had brought a lantern. He hoped to see her clinging to the mortared rocks on the parapet. The cold rain beat down on his face from the opening as the angry wind howled menacingly over the top. He couldn't see her through the shadows. He called again, his voice, echoing eerily off the ancient stone walls, mingled with the wail of the wind. As he climbed the mossy stairs, he saw only the foreboding gloom of the raging black sky at the top of the tower.

"Ana!" he cried out as he rounded the winding stair in the hope of finding her still atop the tower. The storm ripped at his clothes and face; his hat having blown away long ago. Pushing the dripping hair from his eyes he stopped, as the feeling of trepidation gripped his chest. He rushed to the edge. He could barely see in the dim light as the wind and rain hit his face. He frantically scanned the ravine below for some clue, some indication of her whereabouts.

"Ana!" he cried, but his call was carried away by the gust of wind. The crack and crash of a tree roared up to meet his ears it snapped on the slope below. His eyes searched the new narrow clearing which sloped steeply downward, desperate to see something, anything. It was almost impossible to gain a clear vantage below from his position. The trees and underbrush whipped around as violently as the distant churning sea. He was desperate. Where could she be?

"Ana!" he called out again knowing it was futile as a crash of lightening lit up the angry black sky. Suddenly, in the flashing light, his eyes caught a glimpse of something white fluttering in the abyss below.

"My God." He stood momentarily in fear, his eyes searching for some sign of life as the realization of what had happened began to sink into his brain.

"Ana," he repeated, horrified, his voice now husky with emotion. Climbing back down the tower he slipped on the slick wet stones. "Damn it to hell!" he cursed, the water beating on the back of his neck, his hand now scraped and bloodied by the fall. He stopped momentarily, realizing stones had been pushed away from the window. This was where she must have fallen. Exiting the tower, he heard the sound of hooves approaching with another rider. He threw himself back into the shadows of the tower entrance. The cold of the hard rocks permeated his already saturated coat. His senses were keenly attuned to the danger that awaited him in the darkness. He pulled his pistol from his belt, cocked it, making ready to fire at the possible enemy. The sound of thunder rumbled like familiar cannon from distant battles and for a brief moment his mind flashed back to war-torn India. He shook his head to clear his mind.

"Father, Father, where are you?" Geoffrey's voice brought him to his senses.

Letting out a long sigh of relief, Alexander lowered the revolver and made his presence known from the blackness of his hiding place.

"Geoffrey! What the devil are you doing? I damn near shot you. Go home!" he ordered out of frustration.

"Father, I'm not a child. I'm here to help," Geoffrey shouted above the storm.

"You're right. Follow me," he conceded. "I think she's in the ravine. We need to move fast. The water is pouring down into the chasm. She may be drowned."

Standing on the edge of the embankment he studied the situation. He could see her better now, lying on the soft mud below; the streams of the rainwater dangerously rising, the power of the storm increasing their ferocity. Though there was a natural winding path, the fastest way was directly down the incline. Grabbing a rope from the saddle, he tied it onto Cesar for ballast.

"Here," he said, handing Geoffrey the rope and bridle. "Hold Cesar. I'm going down." Grabbing hold of the rope for support, he cautiously but swiftly slid down the muddy and treacherous slope. Once in the ravine, he ran to Ana's motionless body. Falling to his knees, he leaned forward to place his ear on her chest.

"Thank God," he murmured as he felt the gentle rise and fall of her breath.

He took her icy cold hands in his and began to rub vigorously hoping to bring some warmth back into them. "Ana, Ana, wake up." He patted her cheek.

He took off his coat and covered her still form. As he looked up the elevation, he saw the lights of several lanterns appear at the base of the tower.

"Down here!" he yelled up waving his arms.

"I'm coming down, sir," Chesterton called, his voice barely audible above the wind. "I've Doctor Pendleton with me."

The two men made their way to where Lord Luttrell knelt over Ana's still body.

"Is she dead sir?" Chesterson asked, filled with concern and fear.

"No, thank God, just unconscious. I think she fell or was pushed from the tower window and rolled …," he said thinking out loud.

"Step aside Luttrell, let me examine her." Doctor Pendleton quickly began to check her limbs looking for broken bones. "Nothing appears broken here, thank God," he muttered.

Looking up at the dark outline of the tower battlements against the stormy gray sky, "It's amazing she is alive, sir." Chesterton said with some relief.

"Help me turn her over, gentlemen. I need to check for a broken back or neck." Both men looked at the doctor, horror in their faces.

"Gently now, very gently," Dr. Pendleton instructed as he held one of the lanterns high. The men obeyed and slowly, gingerly began to move her over onto her side. "Watch her head. Good. Good. Move aside." Handing the lantern to Chesterton, he leaned over and slowly felt her neck and back. "Hmmm. Ah-hmmm."

"Well, Penny?" Alexander asked with extreme impatience. If she was permanently damaged, even though he had not pushed her, he felt immensely responsible. If he had not been such an angry fool, he would never have left her in such danger. He should have known of the threats against her. He was angry that he had not been made aware by others of his household. He was angrier still at his own inability to see past his foolish pride to realize that the letter and her earlier comment were real signs of danger. But why would anyone want to harm her? How could she be such a threat that they would want to silence her forever?

"Amazing!" Doctor Pendleton said as he stood up and brushed the mud and pebbles from his hands and knees. "Gentlemen, she does not appear to have any broken bones. Frankly, I don't know how that's possible. She had to tumble head over heels. It's just amazing."

"Most likely all those petticoats and such," Chesterton chuckled with nervous relief.

"Perhaps. Well, we need to get her up," Doctor Pendleton said as he assessed the continuous downpour. "The water is coming in quickly. And this storm is not letting up. Get her back to the Castle where I can give her a more thorough examination."

"Chesterton, give me your coat," Alexander ordered as he sprung to his feet. "Sir?"

"Just do it. We'll make a sling to get her up the embankment."

"Quite right, sir," he said as he quickly removed the garment from his back, his white cotton shirt and waistcoat quickly soaking up the falling rain.

They fashioned a hammock and gently cradled Ana in it. Taking the rope that was tied to Cesar at the top of the incline, Alexander made a tight loop around Ana's waist to prevent her from falling again during their ascent.

"Geoffrey," he called loudly. Even with his hands on both sides of his mouth his voice was muffled by the storm, "Geoffrey!"

Suddenly a lantern appeared above them.

"Move Cesar back slowly, we're bringing Miss Pembroke to the top."

"Yes, Father!" he responded immediately, pleased to be of aid.

"Chesterton, take her feet and I'll grab this end. Penny, if you would be so kind as to help with balancing the middle. Now on the count of three let us all move together. And for God's sake, gentlemen, watch your step. One, two, three …!"

Slowly, they lifted the sling and began to move up the face of the hill, the wind and rain hampering their way and making their footing shaky at best in the mud.

"Geoffrey, steady. Steady!" Alexander yelled up to his son.

Taking Cesar by the reins, Geoffrey slowly began to move the steed, keeping the rope taught. He whispered gently into the horse's ear providing encouragement for the task at hand. As they moved forward, he could hear the voices of the men getting closer with their burden. Suddenly, Doctor Pendleton's lantern threw its glow across the ground. They had reached the top.

"Whoa, Cesar," Geoffrey ordered and he ran over to help the men hoist Ana's unconscious form over the crest of the embankment.

Once she was safely on the top, the men barely sat to catch their breath.

"We must get her back to the house immediately. Geoffrey," Doctor Pendleton said, "Return at once and have the women warm her bed. She is half frozen."

"Yes, sir," Geoffrey said and was on his horse almost before the words left his mouth.

Alexander climbed onto Cesar's back. "Lift her carefully," he ordered as she was laid gently across his saddle, cradling her in the crook of his arm. She looked pale and fragile.

"Do you have her, sir?" Chesterton asked.

"Yes, I'll see you back at Dunster." And with that he kicked his heels into Cesar's side and carefully followed Geoffrey down the rutted path. The horse appeared to know his cargo was precious. Chesterson and Doctor Pendleton followed not far behind.

Geoffrey, wet and muddy, ran into the inner hall to find Mrs. C.'s, Bess and Lady Catherine anxiously awaiting the news of Ana's whereabouts.

"We found her!" he cried. "Father's bringing her home. Doctor Pendleton said you ladies need to prepare her room to get her warm," he ordered, his young voice filled with authority.

"Thank God she is found," Lady Catherine sighed with relief.

"She's unconscious," Geoffrey said breathlessly.

"I'll go at once. Alice, build a fire. Bess, boil water," Mrs. C. directed as she scurried up the stairs.

"Unconscious?" Lady Catherine grabbed Geoffrey's soaked arm. "What do you mean? How did this happen?"

"She fell from the tower window. Father thinks she may have been pushed."

"Pushed?!!" Hearing the horses on the drive, Lady Catherine ran past Geoffrey into the driving rain to find the men had just arrived with Ana. She needed to find out more.

"Careful, Chesterton," Alexander commanded as Ana was gently lifted from his saddle.

Looking up he said, "Mother, get inside. You'll catch your death."

"But, Alexander, is everyone alright? Ana…is she…?"

"Mother you're getting soaked. Get into the house!" he ordered.

Picking up Ana's limp frame in his arms, he carried her into the house with Lady Catherine trailing anxiously behind. Ana felt weightless to him.

"Pushed? Alexander, Geoffrey said she was pushed? What does that mean?" Lady Catherine said as she grabbed his shirtsleeve.

"Mother, I will speak to you later. But for now, see that Geoffrey gets warm and dry. And see to yourself. I don't need a household of invalids." He left her to stand at the base of the stair wondering anxiously at the events that had transpired.

Turning to Geoffrey she said, "You heard your father, up to nursery. And I mean now, young man!" She gave him a gentle shove towards the stairs.

Taking two steps at a time, Alexander carried Ana to her room, where Mrs. C. and several others servants were waiting to do the doctor's bidding. A large fire was burning in the hearth, providing a warm glow.

"No, no sir. Don't lay her on the bed. You will soak it with her wet garments. Lay her here on the blankets next to the fire. Oh, Doctor Pendleton, what do we need to do?" Mrs. C. turned her attention to the medical man who had entered the room behind Alexander.

"Let's get her out of those wet things first," he ordered as he dropped to one knee to begin work on his patient.

Alexander stood by watching and uncomfortable, feeling useless as the women began to unbutton her heavy wet dress. He felt he needed to do more but did not know what. Doctor Pendleton looked up at him. "I'll take over from here. You get warm and dry. I'll find you shortly and tend to your hand." He centered his attention back to his patient.

"Alex, you saved her life, I dare say."

Alexander entered his rooms. Chesterton had changed his own clothes and was laying out dry clothes for Alexander.

"Sir, will she be alright?" He asked as he laid out a pair of brown trousers next to a fresh white shirt.

"I don't know. I'm sure Pendleton will do all he can," he said, assuring himself that she was out of danger.

"Sir, would you like a warm bath? I find a bath at times like these most relaxing."

"Chesterton, when have you ever experienced times like these?" He shook his head and chuckled to himself. But a bath sounded inviting. "Yes, a hot bath and a brandy with that."

"Yes, sir, I took the liberty of having water heated. It will be up momentarily."

"Thank you, Chesterton. And thank you for your help. We wouldn't have been able to save her without it."

"Sir, I was only doing my duty," he answered, nodding in Alexander's direction.

Smiling at his manservant Alexander added, "I think you went beyond your duty."

"Thank you, sir," he said as he quietly left the room. For some time now Chesterton had secretly known that Ana had become a special addition to the family.

Within minutes the tub was brought up, and steaming hot water poured to the brim. Finally alone, he took off his ruined clothes. Slowly sinking into the soothing bath, he felt the sting from the cuts on his hand; the drying blood mingling with the water. The wet heat eased the tightness from his shoulders, neck, and aching body. He took a sip of the brandy and felt its heat run down the back of his throat into his empty stomach. It had been hours since he had eaten anything and he hadn't realized how hungry he was.

The sight of Ana lying cold and limp in the ravine filled his mind. She was in his charge; she was his responsibility. Until he knew otherwise, she was still in danger. He knew he could not have her leave under these new circumstances.

He sighed deeply, horrified at his own behavior. They were having a pleasant enough walk. The time appeared to be right to ask for her hand. He was only being honest with her. His mother was right, he needed to take leave of the past and learn to how trust, but that was the question, especially with women. Thinking of her in danger, unconscious and abandoned to the ravages of the storm, possibly even dead, struck him to the core.

Ana's response to his accusation of wanting marriage only for money appeared genuine, though she surely had the ability to cut him deeply with her tongue. Maybe she meant more to him then he realized. The thought sent a chill down his back. No, that's not it, he rationalized. It was only what she meant to his sons and his mother. But someone was out to do her harm; that was obvious. The stones from the window were loosened. Who would possibly wish to do her such harm and why?

If only she had not rebuffed him, this never would have happened. She was different from women in his circle, those ridiculous peacocks. He smiled. She taught Riya about choice. Poor Riya, he would have to apologize to the child. But Ana challenged him on his own decisions with his sons. In fact, she challenged him on most everything. She was most aggravating.

Taking another sip of brandy, he closed his eyes. *Most aggravating*. He thought of her turquoise eyes, and the way they flashed when she became angry. The way she felt in his arms. Her full crimson lips, the way she tasted when he kissed her, her response to him, pushing up against him longing for more, hungering for more. The way she aroused him was most aggravating indeed. He could feel his passion beginning to grow as the direction of his thoughts moved towards taking her to his bed. Still, he couldn't trust her. Surely, she was only out for money. He had learned that from Jacob Sumner, Esq. But this woman made him burn; she stimulated him, challenged him. He wanted her. Further, she was his responsibility and it was his duty to protect her as long as she was in his household. And until this threat was resolved she would be here for a while.

The knock at his door brought him swiftly back to his senses. He quickly drew a towel into the water to hide his growing passion.

"Who's there?" he asked, embarrassed at the possibility of being found out.

"Only me," Dr. Pendleton called, poking his head into the room.

"Penny. Come in," he motioned with a wet hand to his longtime friend.

"Ah, Luttrell, a hot bath, just what the doctor would've ordered," he chuckled. "I've come to report on our patient," he said as he pulled up a chair next to the tub.

Alexander sat up straight, anxious to hear what the good doctor had discovered. Water spilled onto the floor.

"Well, there are no broken bones. However, she has a rather nasty gash on the back of her head which needed a few stitches. She must have grabbed for the bushes and such to stop the fall. Her hands were cut up but now cleaned and bandaged. I had to set her shoulder which seemed to have been pulled from its socket. It'll be sore for a few days. but otherwise she'll be fine."

"But there was no blood?" Alexander asked, confused at this report.

"No, too much shock. She'll sleep for several hours. I gave her some powders to ease the pain. When she wakes, she'll feel groggy. I told Mrs. C. to give her broth for a few days until her strength returns. I also advise that someone be with her at all times. She needs the bed rest. Someone needs to be there when she awakes."

"So, she's still unconscious," Alexander said, concern clearly etched on his face.

"After a fall like that she wouldn't have been able to handle the pain." Doctor Pendleton said as he shook his head. "Luttrell, it's a miracle she only sustained minor injuries." The doctor studied his hands for a few minutes finally responding to his own exhaustion from the event. "I looked in on Geoffrey, Chesterton, and your mother, all doing well. Let me look at that hand."

Alexander extended his injured hand. Penny studied it. "Minor cuts. Have Mrs. C. bandage it when you're done here."

"How can I ever thank you, Penny?" Alexander said as he extended the other wet hand.

Pendleton stood up taking the hand offered and laughing, "I'll send you my bill, ha ha." He turned to leave the room but stopped.

"Luttrell, I'm curious about one thing. At the tower you inferred to the possibility that Miss Pembroke was pushed. What did you mean?"

"Mother and another of my staff informed me that Ana had reported that some suspicious fellow was making inquiries about her in town. In addition, she told me about a threatening letter she received. I had taken it as some foolishness from the boys, you know youngsters and governesses," he sighed.

Doctor Pendleton nodded in full understanding.

"Then only today, she asked me if I had been watching her from a shop window. But she shrugged it off. We both shrugged it off. Then I noticed that stones from the tower window had been purposefully moved. There is no way her fall would have shifted stones of that size. It looks deliberate."

"Well, if someone meant to do her in, they failed today, thank God."

"Yes, thank God," Alexander agreed.

"When they find their attempt has failed, they'll try again," he warned.

"I'm fully aware of that. I plan on doing all I can to find this madman as well as to protect Ana. As long as she lives under my roof, she's my responsibility," he added with determination in his voice.

"Yes, well good night, sir. I'll return tomorrow to check on our patients. Let me know if I can be of any help to your search, will you?"

"Thank you, Penny. I will."

As the doctor closed the door, Alexander rang for Chesterton. He was famished.

CHAPTER 23

The clock struck eleven in the evening as Alexander made his way to Ana's room to relieve his mother from her bedside watch. Softly knocking on the door, he entered to find his mother gently snoring in the chair next to Ana's bed.

"Mother," he whispered, touching her shoulder, "It's time for bed."

"Oh," she said blinking awake, "I'm sorry, I must have dozed."

Looking closely at his mother, he was startled by her flushed appearance. Placing his hand upon her forehead, he felt the heat of fever.

"Mother, you're burning up. I'll send for Mrs. C. to look in on you. You caught a chill from the damp, I'm sure," he said, distressed at this latest development.

"Oh son, it's nothing, just a bit of a summer cold," she answered, attempting to shake off his concern.

"I'll send Mrs. C. up anyway. Now off with you. It's my turn to watch."

Standing up, Lady Catherine admitted she did feel a bit woozy. "I'll have Mrs. C. bring up tea. Sit and I'll get her to help you out."

"You're right, son. You don't need two sick women on your hands."

As he rang for Mrs. C., he asked quietly, "Has there been any change?"

"I think she's resting now. She had been dreaming. I would think it's a good sign, wouldn't you?" Lady Catherine said. He shrugged, not knowing the answer.

There was a soft knock on the door.

"Take mother to her room, she's not well. See to her care. Get her some tea." Mrs. C. took Lady Catherine's arm.

"Don't worry son, 'tis nothing," Lady Catherine said as she flashed her son an assuring smile.

"Let's pray that it is. Off with you both!" he smiled as his mother blew him a kiss and gently closed the door behind her.

He threw several logs onto the dying fire and seated himself in the chair vacated by his mother. It still held residual warmth from her presence. Stretching his long legs out in front of him and crossing them at the ankles, he linked his hands behind his neck, leaned the chair on its two back legs, and rocked ever so slightly while watching the gentle breathing of his charge. He was concerned about the turn in his mother's health. He looked at the bandage on his hand and shook his head thinking what a mess he'd made of his household, all because of his own pigheadedness.

He thought of how Geoffrey came to his aid and felt a sense of fatherly pride in his son's courage. Stretching out his arms he realized he was exhausted from the day's highly-charged events.

As he reviewed the day, Alexander remembered the note Ana had accused him of writing several weeks ago. He stood up and slowly but quietly perused her room, occasionally looking over his shoulder towards the bed.

Where would she keep her letters? he thought as he walked over to her dresser and stealthily began to pull open a drawer. He felt uncomfortable looking through her cotton underpinnings. Not finding anything, he quickly closed the drawer, embarrassed now at getting so personal. He again glanced over to the bed, then silently walked to her dressing table. Lifting the cover, he quickly recognized her hair brush. *That damned hair brush*, he thought.

Yes, he was drunk that night, but not so drunk as to forget that kiss, that hot passionate lusty kiss. Alexander knew if it were not for the overindulgence of whiskey, he would not have stopped, and though his memory was unclear, and he was not sure that she would have stopped either. A sly smile crossed his face as he again looked at Ana sleeping quietly in her bed. He thought with a chuckle, if it were not for the whiskey, he would have never entered her room that night in the first place. And the truth was, he would not be burning for her now, he thought as he frowned.

Alexander returned his gaze to the objects of the dressing table to resume his search. There was a bar of soap. He picked it up to smell it; lavender, just like her hair. Returning it to its spot, there were no letters here. He quietly closed the lid.

Noticing a wooden box on her writing table, he walked over and opened it. There were many folded and well-read missives. He glanced over his shoulder at the still form lying in her bed. He knew he should wait for her to awaken, but duty and responsibility held a stronger pull than propriety. Picking up the box, he returned to the chair where there was better light from the fire.

Shifting in her bed, Ana moaned softly in her sleep. He held in his breath as he glanced up to check on her again. She did not awaken. It must be one of her dreams, he thought. Biting his lower lip, he pulled out the bundle of letters wrapped in soft colored ribbons. Taking them from the ribbons, he slowly turned them over reading the names of the senders: Eliza, Eliza, Charles, Eliza, Sarah, Ana Jane, Eliza. He let out a long soft sigh. Maybe she didn't keep the one he was looking for. He kept looking through the box.

Another letter from Charles. He shook his head. He had never taken the time to find out who these people were. He realized he may have judged her too quickly. It was clear she had family who missed her. Thinking back, he remembered his mother telling him that her brother was killed in the War between the States and that her parents died in some coach accident. Eliza must be her sister, but who was this Charles? Was he the person Sumner described?

Compelled by some unknown feeling, Alexander could not resist opening the letter in his hand.

My Dearest Darling Ana,

My feelings are crushed by your continued denial of my offer. How can you continue to shame me and your family by persisting in these fool-hardy endeavors? How often must I feel the pain of your rejection? Ana, my love, with you by my side we will be able to do so much more than your father ever could accomplish. You know how the join-

ing of our lives will benefit all in our family. Together we can grow strong. You know I will continue to offer my hand as I cannot accept no as the answer. You are mine and will always be mine.

I dream of the day that I can possess you, my darling.

Yours, Faithful Cousin,
Charles

Alexander found that he could not help but read the letter three times. *Cousin Charles?* He glanced up at Ana. *"Dream of the day that I can possess you,"* he grimaced. Immediately he didn't like this Charles. It was obvious that Ana had turned down his offer more than once or he wouldn't be begging so hard. But there was also something about the letter that made Alexander angry. Charles was reaching for something and Alexander realized it was power. And Alexander was well aware women didn't want power alone—they wanted money, which brought them prestige.

Suddenly, a sound from the bed brought his attention back to Ana. He sat very still, horrified at the thought of having her awaken to find him with her box of letters in his lap. She rolled over onto her side; her face illuminated by the firelight. She softly moaned as she lay on her injured shoulder. Alexander stood up, placing the box on the seat of the chair and went over to her. He gently rolled her onto her back to relieve the pressure. Thankfully she didn't awake. The sleeping powders were doing their job. A thick brown curl fell across her forehead; he moved it from her face and noticed that it was still damp from her ordeal. Alexander watched as she remained asleep, noticing the steady rise and fall of her chest as she breathed. He noticed that a rosy color had returned to her cheeks and lips. Her thick dark hair spilled over onto her pillow. He remembered the first time he had seen her. She was sleeping then, too, in his library. He gently smiled to himself at the memory then returned to his task.

He checked the post mark on the Charles' letter. She had received it only a week ago. This Charles didn't give up, Alexander thought.

Alexander returned to the letter box. Finally, he found a letter with a hand that was unlike the rest. Glancing at Ana, he quickly opened the folded sheet of familiar paper and began to read.

Miss Pembroke,

You are in grave danger. Leave Dunster Castle immediately, or your safety will be compromised.

A friend.

His brow furrowed. Nothing on the letter gave any indication of its origination or author. Whoever wrote this wanted to frighten Ana and maybe even harm her if she did not follow his bidding. Folding the letter, he placed it in the breast pocket of his vest. Returning the other letters to the box, he quietly returned it to the table and took up his vigil. He felt certain that whoever wrote this letter had pushed Ana from the tower.

His need to protect was strong. He knew he could not allow this Charles to … what did he say? "Possess her." His sons needed her too much. His mother needed her too. In the past months she had become a very important part of the family, and of the household, though against his will. And Charles be damned to hell if he thought for a moment that he could possess her.

Alexander determined at that moment that he must marry her. It was the only way to protect her. He knew love had nothing to do with it. What was love anyway? Foolish, fanciful ideas that his mother espoused of fluttering hearts and gardens of pink roses? He shook his head. Alexander also knew it was simple lust she stirred in him. Plus, he needed to see to his responsibilities towards her now. And marriage, in his mind, was the only way he could fulfill both needs.

Seeing that Ana's hand had fallen out from the covers, Alexander reached over and took it into his. It was so much warmer now, now that she was safe. There was a bandage wrapped around her palm. Only now did he realize how horrifyingly close he had been to losing her… that they all had been to losing her. He noticed her delicately shaped fingers next to his own large hand, how soft her skin was to the touch. Closing his eyes, he gently brought her hand up to his face to barely brush her silky fingers against his lips. Moaning gently, she began to shift under the bedclothes. Alexander quickly tucked her hand back under the covers. He heard the hall clock strike one. Two hours had moved fast. His time was done.

There was a gentle knock at the door. Mrs. C. had come to relieve him. He was informed that his mother was sleeping soundly. He, too, was exhausted and retired to his rooms for the night.

Alexander lay in bed but sleep would not come to his weary body. He read and re-read the letter he had found in Ana's room, setting it to memory and pondering who would want to harm her and why? Who had anything to gain by this? How could Ana be such a threat that her life needed to be cut short? Who would choose such a dastardly way as to push her from Conygar Tower? Did she know something about someone or something that put her at risk? He needed to resolve this before more harm was done to her. It was clear that accepting the marriage proposal from Charles was distasteful. He'd not protect her. He was out to use her.

And protecting was what Alexander did best. He protected his sons. He saved Riya from a life of demoralization and slavery. He watched over his mother. He tended to his servants and resolved his tenants' needs. He was there for his troops in India and he was always ready to serve and protect his Queen. And now he needed to protect Ana.

Her safety was being threatened, and it was imperative that he do his duty towards that end.

His eyes felt heavy. He knew that he needed sleep. Yet, when he did nod off, vivid lifelike dreams of the smell and violence of battles and screaming men and horses quickly roused him back. The events of the day were taking their toll. His head ached from the flashbacks, memories, and the exhaustion. Finally, sleep did overtake his drained body as the morning larks began to break the night's long silence and the soft pink glow of dawn began to edge its way over the horizon.

The vigorous shaking of his shoulder finally rousted Alexander from his deep sleep. His bedchamber was awash in brilliant sunlight.

"Lord Luttrell, wake up, sir."

"What is it, man?" he groaned, feeling annoyed that his much-needed sleep was so uninvitingly and physically disturbed, the sunlight hurting his bleary and tired eyes.

"She's awake, sir," Chesterton said, as he stood back with a rare smile.

"Awake? By Jove, why didn't you get me up sooner?" Alexander demanded as he threw back the covers and jumped from his bed, suddenly feeling well-rested.

"Sir, she just awoke," he said as he helped him on with his robe.

"How is she? Did she say anything?" he inquired, tying the red brocade garment around his waist while his feet fumbled for their slippers.

"I believe she said she was hungry, sir."

"Hungry? That's wonderful! Chesterton, you know, so am I! I want a big breakfast this morning!" Placing his hands on his servant's shoulders, he said "Chesterton, I knew she'd pull through," his blue eyes twinkling with delight.

"Yes, sir, she's made of strong stuff."

"Yes, that she is, that she is. Did you send for Pendleton?"

"First thing, sir."

"Good man."

"Lord Luttrell, may I suggest you not visit with her just yet," he ventured, not wanting to break the mood.

"Not visit? What? Why?" Alexander's eyes darkened.

"Yes, sir, let the ladies attend to her. I'm sure she's still rather weak from her ordeal."

Sitting on the edge of his bed, he looked up at Chesterton, "Yes, you're right. Of course, you're right," he said, feeling a little rejected. "Well, I think I will take a bit of exercise before breakfast. It looks like a beautiful day. Have Cesar made ready," he said as he pulled off his recently donned robe, "I shan't be long for I'm starving!"

CHAPTER 24

"*L*uttrell, my good fellow, here you are," Doctor Pendleton said, announcing his entrance.

"Get some breakfast, Penny," pointing with his fork to the abundant sideboard. "Take a seat. I demand an update," he said filling his mouth with more food.

"Luttrell, you promised there would be no more orders," grabbing a plate to pile it high. Pendleton had served at the Duke's side in India, attending to bloodied and battered men of the war. Their camaraderie ran deep from their experience of battle and they became fast friends.

"Well let's not call this an order but a strong suggestion, old friend," Alexander mumbled, food in his mouth, again pointing his refilled fork towards the sideboard.

Bringing his filled plate over to the table the Doctor took a seat next to the Duke.

"Frankly, Luttrell, I don't remember a time since returning home that I felt such danger. It brought back some dark memories I must say." Penny remarked as he poured some hot coffee into his cup. "So, did you find anything out?" he asked after blowing on the steaming brew and taking a sip.

"I found the letter. But first, your report on our patient."

"The wound on her head will heal very nicely. Seems chipper enough, I'd say."

"Chipper? How in God's name can she be chipper?" Alexander put his fork down on his plate awaiting an explanation.

"You see, she doesn't remember anything."

"What do you mean?" he said, fearing complete amnesia.

"Well, she knows who she is, where she is, and even why she is here. But she doesn't remember anything about the Conygar incident. When I mentioned the tower, she said that she had hopes of visiting it one day."

"I don't understand?"

"Luttrell, sometimes when someone experiences such an extremely frightening and life-threatening event, their mind somehow blocks it. It's like the mind's way of protecting itself, you see?"

"So she doesn't remember anything of being there? The fall? The proposal? The argument? None of it?"

"Proposal? Whoa, there's something you're not telling me, you sly fox." Pendleton's face was getting red as it always did when he became excited.

"I had asked her to marry me," Alexander said sheepishly.

"Why you old devil! Congratulations!" Pendleton's meaty hand gave Alexander a big slap on the back. Alexander choked from the resounding pounding on his back.

"Don't congratulate me, my friend. She turned me down." He shook his head, still coughing from the piece of egg that had been caught in his throat.

"What? Turn YOU down? A duke? Inconceivable!"

"Penny, she turned me down. She wounded my pride. We had an ugly argument and I left her. I feel like a cad. This would've never happened had I taken her rejection like a man rather than the arrogant fool I am." He began to push the food around on his plate. "But here's the thing. I must marry her."

"By Jove, what what! Alex, you're in love," Pendleton said as he leaned back in his chair and started to laugh at his friend who had sworn off love.

"In love? Never! You should know me better than that, Penny. It's everyone else in this insane house that loves her. My sons are crazy about her. Hugh has grown so attached. I can't afford to have her leave. They'd be crushed. I can't do that to them again. I admit I first tried to get her to leave on her own accord, but she didn't go. And I couldn't be responsible for causing them more pain by sacking her myself. They'd blame me." Alexander took a sip of his coffee, knowing he would not tell of the intimacies they had exchanged nor the scandal which might ensue. He continued, "I really had hoped she would leave before they became too fond of her. But too late. And so, I thought that offering marriage was the best solution. She would be forced to stay and my sons would be safe from further heartbreak." Alexander continued, shrugging a shoulder. "Besides, I find her ... comely enough."

"And she turned you down?" Penny slowly shook his head from side to side. Meanwhile, his odd, all-knowing smile was driving Alexander mad.

"What?" he said with a frown.

"You want to marry her because your sons love her? That's the craziest reason for marriage I have ever heard."

Alexander glared at him through gray slits. He and Pendleton had had some arguments in their day but never had he wanted to knock out his lights as he did at this moment.

"Pendleton, you're on shaky ground," he hissed. "I want to protect them!"

"I'm sorry, old friend. I understand the protection part, but I wouldn't marry you either just because your sons love me. And frankly, wanting your protection would not be enough either," he advised, his guffaws turning into deep bellows. "But that's just me."

Alexander stabbed at the sausage on his plate. "I plan on asking her again," he said flatly.

"What? You are a glutton for punishment!" Penny couldn't contain his belly laugh.

"Well, now that I know that she has no memory of it, I think I have a better chance, don't you? Besides, with this threat on her life, I have to protect her. She's in real danger. I can keep closer watch if we were married. Maybe even discover who this devil is," Alexander said providing his logic to his friend.

"I don't know. Maybe you're right. With everything you've told me thus far, I would have to agree with you there, that the fall was not just an accident. Something really happened out there," the doctor said soberly, "though, I'm not sure marriage is the answer."

"Penny, I rode back there this morning before breakfast," Alexander responded, ignoring the jibe. "Those blocks are too heavy to have just slipped. They had to have been removed. But who would have known that she was going to be there yesterday?" he asked, puzzled.

"Do you have the letter?" Penny said, refocusing more on the important subject at hand.

Taking it out from his vest pocket, Alexander laid it on the table between them. Pendleton picked up the letter and read it several times. "Whoever wrote this wanted it to sound like a warning. But I think it's more like a threat."

"My conclusion precisely!" Alexander exclaimed as his fist hit the table, making the china clank loudly.

"But alone this letter means nothing. Are there any other signs?" Penny said as he handed the letter back to Alexander, who refolded it and put it back in his vest pocket.

"Yes, the first few weeks here, some stranger made inquiries after her in the town. Then, yesterday, Ana thought someone was watching her through a shop window. Ha! She thought it was me."

"What will you to do?"

"I first want to question Ana."

"I wouldn't do that Luttrell, it's too dangerous."

"What do you mean?"

"She doesn't remember for a reason. And when she does it will be on her terms. Questioning her will only confuse her."

"I see," Alexander said, feeling he had hit a dead end, his finger tapped the table. "Well, I'll start with Mr. Goodall at the post. He's the only person who had any contact with this villain."

"Well, that's a start."

"There is one other thing," Alexander said as he pushed his empty plate back. "I couldn't help but read some of her other letters."

"Luttrell, you conniving snoop!" his friend said as he shook his head.

"Penny, she had a few letters from this Charles person. Seems he's a cousin, professing love and all that rot. It appears that he's been offering marriage for quite some time. But I don't like him. Sumner mentioned him."

"Competition?"

"No, you fool. Competition? Really man! I just can't place it. I don't like him. Besides, I believe she's more interested in increasing her fortune as all women are, otherwise she would have married him," Alexander said. Almost under his breath, he added, "Maybe they are in it together?"

The doctor shook his head. "Luttrell, sometimes you worry me. Not everyone is Elizabeth. Well, I'm going to check on my patients and leave you to your plotting. I have to make some rounds. Today might be the day Mrs. Whitlaw is delivering. That will be number nine, you know. She's done this so many times I almost don't have to be there," he chuckled.

"I'll be off to town. Good luck my friend." Alexander said, absentmindedly. "Good luck to you."

"Oh, Penny, just one more thing," He said, stopping his friend at the door. "If you would check on mother, she seemed a bit feverish last night."

"Of course, my friend, with pleasure." And with that Doctor Pendleton left Alexander to his thoughts.

Alexander entered the Dunster mercantile with the direct intent to search out Mr. Goodall and question him on what he remembered about the mysterious perpetrator.

"Come into the back room, yer Lordship. No need to stand out 'ere discuss'n private business." Mr. Goodall rarely received such prominent guests and bowed his head in respect. "The missus will keep watch on the store." Mrs. Goodall was barely able to afford a curtsey as he shooed his frustrated and overly curious plump wife through the door.

"Thank you, Mr. Goodall." Alexander said as he looked around the crowded room filled with boxes, crates and barrels of wares for the store.

"I'm sorry, yer Lordship. Where are me manners? 'Ere's a chair fer ye. Let me dust it off for ye, sir," he said, as he grabbed a rag and swung it back and forth across the seat.

"Thank you," Alexander answered, feeling unusually uncomfortable with all the fuss. "I just want a few words. No need to trouble," he said as he took the seat offered.

"Is Miss Pembroke alright, sir? We 'erd about 'er accident at Conygar Tower. 'Tis a bloody shame that, bloody shame, yer Lordship," Mr. Goodall said as he sat on a dusty barrel.

"Actually, Mr. Goodall, that's the very reason I've come. You see I don't believe it to be an accident."

"Sir?" Goodall said as he moved the barrel closer, interested in this turn of events.

"No, I believe she was pushed," Alexander responded.

"Pushed, ye say? Why that's bloody terrible, yer Lordship." News of this nature was highly irregular in the sleepy town of Dunster.

"I've come to discover that there has been a man here inquiring about Miss Pembroke. I understand that you spoke to him directly."

"Yes sir, 'tis true," he said with a nod of his head.

Alexander sat on the edge of the chair. "What do you remember, Goodall?" His eyes darkened with intensity.

"Well I did think it bit queer, Miss Pembroke being new 'ere and all," Goodall said. He liked a good yarn and was enjoying the attention from the Duke. He leaned forward with his elbow on his knee. "Ye see 'twas a beautiful spring daiy. The streets were filled with the market. I remember because I said to the missus ..."

"Goodall! Get on with it, man!" Alexander barked, and the poor man jumped on the barrel.

"Sorry Milord," he said as he looked demurely at his hand. "Well, I remember 'e were a man of means. I could tell by the cut of his cloak."

"Yes, yes, what did he look like? What did he ask?" Lord Luttrell was becoming obviously agitated.

"I'm get'in to that. Now 'old on and let me remember?" he said placing a boney finger on the side of his nose. Mr. Goodall tilted his head in thought. "Well 'e was an average looking bloke I'd say. Not too young. Not too old, bout average 'ite, brownish 'air...."

"Well that could be anyone," Alexander responded, exasperated.

"Now wait, I remember one thing Milord, 'e was wearing an interesting ring," he said as he shook his head, satisfied with himself.

"Well good, that really narrows it down now. Many men wear rings, don't you think?" Alexander answered sarcastically.

"'e did ask if I knew of the whereabouts of Miss Pembroke, sir. 'e was specific in that I know for sure. 'e knew who 'e was lookin' for, 'e did."

"So maybe this 'bloke' is someone who knows Miss Pembroke?" Alexander was almost thinking out loud.

"Can't say ifin 'e do? Just 'e was specific 's all," Goodall said as he scratched his hairy chin."Good man," Alexander said as he stood up to leave. "You were helpful. I guess I was just hoping for more," he said looking discouraged, "If you remember anything else, anything now, mind you, you tell me," he ordered.

"Yes, sir, govnor … ah Milord," Goodall said as he stood up to walk Lord Luttrell out to the street.

Alexander decided to make further inquiries at the shop across from the town baker and the shop across the way. However, he left there discouraged and with even less information than he had received from Goodall. The sun was beginning to move lower on the horizon providing the sky with brilliant hues of pinks, purples and yellow. Mounting Cesar, he pushed on for home hoping to check on his injured charge.

When Alexander returned home, he was informed that Ana was sleeping. He checked-in on his mother, who was now confined to her bed with a mustard plaster on her chest. Alexander's exuberant mood from the morning was now replaced by frustration. Following supper, he returned to the library to ponder the situation and review the information he had gathered during the day. "Come in," he responded to the knock at the door. It was Chesterton.

"Miss Pembroke is awake, sir."

"Thank you, Chesterton. I will be right up," he said as he put out his cigar.

Ana is not going to remember what happened, he reminded himself as he made way to her room. He stood outside the door thinking about what to say, then knocked and waited for a reply.

Ana was lying in her bed, propped up by an effusion of pillows. She looked well, much better than he expected. He noticed her hair was in a neat braid which flowed down her shoulder instead of the mass of long thick curls that he had seen the previous night. The glow of the candles provided a soft light to the room. She looked inviting as she lay on her bed and it stirred him. There was a warm evening breeze coming through the window.

"Good evening Ana," he said cautiously. He felt awkward as he looked around the now familiar room having searched through her personals just the night before.

"Good evening sir," she replied, also feeling uncomfortable with his presence in her chamber.

"How are you feeling?" He drew the chair closer to her bed and sat down.

"Other than a headache and the pain in my shoulder I'm well, thank you," she said giving him a slight smile.

He smiled back gently, but immediately after there was a thick silence between them.

"Yes, that was … it was an unfortunate … I'm sorry you are in pain." Rarely was he without words. He so wanted to speak to her about what had happened, but Penny had warned him to not push her memory. He believed she may know who did this, but she did not remember and now may never. He felt frustrated and responsible all at the same time.

"Ana, I'm sorry…," he said as his voice was filled with an unknown emotion. Their eyes met and held for a moment.

"Frankly, sir, I don't know what happened. And I for one am not sure that I want to know." She smoothed the covers over her lap indicating her determination to not speak about it. He noticed the bandages on her hand and frowned.

"I understand." But he didn't understand. Suddenly he wanted to shake her. Didn't she want to know? He knew he did, but instead he said, "Well, I am glad you're feeling better." He had nothing else to say. Feeling uncomfortable, he got up quickly and moved towards the door. "Ana, I—" he started but became silent. He sighed deeply. "Sleep well," he said as he left her with her own thoughts and, frustrated, headed to his rooms for the night.

Ana played with the end of her long braid, wondering about the exchange that just happened between Lord Luttrell and herself. His apology was not necessary and most unusual. What was he apologizing for? Was he somehow responsible for what had happened to her? In reality she did want to know. But for whatever reason, she didn't want to talk to *him* about it. Somehow, he frightened her. He had often made her angry, but never frightened. It was unsettling. How did she end up so battered and bruised? No one would tell her. Everyone was so nice and so attentive. She liked the doctor. But she couldn't remember what had happened to her the day before no matter how hard she strained her brain. All she could remember was her walk to town to mail letters. Then she had eaten something at the bake shop. Yes, Lord Luttrell had been in town. And they had walked for a while. She had hoped to go to Conygar Tower but couldn't remember ever being there. And she couldn't remember how she got home. Her head ached from thinking. She could not remember more, as hard as she tried. Where did they walk to? What did they talk about? She leaned her head back on the pillow. Her eyes were getting heavy from the sleeping powders the doctor had prescribed. Where did they walk and what did they say she wondered as she drifted off to sleep?

.

CHAPTER 25

"Wake-up sir, wake-up!" Chesterton urged.

"Can't a man get sleep in his own home?" Alexander grumbled at being disturbed for a second night in a row, his eyes bleary with exhaustion.

"I'm sorry, sir. It's Miss Pembroke." Chesterton's face was lined with worry.

Sitting up, Alexander pushed the covers aside and swung his feet onto the cold floor.

"What time is it?" he asked, rubbing sleep from his eyes.

"It's about four in the morning, sir."

"It's an ungodly hour, Chesterton," he replied, squinting in the bright candlelight.

"Yes sir. Here's your robe." Chesterton stood ready to place the dressing gown on his master, creating a sense of urgency.

"What's happened? Has she taken a turn for the worse?" he said quickly as he tied his robe around his middle, now fully awake.

"She's remembered, sir. Mrs. C. can't console her. She can barely stand and she's packing to leave. If she's not stopped, I'm afraid she'll hurt herself, sir."

"I understand. Thank you, Chesterton. You did the right thing waking me."

"Thank you, sir. Is there anything I can do?" he asked wanting to be helpful.

"Yes, have brandy sent to her room."

"Very good, sir."

Standing outside Ana's room Alexander could hear Mrs. C. trying to control the situation. Not sure he could do much better, Alexander knocked on the door and entered without waiting for entrance. Ana spun around to see who had come in uninvited. She appeared unsteady on her feet, her face was feverish and her turquoise eyes glassy.

"You!" she hissed. "Get out!" she was holding the table for balance and threw her brush in his direction.

Damn brush, he thought. "Ana, calm down." Alexander's voice was stern as he ducked to avoid the object hurtling at his head. He noticed the thin white night shift she was wearing.

"Get out!" Ana said again, louder. Pendleton had warned of something like this.

"See what I'm contending with, sir? I can't get her back into bed. I'm afraid she'll hurt herself." Mrs. C. dabbed at her moist, fatigued eyes. She too was dressed in her nightclothes, her night cap askew from the apparent struggle, tassels of her silver hair hanging limp around her flushed face.

"I'll take over from here. I've sent for some brandy. I suggest you have a dram yourself before you retire to bed. I'll call if you're needed."

"No, Mrs. C.," Ana said as she grabbed for the woman's shawl. "Don't leave me with him," her eyes were wild with fear.

"Miss Ana, he'll not hurt you," she assured, pulling Ana's hand from the cloth. Ana's eyes pleaded with Mrs. C. as she left the two of them alone, quickly closing the door behind her.

Turning her back on Lord Luttrell, Ana returned to her packing. Alexander stood watching her hold onto the furniture as she moved between her dresser and trunk. As she passed the lit fire, the shadow of her naked figure shown through her light gown providing Alexander with a rather pleasant and enticing outline.

Rousting himself from his thoughts he said, "Ana you need to get back to bed. You're unsteady on your feet."

"No thanks to you, sir," she glared at him over her shoulder as she continued to clumsily fill her trunk. All she knew was that she needed to leave. She had to return home where it was safe. What first felt like a nightmare became real as she awoke to memories flooding into her head. Someone tried to kill her. Someone had pushed her at Conygar Tower. She felt desperate to be with Eliza, desperate to feel safe. Henry and Charles would protect her. She couldn't take this any longer. She thought she was strong enough to do this work. But this was more than she bargained for. With the loss of her parents and brother, and now, an attempt on her own life, Ana wanted more than anything to be that safe spinster aunt she had been running from.

There was a knock at the door. A servant girl entered with a small tray on which rested a bottle and two glasses. She placed it on the table where Ana was standing as indicated by her master, then left with a quick curtsey.

"Ana, what are you doing?" he asked gently watching her as she packed yet fearful to reach out to her to make her stop.

"I have to leave. You tried to kill me. Someone tried to kill me." Her hand came up to her mouth as if to stifle a scream. She stopped momentarily to gather her emotions.

Alexander took a step towards her. "Ana, I didn't do this to you." He needed to comfort her and fought to retain his focus to move slowly.

"You hate me. You've made that perfectly clear." Her voice was shaking with emotion as she kept her back to him to avoid his gaze.

"I didn't push you. I left you there, yes, and I'm so sorry for that. But I did not push you."

"I disgust you." Uncontrollable tears began to quietly spill down her flushed face.

"That's not true. I was just angry. I didn't push you," he said softly, feeling wretched that he had hurt her so.

He could see that she had stopped her packing for a moment, pausing to contemplate what he said, her hands rested on the dressing table to steady her shaking legs.

"Who else would've pushed me?" Her voice was barely audible.

A sense of relief engulfed him as he realized she might believe him. He took another step closer. "I don't hate you Ana. I want to protect you. I don't want any harm to come to you." His voice was soft and calming.

"But you … you left me!" her fists coming down on the table in a rage. "Who pushed me?" she said, her body shivering from the stifled sobs as she worked at keeping control of her emotions.

Now, standing directly behind her, his deep voice soft in her ear, "Ana, I will find out who did this. I'll protect you." He wanted desperately to take her in her arms and comfort her in her pain and confusion.

Ana turned quickly, facing him. He instinctively turned his head but stood firm to take the much-deserved force of her anger as her hand came down hard upon his cheek. "Protect me? You left me!" she said through her unsteady pain. "You hurt me!" She hit him again. He deserved it.

His arms suddenly surrounded her, holding her close to prevent her from flailing at him again. "I am sorry, Ana, I am sorry," he whispered into her hair. "If I knew you were in danger, I would never have left you in such a desolate spot. I feel absolutely responsible for what happened to you," he said softly as he felt her body shake with pain, rage, and fear. He began to stroke her head as it lay upon his chest. He could feel the dampness of her hot tears through his robe.

"You've been so brave, Ana, and I've been so stubborn. I never thought about what you've been through all these months. I could only see what I wanted to see. I've acted inexcusably," he said quietly. "Ana I'll make it up to you. I'll make sure you're not hurt again. I'll find who did this. They'll pay for their crime. I promise this." His voice was filled with tenderness. Though noticing that she was no longer shaking, he continued to hold her in his arms, wanting her to feel protected by them.

After a few minutes he loosened his hold and poured the brandy. Offering it to her, he said, "Here, drink this. It will help settle your nerves."

She took the glass and drank, scrunched her face as the alcohol burned the back of her throat.

"Good girl," he said as he took the empty glass.

"Ana, you'll not leave. Everyone needs you here. You belong here. Besides, you're not well." He encircled her in his arms once again not because she needed him to, but because he needed to feel secure. "When you're well, Ana, you'll be returning to your sister's home for a visit, correct?"

He could feel her nod her head against his chest. Ana felt comforted, encircled in his strong arms and allowed herself to relax. She was willing to believe him and accepted his protection. She felt warm and safe. She closed her eyes and leaned against his muscular frame. She could feel his arms tightening around her. He was right, she did feel unsteady on her feet and his supportive arms were welcoming. Exhaustion began to overtake her.

"Mother told me your sister's expecting," he continued. She again nodded against his chest. "This is happy news for your family." He rested his chin atop her head thinking her the perfect height for him. "Ana, I'm so sorry for your losses." He began to gently massage her back with his hand as she lay against his chest. He could feel her body begin to shiver again as relaxation gave way to emotion and she began to silently weep. "You see what a brave girl you've been?" he continued softly. "Even with all you've lost you came here to fight with me, the ogre." He heard a small chuckle at his reference to himself and felt better for it.

"Come, let me get you into your bed." And with that he swept her off her feet and into his arms. In several strides he gently laid her on her bed. He pulled her feet down into the covers and then pulled the blanket up over her shoulders and sat on the edge of the bed. Placing a hand on each side of her by her shoulders, he propped himself up so that he could better look into her face. He could see she was thinner. He saw the dark circles under red swollen eyes. Her cheeks were wet from her tears and he felt sympathy towards her situation.

"How are you feeling, Ana?" he inquired, genuinely concerned for her well-being.

"Dizzy," she answered with a small crooked smile.

"I'm not surprised. That was a nasty fall. It's a miracle I found you alive."

"*You* found me?" she said, now aware of a gentle expression on his face she had not noticed before.

"Yes, you were in the ravine below the tower." He pushed back a curl that had fallen onto her forehead. "Ana, do you remember anything about the person who pushed you from the tower window?"

She seemed to shiver under the covers. "He was wearing a black cape … I think."

"You didn't see a face?"

She closed her eyes tight and began to shake visibly under the covers as the memory of the fall became all too vivid. Realizing he was asking too soon, he stopped. He gathered her into his arms and held her close. Softly, he began to rock her back and forth. "That's alright, Ana, you don't have to remember anything now. We'll wait until you are stronger," he cooed. "I'll keep you safe."

Pulling her arms from under the covers Ana wrapped them around his muscled neck.

"Thank you for saving me," she whispered, her breath warm and soft against his cheek.

The vision of her shapely form through her thin night shift swiftly returned to him. He knew he needed to pull away but she held onto him fast.

"Ana," his voice was deep and husky. He looked into her face. It was so close. His blue eyes darkened with passion. He longed to kiss her. But he knew she was not well. Anyway, he wanted more than just a kiss from her. He wanted all of her. But she was too weak, too vulnerable. He gently laid her head onto the pillow. But she did not let go. And he did not want to let go of her. He swung his legs onto the bed and lay on top of the covers, holding her close to him, feeling the warmth of her body next to his, keenly aware of her supple warm breasts pushing up against him. He couldn't help the stirring of his desire, but was determined not to act on his feelings. He was just going to just allow her to feel comforted by being in his arms until she fell asleep and then he was going to leave.

More than anything, Ana wanted to feel sheltered. She knew she should let him go. But she felt protected in his arms and grateful for his rescue. She was holding on for dear life. And there was something in his nearness that was more than just a safe harbor. There was a gentleness and kindness she had not known from him before. He was showing genuine concern. Her eyes were heavy from emotion, the brandy, and the sleeping powders. Her body was exhausted from the trauma. She quickly drifted off into a deep sleep.

Lady Catherine stood outside Ana's door and listened for movement. The sun had barely broken the horizon. The interior of the house remained dark as the pink and golden rays of dawn had not yet penetrated the hallways and windows. She knocked gently, listening again at the door. Silence. Slowly turning the knob, she entered. Whoever she was relieving was going to get a severe reprimand for sleeping.

Just as the door began to slowly open, so did Alexander's eyes. To his amazement he found Ana still in his arms, sound asleep. He had not intended to fall asleep by her side but own his exhaustion made it impossible to do anything but. Gazing at her, he thought of how peaceful she looked next to him, her auburn curls spilling out over his arm and the pillow. The warmth of her body invited him to remain close.

As he began to close his eyes, he noticed movement near the door of her room. Slowly he lifted his head to see that his mother had entered and was quietly closing the door behind her. He watched as she glanced over at the empty chair. Seeing that no one was sitting there she placed her hands on her hips and shook her head in disgust.

He hoped she'd leave and not notice him. But as he watched his mother draw closer to the bed, he saw her eyes grow wide with surprise.

"Shhh!" he said, silently, placing a finger to his lips.

"Alexander!" she whispered, obviously startled and shocked by the scene before her.

Slowly, Alexander pulled his arm out from under Ana's head where it was resting peacefully. "Shhh," he said again as he slowly sat up.

"Alexander, what are you doing here?" she asked, her voice more husky than quiet. "What has happened here?" she said as her eyebrows rose in speculation.

"Nothing mother, I just fell asleep is all," he said softly as he stood up, not wanting to disturb Ana's slumber.

"In Ana's bed? In your arms?" Lady Catherine said, happily shocked.

"It's not what it appears, mother," Alexander whispered both reluctant to explain and frustrated about the interrogation. "She remembered what happened to her last night. She was inconsolable."

"So, this is how you consoled her?" his mother smiled a knowing grin which infuriated Alexander.

"Mother, I just held her until she was asleep. Don't place too much on what you see. I too must have dozed," he whispered.

"Could it be you're developing feelings toward her?" Lady Catherine said, ever the romantic.

"No, Mother, you know my stand on that," he said through clenched teeth, angered now by his mother's persistent meddling. "Besides, what are you doing out of your own sickbed? You're not well and need your rest," he continued in an attempt to change the subject.

"Nonsense, it's my turn and I'm here to fulfill my duties. Unless you want me to leave the two of you alone," she said.

Alexander shot her a look of contempt.

"No, Mother, I'll return to my own bed. And so shall you, yours. You're not well. Send around another servant. I'll stay here until she arrives. And you, good lady, off to bed." He whispered as he opened the door and unceremoniously ushered her out into the cold dark hallway against her protests. Closing the door Alexander returned to Ana's bedside to stand watch until his relief came.

Quietly pulling the chair closer to the bed, he sat down. He was angry that his mother found him lying with Ana tightly wrapped in his arms, yet he was grateful that it was his mother who had found them, not one of the servants who would gossip.

A thin stream of golden light broke through the curtains and fell softly across Ana's face, illuminating her sleeping features. More and more, Alexander felt drawn to her, rationalizing that it was just a man's physical need for a woman. He found her features to be perfectly formed, the curve of her brow, the slight upturn of her nose, the fullness of her lips, the flash of gold in her turquois eyes when she became angry.

His thoughts again returned to the question at hand—who and why. He shook his head. There was a soft knock at the door. Alexander quickly got up to find Riya standing in the dimly lit hall.

"Riya, I wasn't expecting you," he said, anticipating another serving girl.

"No Sahib. I come after your mother."

Stepping out into the hallway he decided now was as good a time as any. It had been several days since he had seen Riya and he had been cross with her. As a result, she had kept herself scarce, occupying her time with her studies.

"Riya, I need to apologize for barking at you the other day. I was … distressed. But not at you." Alexander began to feel that he owed everyone on his staff some sort of an apology lately.

There's nothing to apologize for, Sahib," she said quietly, surprised that he would make such an offer.

"And another thing, if you're to be an English lady you must stop calling me Sahib."

"What shall I call you, Sahib?"

"Riya, you're more family than servant. Call me … Sir Alexander." He felt uncomfortable himself with the change, however there was no other suitable suggestion.

Yes, Sahib, Sir … Lord Alexander," she said demurely, moved at being considered family.

"No. Not Sahib, Sir. Just Lord or Sir Alexander will be fine." He smiled at his young charge.

"Yes, Sir Alexander," she said timidly.

"Now go in quietly for Miss Pembroke is still sleeping. She's had a difficult night." He opened the door so Riya could enter. His exhaustion was returning.

"Yes, Sir Alexander," she said softly.

"And Riya, thank you," he smiled.

"Thank you, Sir," she smiled back as she closed the door.

Though rays of early morning sun were now streaming into halls and rooms and sounds from the kitchen deep below were softly floating on the air, Alexander knew that his plan was to return to his bed for desperately needed rest.

It was nearly noon when Alexander came down to the dining room. He was genuinely surprised to be greeted by all the womenfolk of his household. He was especially surprised to find Ana sitting, fully dressed, at the table with a full plate.

"Good morning Mother, Riya, Ana," he said as he nodded to them all.

"Good morning Sir Alexander," Riya said strongly.

"It's more like good afternoon wouldn't you say?" Lady Catherine chided lightheartedly as she wiped her red nose.

Ignoring his mother's jibe completely, Alexander walked over to the sideboard to fill his plate as a servant poured coffee into his cup.

"How are you this morning, Mother?" he said, pleased to see his mother in her usual "good humor."

"Doctor Pendleton has already come and gone. He's checked on each of us and determined that we are fit as fiddles," she said, though her voice sounded raspy. Alexander looked askance at his mother, unconvinced at the story on her health.

"Ana, I'm surprised you're up this morning," he said as he made his way to his chair.

"Doctor Pendleton told me I was surprisingly well and free to leave the confines of my bed. So, here I am." Her bright smile dazzled Alexander's senses.

"You're well then?" he asked, studying her face and seeing that the dark circles were gone and color had returned to her cheeks.

"Yes. He did charge me to rest, especially if I felt dizzy or if my head ached. But I hope to resume my duties tomorrow."

"As long as you take it slowly, he said," Lady Catherine reminded her.

"Yes, as long as I take it slowly. I do have Riya to help." She reached over and patted her friend's hand.

"So, you're not leaving us then?" he asked, curious if she remembered the events of the early morning. As a matter of fact, he wondered if she had retained her memory at all of what happened, she seemed so bright and chipper.

"No, not until I hear from my sister. You remember, she is due to give birth very soon."

Alexander could not help but raise one eyebrow at her comment, feeling it was in reference to their early morning encounter. He thought she was playing coy, wanting to keep what happened out of family discussion and just between the two of them.

"Yes, that's right," he said before filling his mouth with a forkful of kippers.

The noise from the hall made them all turn to look as Geoffrey and Hugh both came bounding into the room.

"Boys, what have I told you about running in this house," he reminded his sons.

"Sorry Father," Geoffrey said as he gave Hugh a slight shove. "Good morning Riya," he added shyly. "Good morning Master Geoffrey," she responded, also a bit too shyly for Alexander's liking. He frowned noting he would have to address this budding romance.

"Miss Pembroke! Miss Pembroke! You're up. Are you well?" Hugh quickly ran to her side as she pushed herself from the table to be embraced by his open arms, wincing slightly at the pain in her shoulder.

"Yes, Hugh. I'm well, thank you." She hugged him back. "It's so good to see you. I've missed you."

"I've missed you too. Will you be teaching us today?" His face was hopeful.

"No, sweetie, not today. Tomorrow." He responded with a big toothless smile. "Oh, you lost another tooth." She patted him on the shoulder and again feeling the pain in her own shoulder. Ana looked up to see that Geoffrey was standing close by. "And how are you today, Geoffrey?"

"I'm glad to see you're doing better. We were so worried."

Ana extended her hand to him. "Geoffrey, I so appreciate your concern, I understand from your grandmother that you were very helpful the night of my accident. Thank you for helping to save my life."

Geoffrey looked at the floor, "It was nothing, Father did the real work," he said glancing proudly towards his father.

"No Geoffrey, he couldn't have done it without your help. I'm very proud of you. I'm very proud of both of you," she said as she continued to hold Geoffrey's hand and hugged Hugh with her other arm.

Riya stood up and indicated that they follow her to the nursery.

"Go with Riya. I'll see you tomorrow." Both boys dutifully followed Ana's direction.

Watching their interaction, Alexander was more determined than ever. Marriage to Ana would be the best thing for his sons and the best way to keep her safe. He knew he had to work harder at convincing her that this would be the best solution for both of them, even though love did not enter into the picture.

He glanced up at his mother who had been watching the scene unfold. She had that knowing look on her face.

"What?" he asked her, his old dark scowl returning to his brow.

"Alexander, I've nothing to say, nothing at all. Ana, my dear, shall we take a stroll in the garden? The air will do us both good."

The two women left Lord Luttrell to finish his meal alone with his thoughts.

CHAPTER 26

Within several days Ana resumed her former routine with the boys, who required much-needed attention. The Conygar Tower event left them changed and distracted. Geoffrey's level of increased maturity was tangible; he appeared taller and his voice took on a deeper, richer tenor. Sadly, Hugh appeared petulant and needy. Lady Catherine's head cold was taking its time to heal and had moved into her chest. Otherwise, the household appeared to have returned to some semblance of normalcy. Though Alexander and Ana had several discussions concerning the boys, the incident of the tower loomed unspoken between them.

As the days wore, on the incident returned to her memory. It crept into most of her waking thoughts. She found it even seeping into her dreams: The Duke's proposal, his kiss, his disdain, and the feeling of falling ... falling ... falling.

It was obvious to Ana that the Duke painfully swallowed his pride to protect her. He had been so horribly clear about how he felt about her on that fateful day. And now she was, after all, a member of his household and he was just doing his duty.

She believed he didn't make the attempt on her life. But she remembered the way he wiped his mouth from her kiss. It was more painful than knowing someone might want her dead. And the sorrow of realizing she loved a man who did not love her broke her heart. But she had a job to do and she was determined to do it well. Somehow, she needed to put it behind her. If nothing else, he would protect her.

Secretly, however, she cherished the memory of how gentle he had been with her the night they lay together in her bed. Her memory of his strong arms holding her, keeping her safe and warm often lulled her into sleep. She longed to be held by him again, to feel his hard-muscled body next to hers, to experience the scent of him, and to be kissed by him. But he had kept his distance since that night, confirming her suspicion of what he truly felt for her.

Alexander had not wanted to bring up the Conygar Tower incident until he felt Ana was strong enough to deal with what had happened. He remembered how frightened and fragile she was the night she remembered, the way she visibly shook in his arms when he questioned her. Though she appeared to be on the mend, he did not want to distress her again. But his own need to find out who threatened his household was strong. He knew he was going to have to re-open the subject and today was as good a day as any.

He had continued to make several more inquiries in town, but to no avail. No one at the market or in the shops was able to provide any information. No one seemed to remember anyone with a black cape. Even the innkeeper at the Rose and Crown reported on having only two guests for that week, the two Misses Davenports on holiday to visit with their brother the Reverend Mr. Davenport.

Alexander knew that Ana alone might hold the key to whoever made this heinous attack on her life. He had to tell Ana he had found the letter in her letter box; it was his only possible link to the scoundrel who pushed her. She had to know. He also knew he had to broach the subject of marriage once again. He couldn't accept no for an answer. It was the best solution for his family and the only way he could truly protect her.

But as the days passed, he found it harder and harder to keep his desire for her in check. Whenever they were in the same room, Alexander had to make a conscious effort to keep his distance. He had to force himself not to look too intently at her, yet all he could think about was how she felt l next lying to him and how she looked in that thin night shift with the firelight casting shadows of her form, and how she responded to his kiss.

He was also frustrated with the remarks made by both Lady Catherine and Dr. Pendleton. That they insinuated he had any feelings for this young woman was preposterous. Why couldn't a man just desire a woman? She was, after all alluring and sensual. Why did people always assume that love had to play a part? And who wouldn't want to protect someone whose life was in danger?

Having received a message via Mrs. C. earlier that day, Ana kept the appointed time with the Duke as requested and knocked on the library door. She waited to be invited into the room. Lord Luttrell was sitting at his desk, deeply engrossed in his work. He stopped immediately when heard Ana's gentle tapping at the entrance.

"Ana, come in." He was cordial as he offered her the red leather chair. He enjoyed watching her walk across the room, and could not help admire her in her dress. "You are looking well today," he said, his eyes instinctively scanning her form.

"Thank you, sir. I'm feeling rather well today," she responded quietly, feeling uncomfortable at being in his presence, knowing the disgust he felt for her.

The brief interchange was followed by a more uncomfortable silence. Alexander fiddled with some papers on his desk. As the quiet moments dragged on, Ana began to feel a tightening in her chest. It was becoming an all too familiar pain when she was near him. A longing for something she knew she was never going to receive: his love. She found herself studying her hands so as to not let him see what she was feeling in her eyes. She waited for him to speak. He placed his pen at the top of his desk.

"Ana, we have to discuss what happened that day at Conygar Tower." There, he said it. It was like a weight lifted off his back. *The subject is open*, he thought.

"There's nothing to discuss," Ana said flatly.

"There is everything to discuss. I need to find out who made this attempt on your life. Ana, don't you see, because you are still alive, this person may make another attempt. And the next time you may not be so fortunate. I have a responsibility to protect you and I fully plan on remaining true to my word." He looked at Ana for her response.

She continued to sit quietly in the chair. She almost resembled a lost child, eyes downcast, twisting a button on the bodice of her dress. She was obviously distressed, but he had to talk to her about this.

"Ana," he said softly, "look at me."

Slowly, Ana lifted her head, her turquoise eyes brimming from unspent tears.

"Sir, I really don't wish to speak of this," she begged.

"I understand. But I must continue. I went to town asking if anyone could recall a stranger from that day. I spoke with Mr. Goodall. No one has been able to provide any additional information. I have no clue. I do, however, have a letter." He took his risk.

"What letter? Someone sent you a letter?" fear twisted at Ana's face as the tear silently rolled down her cheeks, her eyelashes glistening from the moisture. Alexander ached to take her into his arms, to comfort her and let her know he would keep her safe. But he knew he had to keep his distance.

"Ana, I have the letter you received all those weeks ago. You remember, the one you accused me of sending to you." He watched intently for her reaction.

"Oh, that letter." Suddenly, an old familiar spark of anger lit up Ana's eyes. "Where did you get it?" she demanded. The intensity in her eyes made Alexander hold his breath.

"Ana, I had no idea how long you would have remained unconscious," he started.

"So, you went through my things? I'll not stand for this. Who gave you leave to go through my personal things?" Using this as her excuse, she stood up to move towards the door.

"Ana. Come back and sit down!" The stern tone of his voice made Ana stop in her tracks. She stood silently, deciding whether to leave or stay. What she wanted most of all was to run. She wanted to leave and get on with her day. She wanted to get on with her life as if nothing had ever happened to threaten to take it away from her. She wanted to forget Lord Luttrell had ever kissed her. She wanted this nightmare of pain to end.

"Ana, you have to face this," he said, his voice regaining most of its calm. "You can't run away from this."

She knew he was right. He could see she knew it. Her head and shoulders drooped. She turned around slowly and walked back to the leather chair to take the seat she had just vacated. She looked completely dejected.

"What do you think I might know?" Her voice was flat and emotionless.

"You may know who did this. Just take a minute and think back. What exactly happened?" he asked in measured tone.

Ana closed her eyes and sat very still. Alexander wondered if she was even breathing, she was so still. He could see that the knuckles of her hands were turning white as she tightly gripped the arms of the chair.

"It's alright Ana. You're safe now," he said softly, wanting to reassure her.

"All I remember," she said, her eyes still tightly closed. "I was … I was confused. I … I remember climbing into the tower to get away from ..." She bit her bottom lip. "The stones were wet and slippery. It smelled of damp moss and earth. I … I had to hold onto the wall as I climbed. It felt cold and slimy. I don't remember hearing anything but the sound of the wind and … my footsteps … and as I climbed, suddenly the stones, the stones gave way. I felt something pushing. It was like someone was pushing me. I tried to turn and grab onto something, anything. I knew I was falling … falling …" She stopped. Covering her face as if to blot out the memory, it felt so real she could smell the sea.

"Please sir, I can't," she gulped for air.

"Ana, you must." His voice was firm yet gentle. "Take a minute to gather yourself."

He leaned over his desk to offer his handkerchief. "Here, blow your nose."

She took the cloth offered and after a good blow she dabbed at her eyes. Taking a few deep breaths, she continued.

"I remember … There was a black cape, a dark hat. His face was completely covered." She looked up suddenly at Alexander. All the color had drained out of her tearstained face. "I remember a ring."

"A ring?" he asked, his brow furrowed as he remembered Goodall mentioning a ring.

"As I tried to grab onto something to prevent myself from falling. I remember seeing a ring. But it couldn't have been." Ana shook her head in disbelief.

"What do you mean?"

"It was familiar to me. It … it looked so like to my brother's ring."

"Maybe this person had a similar ring. Do you know where your brother got the ring?" *Now we're on to something*, he thought, excited by the prospect.

"My father had it made for his sixteenth birthday. No one could have that ring but Miles. And he is dead." Her eyes were wide with fear and disbelief at the possibility of her brother's ghost come back from the grave to harm her. But she quickly shook the thought from her head. The person who pushed her was much more than an apparition.

"Yes, Ana, I know. I am sorry," he replied, sensing her pain.

"He was killed in battle in Virginia in the War between the States. He is not buried here. Who would have been able to get his ring? I don't believe it was returned to Father. And why come here to England and try to kill me? That just doesn't make any sense." Her confusion was evident on her face.

"No, it doesn't. But a coldblooded killer does not make sense, Ana. Insanity never makes sense." He opened the top drawer of his desk and removed the letter. "What about this?" he asked handing it over to her.

Quickly reading it over, "In light of what's happened, this feels like a threat. Whoever wrote it made it sound more like a warning," Ana swiftly handed the letter back, almost as if the paper was burning her hands. She couldn't bear to hold it any longer.

"Ana, do you recognize the handwriting at all?"

She shook her head.

"Look at it again. Maybe the paper … something," He tried to hand it back to her but she refused to take it. "Ana look at the watermark, do you recognize the paper?"

"It's the same paper you use," she said flatly.

"No, it is similar. But it is not my paper. Just look at it," he said as he held it out to her again.

Gingerly, Ana took the letter back and held it up to the light.

"Oh my!" she exclaimed in surprise.

"What?" Alexander stood up and came around his desk to get a better look at what she was seeing through the light.

"It's the same paper maker my father used." She handed the sheet back over to Alexander who stood and studied the watermark through the light of the window.

"My father always purchased his stationary from Shields and Glass in London. But many people must buy paper from them."

"That is true, but it narrows it down some." He was hopeful of any new lead.

There was a knock at the door; Chesterton come with the weekly post.

"What is it Chesterton?" Alexander snapped, feeling a bit peeved at the disturbance.

"There's been a delivery for Miss Pembroke, sir." Chesterton answered knowing Ana was waiting on news from her sister.

"Oh!" Ana stood up, her mood brightening. "It must be from Eliza and Henry." She took the letter from the silver tray and opened it quickly. A beaming smile crossed her face as she looked up at the Duke. "She had a son!" Suddenly all the anxiety of the past conversation dissipated and was replaced by the joyful event.

"Congratulations, Ana!" Alexander was happy for her news, yet fully aware that it also meant she was to depart from under his protection.

"Yes, Miss Pembroke, congratulations," added Chesterton, "If I may take the liberty to share the good news, Miss?"

"Thank you both. Yes, by all means, share the good news." Turning towards Alexander, Ana continued, "Sir, I must get ready to leave. She'll need me," Ana so wanted to leave. For her the conversation had ended. She turned to go without being discharged from his presence.

"Ana you can't go. It is not safe." Alexander moved to stop her. He reached out to take her arm, her soft flesh warm to his touch.

"But I must go. I need to go. I have to see my sister," her eyes grew wide with anxiety. She looked down at his hand encircling her arm as her eyes began to fill with tears.

Alexander could see that she was right. She needed to go. She needed to be with her people. She needed to share in this happy time. He couldn't stop her. Maybe it would be for the best. The visit would calm her nerves. He released his hold.

"You'll take my coach. My men will be with you. You'll be safer that way." He stopped and thought for a minute.

"Where did you say your sister lived?"

"London."

"Shields and Glass is in London you say?" He looked at Ana and she nodded. Alexander bit his bottom lip.

"All the better, I'll accompany you. I can investigate the papermakers and see what I can find out while you visit with your sister." He was determined.

"But sir—" Ana began to protest.

"There's no other way. I'm coming along. Now let's get packing." And in a few long strides he stood by the door ushering Ana out into the hall to make ready for their journey.

The topic of marriage never came up.

CHAPTER 27

*A*na and Lord Luttrell were seated in the coach and four on the long drive to London. They had left Riya with a great deal of responsibility for a young girl of seventeen; Lady Catherine was still unwell and of course there were two rambunctious boys to contend with. Alexander took some comfort that Chesterton and Mrs. C. would be available for much-needed assistance.

Alexander felt anxious leaving his family, especially with his mother now ill. But he believed he had no other choice. He looked over at Ana who had pressed herself into the opposite corner of the coach. She kept her gaze pasted to the passing countryside and remained silent. It was an odd and uncomfortable silence between them.

He realized how fragile she still was from her ordeal and was glad that she would be able to spend some time with her family. Alexander was sure that she would rejuvenate amongst her own people. He noticed her eyes had closed from the sway of the carriage.

Ana was not asleep however. She remained deep in her own thoughts and needed to close her eyes for the sake of privacy. She needed to see Eliza. There was so much to share. She always felt stronger when she was with her sister. Now there was the new baby boy. Ana's arms ached to hold him. They had named him Miles. Miles would have been so pleased to know his new nephew carried his name. It was going to be so different not to have him there to celebrate with the family and not to have her parents there also.

She thought back on that last Christmas Day when they had all been together, when Eliza and Henry shared their news. How things had changed in those months. And now there was someone out to kill her. She wanted to tell Eliza, to rush into her arms and feel her loving protection. But she knew she had to keep it from her. Eliza would be too distressed at knowing. No one in her family must know. Not even Henry; not even Charles.

Ana looked up to find the deep blue eyes of Lord Luttrell studying her. She immediately felt uncomfortable by the intense power of his gaze.

"Sir, I have one request," she said, breaking the cold silence that enveloped the coach since they left Dunster Castle hours ago.

Startled to hear her voice he said, "Oh, I thought you were asleep."

"No," she answered plainly, "just in thought."

"What is your request?"

"Please don't inform my family about what happened," she said with a steady and sure voice.

"For heaven sakes, why?" he answered, surprised by her entreaty.

"They have been through enough. I don't want to worry them," she answered determinedly.

"Ana, they might have some clue. I don't think your request is wise."

"Maybe not, but I'll decide when to tell them, if I tell them. They are not your family. They're mine and I have the right to tell them when I am ready." Her voice was becoming strained with emotion, "I shall not place them in harm's way."

Seeing her distress, he conceded against his will. "I still don't think it's a good idea, but I will abide by your request."

Ana again turned her head towards the window to hide her tears. "Thank you," she said softly.

The coach continued on the roadway as the mist of the approaching evening encircled the silent travelers heading towards their destination for the night.

"It is getting close to nightfall, yer Lordship," Rollins informed them through the ceiling hatch. "We will be entering Salisbury shortly."

"Very good Rollins, we will stop for the night." Alexander ordered.

Ana's turquoise eyes flashed open wide. Stop for the night? She had not thought of the prospect of spending a night at an inn with Lord Luttrell. This was most inappropriate and even more so, awkward.

Seeing the look of shock on her face he assured her, "Don't worry Ana. We will have separate rooms," though he couldn't deny that the thought of sharing a room with her was, however, an intriguing prospect.

He had not broached the subject of marriage again, but concluded that the venue of the inn would be the best opportunity, especially before she reunited with her family. He decided that a public place would provide the perfect setting.

Ana found her room adequate for its purpose and supposed that Lord Luttrell found his room more than sufficient. The bed was clean, though a bit lumpy, and there was a warm fire burning in the grate which provided a small sense of cheeriness to the otherwise drab interior.

There was a light knock at her door. "Yes?" she asked hesitantly, unsure of who would be there.

"Ana, it is I. I have planned for a small supper down in the dining room. Please join me," Alexander announced through the closed door.

She opened the door, "Thank you sir. I am a little hungry," she answered, her smile taking him by surprise.

Allowing her to lead the way, Alexander enjoyed following her down the small hallway to a secluded dining room of the inn. He pointed to the small table set with an array of foods and wine.

Seeing that she was securely seated, Alexander took the place across from her so that he would be able to speak to her directly over their meal. He knew this was calculated but he needed to re-open the subject of marriage in a place where Ana was most unlikely to become emotional.

"How was your carriage ride?" he inquired, trying to make small conversation. He filled her glass with the port.

"It was fine, sir."

"And your room," he said as he handed her a plate of cold meat.

"Adequate also."

He took a long swallow from his glass, feeling frustrated with what he considered his trivial chatter.

"Is there something wrong sir?" Ana sensed his frustration.

"No, Ana, nothing's wrong. It's just I have to bring up one more item with you."

She put her fork on her plate unsure of what else he could possibly discuss with her that would be weighing so heavily on him. "What is it?" she asked.

He picked up his fork and began to push the food around on his plate and put it back down again.

"Ana, remember when we were both at Conygar Tower, before I left you there … alone?" He reached out across the table and covered her hand in his.

A shiver ran up her arm from his touch. "Yes." She looked directly into his darkening eyes. She felt cold and detached. Yes, she remembered. She remembered all too well.

"Ana, I had asked you to marry me."

Ana pulled her hand out from under his and quickly placed it in her lap. *This is too much*, she thought, *how could he bring up this topic?*

"Ana, hear me out. I don't want an answer. Just hear me out," he implored.

"I'll listen," she said quietly yet most defiantly.

"I'll share with you again my reasons for asking you for your hand in marriage. And in light of what has happened, I have more reasons to believe that this is the right thing to do. My sons need you, Ana. My mother needs you. I need to protect you. I will give you a good life. You'll be safe with me." He stopped and studied her turquoise eyes. They seemed as cold as stone and unaffected by his proposal.

"But your feelings for me have not changed. Am I right?" She stated tersely.

"No, my feelings have not changed," he conceded finishing his glass and refilling it.

Ana nodded several times. The thought of being in a loveless marriage was too painful. Especially because she knew she loved him and that he could not return her affections. She opened her mouth to respond.

Alexander held up his hand. "Don't say no yet. Think on it, Ana," he implored before she could speak.

Think on it, he asked. She must talk to Eliza. Eliza could help her decide. Thinking on his request did not mean she was agreeing to a farce of a marriage. All it meant was that she was to think on it. She could do that, she decided.

"I'll think on it," she said as a cold shiver of foreboding ran down her back.

He sat back in his chair feeling satisfied with her answer as if a weight had been lifted off his shoulders. "I promise if you agree to our union, you'll not be sorry."

Ana picked up her fork and poked at her meal, having lost her appetite, while Alexander reached for his glass. He studied her as she ate. Her dark auburn hair had unruly curls, her upturned nose was charming, her full lips inviting and the flash of her turquoise eyes tantalizing. Finally, he attacked his own food with gusto.

Having completed their meal in silence, Alexander led Ana back to her room. Feeling satisfied with himself, he decided to risk one more thing. Before Ana was able to open her door, he took her by the shoulders and turned her around to face him.

"Ana, I'm pleased that you will consider my request," he said, his voice was deep with passion, his eyes dark with desire, "You'll not be sorry." And with that he gathered her into his arms. His mouth came down onto hers, gently at first, longingly. He had wanted to taste her again, impatient to hold her close to him. He wanted to feel her hungry response to him as he had before. He parted her lips with his own, searching for her desire. He had never wanted a woman as much as he wanted this one. But Ana remained lifeless in his arms. There was no familiar surrender to his passion. Confused by her lack of response, he pulled away to search her eyes, and found them unmoved.

"I will think on your offer of marriage and no more, sir. Good night." With that she turned and left him standing speechless in the hallway.

As she closed the door, she leaned her back on the coolness of the hard wood. She could not believe she had been so callous. Lord Alexander Luttrell, Duke of Exmoor, was asking for her hand in marriage. Not once, but twice. She didn't know how she managed to remain so cold when his advances left her hot and shaken, yearning for more. But the memory of his kiss at Conygar Tower had cut deep. Ana knew if she accepted, she would be marrying him for his children's sake, to friend his mother, and for his protection. Only for that. What would happen when he tired of her in his bed? She did not want a life tied to a man who would look to others once the heat of passion died because there was no love to sustain it. She told him that she would think on it. Yet she already knew her answer. Exhausted, Ana slowly walked over to her bed.

The fire had died down in the grate. She slowly took off her dress and placed it on a nearby chair, her petticoats and shoes as well. As she lay in the cold darkness of the drab room looking at the water-stained ceiling, two large drops rolled from her eyes onto the pillow under her head. Suddenly, unable to control the sobs, Ana rolled over into the pillow to have a good hard cry.

Alexander returned to his room stunned by Ana's cold, hard response to his advances. Never in his life had a woman responded so in his arms. If she had slapped him, he would have been able to understand. But this was an insult as he had never experienced. He could not comprehend her unwarranted behavior towards him. They had kissed before. Her responses were always inviting, even demanding more of him. But this? Why would she have cut him so deeply? Hadn't he saved her life? Wasn't he offering his protection? Hadn't he comforted her? If love was so all important to this wench, she was just going to have to find it elsewhere. Alexander took off his coat and laid it across the chair in his room. He threw another log on the dying fire and sat on the edge of his bed. Who did she think she was, treating him thusly? Pulling off his boots, he hurled them into the corner, angry at her for rebuffing his advances. He laid on his bed, with an arm covering his forehead. God, she tasted so good to him. He wanted all of her.

In the quiet of the night he thought he heard the faint sound of crying as he drifted into a deep fitful sleep.

CHAPTER 28

*T*he cold hard rain made the muddied roadway difficult for travel. Neither Alexander nor Ana had said more than three words to each other for the rest of the uncomfortable ride into London. Both were deceptively fixated on the passing gray scenes from outside their respective windows. Both were deep in thought.

Ana tried her best to put on a brave and nonplussed face though her eyes were still rimmed red from crying the night before. She was shocked by his second request for her hand. He continued to insist his proposal was out of a desire to protect her rather than out of any feelings of warmth. And their past contentious relationship proved it to be nothing more. It was too painful to agree to a loveless marriage, especially when she was the one who was in love and the feelings were not reciprocated. Her response to his kiss last night was in harsh retaliation to the disgust that he had shown at the tower. Though she had agreed to think on his proposal, she was angry at herself for entertaining such a painful idea to such a cold, cold man. And yet, she was so drawn to him.

Alexander remained confounded by her negative response to his marriage proposal. He thought because she had agreed to consider it, she would've been more open towards his physical overture before they parted to their separate rooms. He knew he needed to protect her from the danger she was in. But now he was angry that she rejected him so coldly, for he was not just anybody.

He was the Duke of Exmoor. He determined she would be safe with her relatives while he inquired at the paper shop. And if she chose to, she could remain in London. She need not to return to Dunster with him, as long as she was safe. He believed his sons would understand her decision to remain with family. It would be a logical response to what had happened at the tower. Besides, it wouldn't break his heart, though he yearned for her.

"We're here, sir," Rollins called down from atop the coach.

Silently, Alexander stepped out and offered escort to Ana. The rain had stopped long enough to prevent them from getting soaked. The damp air sent a shiver down Ana's spine reflecting her mood. She took his offered hand. It was warm to the touch. He noticed her hand felt cold in his.

"So, this is your sister's home?" Alexander asked, disengaged.

"Yes, sir, it is," she responded. She watched Rollins place her small brown trunk on the doorstep.

"I've decided to go on and make inquiries at the papermaker. I'll be in my apartments. When you're ready to return, if you choose to return, I'll send Rollins. I'll wait a fortnight." His cool manner angered Ana. He was dropping her off at the door as if she were baggage. She was appalled. Didn't he wish to meet her family? Still, she remained aloof.

"Thank you, sir. I'll return for the sake of your sons," she turned to leave but stopped, adding flatly over her shoulder, "And I shall have an answer for your … proposal. Good day, Lord Luttrell."

He silently watched her walk up the stairs to the brick row home. He was uneasy with her coldness, but was appeased that she had not dismissed his offer.

He returned to his coach and waited for Ana to be let in safely. As soon as the door opened, he gave Rollins a tap on the roof to move on to Shields and Glass.

They wound their way down the dirty crowded streets of London. The coach stopped in front of the small shop; a royal crest swung above the door. He knew that whoever sent that letter had to have a decent income to afford paper from this establishment.

"Wait here," he instructed Rollins as he left the coach. It was crowded with many customers, as was appropriate, for a shop where the royal family purchased any of their goods always prospered. Alexander walked around and looked at the wares displayed on the shelves and tables. Much of the paper was bundled with colorful ribbons to keep the sheets in place. There were small writing tablets and books filled with empty pages for accounts, music, sketches or poems, ink, pens, waxes, and other implements. Alexander hoped the paper he was searching for was specially ordered, possibly even for one patron.

"May I help you, sir?" asked a well-dressed clerk.

"Yes, is Mister Shields or Glass available? Tell them that Lord Alexander Luttrell, Duke of Exmoor is asking for them."

"One moment, your Lordship." Seeing the potential for a wealthy patron, the clerk gave a rather deep bow and scurried off to find one of the owners of the shop.

Soon he returned. "Please follow me, your Lordship. Both Misters Shields and Glass will meet with you in their private offices."

Following the clerk into the back of the shop, Lord Luttrell was ushered into a large and well-appointed office. There were two desks back to back. Several overstuffed chairs surrounded a rather large table with books of paper samples spread across its surface. Fine brocades and art decorated the walls. Beside each desk stood a rather portly wigged gentleman, each dressed in the fashion of the day. The shopkeepers were obviously well-to-do. Their business was providing a more than sufficient income for both.

"Good day, Lord Luttrell. I am Bertram Shields and this is my partner, Benjamin Glass. We're here to serve you." Shields nodded his head in respect towards his noble patron as Glass followed in kind.

"Gentlemen, I'd love to say that I'm here to purchase from your impressive stocks, but alas I am not. In truth, I'm doing an investigation concerning a murder attempt on one of my household."

Both men looked at each other with dismay at the very thought of a murder attempt being traced to their doorstep.

"Your Lordship, I assure you, we and our staff are upright subjects of the Crown and would have no dealings with such miscreants," Shields answered as he quickly removed a lace handkerchief from his sleeve to wipe the sudden appearance of perspiration on his forehead.

"No gentlemen, I'm not suggesting either you or your staff has anything to do with this crime. It appears however, the would-be murderer had written a letter on paper supplied from your establishment. I have it with me to see if you might identify the purchaser of this fine stationary." Alexander took the folded sheet from his breast pocket and handed it over to Benjamin Glass who, placing his optical over his eye, inspected the parchment at hand.

Holding it to the light, he carefully studied the markings and color of the sheet. "Hmmm," he commented as he handed it over to Shields who repeated the procedure.

"What do you think Bertram?" Benjamin asked. "It's most definitely one of our stock, of that I am sure."

"Yes, here's our watermark." Shields said as he looked up at Lord Luttrell.

"This letter is addressed to a Miss Pembroke." He looked quizzically at Alexander.

"Yes, she is governess to my sons. Her family has fallen on hard times. Her father was the late Lord William Pembroke, Baron of Milford."

"Oh yes, Bertram, Lord Pembroke. I believe it's the very stock he purchased for his personal use. But this is such a popular paper amongst our patrons. It would be very hard to tell if it came directly from his desk."

"Yes, very popular stock, very popular." Shields added, "But it must be ordered specifically. Isn't that right Benjamin?"

"Yes Bertram, special order."

"I suppose you keep record of you patrons?" Alexander inquired.

"Why yes, we keep very thorough records. We can have one of our clerks make a copy for you and send it around."

"Very good gentlemen, you've been very helpful. There is no need to send the copy. I'll have my man come round in the morning."

"Very good, sir," Bertram added clearing his throat. "Do you have any need of stationary, sir? We do service the Queen, you know."

"Not at this time Gentlemen, but I'll keep you in mind for the future. Good day to you sirs." He tipped his hat in gratitude.

Alexander left feeling hopeful. Their list of patrons may provide a clue to lead him to the villain.

Ana stood at Henry and Eliza's front door for what felt like an hour as she waited for Harrington to answer her knock. She knew Lord Luttrell was sitting in his carriage, watching her. The very fact that he was looking at her at all unnerved her to her very core. Yet she refused to turn around to look at him. How dare he treat her so, she thought.

"Harrington, where are you?" she muttered through her teeth. Finally, she heard the familiar footsteps at the door. Her heart raced with excitement at the thought of seeing her sister. She'd also be glad of the relief to be well rid of the dark penetrating eyes that were burning into her back.

As the door slowly opened, Ana pushed in and threw her arms around the neck of a surprised but happy Harrington. As she did, she heard the sound of Lord Luttrell's carriage pull away and was surprised to feel her heart sink, knowing that he was leaving her, albeit safely with her family.

"Miss Ana!" Harrington laughed. "Miss Ana, I have not had such greeting from you since you were in pinafores and ringlets."

"Oh Harrington, it's so good to be home!" she said through tears that welled up in her eyes as she looked at his familiar lined face.

"Aunt Ana! Aunt Ana!" Sarah and Ana Jane came running down the stairs and rushed into Ana's open and waiting arms, and for a few minutes they clung together in the joy of their reunion. Finally, pulling apart, Ana was able to see how her nieces had grown in the months she had been away. She felt a twinge of pain realizing she had missed so much of their lives.

"Aunt Ana, we have a new bother!" Ana Jane said as she jumped in her excitement.

"I know, Ana Jane. That's one of the reasons I've come," she said as she took their hands, allowing them to lead the way, "And the other is because I've missed you both so very much. Look how you've both grown. And Sarah you're looking so much like your mother."

"Mama says I look like you, Aunt Ana," Ana Jane added.

"Yes, I see a resemblance, sweetie," She pulled on one of Ana Jane's long ginger curls.

"Come up and see baby Miles!" They began to tug on her arms in their excitement to introduce their new brother. She barely noticed the pain in her shoulder as they pulled her along.

Ana could not help but laugh at their enthusiasm. It was such a long time since she had laughed that it actually hurt her face.

"I'll put your trunk in your old room, Miss Ana," Harrington said from behind the scenes, smiling at the family reunion.

"Oh, thank you Harrington," she smiled as she allowed her two nieces to spirit her away.

"You will find Miss Eliza in the nursery I'm sure," Harrington added.

"Yes, come up to the nursery," Ana Jane tugged again. And with all the excitement of a young girl, Ana joined her nieces in a run up the stairs and down the hall.

But as they closed in on the nursery, Ana Jane and Sarah slowed down. "Father said we have to be quiet or we may wake our new brother," Ana Jane instructed, putting her finger to her lips.

The anticipation of seeing Eliza again was almost more than Ana could bear. She waited as Ana Jane slowly pushed open the door and they all peeked into the room.

"Mama. Aunt Ana is here," her whisper almost louder than her normal voice.

"Ana? Oh Ana, come in!"

Just the sound of her sister's voice brought tears to Ana's eyes. Pushing past her nieces, Ana and Eliza fell upon each other with a combination of laughter and tears, each looking longingly at the other, and then falling again into a tight hug.

"Ana, let me look at you," Eliza again studied her sister. She was suddenly struck by the change in her. She was still as young and beautiful as ever, but she looked thinner, and tired. "Ana, are you well?" Eliza was concerned.

"Oh Eliza, I'm very well. I'm home. How can I be any better?" She again reached for her sister's protective arms. Moving back, she looked at Eliza. "And you look wonderful for a woman who has just given birth to your third child. I want to see the baby."

"He's over here." Taking her hand, she led her to the cradle. "We named him Miles for our brother," she said proudly.

Ana looked over the rim of the crib to see her new nephew. He was a tight bundle of soft blue blankets all but for his bright blue eyes, round cherry lips and soft pink cheeks.

"Oh Eliza, he is so sweet. May I?" she said as she reached in to pick up the new life.

"Be careful of his head," Eliza warned as she led Ana and the babe to the rocking chair in the corner of the room.

Ana could not have been happier as she held her new nephew in her arms, surrounded by Eliza, Sarah and Ana Jane. She was home. She laid her cheek on the sweet small head of the babe. She was finally safe.

The next day, Rollins returned to Lord Luttrell's townhome with the list of patrons from Shields and Glass. As Alexander perused the long list of names, he slowly felt his heart sink. There were only two names on the roster that were familiar to him. The first was Ana's father, Lord William Pembroke, the second was Henry Colwell, Ana's brother-in-law.

Well, Henry would have no reason for writing such a letter. And Lord William was gone, so that was a ridiculous idea. Still, Charles would have access to Lord William's stationary. But as much as Alexander disliked him, he was doubtful Charles had anything to gain. He was already the new Baron. Besides, the letters he had written were on different paper and his handwriting was most definitely different.

He took the letter from his breast pocket. He didn't know this Charles, but he knew he didn't like him. Charles had asked for Ana's hand in marriage. He was a rival. But she had denied him. That alone would not be reason enough to want her dead. Men were often turned down when they extended a proposal of marriage. Ana had turned him down, once. He had been angry about it, but not enough to want to kill her. He knew about killing. He had seen enough of it in India.

His thoughts returned to that day at Dunster Castle. He had never asked a woman to marry him before. His marriage to Elizabeth had been arranged through their families. He never anticipated that Ana would refuse him. The rejection had stunned him; hurt his pride. He was furious at her for her response. He wanted to hurt her in return. He remembered his behavior towards her. He had never been so insulted; he was the Duke of Exmoor. He wanted to retaliate somehow.

So, what did I do? I kissed her. Then I wiped her kiss from my face as if she repulsed me.

Suddenly, Alexander sat back in his chair. *No wonder she had been so cold.* He realized, at that moment, that she believed he had found her to be repulsive. He could not help but laugh at the irony of the situation. She had no idea how strongly he desired her. And she had shut herself off out of fear of further rejection. He deserved the punishment she was giving him, and more. His reaction had been cruel and unseemly and he didn't like himself for it, he thought soberly.

"What a tangled mess we are," he said to himself as he shook his head. But he had to admit it was going to be exciting to recapture her and rekindle the flame of desire within her to meet his own.

Picking up the papers, he glanced at them again. Nothing. It would be a fortnight before he would rejoin Ana and take her home to Dunster. Discouraged at the lack of a lead, Alexander pulled the bell.

"Andrews!"

"Yes, sir," the townhouse butler responded.

"Tell Rollins to ready the carriage. I'm off to visit with Her Majesty."

"Yes, sir"

"And Andrews, have my uniform made ready. I will be attending the ball."

"Yes, sir," Andrews said, bowing as he left to fulfill his new tasks.

Previously, Queen Victoria had generously excused him from attending the Helena Augusta Victoria sixteenth birthday coming out ball. But now he was in London with no further leads and with time on his hands. Plus, he had a request to make of Her Majesty. Maybe a distracting visit with the Queen would clear his head and the solution to this riddle would become obvious, or at least provide another lead. He tossed the stationer's roster across his desk, the sheets scattered over its top.

CHAPTER 29

With tea cleared away from the table, Eliza finally had Ana all to herself. She was concerned for the dark circles under her sister's turquoise eyes, concerned indeed for her health. She had never seen Ana this thin and pale. She sat next to her sister on the settee and took her hands.

"Ana, are you happy? I mean are you truly happy where you are?" Her worry was etched across her pretty face.

Eliza's deep compassion for her sister's well-being opened the floodgate of Ana's heart. She put her hands to her face and began to sob. Eliza wrapped her arms around her distressed sister.

"There, there. I know it's been hard," Eliza cooed as she gently rocked her sister back and forth. "There there, now."

Finally, as the tears subsided, Eliza gently took Ana's face into her hands and looked deeply into her beautiful sparkling eyes now laced with wet lashes.

"What have they done to you?" was all she could ask.

"Oh Eliza, I have done such a foolish thing. And now that it is done, I cannot turn back."

Eliza's blue eyes opened in shock, for she could only think of the worst. "You are with child?"

Ana stared back, equally shocked, "What are you talking about?"

"The foolish thing that you cannot undo," Eliza repeated.

"Oh no, no. It is not that foolish. Not yet anyway," she assured her sister.

"Oh, thank goodness," Eliza was so relieved. "Well, what could be so terrible then? And what do you mean by 'not yet?'" Her curiosity was piqued.

"Eliza, I have fallen in love with a man who does not love me," she said simply, tears still staining her flushed cheeks.

"The Duke?" Eliza whispered as her eyes grew wide. "Not the Duke!"

Ana nodded yes, feeling ashamed of her traitorous heart.

"Oh, Ana it was the very thing I was afraid of. What has he done to you? Has he dishonored you?"

"No Eliza, he has not dishonored me." Ana was deeply frustrated by her sister's accusation.

"Thank God. Ana, I knew you shouldn't have gone. His reputation preceded him. See how it's affected you? I just knew this wouldn't end well for you. I was so angry with Henry for setting you up like this!" She studied Ana's face, "Is there something else? There is something else."

"He has asked me to marry him," her eyes beginning to well up again.

"Oh, Ana, no. This is terrible. Why would he do such a thing? You just said he doesn't love you." Eliza didn't know how to respond to her sister's news. "Oh, dearest, I am so confounded by you. How could you love such a scoundrel?"

"I do love him. I never knew anyone could feel this way about another person. But Eliza, he doesn't love me!" A tear cascaded down her cheek.

Moved by Ana's distress, Eliza hugged her sister tightly. "He doesn't love you but he asked you to marry him? I don't understand."

"He has asked me twice," she stated quietly.

Eliza pulled away to look into her sister's face. "Twice? You say he's asked you twice to marry and yet he does not love you? Ana, you must be mistaken. A man does not ask a woman to marry twice if he has no feelings for her."

"He only has contempt for me." Ana's eyes began to well up again as she remembered his reaction to her at the tower.

Eliza shook her head. "If he only had contempt for you then why in heaven's name would he ask you to marry him … twice?" She said as she handed her sister a handkerchief to wipe her eyes and blow her nose. "Henry's just going to have to fix this," Eliza said under her breath.

After a good long blow Ana continued. "Eliza, please don't be angry with Henry. He was only trying to help."

"But why would he ask you twice?"

"He wants to marry me so that I can be mother to his sons," dabbing at her damp eyes.

"Really now, and he has contempt for you?" Eliza was really struggling to follow.

"He wants to protect them. They have grown attached to me. He wants to assure them I will not leave them as their mother had. So he wants to marry me."

"Oh," Eliza said quietly, finally beginning to understand. "But who's to say you would stay with him, or him with you for that matter? Obviously, marriage does not guarantee that. But how did it come about that he asked you twice?"

"Eliza, I turned him down the first time. I just couldn't marry a man who does not love me. If I was able to do that, I would've married Charles ages ago."

"Well good for you. But I still don't understand why he asked you a second time then, especially if he doesn't love you, the cad. I thank God Henry and I have the kind of marriage where we love each other. So you turned him down because he clearly said he does not love you. But what I still don't understand is why he asked you again?"

How could Ana tell her sister that he wanted to marry her now to protect her and that her life was in danger?

"Eliza, he is such a wonderful father to his sons. He is very involved with them. We have discussions nearly every day about what they are learning and what I am teaching them. He's very caring to his mother; indulges her really. All his servants adore him. And remember that story about the Indian girl?" Eliza nodded vigorously, interested in the gossip. "Well there *is* a girl from India. Her name is Riya. He was wounded and she mended him. He then rescued her from a future of shame and degradation. Her whole family was killed and she was left alone to fend for herself. And she's ever so sweet and helpful. It's so very confusing, I know. He has me teaching her also to be an English lady." She started to cry, "Oh Eliza, he has these most wonderful expressive blue eyes!" Eliza's eyes were wide with surprise at the story as Ana began to weep.

"Oh, dear, you most definitely adore him," Eliza stated frankly, her heart going out to her sister's dilemma.

"I've kissed him," Ana added quietly looking at the handkerchief that she was twisting in her hands.

"You've what?" Eliza was stunned.

"Yes, I have kissed him, several times." She looked at her sister through wet lashes.

"And?" encouraging her to continue.

"I've never felt that way before. Oh Eliza, when he held me in his arms and kissed me … I wanted him never to stop."

"Oh, Ana, you are in love with him. But how do you know he doesn't love you? I mean he has asked you to marry him, twice. Plus, you just said he kissed you."

"He told me," Ana's voice again quiet.

"He told you he didn't love you?" Eliza was incredulous, her eyes widened with this tidbit. "What exactly did he say?"

"He said that his sons needed me, and his mother needed me too. But he didn't believe in love."

"Ana, that's nonsense," Eliza stopped and thought for a few minutes. "And the boys' mother abandoned them," her mind was working.

Ana nodded her head as she again dabbed at her nose.

"That means she left Lord Luttrell too."

"Yes, but he said he never loved her either. It was an arranged marriage when he was much younger. Lady Catherine told me that." Ana explained.

Eliza stood up and began to pace back and forth, her smooth brow furrowed in deep thought.

"Hmmm … he never married again; we know this."

"No," Ana answered watching her sister crossing the floor.

"Has he taken on a lover or a mistress?" She stopped in front of Ana.

"Not that I have heard. He doesn't come into town unless called for service to the Queen." Watching her sister resume her stride, "Eliza, what are you up to?"

"Well, I am sure he must've visited the brothels. He is a single man. But that's unimportant." Eliza stopped and bit her bottom lip. She looked directly into her sister's tear-stained face. "Do you know what I think? I think that he does love you. I think he just doesn't know it yet. It may be that he has never been in love and cannot recognize the feelings he's having towards you. But he's kissed you several times and obviously wants more. And THAT's why he has asked twice." She grinned from ear to ear, feeling like a sleuth who found her villain.

Ana's eyes lit up. "Oh, Eliza do you think so?" suddenly feeling hopeful. "You know Lady Catherine says the same thing."

"Tell me, what happened for him when he kissed you?"

"He seemed very passionate." She felt exposed sharing such intimacy with her sister. *Except for the kiss at Conygar Tower*, she thought. But no, the kiss itself was passionate … very passionate. It was what he did after the kiss that was so painful. Ana felt her face blush at the intimacy of the conversation she was having with her sister and was saddened that she wasn't able to share all.

"Well, there you have it. I know I'm right." Eliza felt very proud of herself for her discovery and rocked back on her heels. But playing the devil's advocate she added. "Is it the same when Charles kisses you?"

"Oh Eliza, how can you even say that?! Charles makes my skin crawl. I want to push him away from me. And he seems to claw at me like I'm a possession or something."

"What do you want to do about this, Ana?" She sat down again next to her sister.

"Eliza, I … I just don't know what to do," studying her sister for any hope of an answer.

"Well, first, you DO know that you cannot make him love you. And what I would want you to do is come home. But that is just being selfish on my part." Eliza took Ana's hands in hers. "Ana, you have to follow your heart. What does your heart say?" She looked intently at her sister.

Ana sat silently. A tear ran down her cheek as she looked at back at Eliza. "I love him, Eliza. I don't know why I do. I just do."

"It is settled then. I think you should accept his second proposal. Oh, Ana what an extraordinary turn of events. You will be a Duchess. And I think he will come around. He will realize that he does love you. I know he will." All thoughts of scandal left Eliza's mind at the thought of her sister's new found position.

The two sisters embraced with joy, though Ana remained somewhat skeptical of the idea of accepting his proposal. She had not told Eliza the complete story.

Suddenly, there was a knock at the door.

"Lord Charles is here to see you, Miss Ana," Harrington announced.

"Eliza, let's not mention this to him. I don't want him to pester me," Ana implored in a whisper.

"Ana, Cousin!" Charles entered directly behind Harrington. "Come let me look at you." His arms hung open for a hug. He pulled her up to stand before him and embraced her closely.

"Charles." She extended her cheek to receive his kiss. "How good of you to come for a visit."

"Ah, Ana, you are as beautiful as ever, I would say that work agrees with you. You look hauntingly appealing. How was your journey home?" He found her pale skin and dark eyes alluring.

"It was a difficult ride. The weather, you know," she said answering his question.

"Yes, the weather yesterday was relentless," he said.

"And Charles, you are looking fit as usual. I would say being Baron is agreeing with you," she continued, forcing conversation that she wished would end.

"Oh, Ana my dear, you know what would make it more agreeable. I know, I never give up. Hope never gives up." He smiled his crooked smile, keeping her in his grasp.

Finally releasing his hold, he said, "And Eliza, how is the new mother and her son today?"

"We are doing very well, thank you, Charles."

"I really can't stay and visit, though you know I'd love to." His eyes flashed with a devilish twinkle. "I came because I have a special request of you Ana. You have been working so hard. It is time for some cultured society, my dear. There is to be a ball in less than a fortnight and I want you to give me the pleasure of accompanying me."

"Well, I don't know, I've just arrived. I'm tired from my journey. Besides I have nothing to wear." Ana was looking for excuses.

"Nonsense! When you are rested you will be screaming for diversion. Helena Augusta Victoria has turned sixteen, and Her Majesty has invited me to the ball. Can you imagine, I have been invited by the Queen to a Royal Ball? You must come as my guest. I'll not take no for an answer." He smiled while nodding his head, his brow lifted in hopeful expectation.

Ana smiled at Eliza. It had been such a long time since she had been to any gala affair, and this did sound magnificent.

"Oh, go." Eliza encouraged her. "What fun we'll have dressing you up. Charles is right, you do need a diversion."

"Alright Charles, I'll accompany you. Promise to be on your best behavior."

"Splendid, Ana, splendid. I knew you would not disappoint, my dearest cousin. I have already contacted the dressmaker for you and the fabric and style has been picked. All you need to do is go for a final fitting. You'll be the most beautiful woman there and I the most luckiest of men." He pulled Ana to him and kissed her on the lips. She could not help but pull away.

"Charles, you promised to behave," she admonished.

"I know, I know. But you've just made this man very happy, very happy indeed. Well ladies I must be off. Business you know." He flashed a smile as he turned to leave. "Have a good day my beautiful cousins."

When he had gone, Ana considered Charles' proposals and realized she had treated him exactly as Lord Luttrell had treated her. She was saddened by her behavior towards her very own cousin and understood she must have hurt him terribly. She decided that, though she would not ever marry him, he did deserve her apology for the pain she must have caused him. In the meantime, she was going to prepare for a ball, and more importantly, accept Lord Luttrell's proposal of marriage.

CHAPTER 30

The days sped by and Ana soon returned to her familiar routine. She took great joy in helping Eliza with her nieces and Miles. She was warmed by the love and safety of her family. However, she looked forward to being reunited with Lord Luttrell and his family. She was surprised at how deeply she missed all of them and she longed to be in Lord Luttrell's presence.

Tonight was the Royal Ball. Ana admitted that she was excited by the prospect of being out in society, dressed in her new forest green taffeta silk, trimmed with fawn colored lace and an underskirt of striped buff and light green with delicate embroidered pink rosebuds along the hem and neck. It had been a long time since she had worn a ball gown and she was a bit uncomfortable exposing her shoulders and arms.

She and Eliza spent hours perfecting the ringlets in her hair that cascaded down either side of her face. Mother's Spanish comb added just the right touch of elegance along with Eliza's pearl and emerald ear bobs. Ana felt exquisite.

Charles, prompt as ever, had not wanted to miss any time he could spend with Ana. He was insistent upon impressing the Queen and refused to be late to such a momentous celebration.

"You look very dapper, Charles," Ana complimented him. *Dapper never handsome*, she thought, as he placed her cover over her exposed shoulders.

"Why thank you, Ana, and you are ravishing tonight." His black eyes were hot and penetrating as his gaze roamed over her figure. He could not help but notice the gentle curve of her white shoulders and the soft full mounds that pushed up from the low bodice of the dress. "Your gown fits you to perfection."

"Thank you, Charles." She smiled at him, though she felt exposed by his glance. However, she had to admit that she felt sensual in the gown. "Thank you for this beautiful gown."

"You are most welcome Ana. Shall we then?" He led her to the front door, impatient to get going.

"Good night Eliza," Ana said as she kissed her sister on the cheek.

"Have a good time Ana, you deserve it. You look beautiful." She whispered into her ear. "And be careful with her, Charles. She is precious you know."

"Not to worry dear Eliza. She's precious to me too," he grinned a crooked grin and the two were off to the Buckingham Palace in a Hansom cab.

"Is the Queen really going to be here tonight?" Ana asked, feeling as excited as Charles at the prospect of meeting the Queen.

"Why of course, silly. We shall be presented together to Queen Victoria." Charles took Ana's hand, but she casually pulled it away not wanting to hurt his feelings.

"I have never been to a royal ball; nobles of course, but never royals." Ana's turquoise eyes glistened with excitement.

"Ana, you know for you I would do anything," he said in her ear, again, reaching for her hand.

His familiarity towards her made her uneasy. "Now Charles, you said you'd behave." She chided him again, pulling away her hand and giving him a gentle yet playful push back towards his seat.

Her smile disarmed him. He leaned back into the cushions. "Yes, and I always keep my promise," he said flatly as he glanced out the window. "Ah, we should be there in a moment." His mood lightened. The cab pulled to a halt. "And here we are."

The door opened and the footman helped them out onto the wide, well-lit portico. The marble of Buckingham Palace was brightly festooned with torches, garlands, ribbons and flags. It glistened like a brilliant star in the heavens. Ana was dazzled by its beauty. There were throngs of couples cued up to enter the golden doors. Londoners were on the street pressing their faces to the palace gates just to get a peek at the ladies and gentlemen in their finery. The guards stood unflinching, keeping watch for their monarch and her family.

Charles took Ana's elbow into his white gloved hand and began to lead her through the door. Ana was awed by its beauty.

The sound of music floated down the crowded divided golden staircases that encircled the grand entrance, with couples ascending as they headed towards the ballroom. Ana and Charles followed the throng that was rising to meet the Queen. Each couple was formally announced as they entered the ballroom by a splendid master of ceremonies holding an ostentatious golden baton.

"Lord and Lady Linton of Derbyshire"

"Lord and Lady Barnet of Middlesex"

"Lord Malin and Miss Pembroke of Milford"

Ana's eyes widened at the enormous space that opened up in front of them. The Buckingham Palace ballroom walls were ornately decorated in red brocade fabric trimmed in gold. Tall branched candelabras lit the room from both sides of the hall. The ornate white plaster ceiling was resplendent with deep maroon and golden leaf accents. On the far side of the room, a gilded arch hung over an impressive dais for the Queen. Beautifully dressed women and elegant men filled the room with grace and sound. The grandeur took her breath away. She was hardly aware that Charles was guiding her through the crowd to the dais upon which sat Her Majesty, Queen Victoria herself, surrounded by her husband, Prince Albert, and royal family members and nobles.

"We are here," Charles whispered in her ear as he guided her to the group.

Suddenly, they were standing in front of Queen Victoria. Ana made a graceful and deep curtsy to acknowledge the Queen's royal lineage. As she stood up, she was shocked to see, standing behind Princess Helena Augusta Victoria, none other than Lord Alexander Luttrell, Duke of Exmoor. The curtsy she had been practicing all week nearly came to an embarrassing stumble as their eyes met. It was apparent that he was just as shocked to see her as she was to see him. His left brow arched and his blue eyes widened with recognition. She looked beautiful in her dark green gown. The warmth of the candles highlighted the golden threads of her auburn hair. She was most pleasant and alluring. Quickly, her gaze dropped to the floor as she could feel her cheeks warm with the color of embarrassment under his intense gaze.

"Your Majesty, thank you for the honor of inviting us to celebrate your daughter's birthday. We are your humble servants," Charles said with deep bow.

"So, you are the new Baron of Milford?" Queen Victoria inquired.

"Yes, Your Majesty, and this is Miss Ana Pembroke, my cousin."

Ana had to drag her stare away from the floor and refocus on the Queen. "Your Majesty." She again bowed down low feeling the Duke's eyes on her every movement.

"We are sorry to hear of your loss, my child. We knew your father. We shall miss him," the Queen said.

"Thank you for your condolences your Majesty," she said sincerely.

"We hope you enjoy the ball," she added waving them on with a gloved hand.

"Thank you, your Majesty," Charles said as he led Ana off towards the large dance floor filled with guests.

"Ana, isn't it exciting? The Queen knew who we are." Charles was filled with an extraordinary sense of self-importance and mistook Ana's paling features as awe at meeting the Queen.

"You see, I can give you the world Ana." His beady eyes sparkled with the lust for power.

"Oh, Charles, really, you promised!" Ana said as she looked over her shoulder towards the Queen and her entourage. Lord Luttrell was standing tall and proud over the Princess, his gaze directed at the next couple who were being presented to the Queen.

"Besides, are we not here to dance?" Her heart dropped a little in hopes that he was still staring at her.

"Yes, my dear and beautiful cousin. We shall dance the night away. I shall claim all dances on your card."

"Oh, no you won't. I want to dance with others too. Charles, I want to have fun." It was obvious to her that the Duke was going to be otherwise occupied for the evening and might not have an opportunity to dance with her. He might not even want to dance with her. But the thought of dancing only with Charles was not her cup of tea and he was going to have to deal with his disappointment. She wanted to enjoy herself and was annoyed that Charles wanted to monopolize all the dances.

"May I have this first dance then, cousin?" He took her hand in his and led her to the dance floor as the Dance Master announced the Grand March. All couples lined up behind the Queen and her family. Ana could see the top of Lord Luttrell's dark chestnut hair since he was taller than most. Helena Augusta Victoria was securely ensconced on his arm as he was her obvious partner for the evening. Ana's heart dropped all the more as the hope of a possible dance with him began to fade into the distance.

Suddenly, the music commenced as the couples began to follow the directions of the Dance Master. They were led by none other than Queen Victoria and Prince Albert. As the couples linked arm in arm with other couples, the line began to form. Ana was able to admire all the beautiful gowns, the graceful women and the elegant men, as they passed by in review. It was the opportunity to see who had been invited and who had come. The bright gowns and dark cutaway coats and tails flew past her in a whirlwind of colorful motion and sound. Suddenly, before her were the Queen and Prince, followed by the Princess and Lord Luttrell. Their eyes met for an instant. Ana could not help but give him a warm smile as they passed. She could see a glimmer of humor in his blue eyes as he nodded his head and was gone.

Her heart leapt with joy. She could feel color rise to her cheeks. She had not expected to see him until her return to Dunster Castle. She had missed him greatly in the last several days. She knew Charles thought her to be beautiful tonight. But that was unimportant. She wanted to be beautiful for the Duke. She hoped that her gown was doing her justice. And suddenly, again, he was before her. Only this time it was Lord Luttrell who smiled as they passed. To Ana it felt as if everyone in the room was fading away and she and the Duke were the only two on the dance floor.

The music stopped and the Grand March was over. Charles took her by the hand and led her onto the dance floor for a reel. Mechanically following Charles' lead in the dance, she couldn't help but search the crowd for the Duke. When he disappeared from view, her heart sank just a little.

"Ana, are you having fun?" Charles asked as they crossed arms in the dance.

"Oh, yes," Ana said breathlessly.

"Good," he said as he took her hands and steered her around the other couple.

"Let's just dance," she said, not wanting to engage in the usual banter.

After several dances, Ana requested to sit one out in hopes that someone else would request a dance with her.

"I'll get us some punch." Charles offered. "Stay put." He added, a note of warning in his voice. "Remember, you are with me tonight."

As she had indicated to Charles, she was not going to save her dance card for him alone, however, no other gentlemen had yet come over and asked her for her hand. It was so often that way when Charles was her escort, Ana thought. She almost always ended up dancing all the dances with Charles.

Soon he returned to find her where he had left her. She took the fine crystal glass filled with ruby punch. Charles' voice droned on in her ear as she scanned the crowd for one small glimpse of Lord Luttrell.

Eliza was right. She was very much in love with the Duke. So much so that if she could will him to leave the Princess and come dance with her, she would. She also realized that in her joy at seeing him, she had forgotten how much he had hurt her. The thing she wanted most of all was to accept his proposal of marriage, even if it meant living with and loving a man who could not love her back. She was willing to accept the consequences of that kind of union as long as it was with him.

Ana became aware that Charles had pulled the cup from her hand. He led her back to the dance floor for more waltzes, and dances. The night seemed to go on forever. And each dance seemed to be with Charles. Ana was beginning to feel annoyed at the way Charles monopolized the evening; never allowing another gentleman to break in. The longer the night wore on, the more Ana's heart sank as she realized that Lord Luttrell was never going to ask her for a dance.

At the end of the next quadrille, Ana asked Charles for a reprieve.

"I am so thirsty, Charles, I would love more punch," she said, a smile pasted on her face. She looked down at her dance card once he departed. Her heart sunk completely at the realization that it was to be the last waltz of the evening and the Duke was not going to leave his charge even for one dance with her.

Suddenly before her were two dark shoes that did not belong to Charles. She looked up and there standing before her was Lord Luttrell.

"May I have this waltz?" he asked extending his arm to lead her to the dance floor. "I believe we danced to this melody once before." His voice was warm in her ear.

Ana's heart skipped a beat as she took his arm and allowed him to take her onto the floor. The music began. It was indeed the same waltz played by Lady Catherine on that stormy and fateful afternoon. His arm encircled her waist as he gently pulled her towards him. He stood still for a moment holding her close, his intense eyes fixed on hers. Ana's heart quickened under his stare. He started to glide them both gracefully around the floor.

"You must imagine my surprise to see the governess of my children standing before the Queen," he began with a humorous twinkle in his eyes.

"Sir, you must imagine my surprise to see you standing behind a Princess," she replied, smiling up at him.

"So how is it that you find yourself at this ball?" he asked as his eyes drifted down to study her full lips as she answered.

"My cousin Charles, the new Baron of Milford, was invited, so he asked if he could escort me. And yourself?" Their conversation flowed easily, yet their gaze was intent upon each other.

"While here in London, I felt it necessary to visit with the Queen. She said she needed my services, so here I am." He added, "I am on a quest, Ana.

"Always at the Queen's service," Ana smiled up at him as they danced.

"I am on a quest for you," he said. "Are you having a good time, Ana?" His voice was warm and gentle.

"I am now," she said as they glided across the dance floor in time with the music. To be in his arms again was heavenly. She wanted never to leave them.

They moved towards the rows of glass doors that opened up onto the Palace gardens. Ana could feel the cool breeze of the night air on her face as they danced closer to the opened doors. Suddenly, Lord Luttrell was leading her onto the marbled terrace. He pulled her closer as he slowed down his step.

"Ana, walk with me in the garden." His voice was deep and warm as he whispered in her ear. He took her hand and led her down the moonlit stair. The garden was filled with sparkling fountains and glowing torches. The music of the waltz began to drift gently into the night. The early scent of autumn and late summer roses perfumed the air. Ana felt she was entering a fairytale land of starlit romance. She had hoped for a dance, but this was more than she could have ever imagined.

He was pulling her to him, wrapping his arms around her waist. She found that she was unable to resist as she placed her arms around his neck. Their eyes met.

"Ana, you are beautiful tonight." His voice was husky. "I could not think of anyone but you."

He bent his head towards hers, his mouth brushing ever so slightly up against her lips. "Kiss me, Ana," he said in a voice husky with desire, "kiss me." His mouth found hers as he pulled her closer. He parted her lips and allowed his tongue to explore the sweetness of her mouth. He wanted to taste her. Their tongues intertwined as she responded to his kiss. She closed her eyes and felt herself melt into him. Slowly he pulled his mouth from hers and began a trail of moist, hot kisses down her neck and shoulder. Her body responded to his touch as shivers of pleasure began to warm her innermost being. She could feel his desire against her as he pushed his hips into hers, and she responded instinctively by pushing back.

Slowly, he lifted his head, staring into her dark sultry eyes which mirrored his own, "Ana, this is what I want from you." He kissed her again. "What I did at the tower was out of anger. I am sorry I hurt you." He kissed her forehead. "I want you in my bed. I want you to mother my sons. I want you to marry me. Marry me, Ana," his voice quietly demanding.

Ana flashed to her conversation with Eliza—maybe he does not know he loves me, she thought.

"Sir, are you making love to me?" she ventured the question with hesitation at the use of the word.

"When I saw you standing before me this evening, I realized how much I wanted you, how much I need you in my bed. If this is making love to you then so be it." His voice was deep and husky. His mouth again found hers.

Ana felt encouraged with his answer and allowed herself to become lost in his embrace, her own desire for him taking hold, raging to be satisfied.

Pulling away again, he looked deeply into her turquoise eyes, "Do you have an answer for me?"

"Yes, my Lord, I will marry you," she said breathlessly.

"Ana," the resumed fervor of his kiss made Ana's knees weak.

"I promise I will make you a good husband." His whisper was hot in her ear as he held her close, reluctant to part. "The Queen herself has approved of our union."

"You asked the Queen?"

"In my station, I am obligated to get her permission." He looked down at her wistfully, "We must return to the dance before we are missed," as he reluctantly pulled away from her. "Ana, return home with me so we can set a wedding date."

"I shall return with you after I finish my visit," Ana smiled coyly, though not wishing to appear too eager. "There is nothing I want more."

"Ana, there is one thing you will need to change."

"What is that, sir?" she asked looking up at him.

"You must call me Alexander." His heart jumped as she gave him one of her stunning smiles.

"Alexander." She like the sound of his name. "Alexander." She said again with a slight giggle.

He threw his head back and laughed. "Come on, we must return. You get to practice saying my name for the rest of your life."

Ana found Charles standing where he had left her. His face was flushed with anger as he stood there holding their two glasses.

"Where the devil have you been? I have been standing here like a fool, holding these cups." His voice was cold and harsh. His anger took Ana by surprise.

"Charles, I'm sorry. I didn't realize it but my employer is here tonight. He must've seen us dancing. And when he saw I was sitting alone he came over and requested the last waltz—a turn on the floor. That is all."

Charles closely studied Ana's face. It appeared to him that she gave her employer more than just a turn on the floor. Her hair was just a bit mussed, and her lips appeared redder and fuller, as if she'd been kissed, and kissed hard.

He all but smashed the cups down on the window sill behind her as he grabbed her arm. "Just a turn you say. When will you give me a turn?"

"Charles, please, you are hurting me." Ana was surprised by the violence of her cousin's response. "I told you, we waltzed."

"It is time for us to go," he growled as he began to drag her from the ballroom.

"Charles, please? Don't do this. Please don't spoil the evening. We were having such a good time." She could feel her face turn red as other guests and couples began to watch Charles pull her through the crowd as if she were an errant child

But Charles was not listening to her pleas. He was angry and jealous. He searched the crowd for his possible rival. Turning around, he stopped and grabbed her by the shoulders. "Who is he? Who is your so-called employer?" He demanded as his face twisted with rage.

"Charles, please, this is embarrassing," she answered as tears welled up in her eyes.

"It should be you who is embarrassed, behaving like a who—."

"What seems to be the trouble here?" It was Alexander. Ana looked up, silently imploring him not to take any action against her cousin.

Charles spun around and found himself facing a man at least a head taller than himself.

"We're leaving. It's time for us to leave," he hissed.

"It appears that the lady does not yet wish to go," Alexander responded coolly.

Ana quickly shook her head. The last thing she wanted was any trouble between these two men. "No, no I am ready to go. But thank you for your concern, sir."

Alexander took a step forward. "Let me introduce myself. I am Lord Luttrell. Miss Pembroke is governess to my sons. And you are?" he extended his hand toward Charles.

Charles looked down at the hand offered with contempt. It appalled him to have to take it when what he really wanted to do was call this fellow out. But this was a royal ball and the Queen herself was present. He could not afford to do otherwise. "I'm Charles Malin, Baron of Milford. Miss Pembroke and I are cousins."

Ana could see by the look in each man's eye that they despised each other because of her. However, Ana let out a silent sigh of relief as the two men tentatively shook hands. She loved them both and was horrified at the possibility of what might have happened.

"You see Charles, I told you my employer was here. He was kind enough to ask for a waltz. Again, thank you, Lord Luttrell," she acknowledged with a small curtsey. "Please give my regards to your mother and sons upon your return." She took Charles' hand and gently pulled him towards the door leaving Alexander to stare dumbfounded at her response and at their exit, together.

CHAPTER 31

With squinted eyes, Alexander watched, appalled, as Ana and Charles were swallowed up by the crowd. He didn't like what he knew of Charles, and now that they had met, his disdain increased. He felt betrayed and deceived by Ana's cool handling of the situation. Alexander had witnessed how he had forced her to leave. But she sided with Charles and even protected him by taking his hand and leading him out. She had just agreed to marry Alexander. And yet, he was not keen about letting her leave with this man, cousin or not. Having observed his aggressive behavior with Ana, Alexander determined to follow them.

"Your Majesty, I find I must leave. I believe Miss Pembroke is in danger," he whispered into the Queen's ear.

"Yes, we met her earlier this evening, lovely girl. Danger you say? By all means do your duty, Alexander and see to her protection." Her bejeweled hand waved him on.

"Your Majesties," and with a grand bow, Alexander turned on his heels and raced to follow the carriage containing Charles and Ana.

"Rollins, stay at a safe distance, I don't want us to be discovered," he instructed.

Rollins stopped his coach more than a block from the Hansom cab that was parked in front of the familiar townhouse.

Alexander sat and waited. No one left the carriage. He glanced at his pocket watch. He had been sitting, watching for over ten minutes now. He could not help but wonder what was going on in that carriage. He knew they had not left the cab, for Rollins had pulled up just as they came to a stop and the coachman had not come down to open their door.

Looking at his watch again, Alexander began to feel small twinges of jealously as he realized that they had been in the cab for seventeen minutes. The carriage rocked back and forth on its springs.

He thought he could trust her. She agreed to marry him just this night. Could she really be that fickle? He looked at his watch; nineteen minutes. A lot can happen in nineteen minutes. He knew he needed to stop this train of thought. He was here to spy on Charles, not Ana. Suddenly, the carriage before him lurched side to side. His brow lifted in disbelief.

Her kiss was so ardent not an hour ago. He could still taste her on his lips. She could not be the innocent he had thought following that display of movement from the vehicle in front of him; that was apparent. Twenty-three minutes had now passed. Now that they were betrothed, if she offered herself, there would be no reason to wait for the wedding night. She was obviously free to give her charms to any man who showed interest. He hated that he needed her so much. But have her he will. His jealousy raged.

Twenty-eight minutes. His fist hit the door of his coach. More than anything he wanted to pull that cad from the carriage and call him out.

"Sir?" Rollins opened the top hatch.

"Nothing Rollins, we will wait." His voice was tight with anger.

Alexander knew that Charles had asked Ana for her hand. He also knew she had turned him down, and had just agreed to marry him. He sat confounded as the minutes ticked by.

Just then the cab driver jumped down from his seat and opened the door. Alexander watched as Charles and Ana exited the cab and walked up the steps to the door. Ana turned around and gently caressed Charles face. He bent his head low as he allowed her to give him a kiss on his cheek.

Alexander's anger spiked. *What a tender scene. She has been playing me for a fool! Well, two can play at this game.* His thoughts were becoming darker with each passing moment. *Women are fickle deceivers.*

Ana opened the door and entered the hall. Alexander watched as their hands slowly released. He felt vile. His stomach churned. Charles returned to the cab.

Rollins reopened the hatch, "Shall I follow him, my Lord?"

"Yes, follow that bastard," Alexander hissed. "And Rollins, once we find out where he's going, make ready to return home to Dunster. I'm tiring of this folly."

"Yes, sir," The sound of the whip snapped as the team began to move them along the dark swirling streets of London.

Ana was horrified at the brutish behavior Charles had displayed at the ball. She had specifically requested that he be on his best conduct. But instead, he became jealous, controlling, and overbearing as usual. Ana was so angry she found that she could not look at him at all during the ride home. Finally the cab pulled in front of the town house.

"Ana we must talk. I must apologize. I don't know what comes over me. I get so jealous when another man looks at you," he pleaded.

Ana looked at her cousin; there were genuine tears of shame in his eyes.

"Oh, Charles, I don't know what to say. You are too possessive of me."

"Ana, I love you. I want you to marry me. I don't understand why you can't see that."

"I love you too Charles, but not like that. We grew up together. You are more like a brother to me. I am sorry, but I can't see you in any other way."

"Ana, you hurt me to the quick. Is there no hope for us?"

"You've known how I have felt for a long time now, yet you continue to persist. Take tonight as an example. You're a young man. You have a lot to offer a woman. You're now the Baron of Milford. But you insisted upon not leaving my side. You had such an opportunity to dance with other single ladies tonight. But you chose to stay with me."

"I didn't want to dance with any other woman. Ana, I love you," he cried, again insistent.

"Yes, Charles, I know. But I don't love you ... not in that way. Please understand."

Charles knew that he was not going to win when the sudden realization of the events of the past hour struck him. "You love that Luttrell, don't you?"

"Charles, I don't want to hurt you. I know what it feels like to love someone who does not return your love. I'm sorry for the pain I'm causing." Her apology was sincere.

Anger replaced the pain on his face. "That's why he came to your rescue tonight," he hissed. "I don't want to hurt you, Charles," he mimicked, "I know what it feels like, Charles," his voice in a whiney falsetto. "Have you slept with him?" he demanded. "Have you?"

"No, how could you say such a thing to me?" She was horrified at his reaction. "Maybe you can be happy for me," she implored.

"Happy? How can I be happy when you have rejected me for another?" He shook his fist in her face. "You know I've wanted you my whole life. I've waited for you to grow up. I've put in my time waiting for you. I can take you right here if I want! You owe me." His face twitched, spittle flying from his mouth as he raged.

Ana pulled back in her seat. His interest in her had been apparent for a long time, but she never expected him to become so violent, so obsessed.

"What is it with you men?" she asked, thinking about Alexander's initial reaction at her first denial of his proposal. "Why can't a woman make her own choice? It's very simple. You asked me and I said no. So stop this foolishness. Stop it at once," she cried.

Charles leaned in closer to Ana, his face very close to hers. His beady eyes were twitching with rage. "What is going to prevent me from taking you now," he hissed.

A rush of genuine fear suddenly flooded to Anna's core and flashed across her face. Somehow she needed to stop him. He was out of control. She raised her hand and slapped him hard across his jaw. The strike surprised him instantly and he pulled back.

Tears again welled up in his eyes as he grabbed her hand and brought it to his face. "Ana, Ana, please forgive me. I don't know what I'm doing. I want you so badly. I just can't imagine my life without you as my wife. I didn't mean to frighten you. I don't want to hurt you," he kissed the palm of her hand and brought it to his cheek which was starting to show signs of her strike.

"Charles. I told you. I don't want to hurt you. It's just that we are not meant to be together. Cousin, you'll find another. You have much to offer, I told you." She looked at him as tears began to spill down his face. She felt sorry for him. In so many ways he was so alone.

"But Ana, I have no one, no one but you. And you too have no one. We are both orphans now. We are alone. You are my only family." He was desperate.

"No Charles, we have Eliza. Now don't be ridiculous," she chided gently, aware that he was still very fragile. "Come now, I do love you. You're now more my brother than ever since Miles died. How can I not love you?"

Charles leaned into her and laid his head on her breast like a young boy. "You are not alone Charles. You have me and Eliza, and Henry. We all love you. We all want your happiness." She gently stroked his head, comforting him and quieting him.

He lifted his head and looked into her turquoise eyes, the eyes he longed to hold passion for him. He knew she was right. He had to let her go. "Can you forgive me?" he asked sheepishly.

"Of course I can," Ana smiled at him. He was always dazzled by her smile. Only this time it struck pain into his heart. Slowly, he reached up and knocked for the driver to open the door to let them out.

They walked up the stairs to the door. Ana turned to Charles, "I am truly sorry that I've hurt you and disappointed you." She reached up and caressed his cheek where she had slapped him earlier.

"I deserved that slap, Ana," he said tenderly.

"Let me kiss your cheek."

He lowered his head and received the gift as he felt his heart break into a thousand pieces. "Good night, Ana. I'll always love you."

"And I you." she said as she entered the house, still holding his hand. She slowly closed the door as their hands parted.

Charles stood outside the door for a few moments then returned to his cab. The carriage which had been parked more than a block back began to move.

Rollins managed to stay a safe distance behind the Hansom cab as it wound its way down the dimly lit streets of London. To Alexander's surprise, he found they were entering Cheapside rather than returning to the elegant apartments and townhomes he had expected.

The fog swirled around the lamps like eerie gray ghosts while the smell of the filth accosted his nostrils. It was not quite the direction he thought Charles was going to take following an evening of lust and fornication. But perhaps he was not yet finished for the night, Alexander thought with disgust.

The coach stopped in front of one of the many rundown Turkish bathhouses. Alexander recognized this one as it was well known for its dark trades and shady patrons.

"Rollins, slow down. Pass by slowly but keep going. I need to return home." Alexander ordered his driver; his head pounding. Sure enough, Charles exited the cab and entered the building to enjoy the dark and seedy delights of the night. Alexander's stomach churned at the thought of what awaited inside to entice and fulfill the lusts of the man he was so learning to despise. Though not a stranger to needs of the flesh himself, Alexander had never stooped to such sordid and unholy establishments, which ran rampant with corruption, abuse, and disease.

Maybe he was wrong about Ana. Maybe nothing had happened in the coach and this churl came down to this "great square of Venus" to finish what she had only started. Or maybe his sick and twisted lusts were more then she could satisfy. However, Alexander was now convinced about one thing and that was she was no innocent if she kept company with this debauched libertine. They were playing him for a fool. He fell into that trap with Elizabeth and would not do it again. He had to keep his guard up. He knew his first instincts were right. Women can't be trusted.

He felt exhausted—he was done with this madness! Returning to his own townhome, he arranged to leave for Dunster Castle before dawn. He had been too long away from his sons, and his mother had still been ill when they had left less than a fortnight ago. Whatever game Ana was playing, she was safe with her family for now. He would send around a note telling her he needed to return home without delay. He had a whole new picture of the woman who had just agreed to marry him, and he hated it. He hated all women.

Sleep eluded him as thoughts whirled about his brain. He was a fool to press Ana for an answer. He should have accepted her initial rejection back at Conygar Tower. Why did he have to push? His foolish pride was again his undoing. His sons could live without her. They were already without their mother. He didn't need an heir. He could resume teaching them himself. His mother could employ a new companion. Better yet, she can go visiting. Riya could be sent off to school. The less women in his life the better. He could get his life back. She was only a silly woman. He rolled onto his back.

But her body had pressed against his tonight with such yearning. She would not have responded with such intense passion had she not wanted him. The taste of her mouth was ecstasy. The feel of her warm supple breasts made him ache for more. He was an idiot to want her so much and hated himself for it. Maybe she was so responsive to him because she had already known a man's touch. Certainly, Charles had seen to that, many, many times. His face twisted in rage and jealousy. Was it his need for her that pushed him to want to protect her? Maybe it was her need for protection that made her so desirable? Alexander rubbed his aching head. He needed sleep. Dawn was breaking soon and he was going to have a long ride home.

He shifted to his side. She was a woman like all others, enticing him with her charms while her heart belonged to another. Charles, that vile excuse for a man, most likely stole her innocence. She was probably a mere child of fourteen who now feels some sort of allegiance to that Cretan. What else could be the possible reason for their unholy and unnatural union?

She agreed to marriage with me, Alexander posited as he rolled on his back. Maybe she was unaware? No, women were never unaware. She played the innocent so well. Charles must be a very adept teacher and she must be very cunning. They were scheming against him just as Elizabeth had done with Abernathy, using him for his wealth. Again, he'd been stabbed in the back.

Alexander drifted off into a fitful sleep. The sound of cannons raged in his dreams, the smell of death and smoke filled his nostrils. He was left with his dead comrades. There was no one coming to give him aid. The enemy was descending in waves, dressed in filthy robes and turbans. Thousands of hungry enemy faces. Charles and Ana, Elizabeth and Abernathy. All coming and coming, to bleed him dry.

He woke with a start. His heart raced in his chest. Closing his eyes tightly, he tried to erase the picture from his mind as he returned to his side and thought again of Ana. She was enchanting in that dark green gown tonight and she knew the effects she had on him. That loathsome cousin of hers monopolized her the whole evening. Charles waited for his chance with her and took it at the end of the evening. She's no young innocent. Her passions were as strong as his, her kisses were proof enough.

"When offered, and surely she will offer, I will have her."

CHAPTER 32

As she locked the door, Ana realized there was a light shining from the drawing room. Quietly, she tiptoed to take a peek.

"Henry, what are you doing up at this ungodly hour?" She was surprised to see her brother-in law sitting in front of the fire, dressed in his smoking jacket and reading a book, an empty glass and smoldering cigar on the table next to him.

"It's about time you are home, young lady. I'm exhausted. And if you thought for one moment that your sister would've let me sleep with you out on the town, you're greatly mistaken," he said, snapping his book closed and laying it on the table next to him.

"Oh, Henry, you're such a dear," Ana bent down giving him a kiss on his forehead.

"So, did you have a good time?" he asked looking up at her.

"I did. But I have something I must share with you and Eliza. And I don't think it can wait till the morning." She broke out in a brilliant, joyful smile.

"Well I'll not be the one to awaken her. The babe does that enough and there'll be no living with her on the morrow," he warned.

"What is all this noise and no living with whom on the morrow?" It was Eliza at the door dressed in her night clothes. "How can anyone get any sleep around here with so much commotion?" she said as she proceeded to indulge herself in an enormous yawn, fully aware that she had not slept one wink.

Ana rushed towards Eliza grabbing her hands, "Come, you must sit down. I've something to tell you both. If I wait, I'll simply burst."

Eliza allowed her sister to lead her to the small settee. She sat and observed her sister's face flushed with excitement.

"You'll never guess what's happened," she looked at both of them.

"Well?" Henry pushed.

"Lord Luttrell was at the ball. He was there to escort the Princess."

"That's nice dear," Eliza drowsily leaned back into the cushions.

"Charles was such a boor. He didn't let me dance with anyone but him." She glanced at their faces.

"Then it was the last waltz of the evening. And who do you think asked me to dance?"

"I don't know. Who?" Henry asked flatly, just not getting into her romantic mood.

"Why it was Lord Luttrell himself. Oh, it was such heaven. He glided me across the floor ... and the music ... it was perfection itself." Ana couldn't help but picture the scene in her head.

"Ana, what are you getting at?" Henry was exasperated by her long-winded story and most concerned about its direction.

"Then he guided me out to the palace gardens. Oh, Eliza it was like a fairytale. There were fountains and torches. The music floated on the air and the smell of the roses ... It was so perfect."

Now Eliza's interest was piqued as she sat up on the edge of the seat. "Then what happened?"

"He kissed me." Ana stood up and could not help but twirl.

"What?" Henry was shocked. "Oh no, this is too much ... you will quit that position at once."

"No Henry you don't understand. He asked me again."

"He asked you a third time?" Eliza was now wide awake, "And?"

"Asked you what for the third time?" Henry agitated at having been left out of the loop.

"I said, yes. Henry, Eliza, I'm to marry Lord Alexander Luttrell, Duke of Exmoor."

"God's teeth, this is terrible!" Henry's fist hit the book. "The gossip will be the ruin of us!"

"Henry!" Eliza scolded "This is wonderful news. Our Ana is getting married." She jumped up and threw her arms around here sister in a warm embrace. "Be happy for her."

"What happened to all the scolding I received months ago for coming up with this fellow in the first place?" Henry felt befuddled as he scratched his head. "I thought he was a cad?"

"Just look at how happy our Ana is, dear, and you have your answer," Eliza said over Ana's shoulder.

"Well, if you are happy and Eliza thinks it's a good thing, then congratulations are at hand!" Henry stood up and joined the two women in the embrace. "First our son is born and now Ana is getting married! Yes indeed, things are looking up!"

"Cheapside," Charles directed the cabby as he pulled away from Eliza and Henry's home. In his mind, Ana had teased him enough. His anger and passions were raging out of control and he knew exactly where to go to find his release. Madam Molly always had a new convert for him to use. She, more than anyone, knew what he needed to satisfy his desires and never got in his way.

The cab pulled up to the familiar door. Charles barely had enough patience to pay the cabby. Molly greeted him at the entrance, her large full breasts spilling out from the bodice of her tight corset; her full figure made to entice her patrons. Charles nipped at each breast. "Oy Charlie, you're a randy one tonight," she laughed pushing him away.

"Moll, I need that new girl. And bring me some whiskey." He demanded as he grabbed Molly's large rounded rump. "Hee, Hee," she laughed as her own hand reached for his engorged member. "My, you're ready there, Charlie. Money first, always money first," he pushed a wad of bills in between her large fleshy mounds.

"Take the room on the left. I'll send Lizbeth. She's dressed as you requested," pointing down the hall, shaking her head in amazement at his ardor.

The room was not large but ample enough to fit the bed, a chair and a table with a single lit candle. It smelled of lust and sweat, just as he liked it.

He removed his coat, waistcoat and cravat and unbuttoned his shirt. There was a light knock at the door.

"Come in," Charles voice was filled with anticipation of what was to come. The door slowly opened. The girl entered. She had a bottle and two glasses in her hand.

"Put that on the table and stand over there. I want to look at you." Wiping his chin, he licked his lips in anticipation. He poured some of the whiskey in a glass and downed it in one long gulp. Pouring another for himself and one for the young girl, he downed another.

Lizbeth did what she was told, anxious to please her first customer. Her husband had died at sea. She had no family that she knew of. She had run out of options and she needed to survive. She was timid and scared. Her throat burned as she took a drink.

"How old are you?" He asked as he took in her figure with lustful intent. She was smaller than he wanted, her brown hair curled around her young face, her brown eyes big with fear at the conditions of her life.

"I am about seventeen or so, sir." She responded, uncomfortable with his stare.

"Old enough. Take another drink." He sounded sympathetic but cold. "No family to care for you then?"

She began to relax under his questioning and followed his directions "My mother put me in a workhouse when I was but a babe. They said she was a lady. I had no father. Then my husband died at sea." She could feel the whiskey taking hold. "Do you like the dress, sir?" she asked, knowing it had come from him just for her use.

"I love the dress. The green matches your turquoise eyes to perfection." He glared at her.

"But my eyes are brown, sir," she added timidly.

Charles' rage boiled to the surface at her contradiction. "You need to show gratitude for my gift, bitch," he said darkly as he stormed over to her. His hand came up and struck her hard. Her head spun back. Immediately, blood began to pour from her nose as she let out a scream of pain and shock. "You ungrateful little whore," he hissed again. This time his fist struck her jaw. She could feel several teeth come loose as her mouth filled with blood and pain.

"Sir, what have I done?" She began to cry as she cupped her bruised chin. "I needed the money s'all."

"Stop crying you bitch. You'll get what you deserve." His hands came up around her throat and began to tighten. "Stop bawling." She began to gasp for air as she clawed at his tightening grip. Suddenly he grabbed the top of the gown ripping it down to her waist. He grabbed her exposed breasts and brought them to his mouth. He bit hard into the soft flesh as fresh blood began to pour from the new wounds. She pulled at his ears to get him off of her as she screamed in pain, his hand again striking at her face, breaking her nose.

Molly stood outside the door as a sentinel, barring the way of any would-be rescuers. Several of the girls looked at her with horror and concern for what they heard. "'e's paid. 'e gets what 'e's paid for."

The male voice, cruel and demanding, growled "On your knees bitch. Harder. Harder."

They could hear the scuffle of feet and furniture. "I'm not finished. Don't you cry or I'll give you something to cry about." His voice hissed through the door with Lizbeth's painful cries.

"Molly, please make him stop." One of the girls implored, tears in her eyes.

But Molly stood frozen and immune to the goings on behind that door. Money always came first.

"On your belly, whore," Charles sneered.

Lizbeth screamed in pain. The women in the hall could only imagine the horrors that were taking place.

"Please, 'e's going to kill 'er," another women begged.

"'e'll not kill 'er. 'e's done this before. 'e pays well for this privilege." Molly glared at the girls. "Go about your business or I'll throw y'all in the streets. Mens are await'n." She ordered. The women scampered into their designated rooms, fearful of what was happening to one of their own and grateful that it was not happening to them.

A bloodied and pain-wracked Lizbeth was finally released from Charles' cruel grip, when he was exhausted and fully satisfied by the violent explosion and release of his passion. Freed from his grasp, Lizbeth ran from the room, her once beautiful green gown in tatters, her young face bruised and bleeding. Molly reached to grab her but she ran past and out the door into the swirling night, leaving bloody footprints as she ran sobbing down the street, clutching the torn bodice to her bleeding breasts.

Charles emerged from the room, buttoning his coat collar, looking cool and satisfied. He handed Molly an additional note.

"You were terrible rough tonight," she said coldly.

"She'll live and be grateful for what I've done to her," he sneered as he pushed past Molly into the damp stench of predawn London.

"This is odd." Henry said over his paper, his coffee cup in hand.

"What is it dear?" Eliza asked as she spread some strawberry jam over her hot morning roll.

"Ana, that dress you were wearing at the ball the other night, it's described here. It sounds like the same dress on this woman found drowned in the Thames."

"What?" Ana almost choked on her tea. "How can that be? My dress was made just for me. Charles made it for me. Let me see that article." She grabbed the paper. Had someone mistaken this poor wretch for her? Fear and bile rose in her throat.

"The article said she was found floating by the docks. It appears she had been badly beaten and raped." Eliza's eyes were wide with horror.

"My God, the poor thing," Eliza said. "Who could be so sinister?"

"It says here that they think she was a prostitute," Ana read, her face white as a ghost.

Harrington approached at the door, "There are two messages for Miss Ana, sir."

Ana took the sealed envelopes offered from the silver tray.

"From Alexander," she smiled as she opened his letter, but her bright countenance turned to disappointment.

"What's the matter?" Eliza asked.

"Alexander has left without me. He's returned to Dunster Castle." Her heart sank at the information. "Why didn't he come for me?" she asked both Eliza and Henry, knowing full well neither could answer.

"Well, open the second letter, Ana. It might shed light ..." Henry added hoping that there was a reasonable explanation.

Ana covered her mouth with her hand as she read. "It's Lady Catherine. She died Friday morning." Her eyes began to fill with tears.

"Oh Ana, I'm so sorry. I know how you had grown fond of her." Eliza comforted.

"This might change everything." A large tear began to run down her cheek. "Oh, Eliza, it's all my fault." Ana got up from her chair and quickly ran from the room. "I must leave immediately."

"What the blazes? I will never understand that Ana as long as I live." Henry called out to Eliza as she followed Ana out of the room. "Harrington, get a private coach prepared for Ana's departure. I think she'll need it." He reached for his paper which had been dumped unceremoniously on the floor.

"Ana, slow down." Eliza chided her sister as she charged through her drawers to fill the trunk she had pulled from the corner.

"Eliza, you don't understand," anxiety across her face.

"That's right, I don't understand. What do you mean it's your fault? And how can this change anything?" Eliza sat on the edge of the bed as Ana frantically attempted to pack.

"If I hadn't been … then she would not have gotten wet. I knew she wasn't well when we left. Then that prostitute's death …," Ana trailed off. "And now he might change his mind about marrying me." Ana stopped, covering her face, wracked with fear and confusion. Ana couldn't share her anxieties with her sister. She didn't want her to worry.

Sighing deeply, Eliza stood. Giving her sister a hug, she said, "Ana something's not right. I don't know what it is, but it's not right. You're not making any sense. I don't see what Lady Catherine's death has to do with the death of a prostitute?"

Knowing she couldn't burden her sister with the truth, Ana did her best to reign in her fear. "I'm just afraid that Alexander will decide that he doesn't need me any longer. His message was so … cold. He doesn't even mention his mother."

"May I see the note? It may be that he didn't yet know of his mother's passing." Ana pointed towards the bed where both letters lay. Eliza picked up the missive.

Ana,

I am returning to Dunster Castle. Remain with your family as long as is required. I will send for you if you are needed.

Lord Alexander Luttrell

"Ana, what did you expect? A love letter? For heaven sake. He said he'll send for you to return, didn't he? His mother just died. He'll need your help and will call for you. You'll see," Eliza rationalized.

"Where does it say he needs my help? He said if … *if* I'm needed. You don't know how much he wanted to relieve me of my position but for his mother. And now she's gone." Ana began to weep for the loss of her friend. "Oh, and she would've been so happy to know I was going to marry her son."

"Now, now Ana, it's not so bad. If he didn't wish you to return then he would have said … "Lady Catherine died this morning. Your services are no longer required. I'll have your personal effects returned." Eliza felt proud of her rewrite. "Oh, and the marriage is off, Lord Luttrell … without the Alexander."

"Eliza, you're making fun of me. I'm really frightened."

"I'm sorry Ana, but you must admit you're being flighty. Thinking it's your fault. It should be my fault for giving birth to Miles and making you return home in the first place."

"Now that's ridiculous." She glared at her sister for not being understanding.

"Now you can see how absurd you sound."

"Well, even if I am being ridiculous, I must return to him. You're most likely right. He does need me. Or at least his sons will need me," she trailed off as she continued to pack.

Within the hour Ana departed her sister's home to face the unknown. She was afraid Alexander would be angry with her for returning before she was summoned. But she was willing to endure his ire. She was confused as to why he had left without a word other than the simple, cold note he had sent and why he didn't say anything about Lady Catherine. She knew Geoffrey and Hugh would need her. But more than anything, she felt completely exposed in London. She couldn't tell Eliza or Henry of the threat on her life. She was frightened by the article in the paper. Somehow, she knew the woman found in the Thames was supposed to be her. She had to run home for safety. And Dunster Castle and Alexander Luttrell were now home.

CHAPTER 33

*A*na's coach stopped at the familiar Dunster Castle gate. Less than a fortnight had passed since she left for her visit with Eliza and the new baby. Now she returned to black bunting on the gates and to an unknown future. She was anxious to see Alexander. She missed Lady Catherine terribly and was sure that Alexander must be deeply saddened.

"Miss Ana," Chesterton answered the door, a black band of mourning around his arm. "I'm so pleased. We weren't expecting your return."

"Chesterton," she asked as she took off her bonnet, "Why did you think I wasn't returning?" He looked tired.

"We've had sad days, Miss," he sounded so melancholy. Spontaneously, Ana put her arms around the older man's neck giving him a hug. "Oh, Chesterton, I'm so sad for everyone." Surprised by her emotional response, he gently pushed her away, adding, "I'm so glad you are home. His Lordship needs you." His eyes were misty. "The service was yesterday." He looked down at his shoes, knowing she must feel terrible.

"Oh," Ana said, tears welling up in her eyes. "Chesterton, I had hoped…" she faded. "I left as soon as I received your note." She took his hand in hers. "Where is he?" she was anxious to see Alexander and comfort him if she could.

"His Lordship has sequestered himself in the library. The boys are in the nursery unattended and I'm afraid to say, quite wild.

Ana looked up the carved oak stair case and frowned. "Yes, I hear. Where's Riya?"

"Lord Luttrell had her sent her to a boarding school directly after the funeral yesterday. She cried and cried. He has released all the women servants except for Mrs. C." He shook his head. "Poor Rollins is cleaning the scullery. Lord Luttrell said he couldn't bear to see a woman."

"Oh Chesterton, he even let Cook go?" Ana's fears returned full force. Looking down the hall she could see the library door was closed. He had left London without her. And finding now he had let go all the women staff was disturbing to say the least.

"Even Cook! The worst of it is, Mrs. C. can't prepare a meal to save her soul, poor dear. Frankly, Miss Ana, I am very worried, very worried indeed," he said as he shook his head while looking downward towards the floor.

"Oh, my." Stunned, Ana shook her head. She feared the death of his mother had rendered Alexander quite insane. "My trunk is at the gate, Chesterton. I'll think of something. In the meantime, I'll be in the nursery." She needed to think.

"Very good, Miss. I'm so glad you've returned. So glad." Chesterton, stoic as always, dabbed at his eyes. "I'll have Mrs. C. make some tea." She gave Chesterton a gentle smile.

"Thank you, Chesterton, all will work out. You'll see," she said as she slowly began to climb the stairs towards the ruckus coming from the nursery. She felt weary and was not looking forward to what lay ahead. Stopping, she listened for a few seconds. Geoffrey was taking his aggressions out on poor Hugh. She wondered what had happened to the fine young men she had left behind.

She opened the door. Geoffrey was caught with his left-hand gripping at Hugh's hair, his right in a tight fist made ready to punch.

"Miss Pembroke," Hugh managed to pull away and ran to the safety of her arms.

"Geoffrey, come here," she said extending another arm for an embrace.

"Miss Pembroke," he said as he slowly ventured forward, breaking into a run.

"I'm so sorry for your grandmother's death," she said as she held them close.

"I thought you were never going to come back," Hugh said through tears.

"I said I'd come back and here I am," Ana assured him as she stroked his head.

"Father sent Riya away," Geoffrey said, distressed.

"I know, Geoffrey. I'll talk with him about that. Have you boys had supper?"

They nodded their heads. "It was awful," Hugh added.

"Well it's getting late. After a short read, you both need to go to sleep. Tomorrow we'll need to get back onto a schedule. By the look and smell of things, we'll have to start you both with a bath." Their care was obviously neglected and Ana decided they were first on her list.

Finally in their beds, Hugh reached for a hug. Ana happily obliged.

"I'm so glad you've come home," he said looking up at her lovingly.

"So am I Hugh, so am I," Ana responded brushing back his blond curls.

"Miss Pembroke," Geoffrey called from the other bed.

"Yes, Geoffrey?"

"I'm glad you are home, too," he added with a boyish smile, his blue eyes so like his father's. Ana gave Hugh a kiss on the forehead then gave one to Geoffrey.

"Thank you, Geoffrey. Get some sleep. Tomorrow is promising to be a busy day." She blew out the lamp and quietly closed the door behind her. She felt satisfied that the boys were in their beds. Her first order of business was complete.

Ana returned to her room. Her trunk was placed neatly in the corner. She was exhausted from her long ride. The boys had been draining. She took a sip of her cold tea. There was cheese and bread on a plate. As she ate, she pondered her next task. Sleep was a lovely option, she thought, looking longingly at her bed. But Alexander was locked away in his library. She knew she must go to him.

She pulled on a fresh dress, ran a brush through her unruly curls, and tied them up in a ribbon. Looking in the mirror, she hoped she did not look as tired as she felt. She pinched her cheeks for some added color before leaving for the library.

As she stood at the library door, Ana realized her heart was heavy with the memory of Lady Catherine, yet racing with anticipation of seeing Alexander. Alexander, she must get used to that. His mother's death had to be a severe blow for him or he would not have banished all women from his home. He was obviously too overwrought to be thinking clearly. Ana prayed he would not cast her out as well and hoped to convince him she could be trusted. She felt her hands shake as she reached for the knob. It was not locked. She knocked gently as she walked in.

"Alexander?" she said softly. There was silence. He recognized her voice.

"Come in," he said at last. What he really wanted was to send her packing with all the others.

The clock in the hall struck half past ten as Ana closed the door behind her. The only light came from the fire burning dimly in the grate. The curtains were closed tightly. She could barely see him in the shadows of the room.

"Chesterton said you'd arrived." His voice was flat. He was sitting in one of the overstuffed chairs before the fire grate, his boots resting upon the hearth for warmth. His back was to her.

"Yes, sir, I felt I needed to attend to the boys before I came to you," she added quietly, unsure of her next move. She had not seen Alexander since the night of the Royal Ball when he had taken her into his arms and asked her to marry him. He appeared so forlorn sitting there alone with his grief. She slowly walked around his chair to see his face. He looked as unkempt as the boys, with his dark chestnut hair unruly and a beard of several day's growth covering his chin.

"That was good of you. They've been neglected since Mother's death. I'm afraid I've not had the inclination to tend to them." His voice was flat and emotionless. He was sure she had come to finish him off with a final blow of deceit.

Ana felt his pain. She knew what it was like to lose loved ones. She gently knelt down by his chair and took his strong hand in hers and held it to her cheek. She looked up into his face. He watched her closely through darkened eyes.

"Alexander, I am so sorry about your mother's death," tears welled up in her turquoise eyes. "Is there anything I can do to ease what you must be feeling?" she asked searching his face for a clue.

He remained unmoved; his blue eyes had turned a cold gray. He watched as a solitary tear cascaded down her creamy cheek. Her eyes were gentle and warm as she looked at him. *She is good at this*, he thought. *Two can play this game. If she can use me then I can use her.* He reached out and slowly wiped the tear away. Her skin felt warm and soft under his hand. Her lips parted as he caressed her mouth with his thumb. She took his hand and kissed his palm. Their eyes met and lingered. Her desire to please him was easily read. His need for her began to stir.

"Yes, ease my pain. Help me forget for a few hours." He reached for her, cupping her face in both hands as he leaned over to kiss her mouth. He knew she would offer herself up to him, for she was a conniving tart. Yet he found her tender and inviting as he kissed her. "Ana, I need you." His voice was deep and husky as his passion for her kindled.

"What?" Ana pulled away, slightly confused at his request. She was at once exhausted and excited, frightened and thrilled. But more than anything she knew he still wanted her. A flood of relief ran through her body.

Alexander was surprised by her hesitant response. "Yes. Now. Tonight." He stood up and pulled her into his arms. "Help me forget my pain for a few hours." His eyes were dark with desire as he studied her full crimson lips. Feeling his hands around her waist, Ana realized that she couldn't say no. She wanted him too much to deny his request. Besides, they were to be married soon. There would be no harm. He needed her. She needed him. She lifted her head, passion lit up her own eyes as his mouth found hers.

His kisses were deeper than before. Ana felt his hand untying the ribbon in her hair. Her dark curls cascaded down her back, his hand entwined in her tresses. His tongue explored the sweetness of her mouth. He pulled her closer, his passion hot and hard against her.

"I need you," he whispered again as his mouth trailed fiery kisses down her throat, lingering, hot and sensuous to the opening of her dress, his hand cupping her supple breast. Her body became more alive with every kiss, her own desire growing with his caresses. Their eyes met. He felt jealous knowing she was spoiled. Again, his mouth found hers, searching ever deeper and deeper. Her hands were around his well-muscled neck pulling him closer. She ran her fingers through the curls at the back of his head sending shivers down his spine. Following his lead, she began to kiss his face, her tongue and lips nibbling at his ear. He lifted his head as his passions ignited at her sensual teases. He moaned and again found her mouth, hot and inviting, his hips pushing his manhood into her soft flesh and the folds of her skirts.

Suddenly, he swept her off her feet and into his arms. "I will have you this night," he said, his voice husky in her ear. He carried her as if she were a feather, up two stairs at a time. Pushing open the door to his rooms he laid her gently on his bed.

Ana looked around the room as he closed the door. There was a fire burning brightly providing a warm sensual glow. She had been in his room only once before, following that first kiss. He had been drunk. But there was no alcohol on his breath tonight.

Returning to the bedside he pulled off his boots. Standing over her he began to unbutton his white cotton shirt. Ana watched as his long fingers systematically unfastened each button revealing more of his muscled chest lightly covered with dark black curls. He noted the rise and fall of her bosom, realizing he was tantalizing her with the unfastening of each closure. He pulled the shirt from his broad shoulders and threw the garment into the corner, the muscles in his arm rippling with the movement. He reached for her foot and slowly loosened the tie of each shoe, seductively removing each and carelessly tossing them onto the floor. His hands slowly caressed her calves, reaching up each leg of her pantaloons and removing each stocking. She shivered at his touch. He then knelt on the bed and reached for the brass buttons on Ana's dress.

Her heart raced as he slowly began to undress her, button by button, his light delicate touch teasing her flesh, exposing her white underpinnings. His finger gently traced the soft white mounds that pushed up from her corset, sending waves of desire to the pit of her stomach. She grabbed the fabric of the bed covers as he slowly kissed each mound allowing his tongue to explore the cleavage of her warm supple breasts. She moaned. He reached down and gently pulled the ribbon that held her petticoats in place, his dark eyes never leaving hers, enjoying the desired effect on her face, his own desire hard and strong.

Ana watched him as he bit his lower lip while pulling the heavy garments from her hips and dropping them in an heap on the floor beside the bed. He straddled her. His hands started at her breasts and slowly moved down to caress her sides, her narrow waist, her rounded hips and her shapely bottom, enjoying the warm sensuality of her soft feminine curves. He leaned forward and found her mouth, teasing her with his tongue as fires of desire burned deep within her, his tongue probing, exploring, exciting. Ana closed her eyes, feeling lost in his sensual exploration of her. The smell of musk and spice filled her nostrils. He kissed the graceful curve of her throat and allowed his tongue to deeper delve into the cleavage between her breasts, tasting, teasing, igniting. His hands began to untie the ribbons of her corset releasing her soft round breasts for his pleasure. His mouth began to taste them and tease them through the cotton of her chemise. They responded by giving her intense pleasure, her nipples taut under his tongue.

From somewhere within, a deep moan of pleasure escaped her mouth. Alexander sat up and looked into her dark lust-filled eyes. He smiled at seeing her response to him. *No, she was no innocent*, he thought to himself as he again found her mouth. Only this time he was determined to release her completely from the confines of her corset. His experienced hands slowly continued to undo the bindings that kept her locked in. Finally, the garment was released. He cupped each breast through the cotton chemise, teasing each peak to hardness with his thumbs and teeth.

"Raise your arms," his voice was throaty with awaiting passion. Ana obeyed as he pulled her chemise over her head and added it to the pile on the floor. His approving gaze roamed down her half naked frame, her supple breasts were mounds of perfection, her skin white as alabaster.

"You're beautiful," he bent down, cupping one bare breast with his warm hand as his mouth and tongue teased and tugged at the hard nipple of the other. Instinctively, Ana pushed her hips up as her passions began to take full control of her body. His tongue continued to trace exciting circles, enticing, thrilling as his hand slipped down her flat soft stomach to the button at the top of her pantaloons. Soon she lay completely exposed to him on his bed. But he did not stop with the removal of her last garment. He slipped his hand between her soft milky thighs.

Her initial instinct was to close her knees tightly together. But slowly and gently he began to entice her to open up to him with his massaging hands. She gasped slightly as he found the hot, velvety wetness of her charms.

"Ana, you are so warm, so ready," he said as he enticed the center of her desire with his long fingers. Slowly he massaged and teased her, bringing never-before experienced ripples of exquisite pleasure to her body. Her whole world disappeared into this very moment. There was no past, no future. There was only what she felt as his hand caressed her towards ecstasy and his mouth taunted her breasts. She ran her fingers though his hair.

Ana had no idea that she could ever feel such pleasure. She felt lost in what he was doing to her. Yet somewhere she wanted to please him too. She let her hand reach down to the buttons on his trousers. She could feel the hot thick hardness of his passion as she undid each button. He helped her pull his trousers from his body. Taking her hand, he led her to him. Wrapping her hand around his thick hard flesh, she gently squeezed and released, he moaned as the pleasure of her stroking touch tantalized his passions even further.

His knee pushed her legs apart. "I can't hold back. I must have you now," his voice was deep and seductive. He found the warm velvety opening and slowly began to enter her, but stopped suddenly as he realized he had reached her maidenhead.

"Ana, I thought ..." He looked down at her, surprised by what he found.

"Don't stop," her voice was sultry and imploring. She reached up to his neck to bring his mouth to hers, her lips soft and caressing. Her invitation to continue was all he needed. He couldn't stop now. He pushed through the veil of her virginity. He could feel her body tense at the pain of entry. Slowly, gently, he began to move within her as her pain gave way again to intense pleasure. He felt like a cad. He had misjudged her and was using her for his own pleasure. Oh, but what pleasure it was and how willing she was to give into it.

Slowly he began to move forward and back, bringing her once again towards ecstasy. Instinctively, she wrapped her legs around his thrusting hips as if trying to bring all of him into her. His pulsating movements increased as his passion began to climax.

Wave after wave of sensual pleasure swelled through her body until she cried out from bursts of ecstasy. She held onto him as his own desire exploded along with hers. His eyes closed, he groaned from deep within his chest as he found his release within her.

Gradually, his strong thrusts became gentle. He saw that her eyes were open, watching his face. He leaned down and softly kissed each turquoise orb before he again found her mouth. Lightly, he kissed her. Studying her face, he pulled away a lock of hair that clung to her damp brow. He smiled at her. Ana retuned the smile, her legs remaining entwined around his back. He gently thrust himself into her once again. A small aftershock of pleasure ran down her spine. It pleased him to see the response she had to him.

"You realize you may not sleep in your bed again, not after this," his voice was soft, a glint of future encounters glistening in his eyes.

"What would the household think?" she caressed his face feeling the roughness of his beard.

"Household be damned," he smiled down at her.

Finally, yet unwillingly, he pulled himself from atop of her and rested on an elbow. He traced the form of her brow with his finger, then the curve of her nose.

"You have a perfect nose," he said.

"I always thought it too long," she responded.

"You're supposed to say thank you with a compliment," he teased.

"Thank you," she smiled up at him.

"His finger then traced the curve of her lips. And your lips … made for kissing." Suddenly he cocked his head ever so slightly.

"Did I do that?" he asked as he gently traced the rough and raw flesh of her chin and then felt the growth of his own beard.

"Next time I will be sure to shave," he smiled down at her, his eyes growing gentle, "I didn't mean to hurt you Ana. I didn't know. I just assumed …" He suddenly felt awful that he had been so terribly mistaken about her honor and had taken her out of jealousy and bitterness. He realized his ability to trust was sorely missing and the idea of trusting was as foreign to him as speaking Chinese. He had no concept of it.

"Ana, why did you give in to me? I don't understand and feel such a cad …"

"Alexander—*calling him by his given name was strange*—though you say you don't love me, I love you." She caressed his cheek as she looked up at him. "I'm in love with you. I want to please you any way I can," she said simply.

He shook his head. "Though you know I don't love you. you were still willing to give yourself to me? I don't understand," he said honestly, as he encircled her in his arms.

Ana remained silent. She didn't know how to respond and did not wish to turn a beautiful moment sour. She bit her lip.

Following a long silence, he said, "You're my perfect match," wanting to move away from the uncomfortable topics of love and trust. "See how well you fit into my arms with your head on my shoulder?" She snuggled up against his warm skin, feeling the safety and security of his arms and knowing he moved on from the topic of "love."

His hand came down to caress her breasts once again. "They are also perfect." He lifted his head, there was a glint of folly in his eyes as he raised one brow, "I will name this one Abigail and the other Begonia."

Ana was taken aback at this unexpected and unfamiliar humor that he was displaying.

"That is the funniest thing I've ever heard," she said and began to giggle. Her laugh made him relax all the more.

Then suddenly they found themselves laughing at the humor of his naming, finding a new ease with each other they had never experienced.

He had misjudged her, he thought, as he wiped the tears of laughter from his eyes. His mother always had some romantic scheme. Elizabeth was unfaithful and abandoning. The whole British army had left him on the battlefield. But other than the Queen, who was completely untouchable, he had no close knowledge of true intimacy, especially not with a woman. He studied Ana. Was it possible that she was just who she appeared? Chesterton and Mrs. C. were happy. He loved his sons, at least he knew he needed to protect them from getting hurt. But was that love? Was it possible to love this woman lying in his arms, whatever that was? Her passions matched his. Could he trust her? That was the problem. He gently caressed the top of her head as it lay on his shoulder and tenderly kissed her forehead.

Ana wondered at his relaxed humor. Was it possible that he really could love her? She had again snuggled against his side. He was so gentle with her, he cared about her well-being, he wanted to please her; to protect her. Wasn't that love? She allowed her hand to caress his muscled chest and stomach enjoying the feel of his warm naked flesh. But he struggled with trusting her. She wondered what she could do to gain his trust.

Soon the silent introspection faded, replaced by the rekindling of newborn passion. Her roaming hand had reawakened his need of her again; her warm, soft naked body laying against his tantalized him. He began to kiss her softly at first, them more ardently as his passion increased. And soon his body was over hers, taking her, exploding with ecstasy and she was yielding once again to his desire, her own climax meeting with his until they were both spent.

CHAPTER 34

*I*t was past noon when Ana finally found time to speak with Alexander about the conditions in the Castle. Finding him at his desk in the library she knocked on the door.

He looked up and gave her an engaging smile. "Come in Ana," his face taking on a boyish charm, his eyes soft.

She walked up to his desk and placed her hands on her hips, "Alexander, I don't know why you have sent all the women away. It's just … well … just ridiculous. Mrs. C. can't do it alone and I for one am completely ill-prepared to help."

"Whoa, slow down. Is this what I get after a night of passion—a shrew? And look at you? What have you been up to? You look more like a washer woman then a bride-to-be," he said, as he observed her hair in disarray, sleeves rolled to the elbow, and no petticoats. His eyes sparkled with devilish humor.

"You haven't heard me. You sent all the women away. One of the footmen had to help Hugh bathe. Thank God Geoffrey is old enough to look after himself. And that nursery was a disaster. Rollins can't possibly clean the scullery. I had to scrape out the cinders from three fireplaces," showing the black streaks on her arms. "And poor Mrs. C. is beside herself in the kitchen. What were you thinking?" she pushed a stray curl from her hot face, getting a smudge of soot on her forehead.

Alexander covered his mouth with his hand to stifle the laughter that was bubbling up. He continued to retain the ease of their relationship from the previous night. And, of course he knew she was right.

"You're laughing at me?" She could feel her anger begin to kindle as her turquoise eyes flashed daggers towards him.

He stood up taking on a more serious stance and walked around his desk, taking her by the shoulders began to pull her close, but Ana pushed him away.

"Don't hug me when I'm angry. And I'm angry!" she said as her chin lifted defiantly in the air.

Alexander's eyes opened wide at her reaction to him as he lifted his hands in the air, a smirk lingering on his lips and twinkle in his eyes. "No hugs." Then mocking, "You're right Ana, I've been, once again, the fool. What can I say; the gentle sex brings out the irrational man in me."

"Piffle!" Ana said, stomping her foot trying to control her feelings.

Alexander placed his hands again on her shoulders and looked deeply into her eyes, forcing his face to become very sincere. "I've already had Chesterton send to town for the women. They'll be back tomorrow. They'll be paid for their time away and to make up for any misfortune my impulsivity has done them, I've decided to give them each an additional week's wages. Does that make you happy?" His eyes flickered and a small smile tugged at the corner of his mouth.

"Oh Alexander!" She threw her arms around his neck. "That is most generous and it does make me happy." Looking into his eyes she added, "Mrs. C. will be so relieved."

"Is it alright to pull you close now?" he said as he did so, feeling Ana lean against his frame.

Ana loved the feel of his strong arms around her. Her body next to his aroused his passions. There was never a woman who so stimulated him.

"Well, I must get myself cleaned up. I have two savage boys to teach," she said as she pulled away to leave.

Reluctantly, Alexander let her go and watched the sway of her hips as she walked towards the door. Stopping, she turned around to look at him. There was such a smoldering look in her turquoise eyes that he was sorely tempted to throw caution to the wind and take her now, on the library floor.

"Alexander, one more thing," she said sheepishly.

"Anything," with her looking at him like that he was willing to get her the moon.

"Bring Riya back."

"What?" That was one thing he was not expecting. "Absolutely not!"

Ana replied, "You just said anything."

"Ana, surely you couldn't have missed the flirtation developing between Riya and Geoffrey. I'll not have it." Anger was now sparking in his eyes.

Ana re-entered the room. "That … simple and innocent thing? Riya knows she's too old for him. He's just fifteen. She's almost an adult. There's no harm done."

"I won't have them hurt." His voice was taking on its old familiar coolness.

"Alexander, life has broken hearts. We can't escape it. Shielding your sons from pain will only cripple them. You need to let them learn to feel all their feelings to be complete human beings." Her voice was gentle as she continued, "Look at how you crippled this household by putting the womenfolk out even for one week. You are teaching them to push life away rather than embrace it with all its joys and tears."

Alexander studied the young woman standing in front of him, amazed at her wisdom.

"I'll send for Riya. I can't fight with that reasoning," he conceded, enjoying the renewed embrace and kiss he was receiving. Pleasing Ana definitely had its benefits.

The rest of Ana's day was filled with Geoffrey and Hugh returning to their studies. Finally, the day had come to a close. The boys were tucked in their beds for the evening. She realized she too was hungry and tired after a day of washing, organizing, and getting back on schedule.

It was hours since she had seen Alexander. She thought she might find him in the library; he was not there. Nor was he in the dining room or drawing room. Feeling disappointed and weary, Ana decided what she really needed most was a hot bath. Her stomach growled; but first the bath. Soon Chesterton had several houseboys engaged in filling the copper tub to the brim. The fire in her grate was lit. Her room was set.

Once all were gone and her room was quiet, Ana eagerly removed her dirty clothes. Walking to the window she opened it slightly, allowing a cool evening breeze to gently enter the room. Lighting a match, she lit several candles. The atmosphere was relaxing. Mrs. C. had provided dried rose petals which Ana generously sprinkled into the steaming water, their aroma quickly filling the air. Naked, she sat on the edge of the tub. Removing the pins from her hair she allowed the thick dark tresses drop down her back. Swinging her shapely legs over the side, she slipped into the fragrant hot water for a long relaxing soak. Her hair draped over the side of the tub. Until this very moment, she did not realize quite how tired she really was. Ana closed her eyes and allowed herself to unwind as her tired muscles eased in the swirl of the scented bath. She felt herself beginning to drift off into a light sleep. But the sound of her door closing brought her back to senses.

"Mrs. C. the rose petals were a perfect touch, thank you," she said, her eyes half closed.

"Shhh," it was a male voice.

Ana's eyes flew open wide, her wet hands came out of the tub and took hold of the sides, splashing water over the sides, but she dared not sit up from the tub.

"Just stay where you are," Alexander said. His voice was almost a whisper. "Chesterton told me you were here. I thought you might be hungry. You didn't come to supper. So, I brought you some dinner."

"Alexander?" It was both a question and a statement of surprise. "I'm bathing. I can't eat now."

"Yes, I know. I'm going to feed you," he said as he used his foot to pull a chair against the tub. Ana watched dumbfounded. Placing the tray of food on top of it, Alexander went to fetch another chair for himself. Taking a seat by the tub he said. "Let's see, we have some potatoes, carrots, and a nice slice of beef. And here's some wine." he said as placed the goblet into her wet hand.

"What are you doing?" she asked, quite embarrassed at her predicament.

"I told you, I'm going to give you supper. Now, take a sip of wine. Good girl." She obeyed. He took the glass and placed it on the tray in front of him.

"Let's start with a nice piece of potato, shall we?" His voice was warm and deep.

Ana studied him as he took the fork and pierced the potato. The light of the fire lit up his face. His dark chestnut hair looked almost black. A curl had fallen onto his brow. There were soft lines across his forehead; she had never really noticed them before. His dark eyebrows and thick lashes framed his smoldering blue eyes, where there also were creases created from laughter. Ana silently accepted the forkful of food he offered, but continued to examine his face. He was intent on his project and appeared unaware of her scrutinization. He had a strong nose. Directly below were his full lips and square jawline.

"What happened to your mustache?" She just realized it was gone.

"Here are some carrots. I told you I was going to shave. Remember?" he smiled a beguiling crooked smile. Ana noticed the creases in his cheeks as he did.

Ana nodded her head as she looked into his eyes. There was something in those eyes, something gentle. It made her heart leap. *Maybe Lady Catherine had been right. Maybe he was learning to love. Maybe Eliza is right also.*

"And now for some beef," he said. The loaded fork came towards her.

"I looked for you a while ago. Where were you?" Ana asked opening her mouth to receive the next bite.

"Someone had to cook today." he said with a smile. "Mrs. C is a terrible cook."

"You were in the kitchen?" she said, surprised.

"Where else would I be cooking?" he replied with a smile. "How's your meal?"

"Delicious. I didn't know you could cook."

"We had to do everything in the army. So, I gave Mrs. C. the night off and made us all supper. While you fed the boys, I ate in the kitchen with the Chestertons. It was rather pleasant, actually, to see how my staff lives."

"But I don't understand why you didn't come and get us."

"I have motives for what I do," he said, placing another forkful of food in her mouth.

She looked at him questioningly. He took a napkin and dabbed the corners of her lips.

"Someone has to towel you off," his warm eyes sparkled with enthusiasm of his plan.

"Alexander, you devil," she smiled at him, flicking water into his face with her fingers.

"I know. Isn't it grand?" He smiled back, wiping the spray from his brow. Having finished the meal, Alexander stood up and removed the chairs. He returned and stood by the side of the tub. Ana watched him as he began to slowly undo his shirt, starting with the cuffs of his sleeves and moving to the buttons down his chest.

"What are you doing?" Her eyes opened wide as he removed his garment exposing his strong shoulders and well-defined chest.

"Where is the soap?" he responded.

"Why?" fearful that she knew the reason.

"Now that I have fed you, it's time to finish your bath." He took the pitcher and filled it with water from the tub.

"Close your eyes," he ordered, a lilt in his voice.

"Alexander. Sto— …," was all Ana was able to sputter as the water spilled onto her head. She sat up as she gasped for air.

"Now where is that soap?" he asked again.

Pointing to the cake on top of the towel, Ana attempted to wipe the water from her eyes but he was pouring another pitcher full. She was hardly able to catch her breath. But soon he had managed to create a thick lather in her hair.

"Alexander, you don't know what you are doing. I am going to have a mass of tangles." But he didn't listen to her protestations and spilled more water onto her head rinsing the suds into the now cooling tub.

"Are you getting enjoyment out of torturing me?" She said, glaring at him through long strands of wet hair.

"More than you'll ever know," he laughed. "And I plan on torturing you even more before this night is through. Where is that soap?" He said as he fished around in the tub. "Ah, here it is." He pulled the soap up from the bottom of the tub. It smelled of lavender. He brought it up to his nose and slowly inhaled the fragrance. His dark eyes locked with Ana's, deep pools of desire. Rubbing the soap in his hands, he pulled her arm from the tub and began to slowly and methodically wash her hand, arm, elbow and shoulder. It sent shock waves of pleasure down her belly.

"Alexander….!" He gave her a telling smile. He moved around the tub and took her other arm and did the same.

"Let me have your leg," he said as he moved to the end of the tub.

Ana silently obeyed as she watched him take her wet foot into his hand and slowly began to lather and massage the sole, sensually pulling on each toe. He reached up and massaged her calf.

"Close your eyes," he said softly.

Ana laid her head back onto the tub and followed his direction. His firm hands moved up her thigh, pressing and rubbing her soft flesh. Ana moaned with the pleasure he was providing. He replaced her leg in the water and reach in for the other. He then silently moved to the head of the tub and began to gently massage her face, back and shoulders. Ana felt relaxed as his hands made gentle circles around her brow, temples and eyes. Finally, his hands moved from her shoulder to the sensual mounds and soft belly that were just below the water. Ana opened her eyes at the touch.

"Close your eyes," he repeated, his voice husky with passion.

Easing back into the tub she closed her eyes. He teased each mound, now slippery with soap. Her nipples responded to his erotic touch. His arm entered the water and he gently moved down toward the velvety valley between her legs. Slowly his fingers found the source of her pleasure. He rubbed gently, bringing waves of pleasure to her body. His arms submerged into the tub, slipped behind her knees and back. He gently lifted her from the tub, water spilling over the sides.

Opening her eyes, Ana wrapped her dripping arm around the thick muscles of his neck. His own passion now throbbing and hard, he laid her moist body on the bed. She watched him as he removed the rest of his clothes, the extended bulge in his trousers evident as he undid the buttons. His clothes now removed, he put his knee on the bed.

"Wait," Ana said. "I want to see you." He stepped back, and smiled, a bit embarrassed yet excited by her request. He watched her as her eyes studied his impassioned manhood.

"Are you quite finished?" he said, anxious to continue what he had begun.

"Alexander, you are …" She was unable to finish as his mouth found hers, searching deeply with his hungry kiss. Her eyes closed at the taste of him.

She couldn't help but obey him as he teased her, increasing her pleasure. His hands moved slowly down her stomach towards her hips and thighs, massaging, teasing, kneading. Ana felt her heartbeat quickening as his touch found the damp folds between her thighs.

Slowly he caressed her, watching her face express the pleasure he was giving, his own passion rising hot at the feel of her. He removed his hand and again teased her breasts sending waves of ecstasy through her body. His mouth was hard on hers as he pressed her soft wet flesh against his own damp body. He kissed her eyes, her nose, and again found her mouth. His passion for her was stronger than ever. He had to take her or explode. Her body was utterly awakened by his touch, his passion throbbing for release.

Ana's legs wrapped around his hips as he thrust himself into her. Her desire for him was as strong as his for her. They were lost in their passion as they moved as one towards that moment of ecstasy, both crying out as their union exploded in climatic pleasure.

"Ana, Ana," he said with each exploding thrust. Finally spent, he lay encircled in her arms and legs. Ana kissed the top of his damp head as he lay on her breasts, breathing heavily from the exertion and release.

Finally, he rolled onto his side. He pulled the blanket over their naked bodies and gathered her into his arms.

"Ana, you exhaust me," he whispered into her ear.

Ana lay quietly in his arms, enjoying their strength and warmth. *How can this man, who had just so passionately and tenderly fed me, bathed me, and made love to me not feel love towards me*, she wondered? She needed to know if his feelings were matching his actions. She had to ask.

"Alexander?" She asked quietly, knowing he was falling off to sleep.

"Yes?" his voice already drowsy.

"I was wondering," she was hesitant, "if maybe…."

"Maybe what?" he looked at her with one heavy eye.

"Maybe you do love me?" her voice almost a whisper.

"Ana," his voice stronger and colder, "you know my answer. Don't ask me again. Don't let your girlish fantasy to get a useless emotion ruin what we do have." And with that he rolled over exposing the scar on his back. "The topic is closed."

"I'm sorry, I won't bring it up again," Ana said quietly as the sharp pain of rejection stabbed her heart. His breath became heavy and rhythmic. But for Ana, a tear slowly began to form in the corner of her eye as she gently traced the long, jagged mark on his back, realizing his outward disfigurement was only a symbol of the wound he carried in his closed heart.

Quickly, Alexander reached around and pushed her hand off his scar. Anger had replaced his gentle tones, and his eyes were now menacing. "Do not, ever, do that again." He threw the covers from his body and gathered up his clothes, leaving Ana alone in the dark to deal with her confusion and the pain of what had just transpired between them.

CHAPTER 35

*A*lexander arrived in Bath later than anticipated. The town was bustling with visitors for both the society and the waters. He felt guilty leaving Dunster so quickly. His only explanation was to Chesterton of his meeting with the Knights of Bath, with strict instructions not to tell any others. With his mother barely cold, his sons devastated by her death, it was irrational at best and he knew it. He could have skipped this; the others would have understood. But he needed to give himself distance from Ana's idiotic romantic notions. Having to deal with her foolish emotions when bedding her infuriated him. She shouldn't have touched his scar. It was more than he was prepared to handle. It was too raw, too close. As a result, memories flooded into his consciousness, memories he had never shared with another living soul. They were too real, too vivid; the sights, the sounds all flooded back. Even Riya was not allowed to touch his scar when she was massaging the kinks from his neck, though she had been instrumental in healing the jagged wound. He felt like a coward, unable to stand up to a silly woman's notions, unable to understand the reasons. He just had to leave.

It was late afternoon when he made his way into the Pump Room to partake of the waters, clear his mind, and wash away his dark memories.

"Sir Alexander Luttrell?" he heard a voice behind him say. He turned to see who called his name.

"Why Jacob Sumner, you sly fox, what brings you to Bath?" Alexander reached out his hand for a firm grasp. "I wouldn't have expected to see you here taking the waters." He was both glad and annoyed at seeing his friend, hoping to be alone.

"You caught me, my friend," he said with a gap-toothed grin. "I'm here because I've been smitten … by love."

"What? You? Love? Come now, man. Have you lost your senses?" He knew Jacob was a confirmed bachelor and chuckled at the announcement of his friend's foolishness.

"Yes, yes me, a Miss Stockbridge. See her there with her family?" Jacob nodded at the direction of the table nearest the window where a pretty plump girl sat with two older people. "They came to me on some legal matters and brought the sweet Miss Stockbridge along. I was so taken with her. Possessed really, I've never been the same."

"I'm speechless, truly." Alexander looked as stunned as he sounded.

"It's true," shaking his head in his own disbelief. "You know I swore off women and especially marriage. But here I am and there she is."

"How in the name of all that is holy did this happen to you?"

"I told her something … something I never shared with anyone in the world." He glanced in her direction. "I trusted her, I guess. And then she stole my heart." He gave a sheepish smile.

Alexander looked stunned. He was confused, completely and utterly dumfounded by what he heard and for once was utterly speechless. He told her something he had never told another? And this caused him to find love? Ridiculous, Alexander thought.

"By the way, I understand congratulations are in order for you? Henry Colwell, Miss Pembroke's brother-in-law and I go way back. We're at the same club. He's why she's now in your life. It's so odd how circumstances can change our lives. Where is the charming Miss Pembroke?" looking around the room for her, assuming she would have accompanied him.

"Ah, Jake, there's a long story attached I am afraid. It's been a trying time."

"Can I be of assistance?" he asked, worried at what might be amiss.

"Jacob, I wouldn't want to keep you," Alexander demurred, not sure if he could share with his friend. He was not in a position to open up to anyone. It was his fate, to face things alone and to protect those around him. He was the

Duke of Exmoor, to be leaned upon and not to lean on others. Alexander shook his head.

"No, I can tell … something is amiss." Jacob looked genuinely concerned.

Alexander looked at his friend for a few seconds, trying to decide if he should take him into his confidence. It was something he had never done with anyone.

"So, if I tell you will I be smitten by you?" he jested. He could see his humor was lost on his friend. Trust, he thought. Jacob Sumner was a good and trusted lawyer. And more importantly, he was a friend.

"Well there are several things. First my mother's passing …"

"Oh, I hadn't heard. I'm truly sorry at this news. It must be hard on your sons. She was their only mother figure. My sincere condolences, my friend." Jacob said, obviously saddened to hear of Alexander's sorrow.

"Yes, that's one of the reasons I have asked Miss Pembroke for her hand. My sons can't suffer more loss if she were to leave. But the other is much darker, I'm afraid. I believe she's in danger. There have been … threats," he said tentatively.

"Threats, you say? Go on." The lawyer was now intrigued, his legal mind engaged.

"Yes, inquiries in town by an unknown man, letters of warning, even an attempt on her life. I did a bit of sleuthing and found only dead ends."

"Attempt on her life, you say? My God man, this is more than a story." Jacob was shocked.

"After she was pushed from Conygar Tower, I vowed to protect her. She is under my care."

"Pushed, you say? Was she hurt badly?"

"No, surprisingly. Some slight bruises. Frankly, I don't know how she survived it. It truly was a scare for everyone in my family. I believe it ultimately led to my mother's untimely death. She would have never taken ill except for the chill she caught," he added, the sorrow obvious in his tone. "Then there's this cousin of hers, Charles. I can't put my finger on it."

"I know the one, the new Baron. Lucky fellow I'd say to inherit such a title and properties."

"I met him at the royal ball. His treatment of Miss Pembroke was ill-mannered at best. I wouldn't call him a gentleman, that is for sure. I followed him that night to Cheapside. Foul man."

"Cheapside, you say? The night of the royal ball?" Jacob parroted; his legal mind fully engaged.

"Yes, Queen Victoria's daughter's coming out into society. I don't understand why she didn't stand up to him." Alexander said, almost thinking out loud.

"Hmmm … the night of the royal ball." Jacob said, obviously thinking out loud. "You know, there was a young woman found dead, a Cheapside prostitute, badly abused. Or a possible courtesan based on the way she was dressed. It was all in the papers. Drowned she was, maybe a suicide. Found a few days following that ball. Floating in the Thames. Very sad case, very sad indeed."

"You don't think this Charles fellow could have anything to do with that?" Alexander asked, rather horrified at the idea. "He entered a brothel there. I dislike like the man more and more."

"Nah, Charles? No, he wouldn't hurt a fly. Though he's an odd duck. We really thought he was going to marry your Miss Pembroke. He was after her like the plague. But she chose you."

Alexander sighed. "Why, then, did you tell me about this dead prostitute?" He was feeling a bit exasperated.

"I'm a lawyer and you triggered a memory of that night." Shaking his head, he continued, "Charles has had his heart set on Miss Pembroke for years. He must have been devastated to hear of your upcoming nuptials." Jacob cocked his head. "Speaking of which, now wait, didn't you say you were marrying Miss Pembroke for your sons and to keep her from danger? Sir, I might be out of line here, but that's no reason to marry." A quizzical smile played on his face.

Alexander bristled at the judgement. So much for trusting a friend he thought, as he abruptly ended the conversation. "Mr. Sumner, you are out of line. My choice to marry is valid … for me. Return to your Miss Stockbridge. I see she eagerly awaits your companionship." His tone was now dismissive, "Good day, sir."

"Call on me if you require my services your Lordship. Please," Jacob Sumner implored. But Alexander remained silent. "Good day to you, sir," Jacob nodded. Remorseful for his improprieties, he turned to leave.

"Jacob," Alexander said, seeing he had wounded his friend, "You're a good man."

"Thank you, sir." Nodding again to accept the compliment, he returned to his party.

Reaching for his glass of mineral water, Alexander studied Jacob Sumner and his Miss Stockbridge. There was a gentle intimacy about them that felt unfamiliar and uncomfortable to observe. It wasn't the same romantic flirtations his mother imagined or the melodramatic stuff and nonsense she would endlessly reminisce about. There was something genuine about their affection; a closeness and familiarity that was endearing and attractive, something of which Alexander had no experience with or true understanding around. It also was not something he had ever truly noticed in other couples. All for sharing a confidence? Utterly confused, he drained his glass and left for his rooms. The bitter waters matched his mood.

It had been several days since Alexander had left Dunster. Ana was distressed by his quick and unspoken departure, sensing it was related to her questioning his feelings towards her that last night they were together. He had been so gentle and loving that his reaction was painful and bewildering. And he had turned so angry so quickly when she touched his scar, that it was actually frightening. She was so confused by his sudden turn. They had had less than two days of something that felt like love. And it was gone in a flash. She was becoming unsure of her ability to sustain a relationship where her love was not returned, and where his anger was so easily triggered. She was angry at herself for succumbing to her desires and was very concerned about what might happen to her if this marriage did not occur. She had ruined herself with a man who didn't love her. Her fear and shame were almost unbearable.

Ana struggled to keep her focus on Geoffrey and Hugh as they grappled with the loss of their grandmother. She looked forward to Riya's return. She was lonely without Lady Catherine and missed her sister Eliza terribly. Her world and future felt bleak and it was hard to maintain a positive front for the boys. The past few days were especially long with Alexander gone. This day had been no exception.

It was late at night and Ana made her way to the library to search for some new books for the boys. As she opened the door, her candle illuminated the room to reveal Alexander sitting alone in the dark in one of the chairs by an open window. A gentle night breeze filled the room with the evening scents of the garden.

"Oh, I am sorry. I was unaware of your return," she said as she began to close the door to leave.

"Ana, come in," he gently called after her. She almost didn't hear his voice.

Tentatively, Ana re-entered to room, "I was coming to look for some books for the boys," she explained.

"Come sit by me," he said softly.

"No, I would rather just look for some books." She walked to the shelves and began to peruse the volumes, her heart beating with anxiety at denying his request. Remembering his angry and cold departure, she remained fearful of his mood.

He watched her back for a few moments and could feel the tension between them. Alexander knew her fear of him was not the way to offer his protection. He stood up and walked over to her. "Ana." He placed his hands on her shoulders as she faced away from him. His touch warmed her. She bit her lip. He thought of Jacob Sumner and his Miss Stockbridge. He didn't know what to do next.

"I saw Jacob Sumner in Bath," he said, breaking the silence.

"Oh," she responded quietly, standing very still. "Is that where you went?"

"I told him about Mother."

Ana remained silent.

"I told him about you."

"Me? I don't understand."

"He congratulated me … us." He inhaled. "I told him about … the letter and the attempt …"

Ana turned to face him. "Why?" she inquired. She looked utterly frightened.

"I thought he might help. I told him about the letter. Ana, the paper was a dead-end lead. He told me about a murder in London the night of the ball. A woman found raped and drowned."

Ana's face paled. "That's why I came back." Her voice was quiet.

"What?" He was surprised that she knew of it. "And you didn't tell me?" his brow furrowed with concern. "Why did you say nothing?"

"She was wearing an emerald green gown, much like mine. I … I needed to come home." She looked down as her eyes filled with fear.

Lifting her face, he looked into her eyes, her dark lashes wet from tears. "I wish you had told me. You know I'm committed to protect you." He kissed her forehead, then took her into his arms. Ana felt confused by his gentleness and protection. It so felt tender and safe.

Holding her close had aroused him and his need for her became stronger. He kissed her again, igniting passions neither of them could not ignore.

The large clock in the main hall struck three in the morning. Ana awoke to find herself encircled in Alexander's arms. She was taken aback as he was wide awake, studying her face. His eyes were gentle as they looked at her. She wondered how long he had been watching her sleep. He traced a finger across her lips to keep her from speaking.

"It was a terrible day." He began as he took hold of her hand and softly kissed her fingers. "My men were being slaughtered. I was helpless to protect them. The battle raged on for hours. The screams of men and horses mixing with the explosions of battle were deafening. As it was nearing its end, I found I was alone with two of my men. It was a bloodbath. I realized my comrades were mortally wounded. Dying. I had no choice. I couldn't protect them. Ana, I had no choice." She reached out and touched his face as he closed his eyes as if to block the image. "I had to release them from their painful misery, I had no other choice. There was no help on the way. We were left on the field to die. I shot two of my own men." His eyes were dark and in some faraway place, Ana longed to take his pain away. He continued. "As I did so, an unexpected rider came from behind and knocked me down with his saber. The cut was deep. Fortunately, I was able to take him down with my last shot." He became silent for a moment struggling his emotions. "I lay with my two dead comrades for several hours. I don't know why I wasn't the one killed. I don't know why I couldn't save my men. I thought I'd go crazy with the knowledge that I killed them." His voice was almost inaudible. He was silent for a moment, visibly shaken by his own statements.

Sighing deeply, he continued. "I knew I was losing a lot of blood and needed help. No one was coming. I was left to die on the battlefield, with death all around me. I mustered up all the strength I had left in me and staggered across the bloodied killing fields until I found a small hut. That's where I found Riya. She was just a skinny bit of a thing with long black hair and the biggest black eyes I had ever seen. I don't know how she did it. She was a mere child. But she managed to nurse me to health. God, the worst of it was her dead grandmother stinking in the closet. That poor child! Finally, I was well enough to help Riya bury her. I couldn't leave her to the degradation that would've become her life. I needed to protect her." His voice became cold. "Then I returned home only to find Elizabeth had left. She abandoned me. Stabbed me in the back. She abandoned her sons and ran off with the man I left in charge of the estate. I left my family in the care of that bastard. She was my wife. How could she do such a thing to her sons. My family was destroyed. Devastated. My poor sons were motherless."

Ana took his face into her hands and looked at him intently. She then kissed each eye as if her action could take away the memory of his visions. "Alexander, I'm so sorry," she said gently. "I think I understand," Her hand softly caressed his cheek. "Thank you for telling me. I understand now." She hurt for him. She stroked his dark hair, hoping to soothe his pain.

"Ana, I don't know what love is," he ventured, his voice husky and deep. He rolled on top of her and began to tenderly kiss her face. "I need you to show me."

CHAPTER 36

The day was bright with late summer sunshine and the air was crisp with the coming of autumn. Ana was filled with hope at Alexander's return the night before. His story gave her insight and encouragement of the possibility that her feelings might be returned. She also felt optimistic that he trusted her with such painful memories. It showed her he was willing to open up. It was a move in the direction of love, at least. Though he didn't say the word, the warmth in his eyes and his gentle expressions were undeniably loving and kind. Her optimistic mood and the memory of their love making restored her confidence in the nuptials soon to follow and her fears of ruin faded away. However, it also made it difficult to focus on the lessons of the day.

The knock at nursery door brought Ana's thoughts back to the present. The post had come. Lord Luttrell requested that Ana join him in the library.

"I wonder what it could be?" It was unusual for Alexander to interrupt lessons especially for the post. Ana looked at Geoffrey and Hugh her eyes wide with questioning.

"Maybe the Queen will be attending your wedding?" Geoffrey quipped. The boys had been informed of the impending nuptials and were very pleased to have Ana become their stepmother.

"Now that would be quite a spectacle," she smiled at the boys as she left the room.

"Riya, you're home!" Ana said as she met the young woman at the bottom of the grand staircase. Alexander was as good as his word and Riya returned from school. Giving her a hug, Ana added, "I'm so glad you're back. There's so much to tell."

"I'm too, glad to be back." Riya said as she hugged her friend in return. "I didn't like being away at school."

"Geoffrey will also be glad, you know," Ana added, watching the expression of embarrassment color her young friend's face. "The boys are in the nursery. Join them once you're settled in."

"Yes, I so missed everyone. I'm so happy to be home again."

"I'll be up in a few minutes. We've missed you also," Ana added as she made her way to the library.

Lord Luttrell was standing by the window looking intently into the garden when Ana quietly entered the room. His hands were clasped behind his back and he was holding a letter. He was so intent in thought that he didn't hear her enter. Playfully tiptoeing into the room, Ana snuck behind him pulled the note from his hand. He spun around.

"Ana, no…"

But it was too late. Ana had begun to read. "Why, is it about my would be kill—." The words blurred as the room began to spin. Her knees buckled under her in shock as her world caved in. Alexander reached out and grabbed hold of her as she began to fall.

"Chesterton! Chesterton, send for Doctor Pendleton." He called out as he gathered her limp body in his arms and laid her gently on the couch.

"Sir?" Chesterton appeared at the door.

"Send for Doctor Pendleton. And get Mrs. C. in here quickly!" he ordered.

"Ana!" His deep concern was obvious and he gently slapped her pale cheek hoping to awaken her. "Ana!"

"What happened sir?" Mrs. C. rushed into the room, smelling salts in hand.

"I think she may have thought the post was positive. It was anything but!" He moved away slightly to allow her to wave the bottle under Ana's nose.

Ana responded quickly, as the bitter salts jarred her senses. She pushed the bottle away, shaking her head at their offensive odor. She looked up at Alexander's concerned face with a quizzical look.

"What … what happened?" she stammered, genuinely confused at finding herself awakening on his couch to an obnoxious odor.

"Ana, there's a letter …" was all he said for Ana quickly remembered what she had read as her hands covered her face.

"No. No. No!" She began to sob, her body shaking with shock and grief.

"My God, sir. What has happened?" Mrs. C. said as she poured the nearly hysterical woman some brandy out of Alexander's decanter. "Try to have her take some," she said as she handed a glass over to Lord Luttrell. But Ana was too consumed with grief to take the snifter and pushed it away.

"Ana please, have some brandy. Chesterton has gone for Doctor Pendleton. He'll be here soon."

"No." She curled up on the couch, her face awash with tears. Alexander felt helpless.

"Sir, what has happened?" Mrs. C. asked again. He pointed to the letter now lying on the floor where it had dropped.

Mrs. C. picked up the paper:

Lord Alexander Luttrell,

This is to inform you of an unfortunate accident which took the lives of Miss Pembroke's sister, Eliza, and of her two children Sarah and Miles. The fire was of an unknown origin at their Cherry Street home. Thank God, Henry and Ana Jane were spared.

Henry requests Ana return as soon as possible. I send my condolences.

Please let me know if I can be of any assistance to you during this time of grief.

Faithfully,
Jacob Sumner, Esq.

"Oh, sir, what a tragedy!" Mrs. C. said as she dabbed tears from her own eyes. "Miss Ana has lost so much."

"I fear the shock may be too much for her. Ana please, take some brandy." But she again refused.

He knelt down by the couch to gather her in his arms and held her close. He could feel her body shake with emotion, the tears hot on his chest.

"It will be alright. I'm here." His voice was gentle as he held her trembling in his arms.

"Sir, I think we should move her to her room." Mrs. C. suggested. "I will make some tea for her and will bring up a compress for her head."

"Yes, very good," Lifting Ana into his arms, he carried the sobbing woman up the grand stair.

Riya had come in from the nursery. "What's happened?"

"Riya, Ana received very bad news. Please stay with the boys. I'll explain later."

"Yes, Sir Alexander," she said with a small curtsey and returned to the nursery, though she was clearly anguished.

Alexander gently laid Ana on her bed, gingerly removed her shoes and pulled a blanket over her. Sitting beside her, he felt helpless as he held her hand. She looked pale and shocked as tears continued to stream down her face.

"Eliza, Oh God, Eliza, Sarah, and Miles," Ana wept again.

"Here is some tea, sir. I added some brandy to it," Mrs. C. whispered quietly.

"Ana, please take some tea," Alexander pleaded. But still she refused. He felt utterly helpless and looked at Mrs. C. for direction.

Mrs. C. sat on the edge of the bed and began to soothe Ana's head with the cool compress. "There, there, Miss Ana, have a good cry. You have lost so much. I know it hurts. You haven't lost everyone. You and Lord Luttrell will be married soon. Everyone here loves you," she cooed, but Ana was inconsolable.

Mrs. C. looked up at the Duke, feeling as useless and helpless as he did. They silently agreed to just wait vigil until the doctor came, Mrs. C. on the bed petting Ana's head and Alexander pacing back and forth, muttering under his breath. "Why the hell is taking Penny so long?"

Doctor Pendleton was brought directly up to the room as soon as he arrived. He quickly assessed the situation and mixed a few drops of sedative in a glass of water. "Take this. And don't refuse me young lady." His voice was stern.

Ana was barely able to drink the liquid through her tears.

"That's a good girl. You will be asleep shortly. Luttrell, we need to talk. Mrs. C., if you wouldn't mind staying with her?"

The older woman nodded as Alexander followed the doctor into the hall.

"Luttrell, she is not a strong as you think. She's been through too much trauma. She is going to need a lot of rest," the doctor said, his voice full of concern.

"The letter requested she return home."

"I wouldn't suggest it. She's too vulnerable. She's still recovering from that fall, and the loss of your mother. The added loss of her sister and her children will be too much to bear."

"She is headstrong. She'll not listen," he warned.

"If she must go, go with her. And keep it brief. I don't understand why some have such tragedy in their lives. How could something like this have happened?" He turned to go back into the room and stopped. "Luttrell, do you think there is any connection to the attempt on her life?"

"Penny, I can't say. I hope it was just a tragic accident. She's safe here. She's safe with me," he said, hoping to assure himself.

"Well, I wouldn't call this safe."

"What do you mean?" Alexander's brow furrowed.

"It looks to me that her whole family has been plagued by some cruel and twisted curse. Frankly, I'm not sure at all that it was accidental," Penny added. "I mean her whole family has been decimated in less than a year."

"I've grown lax with her safely under my roof. I'm to blame." Alexander was angry with himself and felt helpless with the current situation.

"Nonsense, man. You can't take this on. Just do your best keep her safe. You can only do your best," Pendleton said.

Mrs. C. joined them. "She's asleep now Doctor."

"Thank you, Mrs. C." Looking now at Alexander the doctor said, "Luttrell, let's get a brandy. You need it. She'll be awake again in several hours. I'll re-examine her then."

I'll stay with her sir," Mrs. C. offered. Alexander nodded in agreement.

Once in the library, Alexander showed Pendleton the letter.

"Have you informed this solicitor of your other concerns?" he asked taking the brandy handed to him.

"Yes, I saw him in Bath. He told me of a murder the night of the royal ball. Penny, I can't help but feel I've become too remiss. What kind of soldier have I become? I can't even protect my own walls, my own family. I traced the first note she received over a month ago; a dead end. I've no other clues. A menacing figure in a black cape; well that could be anyone. I don't like Charles. But he has nothing to gain. He already holds the barony."

Taking a drink of brandy, he offered Penny a cigar. Remembering his feelings of jealousy as he watched Ana with Charles, he finally said, "I just left her in London when Mother died. Then she mentioned something about a woman found drowned in the Thames. I just dismissed it to her fears. That was stupid."

"Why? Do you think there is a connection?"

"I don't know. I thought she was being nonsensical when she first mentioned something about a green gown like hers," Alexander added. "And maybe it is nothing. I'm just blocked."

"Maybe, maybe not." Penny said as he took the cigar and lit it. "So, who is this Charles?" He didn't remember having heard the name. Fragrant smoke circled his head.

"Ana's cousin. He gained the title and lands at Lord Pembroke's death. Just because he is a distasteful fellow doesn't mean he is the villain here."

"That is true," the doctor agreed.

"He's had interest in Ana's hand but she refused him, on several occasions. But he'd have to be crazy to take out such ghastly retribution for her refusal. He would have everything to lose."

"Sadly, there are such men, I'm afraid," the doctor replied as he looked up over his snifter.

"Penny, I met the man. He's a cad for sure, but murder? Sumner said he was harmless. I don't know…" Alexander drifted off as he stood by the window watching the clouds float by. "How can I even broach this subject with Ana? As you said, she's too fragile…," his voice barely audible. Then he added strongly, "My God Penny, I left her in London. I returned here and I left her. What if that dead woman was supposed to be her? What if that fire was meant for her?" He shook his head again. "I didn't stay. I didn't protect her. I was in a rage with jealousy because of Charles. I abandoned her. I could have lost her." Alexander's eyes were wide with the realization.

"Why Luttrell, I dare say, you are in love. What, what!"

Alexander swung around and glared at Pendleton. "God's teeth Penny, not that again. I told you that's a closed subject."

"Admit it. old man. If you could only hear yourself. You care for that woman. Deeply." He squinted at his angry friend, giving him a crooked smile.

"Protecting someone's well-being is not being in love. She's under my care and protection. I would do this for any of my family, tenants and staff. And I am not an old man." His eyes were icy pools of steel.

Pendleton walked over to his friend, placing his hand on his back. "Call it what you will, my friend. Call it what you will. It's time I go check on the patient." Pendleton walked out of the room laughing to himself and shaking his head at his pigheaded friend.

Just as Alexander predicted, Ana insisted on returning to London. He tried his best to dissuade her, but she would have none of it. He felt helpless as she packed, refusing all assistance. Dr. Pendleton provided a tonic which Alexander, who was prepared to accompany her, made sure to pack.

"Ana wait a few days," he cajoled. "You'll be able to travel more comfortably."

"Dr. Pendleton said you need rest, dear." Mrs. C. added.

"No. No. No!" Ana said through tears, "My family needs me."

"Maybe some more tonic dear," Mrs. C. tried again.

"Please, let me pack. Where's my hairbrush? My father gave me that brush," she lamented. "Alexander, are you packed? Is the carriage ready? Oh, Eliza!" She sat on the side of the bed and put her hands to her face. "Don't you understand, I need my family, I need my family." She rocked slightly on the bed.

"Ana, please …" Alexander pleaded.

"No, I need my family!" The forcefulness of her voice almost startled him.

"Alright, alright." At odds with what to do, he said, "I'll check on the carriage." Looking imploringly at Mrs. C. he shook his head in dismay.

"I'll stay sir," dabbing her own eyes, "Poor child, poor, poor child."

Barely down the staircase, Alexander's voice boomed through the halls, "Rollins where's that damn carriage?"

"Mrs. C. I can't find my brush. Where's my brush?" She looked around the room.

Mrs. C. looked at her quizzically, "You packed it dear."

"Oh, Mrs. C. what shall I do? My whole family is gone! What's happened to my family?" Ana was devastated; she needed to get home.

Suddenly, Alexander appeared at the door, followed by Rollins and Chesterton. "Let's get you home." He handed her a small glass. "Drink this and don't argue. If there's something you need, we'll buy it. Rollins, Chesterton, grab that trunk. Ana, where is your cloak?" Surprised by his action she pointed to the wardrobe, took the glass and drank the tonic. "Ana, you want to get home? I'm taking you home." Grabbing her cloak, he wrapped it around her, sweeping her into his arms. "Gentlemen, make way!"

Gently placing her in the carriage, Mrs. C. covered her with several blankets to keep her warm. The plan was to go without stopping. Rollins was glad of the brilliant white moon to lead the way as he spurred the team onward. Alexander sat next to Ana, his arm secure around her shoulder, her head against his broad chest. They charged into the swirling night.

Ana was finally asleep as the coach rocked back and forth. It gave Alexander time to think. The fire had to be an accident. There was no explanation in the note. Fires happen all the time. He had seen many die in battle, but he cringed at the idea of meeting death in fire. There was something honorable about dying in battle. There was something evil about this.

Alexander looked down at the woman sleeping in his arms. She looked so young and frail in the moonlight. Dried tears stained her pale cheeks. Alexander wanted to see to her safety. He wanted to protect her and see to her needs. He wanted her to be happy. Glad to see she was sleeping soundly he softly placed a kiss on the top of her head. The tonic was doing its work. She would need all her strength.

What if she wanted to remain in London? What if she didn't return with him? The thought stabbed at his heart. He took her hand and brought it to his lips. No, she must return with him. He wanted her too much, needed her too much. Maybe Penny was right; she had taken his heart. Maybe this was love. He looked at her again as she leaned against his chest. He had shared with her as Jacob Sumner told him to do. She did not reject him, but offered kindness. The thought of living without her now was preposterous. She was part of him.

Suddenly, he felt lighthearted. He wanted to wake her and tell her. He wanted to shout it out to Rollins. What a fool he'd been! She had confessed her love to him and he had pushed her way. He looked down at her as she slept.

"Ana," he whispered into her hair, "I think I'm beginning to know what love is." He gently kissed her head. He had never been happier. He let his guard down and was swept away by a sense of relaxation he rarely felt. Finally, he too slept, content with the knowledge that Ana would be his forever.

CHAPTER 37

Rollins drove the team hard through the night. Late in the afternoon, distant spires revealed themselves above the brown haze, and the sounds of the London streets finally woke the sleepers. The bustle of activity around them and the objective of their journey made it such that Alexander knew he had to wait to tell Ana about the realization of his feelings towards her.

"Ana, how are you?" Alexander asked, concerned about what lay ahead of them.

"Remarkably, I slept soundly and do feel better." She fussed with her skirts and hair preparing for their arrival. It felt an eternity for the carriage to draw to its destination. Her heart dropped when she saw the black bunting draped from the windows and door of her family home. She had hoped it was a bad dream. Her eyes welled up with tears.

"It's real." She pressed her head into Alexander's chest. "I can't go in," she cried, sounding young and afraid. Alexander lifted her face, his hand on her chin. He gently looked into her tear-filled eyes. He wanted to tell her how he felt, to let her know he loved her.

"Ana, I have something to say before we go in," his handsome face was filled with gentle emotion, his steel eyes turning a warm soft blue.

"Yes?" Ana held her breath.

"Ana, I … I …" Glancing past her through the carriage window, he realized Ana's childhood home was Charles' house now and his jealousy arose anew. Maybe the time was not right. "I won't leave your side," he said finally, kissing her forehead.

"Thank you." She slowly exhaled. "I'm ready now." Alexander knocked on the carriage roof. Rollins climbed down, pulled down the step, and opened the door. Ana trembled as she took Rollins' hand.

"It'll be fine, Miss," he assured her with a friendly smile.

"Thank you, Rollins." Alexander took her arm to steady her as they walked up the marble stairs of her childhood home and knocked at the door. The wait felt like years. Ana was expecting to see Sedgewick's familiar face at the door. But instead, a stranger answered.

"May I help you?" he asked coldly.

"Who *are* you?" Ana couldn't help herself. Her heart stopped, stunned at her own rudeness.

"Madam, who are *you*?" he replied, even more coldly than before.

"This is Miss Ana Pembroke, you fool!" Alexander pushed through the door.

"Oh, I'm sorry Miss. It's just … I've never met... You were expected," he stumbled.

"And you are?" Alexander queried, his voice stern as they walked into the hall.

"Coleman, sir. Please, Mr. Henry's in the drawing room. I'll tell Lord Malin you've arrived."

"Henry?" Ana ran down the hall leaving Alexander to follow in her path.

Entering the room, Alexander saw Henry and Ana embraced, both in tears, his one remaining child holding on to his coat tails. Seeing Henry's tears flowing freely, Alexander was awkward amidst the emotion and familiarity—it was all so foreign to him.

Only moments later, he felt a cold presence next to him drawing his attention away from the scene. It was Charles. The two men looked guardedly at each other. Each saw the other as a rival. Never would there be trust between them.

Taciturn in his demeanor, Alexander finally said, "Lord Malin, condolences to your family."

"Thank you. Luttrell, isn't it?" Charles said with disdain, purposefully ignoring Alexander's higher rank.

"Oh, Charles!" Ana said as she threw her arms around his neck. He in turn hugged her back and held her close. "Ana, my dear, dear cousin." His eyes never wavered from Alexander's cold icy stare. He knew exactly what Alexander was thinking and was enjoying every moment of it. He pulled Ana even closer for greater effect. Alexander's jealousy raged, but he suppressed the urge to call the cad out. He knew another death would be more then Ana could bear.

Finally, Ana pulled away from Charles and dabbed her eyes with her kerchief, "Where are my manners?" She took Alexander by the hand and led him further into the room. He hadn't met Henry or Ana Jane. "You remember Charles?" she said. Alexander gave him a customary nod which was coolly returned.

"I remember." His steel gray eyes slowly sized him up.

"I'm told congratulations are in order, my sweet?" Charles' sarcasm went unnoticed by Ana. However, Alexander knew exactly the game he was playing.

"Yes, thank you, Charles. You are such a dear to say so. I only wish…" She smiled tearfully at Charles and continued in Henry's direction.

"This is Henry, my dear sister's wonderful husband and such a good friend." Alexander extended his hand. Henry had a good hearty handshake but his rumpled exterior and the dark circles under his eyes showed plainly that he was sorely devastated by the losses he had just suffered, and he was oblivious to the hostility brewing between the other two men.

"I am truly sorry for your losses," Alexander said, deeply moved by Henry's sorrow.

Henry introduced his daughter, "This is Ana Jane," he said. To Alexander, she looked like a lost and forlorn waif.

"Hello, Ana Jane." Alexander's voice was soft and gentle as he bent down to shake the young girl's hand. She looked as unkempt as her father. He knew she was suffering and his heart went out to her. His sons, too, had lost their mother. It was a heavy burden for any child to bear.

"Well, I would love to stay but I've a previous engagement," Charles said as he broke into the scene.

"Charles, you're not leaving? We've just arrived." Ana was incredulous. "You must stay. You just must," she insisted.

"It's business. Henry will explain. I shall return before supper, my sweet." His smile became contemptuous as he looked in Alexander's direction.

"Charles, please, do, do hurry. I need my family around me," Ana pleaded with him, her eyes again filling with tears. "We need to be together at this time."

"Coleman will see to your needs, my sweet. I'll return shortly. I'll not disappoint. Ana, I can never disappoint you." He gave her a tender kiss on the cheek, and then he left the room, glaring all the while at Lord Luttrell, who glowered back at him.

"Oh, Henry! Henry, what could've happened?" Ana returned to her beleaguered brother-in-law, taking his hand as she sat with him on the settee.

"Ana, I really don't know. When I think of my babies, my wife ..." he trailed off. His eyes brimmed with tears.

"Oh, Henry!" Ana cried and began to weep as she embraced him.

"We were so fortunate. And now I have nothing ... nothing." Henry began to sob, his face in his hands.

"Dear, dear Henry. Thank God for Charles," Ana said.

Henry looked up at Alexander, "I'm sorry, sir," he said, apologizing for his emotional outbreak. He took out a cloth and wiped his damp face. Alexander nodded his head. He understood Henry's deep loss but he was unsettled by Ana's remark.

"Henry, let it out. Don't hold those feelings in. It's not good for you," he said. Ana couldn't help but stare at Alexander, for sharing feelings were not his strong point.

"Charles has been wonderful. He's taken us in; made all the arrangements. The fire all but ruined me. Charles is backing a ship for me. I'll be putting Ana Jane into school. I can't stay. I'm returning to sea."

"Henry, the sea? You can't." Ana was dumbfounded.

"I must. I don't know any other way for myself. It's all I know. Charles is off finalizing the venture now. Ana Jane will be fine." He looked down at his hands, knowing he was all but abandoning his only living child, but he felt completely unable to do anything else.

"Nonsense! Ana Jane will live with me ... us. Isn't that right Alexander?" Her moist eyes pleaded.

"Yes Henry, we'll take her home with us." He was in full agreement. He couldn't imagine abandoning such a sad child to a lonely painful life.

"No, I couldn't impose ..." he trailed off.

"Father please," was all she had to say, her blue eyes large with the fear of being sent off.

"Yes baby, yes, you'll live with your Aunt. You will. I can't even begin to tell you how generous your offer is to us." Henry began to cry. "I'm sorry," he choked.

"Nonsense, man. With my two boys she'll have a ready-made family," Alexander offered, tying to bolster the distraught man.

"She'll return with us when we leave," Ana stated, resolved.

"No, I'll keep her with me until I embark. She's all I have left of my Eliza." He dabbed his eyes.

"I understand, she's all I too have left too. Along with you and Charles," Ana said.

Alexander scowled. He was getting sick of hearing of how Charles was coming to everyone's rescue.

"Aunt Ana, I'm staying in your room now. Would you like to see?" Taking her hand, the young girl began to lead Ana down the hall.

"Yes, dearest, I'd love to. Excuse us, gentlemen," she smiled as Ana Jane pulled her aunt from the room.

Alone with Henry, Alexander saw an opportunity to get more details on the accident and to relay his own concerns about Ana. He knew Ana did not want to burden her family, but he was tired of hiding information. And Henry might have some knowledge that could lead to the person trying to harm Ana.

"Henry, what really happened?" he asked, genuinely concerned.

"Eliza wasn't feeling well. I offered to take the girls to the park, but Sarah chose to stay behind to help with Miles. When I returned, the house was ablaze. I just don't know what happened." Henry indeed looked dazed.

"What about servants, weren't they home? Couldn't they reach your family?"

"They were able to get out from the kitchen, but both staircases were burning. I just don't understand what happened. Eliza or Sarah, I don't know … someone must have knocked over a lamp. It just doesn't make sense. And now I have lost everything!"

"Odd … both staircases you say?" Alexander took a chance, thinking about the attempts on Ana's life. "Do you think this was planned? Could someone deliberately set those fires when you were gone?" Cautiously, he added, "How does Charles fit into this?"

"Charles? I don't understand? He has been wonderful. What are you getting at? Are you saying the fire was intentional?" His face twisted with pain.

"You are wrong, sir. Charles was there to help. He was burned himself trying to get to my family."

"I'm sorry I mentioned it." Alexander studied his hands, deciding to fully broach the subject. "I realize it's a bad time to bring this up, but I have concerns for Ana's safety."

"Ana? What do you mean?" Henry stood up, alarmed by this new information.

"Henry, there was an attempt on her life a number of weeks ago, and a suspicious letter." He looked directly at Henry for his response.

"My God, man, why weren't we told of this?" Henry began to pace, wringing his hands.

"Ana refused. She didn't want to worry you," he said, though he was glad now that he brought it up.

"That's preposterous, we're family. We must know these things … we need to know these things." He stopped in front of Alexander.

"I realize that. I urged her to tell, but she's obstinate sometimes." Alexander shook his head.

"Sometimes? Ha! I see you're getting know her well," Henry exclaimed.

Alexander gave him a weak smile.

"But why Charles? He's like a brother to Ana."

"Maybe … because I don't like him."

"What are you trying to say? I don't understand. I know he's asked Ana for her hand, and often. I could see why you wouldn't like that." The two men were standing eye to eye. "I think you're mistaken about Charles. You don't even know him."

"Well, I've had some contact with him, and frankly I didn't like what I saw."

"Yes, he can be a bit rough around the edges, but he too has lost so much."

"What do you mean? He inherited everything."

"Don't you know? He lost both his parents when he was twelve. It was tragic, and now all this loss. He and Miles were like brothers. Of course, he wants to keep Ana close. Wouldn't you want to keep your family close?" Henry was doing a fine job arguing for Charles, but Alexander couldn't forget the night of Queen Victoria's Ball and Charles trip to Cheapside.

Henry was distressed. "He's family. He's letting us stay here, funding my ship. Frankly, sir, I don't like your line of questioning. And now *I'm* concerned for Ana's well-being." Henry was visibly agitated. "Do you think the fire was intended for Ana and they got the wrong sister? Oh, my God!" Henry was clearly on the brink of hysteria.

"No, no. I apologize, Henry. Put your mind to rest. I don't think anything of that sort. The fire was an accident I'm sure. My concern is to protect Ana; I meant nothing. Now was not the time. I'm sorry." Alexander recognized Henry was in no frame of mind to continue the discussion.

"I would hope not … Apology accepted, sir," Henry said, now sounding a bit calmer. Returning to his chair, he sat with his head in his hands.

The voices of Ana Jane and Ana could now be heard in the hall along with a male voice. Charles had returned. However, only Ana Jane returned to the salon. Alexander felt uncomfortable knowing Ana and Charles were alone on the other side of the wall. He wished he had an excuse to join them. Even more, he wished he could hear their conversation, but Ana Jane was prattling on to Henry about Ana's visit to her room which made it difficult.

Nonchalantly, Alexander began to meander around the salon as if looking at paintings, books and bric-a-brac, making his way closer to the door in hopes of hearing more clearly. Finally, nearing his goal, he picked up a book and acted as if he were reading. He could hear their voices distinctly now.

"Charles, you know how I feel; I love you." It was clearly Ana's voice.

"I can't stand the idea of you being with him; you know I'm the one who loves and adores you."

"Charles, you know I'll always love you."

There was silence. Alexander could only imagine the romantic scene taking place. He snapped the book shut, put it down on the table and walked to the window. He had heard enough. So, he was right not to share his feelings. His thoughts raged in his head. He heard Ana tell Charles she loved him. She said it twice. Henry said they only have each other now. Even Ana herself said Charles was all she had left. Why wouldn't Ana want to be with Charles? If he hadn't promised to stay by her side, Alexander vowed he would leave right now. Just walk out now while she's there in his arms, and catch her in the act. He wondered how long he was going to be played the fool.

Supper was decidedly hostile. Charles maneuvered his seat next to Ana causing Alexander to sit across the table. It was apparent that the two men despised each other; their conversation was cool and calculated. Ana noticed Alexander's mood towards her changed. His eyes reverted to their familiar cold steely blue, which left her concerned and confused. Following dinner, they returned to the salon.

"Ana, play for us?" Charles directed, motioning towards the piano.

"I've not played for a while," she responded. "I'm afraid I'm a bit out of practice."

"You've not played for Lord Luttrell? I'm shocked." He looked over towards Alexander with penetrating beady black eyes.

"Charles, it never came up," she defended.

"Nonsense! I remember a time we couldn't pull you away from a keyboard. So, play. Give us some much-needed entertainment, Ana. I desire it." He was smug and condescending.

"Ana, we don't need you to entertain us." Alexander's blood was boiling at Charles' demands.

For his part, Charles glared at Alexander.

"How could Ana have even considered marrying this pompous ass?" Alexander thought.

"No, it's fine, I'd love to play," Ana said to appease them both. She was very uncomfortable with the immature way the men were behaving and was disturbed by it, as she loved them both. She sat at the pianoforte and decided to play a simple Bach sonata. The music kept the men from further discussion and Ana felt a bit of the tension leave the room. She then played a rondo. When she finished, she closed the case.

"There! Isn't that better?" she smiled. The clock above the fireplace struck nine.

Alexander stood up. "Ana it's late. We've had a long day. It's time we depart to my apartments."

"I'll have none of it!" Charles demanded, bringing his fist down on the side of the settee as he stood up. "My cousin is an unmarried woman and will be sleeping under her family roof." His black eyes became wild and dark with the threat of violence. "Ana, I demand you remain here."

Alexander took a threatening step towards Charles.

Ana was visibly shaken at Charles' anger and frightened by Alexander's cold hard glare. "Please, both of you stop! Alexander, Charles is right, we're not yet married. It would be highly inappropriate."

Alexander frowned. It was the second time she stood up for Charles. "I told you I'd not leave your side. But I see you're making a choice … Good evening. Henry," he nodded, then turned on his heels and left.

Now feeling trapped, Ana's eyes welled up with tears. She wanted to run after Alexander. She looked at Charles and suddenly felt unsafe with Alexander's departure.

"Charles, I don't know who you are!" she stammered, her voice shaking. "Henry, I'm sorry." She realized she couldn't stay. Gathering up her skirts, she ran from the room and into the dark night.

Rollins was about to flick his switch at the team when he saw her run out the door. He opened the hatch. "Sir, it's Miss Pembroke. Shall I wait?"

"Move on." Alexander slammed the hatch closed. But carriage didn't move. Alexander banged on the roof. But instead of the carriage lurching forward, the door opened, allowing Ana to enter. Her face was flushed and streaked with tears. Alexander turned his head to the window, furious at Rollins and livid with Ana.

"Alexander, please, I'm sorry. Please," she pleaded.

He continued to stare out the window.

Her heart was breaking. All the men she loved were strangers to her. Biting her lip to stop from crying, she put her hands to her face but she could not stop the flood of tears.

With silent sobs, Ana watched the passing shops, homes and churches from the window of the carriage as they made their way to Alexander's apartments. His silence was painful but she was too spent to try to talk and Alexander was too angry to notice.

"Rest the horses Rollins, we're leaving in the morning," Alexander ordered as they stopped at his townhome. He remained cool and aloof for the entire ride. Ana had regained control of her emotions, yet felt nothing but exhaustion.

Rollins opened the door and offered his hand to the depleted young woman, who wearily followed Alexander up the steps and into the foyer. It was not as grand as Dunster Castle; however, it was impressive with its white marble stairs and black wrought iron balustrades encircling the hall.

"Andrews, show Miss Pembroke to the blue room," Alexander ordered.

"Yes, My Lord," the elderly gentlemen replied.

He must be the butler, Ana thought.

"I'm going to bed straightaway," Alexander announced, leaving Ana to follow Andrews in silence.

It was a lovely room. A cheery fire was ablaze no time. But Ana was too tired to think or feel; she was barely able to say "thank you."

"Here's hot tea, Miss. There are several pitchers of warm water for the basin. Lord Luttrell has instructed that you take this medication." Andrews nodded toward the small glass on the tray.

Ana dutifully drank the tonic.

"Is there anything else, Miss?" Andrews added.

"No thank you," she said shaking her head. After he vacated the room, Ana walked to the bed, plopped down on the soft feather mattress, and fell quickly to sleep in complete exhaustion. She doubted the need for the tonic but didn't have it in her to fight. She was sound asleep within minutes as the sedative took hold, amplified by her own weariness.

CHAPTER 38

*A*lexander angrily paced the floor in his room. How could he trust Ana if she told another man she loved him? Plus, this was the second time she rescued Charles—first at the ball and then tonight. Hearing her words with him made him sick. He had to get out and get some air.

The London fog swirled around the golden light of the gas lamps. The cool damp air felt good against his flushed face as he made his way up the street. The smoke from wood and coal fires filled his nostrils. The sound of his boots resounded loudly on the empty pavement, echoing through the thick dank air. Finally, he was alone with his thoughts on the deserted streets.

He hated Charles and knew the man would go to any length to get Ana into his bed. Of course she would feel some allegiance towards him. He was her cousin. But he wasn't to be trusted. Alexander had observed him at the ball, followed him to Cheapside. What did Ana say? A prostitute found in the Thames several days following the ball wearing an emerald green gown? Was there was any connection? Was she murdered? Did she throw herself into the water to escape the horrors of her life? Was she from the same brothel that Alexander had observed Charles enter that night? Charles was not the saint that Ana thought he was. He was the enemy. And if anyone knew what it felt like to be in danger from an enemy, Alexander knew.

Suddenly from behind, the sound of a galloping horse put Alexander on full alert. He quickly found a doorway and hid in its shadows; his heart beat wildly in his chest. As the rider disappeared into the swirling fog, Alexander slumped to the ground. In a flood of memories, he was back in India. The distant sound of battle engulfed him as he lay in the trench with his two dead comrades. Hours passed. No one came to his aid. He was abandoned; the smell of death and gun smoke filled his nostrils. The pain in his back was searing hot, as thick blood poured from his wound. Gradually, the faint sound of a nightingale echoed in his head. He became aware of its bright song, bringing him back to the present. He was wet from perspiration and needed to get home.

It was almost four in the morning when he returned. Exhausted and conflicted, Alexander decided to look in on Ana; she had been spent and emotionally overwrought when they returned from the visit with her family earlier that evening. He remembered what Dr. Pendleton had said about her frail state. Alexander determined his action was only out of courtesy and not out of caring.

He tried the knob of her door; it turned quietly. He cautiously pushed the door open. The room felt cool and still. He walked silently to the hearth and placed a few coals onto the smoldering embers. It quickly caught flame. A comfortable glow filled the room. He looked over expecting to see Ana wrapped in coverlets but was surprised to see her curled up on her side fully clothed. He sighed, realizing she must have been beyond exhaustion to have fallen asleep in such a fashion. He walked over to her and untied her shoes. Concerned he would awaken her, he removed them gingerly. She did not stir. He straightened out her legs on the bed and began to undo the fastenings of her dress. He knew that she would sleep better if she were removed from her binding clothes. He undid the buttons around her wrists and bodice. He gently lifted her to remove the dress from her shoulders. She remained in a deep sleep. She must have taken the tonic, he thought. He began to undo the corset that bound her tightly. He pulled the garment from her back. He untied the layers of petticoats and pulled them off along with her dress, leaving her in her chemise. Placing the clothing on a nearby chair, he returned, gently pulling the covers back so she could sleep comfortably. As he pulled the blankets up over her shoulders, he leaned down and placed a kiss gently on her forehead. Immediately, he regretted his actions.

Alexander felt himself stir at the intimacy of undressing her while she slept, yet he knew he would not wake her. He was angry with himself for thinking he loved her. He had taken Jacob Sumner's advice and had opened up to her. She had responded so warmly that he had dropped his guard. But he had every right to be cautious. She was in league with the enemy. He did not trust Charles, so how could he trust Ana? They were too closely aligned. He frowned. Why would he even consider telling her his secrets? She would only use him.

He heard the clock strike four thirty. Weary, Alexander made his way to his room and quickly fell into a fitful sleep filled with more unsettled dreams.

Ana awoke to a room she did not recognize. She remembered; she was in Alexander's London home. She felt groggy from the tonic. She heard the clock strike six. It was so much earlier than she thought. She pulled the covers back. Her clothes were neatly placed on a nearby chair but couldn't remember undressing. She must have been sleepwalking. She stood up and poured water in the basin. It was cold on her face. She noticed the pot of now cold tea on the tray and took some refreshment.

Remembering passing several churches, Ana decided she needed a place of spiritual rest from the turmoil and pain in her life. Finishing her cold refreshments and morning ablutions, she quietly left the privacy of her room and went down to the entrance. There was no one about, and not wanting to disturb anyone, she walked out into the cool foggy morning. She took a moment to get her bearings. Remembering the direction from which they came, and she began to walk towards her goal.

Saint Stephens was a short walk away. There were several people gathering for the early morning service as she made her way into the ancient building and took a seat in a back pew. Making the sign of the cross, she closed her eyes and began to pray. She prayed for the souls of her family and for the peace which she believed they now enjoyed. She prayed for Henry and Ana Jane. She prayed for Charles. Hot tears streamed down her face.

"Dear God, please help me," she prayed. "Please help me to love better," she prayed for Alexander.

"Please rise." The priest and acolyte had entered the sanctuary, his voice resonating off the stone walls. She stood to participate in the familiar Anglican service. The minister's voice was clear and soothing as he began Morning Prayer. Ana felt her shoulders ease as the service continued, soothing her.

"For the Lord is gracious, his mercy is everlasting:
and his truth endureth from generation to generation."

Psalm 100

"Yes, she thought, the Lord is merciful and gracious." She believed this truth and took strength from the words. When the service was finished, Ana quickly slipped out the door before the priest made his way to greet the congregants on their way out of the church. With a renewed spirit, Ana walked briskly back through the bright morning sunshine.

"God's teeth, woman!" greeted her as she entered the front door. Alexander and Rollins were standing in the front hall beginning their plan for a search, having found Ana missing. "Where the hell have you been?" he raged, though his anguish was quickly dissipating with relief.

"Church," she answered, surprised at such a welcome.

"Church?" His blue eyes flashed. He looked at Rollins.

"Church," Rollins repeated, raising his shoulders and lifting his hands.

"Ana," Alexander boomed, "WE ARE LEAVING. Get yourself ready." How can he trust someone who sneaks around, he thought? She made him crazy. For good measure he added angrily, "And next time you decide to go to church or anywhere else for that matter, for God's sake, tell someone."

"No one was up so I thought ..."

"Ana you think too much. Now go get ready." He stormed out.

"Alright, just don't get your ... Oh, never mind," she quipped as she made her way up the stairs to her room. Her moment of spiritual peace was gone, replaced with her own frustration.

"We'll be stopping at Salisbury for the night," he yelled up giving her fair warning of their return trip.

"God's teeth!" she responded from under her breath. She was not looking forward to the ride back and was frustrated with herself for so quickly losing the prayer request she had made.

The ride to Salisbury was cool and distant. Periodically Ana glanced at Alexander. He remained occupied with the view from his window. Ana noticed Alexander wince occasionally as the carriage bounced as if in pain.

"Alexander?" She broke the silence. "Is everything alright?"

"Hmm?" he looked at her, having been deep in thought.

"You seem to be in some discomfort," she ventured.

"It's nothing, just that old wound." He turned his head back to his view making it clear that he did not wish to speak. Ana wanted to reach out to ease his pain. She was not sure how to bridge the gap between them and returned her own gaze to her window. She felt exasperated and hurt by his disposition. It was a long silence.

"It was in '57, June 30th, the battle of Chinhat to be exact," he began. Ana turned towards him surprised to hear his voice. He continued gazing out his window, his voice somber and flat. "We were approaching Ishmael Ganj. We were outnumbered, six hundred against six thousand. Sir Lawrence was commander of the Thirty-Second Foot. There was a mutiny. The Indian artillery betrayed us." His voice became distant as if he were in another physical place. "The rebels were well prepared; positioned behind stone walls and entrenched in a nearby village. Lieutenant Case was killed instantly. I watched as several of my fellow officers were viciously cut down. We were ambushed by our own men." His voice remained flat and emotionless. "Many of the Sikh cavalrymen fled. The little artillery that remained was ordered to protect the bridge for retreat. But I had been separated from the rest. I watched, helpless from my position. My men around me ... wounded ... dying. We were betrayed. We had no ammunition. The only place for them to go was Lucknow. I watched as they retreated over the bridge. They were not returning for me. I was on my own." He continued to stare out the window.

Ana listened quietly. What was the point of this story she wondered? Though her heart went out to him, she dared not open herself up. She had no response and said nothing but turned back to her own window.

After a bit of time, Ana turned to him and said, "Alexander, I am not sure about the point you're trying to make with telling me about your war stories. Don't you think I know about the devastation of war? Don't you know I too have suffered because of war? Miles is dead. He is dead and you are here. And I am here. I don't understand. Do you think that telling me these stories is going to push me away? I know you don't want pity from me. I don't know what I'm to give to you? I have given you my heart, but you don't want that. I've given you my ... I don't know ... I just don't ..." She turned back to the window. He never looked at her, but kept his gaze on the passing view.

The sun had dipped into the west as they pulled up to The Swan in Salisbury. Ana was given her now familiar room for the evening, Alexander his. Only this evening he requested separate meals be brought to each. He had remained cool and distant.

Ana's heart was heavy. Any hope she had of Alexander's unspoken love for her was fading fast. She didn't understand what he wanted from her. She sat on the bed; undid her hair. Silent tears stained her cheeks as she paced. She picked at her food and paced again. She undressed and slept for a short while. She awoke then paced some more. She needed to feel safe. She was unsure if Alexander was safe, but she couldn't be alone. It was now well into the night as she made her decision.

As she opened her door, she looked up and down the hall, making sure she would not be observed. Tiptoeing up the hall, she stood in front of Alexander's door. Gently knocking she heard his voice.

"Who's there?"

"Alexander, it's Ana," Ana said in a raspy voice hoping no one could hear her. The shame to be found knocking on his door in the middle of the night was appalling, but her need to feel safe was stronger.

"Yes." His voice was muffled through the door. Ana turned the knob and poked her head in. "May I come in?" she requested. The weakness in her knees was uncomfortable.

"Yes, yes, come in." He sounded exasperated.

Ana quickly entered the room and closed the door, leaning on it for support. The room had a familiar sweet smoky scent. Alexander was sitting cross legged on the floor before the fire as she had seen him before with Riya. He said his back had been hurting and she wondered if this was the way he eased the pain.

"Riya taught me some of her arts. I ... I thought I might try to ease some of the discomfort you mentioned ... while we were in the carriage." She swallowed hard. He looked at her over his shoulder through dark silver slits.

"Please Alexander, I'd like to try." She said softly as she continued to wait for an invitation to approach. He looked at her again and noticed that her hair was loose and flowing freely down her back. He also could not help but notice that there were no usual garments under her dress. Her bare feet were poking from her skirts.

"Just don't touch the scar," he warned.

Ana came to him, pleased that he was willing to let her try. "Is that Sandalwood?"

He nodded.

"Riya told me about it. I like the way it smells." She felt frustrated with herself for prattling on. She knew it was her nerves. She needed to be quiet. "I won't touch your scar," she added gently.

Kneeling on the floor behind him she began to methodically knead his shoulders. She could feel how tight they were and almost commented but decided to remain silent. Using her thumbs, she began to work the back of his neck. He tilted his head forward a bit. She felt pleased as she believed that meant her touch was working and easing his tension.

"May I remove your shirt?" she said softly, "I don't want to mistakenly hurt you." On her knees, she moved around to face him and slowly began to unbutton his shirt before he had a chance to answer. He watched her face intently as the fastenings were undone. His sleeves had been rolled up to his elbow and once the shirt was unbuttoned, she reached for his well-formed arms. She ran her hands over his exposed skin. His dark hair was soft to the touch.

"Ana, be careful of what you start." His eyes were a deep gray as Ana looked up into his face.

"I'll be careful," she said, thinking again that he was referring to his wound. But she then blushed ever so slightly as she began to pull off his shirt. Taking his right arm into her now warm hands she began to massage the muscles as she was taught.

"That feels good," his relaxed voice was soft. His eyes closed.

Ana worked her way up his arm to the strong muscles in his neck. She noticed how his hair curled at the base of his head and around the back of his ear. Being so close was warming more than her hands. She traced his ear with her finger. She began to gently run her fingers through his hair and over his forehead, down his nose and to his lips. He grabbed her hand and opened his eyes.

"I told you to be careful." His voice was filled with passion. He took her hand and opened it to expose her palm. Bringing her palm to his lips, his kiss was soft and warm. It brought a shiver of excitement down to her belly. Their eyes locked. His arm wrapped around her slim waist and he pulled her close.

"You are a vixen." His voice was husky as his mouth found hers. His kiss was deep and passionate. His other hand ran down the front of her dress. Feeling her supple breasts through the thin fabric was tantalizing. She responded to him, passion meeting passion. His kisses traced down her neck until he found the valley between the soft mounds. He caressed them as he softly nibbled at their hardening peaks. Ana held his head to her as he teased and stroked. Alexander looked up at her. His smile was wickedly delicious. Ana responded, smiling back at him, her tongue seductively moistening her upper lip. Alexander pulled her to the floor and rolled on top of her. She could feel his manhood hard against her thigh as his hips began to pulse ever so gently. Ana could feel herself ache for him, her desire growing with his movements. But he was going to make her wait. He slowly undid the buttons of her dress, exposing the round pointed mounds. His tongue made slow teasing circles as his hand worked at removing her dress. Ana's hips instinctively lifted in anticipation of his passion. But he continued to entice her, moving her to greater heights. Alexander sat up and began to slowly unbutton his trousers freeing himself of the confines of the fabric. Ana reached down and took hold of him. He moaned as she slowly began to squeeze and massage his throbbing manhood. Her desire for him grew even stronger as she watched his response to her touch. He pushed open her legs with his knee and began to gently fondle the folds of her flesh, bringing her to higher ecstasy. She moaned softly as he caressed and enticed her.

"Alexander, please." She needed him to release her from her desire, her hips lifting to accept him. He slowly entered her velvety hot center. She wrapped her legs around his narrow hips, pulling him deeper and deeper into her core. They began to move together with the rhythm of their heat, their passion building, increasing, exploding together into uncontrolled ecstasy and release. Wave after wave of pleasure and joy rocked both their bodies until they were spent.

Alexander pulled up on his arms and studied Ana's face. She was the most beautiful woman he had ever seen and she was his. He knew she was his and he wanted to trust her, love her, keep her for the rest of his life. He wanted to tell her. She reached up and caressed his face.

"Alexander, I love you so. I so wish you believed me," she said as a tear slipped from her eye. She was fearful of his response and his distain.

"Ana, I can't." He rolled onto his back. He hated that he could not yet trust her. He couldn't tell her of his feelings. Trust was so hard. How could he be sure she would not abandon him or his family, especially when there was Charles waiting in the wings, so ready to pull her away. *She says she loves me— but I've also heard her say the same to Charles. How can I trust her?* He felt at war within himself.

"I'm so sorry that Elizabeth hurt you so much," she said quietly. He rolled onto his side exposing his back and the angry scar.

"She meant nothing to me." His voice was flat.

"I don't understand?"

He rolled again onto his back and looked at her over his shoulder. "No, you don't understand." Didn't she hear his story? Wasn't she in the carriage when he told her?

"Ana, I'm tired. I need sleep. You need sleep. We will be home tomorrow."

CHAPTER 39

Grief filled Ana's days with a gray haze. She missed the arms of her mother and the safety of father. She longed to see Miles. And mostly she wanted to talk to Eliza. Now they were all gone, dead. Henry was leaving for the sea. And somehow Charles too had died that night at Berkeley Heights. She looked forward to Ana Jane's arrival. She was grateful for that. But most particularly Ana was concerned about her now distant relationship with Lord Luttrell.

Though Alexander had welcomed her advances at the inn, he had remained distant since their return. If he was not riding Cesar at breakneck speeds, he was ensconced in the library. He had removed himself from the whole household. She was afraid their upcoming nuptials would be cancelled, that he had changed his mind. Fear gripped her heart. If he did withdraw his offer, she would be ruined. She could not nor would not return home. Besides, there was no home. Soon she would have Ana Jane as her ward. But hopes of a life with Alexander were quickly fading.

On this morning however, he requested that Geoffrey and Hugh join him. Ana was relieved that he took some pleasure in the company of his sons. Hugh was always needy, while Geoffrey was finding comfort in his friendship with Riya. And for Ana, there was only one person in the household with whom she currently felt any connection—for her too, that was Riya.

"Miss Ana, there is such sadness in this house," Riya ventured. It was the first time in days that anyone had mentioned any emotion. Somehow it gave Ana permission to let down her own guard. She began to cry.

"Oh, Miss Ana!" Riya wrapped her arms around the crying woman. "I know what it's like to lose all your family." Ana in turn hugged Riya, who also began to cry at her own losses. As they held each other recognizing their similarities, they turned from tears to smiles. They were not so alone.

"Riya, I had a sister. Now I have none. Would you be my sister?" Ana ventured looking into the dark face of the beautiful young woman in front of her.

"Oh, Miss Ana, I'd love being sisters." She threw her arms around Ana's neck.

"Riya, call me Ana." She hugged the young women back.

"Ana," she said.

"We can talk about anything. That's what sisters do," Ana said to her as they looked at each other with growing fondness.

"Miss ... ahh … Ana, Ana I want to talk to you about so many things. I want to talk to you about Sir Alexander. I want to talk to you about Master Geoffrey."

"About Geoffrey? What about Geoffrey?" Ana's interest was piqued.

Riya studied her hands as she played with the fabric of her skirts. She was obviously distressed.

"Ana, I know he's so young. I'm older. But I have feelings for him and I think he has feelings for me." She looked shyly at Ana.

"Oh, Riya, I knew there was something between the two of you. I really don't know what to say. He is so young."

"I know he is only fifteen and I am seventeen. But he has been so kind to me and so gentle with me. And we have so much fun together; he makes me laugh."

"But he is too young Riya." Ana was concerned.

"Back in my country I would be married already four years." Her voice was quiet and shy.

"Why, I have never heard of such a thing." Ana said horrified.

"It is not a bad thing, Ana. It is just my people's way. We do not have love in our country. Not like here in England. Not like I see with you and Sir Alexander."

"Oh, Riya. I don't think there is love with me and Sir Alexander."

"No Ana this is not true. I know you love him very much. I know because you show it and because you stay to be near him."

"I do love him. I love him very much. Riya, you are so wise for one so young. But he does not love me. He has told me so."

"No Ana, he does love you. He just does not trust you. I don't think he knows how to trust."

"That doesn't make sense. How can you love without trust?"

"I have seen him looking at you."

"I don't think that is love, Riya"

"No, I know the difference because I see it in his eyes. Sometimes they are dark and, how to say, passionate? Then other times they are kind and warm, like love."

"Riya, if only it was true."

"I know it is true."

"Do you really think so? Alexander keeps himself locked in that library or riding Cesar since we returned from London. I don't know. It is like he is living in a cave or running away."

"Yes, he has called me to relieve the pain in his back, as I have done in the past. But I think it is the pain in his heart that needs to be healed."

"The pain in his heart?" She stopped and thought about the night in the Inn. Had he been sharing the pain in his heart, about what had happened to him on the battlefields of India.

"Ana sister, Sir Alexander believes he protects everyone. But there is no one to protect him."

"Riya, I've purposefully stayed away from him." Ana said. "I've been waiting for him to call me. I've been wrong, and too caught up in my own pain to see his. I need to go to him. He needs to know that I will protect him too. I've had too much pride, Riya. He has pride too. But if we both have too much pride getting in our way, we will never admit our feelings. We'll continue to hurt each other until there can be no more going back. Oh, Riya, thank you so much for our talk. I now know what I must do."

Ana was newly determined to speak with Alexander. Going down the grand staircase to search him out, she was stopped by Chesterton.

"Miss Pembroke, you have a visitor." He had a small brown package in his hand.

"A visitor? Chesterton, that is odd. Did he bring that package?"

"This? No, it's for Lord Luttrell. The post has just arrived."

"Oh, who is this visitor?"

"He said he is your cousin, a Lord Malin. He is waiting for you in the salon."

"Thank you, Chesterton." She furrowed her brow. Charles, of all people, appearing now when she was going to speak to Alexander. He was last person in the world she wanted to see. That last night in London, Ana felt she saw for the first time what he truly was—cold, cruel, and calculating. What could have possibly brought him to Dunster Castle? It had to be something urgent. She rushed off to the salon.

"Ana. Thank God. You must return home. I'm here to fetch you. Henry has gone mad!"

"Oh no! Poor Henry."

"I'm here to take you to him. We must hurry."

"I must tell Lord Luttrell and pack my things."

"There is no time to pack, he has threatened to take his life."

"Oh, God no. Henry! I'll be ready in minutes."

"I'll wait for you in the chaise." He turned on his heels to leave, not wanting to spend one minute more than necessary at Dunster.

Ana quickly went to the library. She saw the small package on Alexander's desk left there by Chesterton and remembered he was out riding with his sons. She quickly jotted a note. Somehow, he must understand. She leaned it against the package in clear view and ran to gather a few things and to inform Riya of her impending departure.

Alexander rode up the drive, Hugh on his left and Geoffrey on his right. When he recognized the occupant of the unfamiliar chaise carriage, he had Cesar rear up. The steed pawed the air. Charles held the reins of his two frightened dappled mares as he glared at the man on the powerful black stallion. Alexander dismounted quickly. His eyes were filled with rage. He passed the chaise without giving the driver the time of day. The boys following close behind.

"Father, who is that?" Hugh asked as they entered the house.

"Both of you, upstairs," he ordered.

"But Father ...," Hugh pleaded. Alexander's look told them he meant business.

"Hugh, come on up. Let's look for Riya." Geoffrey grabbed his brother's coat and began to pull him up the stairs.

Alexander raced to the library. He saw Ana's note, read it quickly, and crumpled it into a ball. He left the room to confront her.

On her way down, Ana met Alexander at the base of the stairs, her note in his fist.

His blood boiled at having that man on his property. The fact that Charles was here to take Ana away was more than he could comprehend.

"Where do you think you're going?" Alexander said through clenched teeth. He was visibly in a rage.

"I must return home. I'll only be away for a short while," Ana said.

"If you go with him, don't return."

"Alexander, it's Henry. He's threatened to take his life. I must go. Please understand. I am not leaving you. I will return," she pleaded.

"Ana you're making a choice if you go with him." His voice was cold and hard. "And this is not the first time you have chosen that man over me."

Alexander, I'll return. Don't you understand? I love you!" *Why could he not hear her?*

"Ha! Fickle woman. You don't love me. You know as much about love as I do. Leave!" he ordered as he pointed towards the door.

"I will always return to you. I will always return." Her voice was calm and reassuring.

"You don't understand. You're free to go. I release you from your vow. There'll be no marriage. Don't return, Ana. I don't need you. I don't need anyone." He turned away quickly and left her standing on the stairs, shocked and dumbfounded.

He just released her from their engagement. Her knees felt as if they were going to buckle. She grabbed hold of the banister for balance as his words reverberated in her mind. Her world was coming to an end. But Charles was waiting. Henry was in need. She had to gather her strength.

"I'll return," she said to herself. "I will."

Visibly shaken, Ana made her way out the front door and climbed into the waiting chaise. She felt she could not risk losing Henry. She had to go to him. She was barely in the chaise when Charles flicked his switch and the two dappled mares began a quick trot down the drive and out the ancient gate. Ana's heart was breaking at the thought of leaving Alexander, and she was troubled by his dismissal. *"Don't return,"* he had said. Tears stung her eyes. Her life had become a nightmare.

Alexander stood at the window watching Ana leave with Charles by her side. The crumpled note dropped to the ground. He felt dead inside as he watched them disappear into the distance. He walked over to the decanter and poured a whiskey. It had been weeks since he'd had a drink. He brought it up to his lips and stopped. Suddenly he hurled it into the fire grate. Rage replaced detachment. His long arm swiped his desk, contents spilling to the floor. He fell back into his chair. He hated Charles, but he hated Ana more. The brown package spun on the edge of his desk. He reached to toss it but stopped. It was from Jacob Sumner, Esq. His curiosity temporarily piqued and offering a momentary distraction, he tore open the brown paper. There were several letters and marked pages from a diary. On top was a note from Jacob himself.

> *Enclosed you will find a letter from Cecil Sedgewick, the Pembroke family butler under Lord William Pembroke, a letter from General Patrick Cleburne of the U.S. Confederate Army which includes a ring belonging to Sir Miles Pembroke, and a diary entry from Lord Pembroke himself. It implicates Charles Malin in the murder of Miles Pembroke. It is my gravest concern that this may have much deeper indication of further harm done to the Pembroke family by Malin and may implicate Malin in other murders and murder attempts, especially on Miss Pembroke. Please by all means keep Ana away from him and under your watchful eye until this matter has been further investigated.*

Paralyzed, Alexander quickly reviewed the other pages. Sedgwick had written:

> *Following my discharge from Berkeley Heights, I found this letter, ring, and diary tucked into the back of one of my drawers. They must have been placed there by Sir William, prior to Lord and Lady Pembroke's fatal accident.*

Lord Pembroke's words jumped from his diary pages:

> "... *most disturbing letter from General Cleburne; I cannot imagine that Charles would do such a dastardly thing to his own blood; I'll be dividing all my worldly goods between my two daughters, followed by any of their male issue, who will hold both land and title.*"

The word *MURDER* sprung from Cleburne's letter.

"My God, Chesterton!" Alexander called as the pages floated to the desk and ground. "What a fool I have been."

"Sir?"

"Get Cesar back. Ana's in grave danger. Go for help." His voice filled with urgency. "I knew he was no good." He muttered under his breath, loading his pistol. Retrieving the Cleburne letter from the floor, he stuffed it into his coat pocket.

A stable boy was leading Cesar to the house. Alexander jumped on his back and bolted down the drive after the carriage, his spurs kicking the soft sides of his steed, clods of earth flying as the hooves assaulted the ground. He had to get to her before it was too late. As he made the bend in the road, he saw the carriage far ahead of him, rocking and perched precariously on the Gallox Bridge.

Ana turned around to watch Dunster Castle fade into the distance as Charles took her further away from the man she loved. Pain caught in her heart as she brought her hands up to her face to muffle the sob.

"Don't cry my pet. I'm here," Charles said as he spurred the team on.

"You don't understand Charles. I love him."

"You don't know what love is, you simple girl," he growled at her.

"Charles, how can you, of all people, say that to me." She looked at him through her tears.

He reined in the team and turned towards her. "I know you have ruined yourself with him. You were to be mine. You threw yourself at a handsome face. You're a foolish, simple, whoring girl!"

He glared at her, spittle flying from his angry mouth. His black eyes were cold and flat.

"Charles, stop! You're scaring me," she begged.

"Scaring you? You have no idea, love, what fear is."

He sneered as he grabbed her by her shoulders and pulled her towards him. His crooked mouth searched out hers. She turned her head to avoided his cruel kiss, but he grabbed her chin and forced her face forward. His fingers pressed into her soft cheeks. She pushed at him in hopes of freeing herself, but he only held on tighter. She hit him with the heels of her hands trying to escape. He stopped and his hard hand came across her face, twisting her head to the side as his ring cut into her cheek. The pain shot into her eyes.

"Charles! Stop!" she cried. All at once, she saw the ring. "YOU!" she hissed.

"I'll not stop. You're mine. You've always been mine and I'll take you now!" His voice was hard and cruel.

Ana began to kick in her attempt to push him away. Grabbing at the bodice of her dress he ripped it open, sending buttons flying.

"Stop!" she cried. Her voice was smothered as he again attempted a violent kiss, his wet twisted mouth reaching for hers. She bit his bottom lip and could taste his salty blood in her mouth. Reeling back from the pain, he wiped the blood with back of his hand, a snarl across his face. Ana kicked him away. He fell back, giving her the ability to grab the reins and the team began to speed ahead at her urging. Charles wrestled the leathers away from Ana's hands and brought his fist down across her chin. This time Ana saw stars as the pain from the punch spun her head around.

The carriage approached Gallox Bridge at a fast pace and slipped onto the stone platform, the rear wheel caught on the stone siding of the bridge, bringing the carriage to a skidding halt, the team rearing and stomping at the impediment. The lurch from the carriage threw Charles on top of Ana. He grinned at the irony of his position.

She screamed as he ripped at her clothes. His one hand covered her mouth to silence her as he worked to undo the ties of her corset with the other. She struggled for air. She pulled at his ears with all her might, fighting and kicking for her life.

Suddenly, Charles was yanked from her. Alexander had reached in from atop Cesar and grabbed Charles from behind. Charles swung around and threw a punch at Alexander, hitting him in the jaw. Cesar reared up, forcing Charles to fall from the carriage. He clambered to his feet and grabbed Alexander's booted leg, pulling him from his steed. Alexander hit the ground hard. Charles began to run through the shallow stream alongside the ancient bridge but Alexander scrambled up, pulled his pistol from his belt, cocked the hammer and fired a warning shot over Charles' head. Charles stopped dead in his tracks and put his hands in the air.

"Don't shoot! Don't shoot!" He screamed over his shoulder as he staggered forward to gain his balance.

"Move to the ground," Alexander ordered. "On the ground, now!"

"Ana … Ana," Alexander called to her over his shoulder. "Are you alright?" He heard her sobs from inside the chaise.

"Oh, my God, he tried to … Oh, my God. Alexander, how did you know?" Ana sobbed.

Taking a few steps backward, he threw the Cleburne letter into the chaise as he kept the pistol aimed at Charles. Through her sobs Ana read the missive.

Dear Lord Pembroke,

It is with deepest sympathy that I must inform you of the death and apparent murder of your son Miles Pembroke. It was an honor to have him serve in my brigade. He served proudly and honorably. He was respected by his men. It had been reported to me following the departure of Charles Malin, that Miles had been shot in the back. It was witnessed by one of his comrades that Malin took direct aim. We sent out a search party to find him in the hope of questioning and arrest, however, he was able to elude us. I felt that this information is pertinent to you. I have enclosed the ring from Miles' hand. I send my deepest condolences to you in this matter.

Ana's tears ceased. She slowly climbed from the carriage, shaking with rage at what she had read, the letter grasped tightly in her left hand.

"Ana!" Alexander was horrified to see her descend from the chaise in ripped and ruined clothing, a bruise forming on her chin and blood trickling from the cut on her cheek.

"Ana, here take the pistol! I'll give you my coat," he said as he handed her the gun and began to remove his coat to cover her exposed body.

Ana took the weapon offered to her and calmly walked away from Alexander. She waded to the other side of the river to where Charles was laying on his back like the dog he was. She felt numb as she fell on her knees beside him. Pointing the gun directly to his head, she shoved the letter into his face.

"You shot Miles. Didn't you?" Her voice was cold and flat.

Charles' face twisted into a sneer.

"You shot my brother." Her voice was rising. "And mother and father? What did you do to them? What did you do, Charles?!" He remained motionless, as he watched her with his dead black eyes, his mouth in a grimace.

"I took what was mine," he snarled.

She cocked the hammer. "It was never yours. What did you do?" She fired a shot into the dirt by his head. He twisted to his side at the shock of her action, hiding his head in his arms, dust and grass spraying his face.

"You pushed me. It was you. I recognize the ring." Her eyes widened as she motioned towards his hand. "Why? Why?!"

"To frighten you so you would come home to me."

"I don't believe you. Why would I believe you?" she screamed. You murdered my parents!"

"Ana," Alexander said gently as he came up behind her.

"You murdered them! And Eliza?"

"Ana, let me have the pistol," Alexander repeated calmly, his hand outstretched.

The sound of the lock released as Ana again pulled back the hammer. "Did you kill my sister too?" she hissed.

This time she pointed the gun directly at his head, the cold steel resting against his temple. Charles hid his face in his hands and whimpered.

"You coward! You killed them all. I hate you! I want you dead!"

"Ana, let me have the pistol. Ana … Ana …," Alexander crouched down by her side. "My love, let me have the pistol." His voice was quiet and steady.

Suddenly Alexander's words shook her from her rage. She stood up and threw the gun away. Rising to stand, Alexander took her into his arms. She began to sob.

Knowing he had but limited opportunity to escape, Charles began to run.

Alexander dove to the ground to retrieve the pistol, yelling "Stop, Stop!"

Charles continued to run.

Still on the ground, Alexander pivoted, took aim and fired.

Charles finally stopped at the impact of the bullet entering his back. He fell to his knees, thick dark blood shooting out of his chest like a fountain as the bullet exited his body. He looked down at the fatal wound in shock, recalling a distant and hazy memory of Miles. An instant later his eyes glazed over and he fell on his face. Dead.

EPILOGUE

*I*t had been many months since the terrible ordeal with Charles had come to an end. A cool spring breeze fluttered the ruffles of Ana's yellow cotton dress as she and Alexander walked through the pink rose garden that Albert had planted for his beloved Catherine those many years ago.

Geoffrey's deep baritone voice could be heard in the distance reading Shakespeare sonnets to Riya, who was dressed in a beautiful blue gown in the latest English style. Her shoeless but stocking-clad feet feathered the grass upon which they rested.

"Alexander, I received a letter from Henry today," Ana said.

"What's he up to?" He loved to hear about Henry's adventures.

"He said his ship, the Cornwallis, made it to Australia in eighty-three days. Can you imagine, eighty-three days?" Ana said.

"It's amazing times we live in, my love." Alexander said as he smiled down at her.

"He's decided to stay there," she added wistfully.

"Frankly, Ana, I'm not surprised. What does he have left here?"

"He has Ana Jane," Ana said as she looked over to where her young niece and Hugh were playing at cavaliers on the lawn, their wooden swords banging together in a mock fight. Her eyes filled with tears at the thought of her sister and her family.

"I'll miss Henry. I'm so concerned for him. His heart was so crushed. He was a good friend and a fine brother. I miss all of them. If it wasn't for Henry I wouldn't be here." She smiled up at Alexander, who took her arm in his as they strolled down the gravel pathway.

"I like him too. He's a regular sort of fellow I'd say." He patted Ana's hand as they walked, knowing that she still struggled with the loss of her family. "I'm not surprised he has decided to stay and start his life over again. He has the right to find happiness too."

"I hope he can. He has so much sorrow to deal with. He deserves a new life," Ana said.

Alexander added, "Yes, he does deserve happiness too. I laugh when I think of the irony of it all! He never would have thought that his scheme could have brought us such joy. He thought you'd be home in a fortnight!"

Ana looked up into Alexander's warm gentle blue eyes, "Are you happy, Alexander?" she asked, already knowing the answer.

"More than I could have possibly imagined, my love." He gently kissed the soft palm of her hand.

"You know if this baby is a boy, he will take my father's title. You will have sired a Duke and a Baron."

"Hmm, I never thought of that." He smiled.

"Alexander, what an odd little family we are," Ana said as she looked into her husband's handsome face.

"Oh, I don't think so. Maybe a bit different, but not odd," he chuckled, glancing at his sons.

"Alexander, if it is a boy, would you mind if we named him Miles?" Ana asked.

"Not as long as you don't mind naming her Eliza, if she is a girl."

"Maybe we will have enough children to give them the names of all our lost and beloved family members." She gave him one of her brilliant smiles, her turquoise eyes glistening.

"At least we'll have fun trying, my love," Alexander said, his eyes darkening with passion as he bent down to kiss his bride.